Swansea's Grand

Swansea's Grand

By Ian Parsons

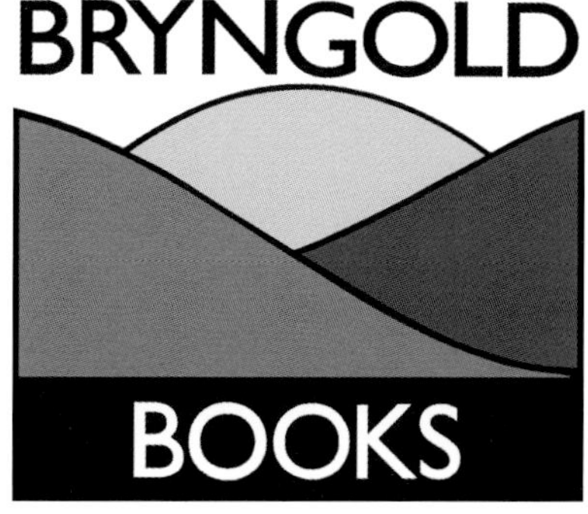

www.bryngoldbooks.com

First published in Great Britain in 2010 by
Bryngold Books Ltd.,
100 Brynau Wood, Cimla,
Neath, South Wales SA11 3YQ

www.bryngoldbooks.com

Typesetting, layout, editing and design
by Bryngold Books

ISBN 978-1-905900-17-6

Printed and bound
in Wales by
Gomer Press,
Llandysul, Ceredigion.

Contents

About the author

Ian Parson's earliest memories of the Grand Theatre, revolve around family visits there during the 1970s for the popular pantomimes that starred the inimitable Ryan and Ronnie. He fondly recalls laughing until tears streamed down his face and being in awe of the stars on stage just a few feet away. As the years passed so the magic of the Grand grew. His fascination for the theatre and those who performed there led to regular visits and a desire to discover more about how it all came about. In Swansea's Grand he shares many facts and fascinating discoveries together with the memories of many who have performed at The Grand. The former Penlan School pupil has compiled one of the most comprehensive theatre and entertainment websites in the UK — www.swanseasgrand.co.uk. Ian works in media marketing and in his spare time is seldom far from anything to do with the theatre at large. He lives in Neath with his wife Rhian and their three children.

Appreciation

The inspiration for this book has a number of sources, not least a pride in Swansea, the city of my birth and a determination to highlight the talent it has produced down the years and continues to do so in profusion.

Added to that is my passion for live theatre. Good, bad or indifferent, for me there is no other entertainment medium to match it. Then of course there is the Grand. As an entertainment venue it is worthy of a salute if only for the enjoyment it has brought so many as the longest surviving theatre in Wales' best seaside city.

Bringing Swansea's Grand to fruition has been an enjoyable experience, but one I could not have achieved without much help from many people. Among those to whom I extended my sincerest thanks are Vivyan Ellacott, who enthusiastically encouraged me to compile the book and in doing so provided me with a wealth of material, wisdom, support and knowledge. Thanks also go to Steve Dewitt, Brian Sullivan, Mike Sterling, Mal Pope, Mike Evans, Ryan's widow, Irene Davies for the use of photographs, the late Peter L Howard, Howard Phillips, Jan Jones, wife of comedian Dave Swan, Sion Probert, Mike and Pam Sayer, Gary Iles, Helen Griffin, Peter Sandeman, David W Kidd, Owen Money, Nigel Ellacott, Freddie Lees, Max Boyce, David Morris and Anne Marie Gay at West Glamorgan Archive Service; Alan W Jones, Griff Harries, Wyn Calvin, Mike Doyle, Stan Stennett MBE, Jess Conrad, Jean Fergusson, Stephen Wischusen, Ceri Dupree, Ria Jones, Gareth Armstrong, Heather Holt, Eleanor Thomas, Gwyn Davies, Islwyn Morris, Margaret John, Ruth Madoc, Melanie Walters, Marty Wilde, Sean Kier, Allun Davies, Kevin Johns, Gerald Morris, Paul Hopkins, Simon Moss, Dreena Morgan Harvey, Kath Rice, Alex Frith MBE, Anthony Lyn, Claire Smith and Jeanette Jones at Neath Library, Frank Vickery, Kenny Smiles, Menna Trussler, Lyn Mackay and countless others.

Finally, I would like to thank David and Cheryl Roberts of Bryngold Books for their help and support, beyond the call of duty on occasions, in transforming Swansea's Grand into something I am immensely proud of and hope you will savour.

Foreword

I am delighted to have been invited to write this foreword as I have been privileged to have worked at the Grand Theatre, as its general manager, for the past 21 years.

Since 1897 the beautiful Grand Theatre has been presenting entertainment, in its many forms, to countless numbers of theatregoers in our region.

The venue holds a very special place in the hearts of many people, not only the theatre's loyal patrons, but all those who have worked in the venue, past and present, and large numbers of performers also.

Des O'Connor, Catherine Zeta-Jones, Ken Dodd, Su Pollard and the late Sir Harry Secombe are just a few of the well known names of the past 50 years who have spoken with great affection of Swansea's wonderful Grand Theatre.

The venue is very special. It combines the great atmosphere of a classic Victorian theatre with the modern day facilities theatregoers, performers and technical staff alike have come to expect, and with its Arts Wing extension, it now offers a contemporary programme of events and exhibitions to complement the more traditional programme in the main auditorium.

Ian Parsons has worked tirelessly over a number of years, to bring together the history, actors, characters, musicians, performers, productions and memories of the Grand, in the pages of this book. He has spent thousands of hours, painstakingly researching the theatre's past, and interviewing many of the people associated with this fine old theatre. The result, I feel, is a splendid book. He has done a magnificent job.

I hope you enjoy it.

Gary Iles

General manager

Swansea Grand Theatre.

Introduction

Swansea and its neighbours have long exerted a strong influence on the world in a multitude of ways, not least in the development of popular theatre.

From humble beginnings in the 1600s, to the city's first purpose built theatre in 1780 and the many theatrical establishments that followed, it has often been the springboard for debuts and developments that have led to greater things.

As a string of theatres came and went they each played a part in the entertainment of Swansea. They provided a launch pad for performers who would achieve fame while at the same time spawned some of the greatest show business impresarios of all time.

Among personalities who have rubbed shoulders with Swansea in their rise to fame are Charlie Chaplin, Laurel and Hardy, Morecambe and Wise, Ray Milland, Maudie Edwards, Richard Burton, Sir Harry Secombe, Sir Anthony Hopkins, Michael Sheen and of course the little girl who grew up to become the city's very own superstar, Catherine Zeta Jones. There are many, many more.

To make it all happen there were the entrepreneurs. People like Sir Oswald Stoll who helped develop the Moss-Empire chain, the Melville family who built up a significant presence in the theatre world and then there was Alfred Denville, who established the country's first repertory seasons at the New Opera House in Morriston.

Today there is a sole survivor of the era we can refer to as the heyday of theatre in Swansea. It is the Grand Theatre which opened in Singleton Street in 1897. Its significance is certainly not in the fact that it was the first, or latest, purpose-built entertainment venue in the city, more that it has survived the test of time and still, continues to entertain and amuse.

The Grand, as it is affectionately known, and its history, forms the backbone of this book which unashamedly devotes space to saluting other theatrical establishments, not just in Swansea, but its surrounding towns; those who created and ran them and those who performed in them, often on their way to greater things.

Add to this the reference lists that have grown with the book, mention of the amateur stalwarts of the musical and dramatic scene together with a multitude of photographs and I hope Swansea's Grand will be a book which will educate and entertain, but most of all be enjoyed by all who turn its pages.

Ian Parsons, 2010

Dedication

I would like to dedicate this book to John Chilvers who worked unstintingly for the survival of The Grand Theatre; to the memory also of my brother, Tony Parsons, his wife Glenys, and to my late father Aubrey Parsons, a stalwart of Swansea Male Voice Choir and Neath Opera Group, to my beautiful wife Rhian and fantastic children Ben, Nicole and Carys. Lastly, but by no means least, to my mum, Mary.

Act 1

Window on a theatrical debut

Nearly four centuries ago a troupe of touring players performing in Swansea's town hall during the annual Michaelmas Fair probably thought that they were simply entertaining just another audience. They weren't. Instead, though they perhaps didn't realise it, they were also securing a place in history. For it is likely that this was the first theatrical performance ever to have taken place in the city.

The event, in 1617, might even have gone unnoticed but for a broken window pane. It seems that it was damaged somehow during the performance and the actors were made to pay for its repair.

There is no hint of what they were performing, or even how good or bad their efforts to please the audience were. A brief entry in the town's accounts book is the only clue to the fact that this was probably Swansea's earliest recorded theatre performance.

Between 1617 and 1633 several more such entries appear in the records that themselves are as entertaining as they are interesting. Sadly however, they only refer to damages or charges and don't give even the smallest hint to the name, nature or programme of the companies involved. It would seem that such visits, playing with permission in the town hall, were regular events. From 1633 to 1669 there were no recorded performances. For much of this time theatre had been banned by the Puritans, along with Maypoles and even Christmas! But when Charles II was restored to the throne, Swansea once more became part of a thriving touring circuit for visiting players and entertainers. The town hall and the spaces outside were used by showmen with bears, puppets and dancing dogs. Before long Swansea Corporation began charging for use of the town hall. A 'dancer on a rope' paid 12 shillings to hire the hall; A 'Frenchman' paid eight shillings for two-day shows.

Most early records refer to entertainers, showmen and mountebanks. However by the year 1715 they reveal the booking of regular annual seasons by actors. These seasons were clearly welcomed by the Corporation, for in the account books of 1736-37 it is recorded as having paid two shillings to treat the actors to a last night party.

In 1737 a new Licensing Act came into force after it was felt by some that it was time to clean up the theatre business. The real objection though seems to have been more the occasional political criticism and satire in the plays than any real indecency. All London theatres came under the control of the Lord Chamberlain while in provincial towns magistrates were given the power to grant or refuse permission for the performances. Licences were required both for the premises and the performers. Actors soon found ways around these new laws. Concerts of vocal music, lectures and the like were allowed. People could pay to attend a concert, listen to a few songs and then stay for the 'free' performance of a play. They could enter a hall, buy food and drink, and

A satirical cartoon of Gabriel Powell outside a Swansea Theatre, something he fiercely opposed. The original of this timely record is at Swansea Museum.

just happen to be sitting there while 'free' dramatic entertainment was provided. Swansea magistrates gave permission for the better class of touring players to perform in the town, but the cost of hiring the town hall increased to 45 shillings. This meant that many of the old favourite companies could not afford to use it.

This better class of player would have included Mr Kemble's Company of Comedians with the young John Philip Kemble and his sister, the future Mrs Sarah Siddons. The company would later include Stephen and Fanny Kemble. These were stars of the 1760s and 70s and are likely to have performed in Swansea. Other touring companies included the Cambrian Company of Comedians and a visiting company from Bath. At this time, however, Swansea had a problem in the form of Gabriel Powell, an over- bearing official. He was Steward to the Duke of Beaufort and Recorder to Swansea Corporation. He appears to have been arrogant, domineering and anti-theatre. Nicknamed the King of Swansea, Powell refused permission for performances to be staged at the town hall. Despite pressure from the town's leading citizens, he claimed that actors seduced the lower classes and were not welcomed by the majority of Swansea's residents. Other leading citizens had a much different view. They saw a future for their town as the Brighton of Wales, attracting visitors for the fashionable sea bathing, and for Swansea to become a popular resort for elegant tourists. They felt that not only should plays be allowed at the town hall, but also that Swansea should build a permanent playhouse. They felt this was essential if it was to become a fashionable resort. Among leading citizens in favour of a new theatre were Lady Mackworth and Dr Charles Collins. In 1780 they managed to convert an existing building into a theatre. It was intended as a temporary structure whilst funds were raised for the building of an establishment worthy of the town.

Gabriel Powell was totally opposed to a proper theatre and assembly rooms and was prepared to fight them tooth and nail. A political cartoon by Moses Harris – a local sign writer – that was later published as a print in London, depicted the general meeting of the burgesses of Swansea held on November 2, 1787. In it Dr Collins is portrayed as objecting to Powell's overbearing behaviour. Dr Collins is being kicked by Powell's son, Rev Thomas Powell, who is snatching Dr Collins wig. Robert Morris, brother of industrialist John Morris, and another thorn in the side of Powell and his ambitions is shown stepping in as peacemaker. The cartoon is the sole record of what occurred at the meeting so it must therefore be remembered that Moses Harris was a long time supporter of Robert Morris and by implication, a critic of Powell.

The first theatre

The first of Swansea's theatres was eventually created at Anchor Court in Wind Street. The building was owned by Lady Mackworth, one of the area's leading socialites who lived at Gnoll House, Neath. It was open for four nights a week during the summer season. Once again Gabriel Powell was totally opposed to the scheme and again it was his old adversary Dr Charles Collins, who led the pro-theatre group.

In order to get permission for their permanent theatre, they needed to prove that the town was properly paved. As both sides became more and more entrenched, the pro-theatre group decided to go over Powell's head and appeal to Parliament. Even though he was more than 80 years old, Gabriel Powell made the long journey to London by horse drawn coach to appear before the appropriate Parliamentary committee, drawing £100 from the Corporation to cover his expenses. A cartoon of the time depicts him standing in an unpaved street. Behind him is a building labelled as the Swansea Theatre. Underneath the cartoon, is a quotation from his

This was how a cartoonist of the day depicted the dispute between Dr Charles Collins and Gabriel Powell that occurred at a meeting of the Burgesses of Swansea on November 2, 1787 when the fight for a theatre was at its height.

evidence to the Parliamentary Committee which reads:

> ***"Swansea is a poor town mostly inhabited with coppermen and colliers, but as well paved as most country towns are. I know of no theatre there. I may have heard of one; I never was at it."***

Unexpectedly, just seven months later Gabriel Powell died shortly before Parliament passed new legislation. With the main opposition hurdles now removed Swansea began the serious business of raising money for a fashionable, purpose built, new theatre. Charles Collins was delighted, but fund-raising suddenly proved to be difficult. Within a few years Britain was engaged in a war with France. Coastal towns such as Swansea were potential invasion points and theatre took second place to national security.

It was to be more than 20 years, and a positive victory by Nelson at the Battle of Trafalgar, before Dr Collins got his fashionable theatre. In the meantime Lady Mackworth's Swansea Theatre took on the role.

The 'Sixty Day' rule was granted in favour of Rupert Calvert for some years. This was an Act of Parliament of 1887 that afforded magistrates of a town 'where the streets are paved and the people well behaved' the power to grant visiting performers or managers the right to stage live dramatic performances for 60 days in any one calender year. After Calvert it was granted to Henry Masterman and his company who would play Neath in May and June, Swansea in July and August to coincide with the growing tourist season, then shorter seasons at a number of nearby towns. Among Masterman's Players around this time were two young actors who later went on to achieve success. They were Charles Matthews and Charles Dibdin. It is likely that the pair would have played an active part in these early Swansea seasons.

Masterman's efforts and the ever-growing attendance figures at his successful seasons led to a renewal of interest in the building of a new theatre. Investors were approached and plans drawn up for one in Goat Street. Sadly Masterman died in 1803 and his successor, a Mr Edwin, didn't enjoy a good start as his replacement. Shortly after he took over, the local newspaper reported a dramatic off-stage quarrel between Edwin and a visiting group – the Bath Company of Comedians. The leading actor accused the manager of cheating him out of money due from his 'benefit' night. Edwin is alleged to have threatened to 'Kick him round Swansea into the sea'

The likely site of the first Swansea theatre is circled in this Thomas Rothwell view of the town in the 1790s.

before attacking him with a cudgel. As a result, the acting company cancelled the remaining shows and left town. The old theatre signed off with a performance of The Wheel Of Fortune and The Doctor And The Jew on October 3, 1806. Some of the would-be investors in the new theatre decided to pull out of the scheme fearing that without Masterman's personal following and careful management, the new theatre wouldn't be a success. The remaining investors, mostly local noblemen and gentry, formed a tontine, a fund where people buy shares and receive a proportion of the annual profits, as a way of paying for the new building. This annual income increases as each shareholder dies, until finally the last surviving investor inherits the entire property.

The new theatre was financed from 500 £10 shares, though at least half of them were bought by just five investors. These included the Duke of Beaufort, Thomas Mansel Talbot and Lord Dumfries. The remaining shares were held by 42 smaller individual investors. Strangely, the Mackworth family didn't invest a single penny. Perhaps Lady Mackworth's 25 years of ownership of the old theatre had made her dubious about the venture's potential. The new theatre in Goat Street was eventually completed in July, 1807 and called the Theatre Royal.

It would be almost a century before the first actors trod the boards at the Grand and the first patrons filled the seats of its auditorium. During that time there were other houses of performance, both portable and permanent, that played their own role. Most of these and the personalities behind them are featured in this book, but it is time to call 'curtain up' on its main focus, the only theatre from those distant days to have stood the test of time and changing trends in the world of entertainment.

Viewed from Wind Street in 2008, this passageway to The Strand and the pub entrance is on the approximate site of the first Swansea theatre.

Act 2

It's curtain up on the Grand

Arguably one of the best in the British Isles, the Grand Theatre is a thriving hot bed of entertainment standing as proudly in the heart of 21st Century Swansea as it did on the day it originally opened in 1897. It has endured a testing roller-coaster journey, survived two World Wars and despite the onslaught of electronic media, retained the ability to transport audiences away from the stresses and strains of everyday life.

Peeling back the layers of history reveals that The Grand is more than just another theatre. It is an institution steeped in theatrical history; one that has nurtured the careers of countless local talents, many of whom progressed to large scale success in the world of showbusiness. Significantly perhaps, The Grand has also developed a great spirit of community among its patrons, something which played a big part in keeping it alive in difficult financial times. It is an extremely intimate theatre and most of those who have performed there would agree that there is an intense warmth which emanates from its audiences.

The theatre's history has brought many highs such as the countless performances from some of the world's greatest stars, but there have been lows too. Times when the theatre's very survival has been threatened, but survive it did when many other establishments were less fortunate.

The creation of the Grand can be attributed to a number of factors. At the end of the 19th Century there was big money to be made in this new entertainment medium and no shortage of entrepreneurs seeking to do just that. Swansea offered them an ideal opportunity. It had a large population, full employment and a growing middle class. What it lacked was a modern, well-appointed playhouse. It did have a concert hall and two variety theatres, one of which frequently staged plays – mostly melodramas written by its owners – but the town's former principal theatre, the Theatre Royal, was unused and lay almost derelict creating a definite need for a high class, elegant and respectable new establishment.

Business partners Frederick Mouillot and H H 'Mackenzie' Morell seized the opportunity to resolve this and hopefully make their fortunes in the process. Morell was the older of the two actor-managers and provided the finance behind the partnership. Mouillot, meanwhile was an enthusiastic 33-year-old who simply oozed the driving ambition that the project demanded. Born in Dublin he was a well-known and popular leading man who had just married 27-year-old actress Gertrude Davison. The trio were rapidly becoming a leading force in theatre management.

Their plan to build a new theatre took a leap forward when they located what they believed was an ideal site – Swansea's former Drill Hall in Singleton Street. The hall had occasionally been used for performances previously. Its owner, Colonel Pike, was as eager to sell as Mouillot and Morell were to buy. With a deal quickly done, the development of the Grand Theatre was

The carriage carrying opera diva Madame Adelina Patti from the Midland railway station St Thomas to The Grand Theatre in Singleton Street crosses the River Tawe. She was on her way to officially open the theatre on July 26, 1897.

underway. Designed by established theatre architect William Hope of Newcastle it was indeed a 'grand' theatre. Decorated with the charming yet intricate style of late Victoriana, it was a tribute to an age of elegance tinged with19th century extravagance.

A journalist writing in The Builder magazine of August 1897, gave a thorough description of the rapidly emerging Grand Theatre as it neared completion:

> **"The building is in the Renaissance style; the materials used for the walls are white stone and red brick, faced with rough cast plaster. Dark red bricks are used at all angles, and terracotta has been freely employed for the ornamental portions. The roofs and towers are covered with Swansea terne plates, layers of steel reinforced with lead, instead of the ordinary slates. The auditorium is in the form of a square, each side 65 ft. long, and consisting of three floors, comprising ground floor stalls and pit, the dress circle, and the gallery. It is estimated that it will accommodate 2,500 people. The exits are such as to enable the whole of a crowded house to leave in two minutes. There are five of these leading directly on to the street, and for each part of the building there is an exit on each side of the auditorium. All the staircases have been constructed of fireproof materials, and 'panic bolts' enable all the doors to be opened by the slightest push from the inside.**
>
> **The principal entrance leading to the stalls and dress circle is in Singleton Street, and will have a marble staircase and decorated walls. The floors and entrance lobby with the landings and foyer will be paved with mosaic tiles. The ceiling is treated in the florid French Renaissance style in finely modelled plaster work, the whole being relieved by massive gilding. Each section of the house is provided with lavatories and convenient refreshment rooms. The height of the stage ceiling from the cellar floor is 80 ft. The gas and electric light arrangements on the stage are controlled from a position above the artistes and stage hands. Electric lighting**

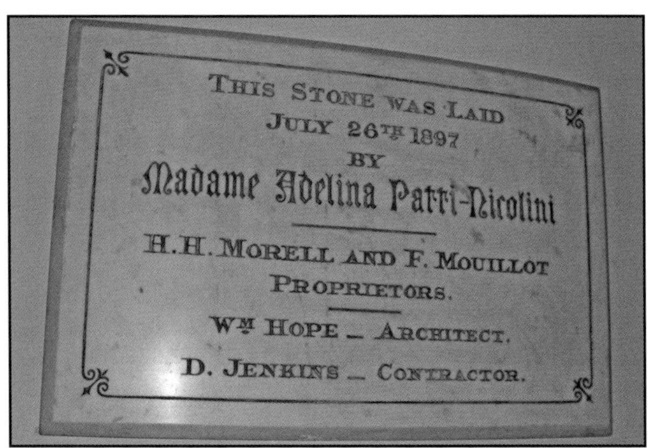

The stone tablet, still on display at the Grand, which commemorates the opening of the theatre by Madame Adelina Patti on July 26, 1897.

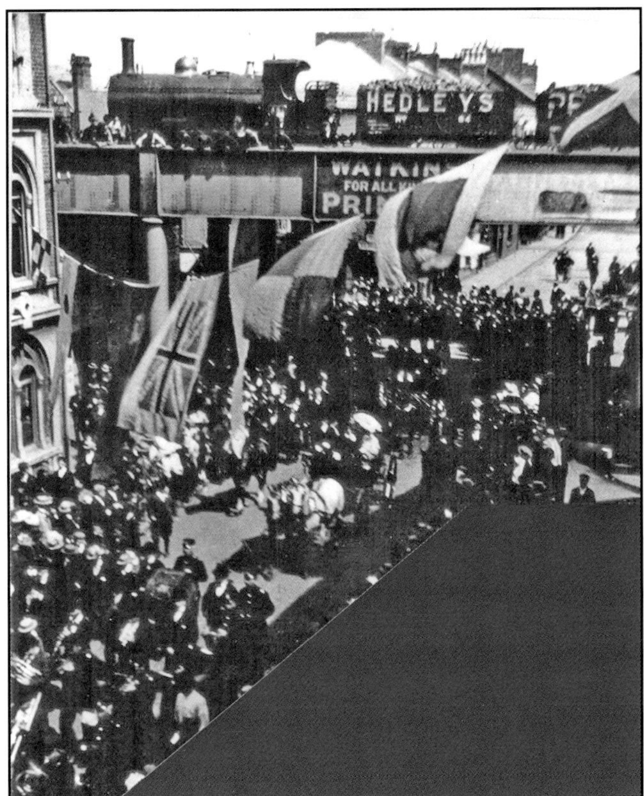

Enthusiastic crowds line Adelina Patti's route through Swansea to the Grand Theatre for the opening ceremony.

Madame Adelina Patti, who unveiled a commemorative plaque to officially open The Grand on July 26, 1897.

arrangements are under the supervision of Mr E Wingfield-Bowles. The cost of the whole building, fixtures etc, when completed, is estimated to be close on £20,000. The contractor for the building is Mr D Jenkins of Swansea. The plaster decorations, the furniture upholstering, and the seating of the auditorium have been carried out by Messrs AR Dean, Limited, of Birmingham. The upholstering, carpeting, and furnishing for the lounges, passages, lobbies, and refreshment saloons have been mainly executed by Messrs. Ben Evans & Company of Swansea. Mr Wm Hope is the architect."

It was an impressive description indeed and reveals just how determined the theatrical entrepreneurs behind the scheme were. The emphasis on the five exit doors, the panic bolts and the ability to clear the entire theatre in two minutes is an interesting piece of theatre history. Just 10 years earlier there had been a disastrous fire at the Theatre Royal, Exeter in which 186 people died, many crushed to death or suffocated because of the number of people who piled on top of them. The exit doors opened inwards and there was only one exit from the gallery. The disaster remains the worst in the history of British theatre. Not only were the building authorities insistent that every new theatre should be as safe as possible, but Frederick Mouillot himself was also obsessed with safety inside his theatres. The Exeter fire happened in the middle of a performance of Romany Rye. The last words uttered on that stage before fire and panic broke out were spoken by none other than Frederick Mouillot himself, playing the leading role. He was determined that such a disaster should never again happen in any of his theatres.

The opening ceremony

The Grand Theatre was officially opened on Monday July 26, 1897. The ceremony began with an orchestra, conducted by Mr W F Hulley, striking up the overture to Ambroise Thomas's Raymonde. Swansea Choral Society followed this by singing Wagner's Hail, Bright Abode. After this, the winning entry in a competition to find the most suitable opening ode for the new theatre was recited. It was the work of a local solicitor, Mr F C T Naylor, and in addition to a cash prize he had the honour of hearing his ode read by Gertrude Davidson, the leading actress of the day who, just three months earlier, had become Mrs Frederick Mouillot.

However, all this paled into insignificance when compared to the main event of the ceremony, the unveiling of a commemorative plaque by world famous opera diva, Adelina Patti. Enormous excitement had been generated by the attendance of someone reputed to be the world's highest paid performer. Patti who married into Italian nobility had chosen to retreat to the solitude of the upper Swansea Valley where she bought

An artist's impression of the Grand Theatre in 1897.

castellated Craig-y-Nos. This was truly a visit from a mega star of the day and the crowds were there to prove it. Patti arrived promptly at 1.30pm at the Midland Railway station on Swansea's eastside – naturally for a star of her magnitude, not by public train, but in her own private railway carriage. She was met by the town's Mayor and an official party, then driven by horse and carriage across the bridge that spanned the River Tawe, up Wind Street down into Temple Street along Oxford Street and eventually into Singleton Street where the carriage halted in front of the resplendent Grand Theatre.

Albert Chevalier, one of the first big names to appear at the Grand Theatre, the week after it opened.

The streets were crowded with cheering onlookers. All the local shops had window displays with Patti's portrait and welcome greetings. Ben Evans' store had outdone them all with giant portraits, flags and bunting draped across Temple Street. The town would have expected nothing less. Its town's evening newspaper – the South Wales Daily Post – reported the arrival of Madame Patti and the attendant excitement along with the plans for the ceremony. However, the newspaper went into print by late afternoon, too early to give full details of one or two hiccoughs, which occurred. It seems the formal opening ceremony suffered from first-night nerves, last-minute hitches and as often happens, some ever-present gremlins to boot.

The first actual performance at the Grand was of the Japanese musical comedy, The Geisha, on Wednesday July 28, 1897. That day the South Wales Daily Post carried a solemn announcement from Messrs Morell and Mouillot stating that 'arrangements had now been perfected, and the curtain would rise, without doubt, at the advertised time of 7.30pm' A perfect opening night must have come as a great relief to the theatre manager, Mr Frank Boyce, formerly of the Theatre Royal, York.

A testament to the popularity of the Grand in the early 1920s. These queues, stretching in either direction from the theatre entrance consisted of patrons keen to see the production The Knave of Diamonds.

In 1972, the Grand celebrated its 75th birthday, and issued a special invitation to anyone who had attended the theatre in its first year. Eleanor Evans, then 82, did. She recalled being at the opening ceremony with her father. He had been in charge of electrical installation work there. Her recollections were recorded, and her words were performed by another Eleanor – the actress Eleanor Thomas – as part of a special 75th birthday Gala Performance.

Her recollections provide a fascinating insight into the opening ceremony and its problems, but they may well have been embroidered a little by the passing of time and the well-known Welsh delight in making a good story even better. This is what Eleanor Evans said:

"We waited inside the theatre for a very long time and people were beginning to say she was not going to come after all. Suddenly there was a very great cheer outside and about half an hour later she entered her box. She was wearing a blue and gold dress with a long white fur cloak and jewels in her hair. The crowd inside cheered for a full five minutes until the overture began. When the red curtains were raised the Swansea Choir sang a very long and quite dull song by Mr Wagner and then Madame Patti rose and left the box. Everyone stood and cheered again, and then we waited a long time before anything happened.

Suddenly the new electric lights on the stage became much brighter and a lady came on. Everyone thought it was Madame Patti and started to cheer, but soon stopped when they discovered it was another lady. She looked most upset when the cheering stopped.

This lady was the wife of the owner of the theatre and she recited a very pretty poem about angels descending from the sky to open a new theatre in Swansea. When this lady left the stage there was another very long pause and finally the orchestra began to play again to fill in the time. A gentleman came on the stage and the orchestra stopped in the middle of an air, but the gentleman only wished to apologise for the delay and to say that the orchestra would play until everything was ready.

After another very long wait the mayor and many other officials came onto the stage and the trumpeter sounded a fanfare for the entrance of Madame Patti

Gabrielle Ray, considered by many to be one of the Edwardian era's beauties.

Sir Henry Irving - his signature survives on a dressing room door.

Gertrude Mouillot, the accomplished actress wife of Frederick Mouillot, first manager of the Grand Theatre

who had changed into a different gown in red and gold. How the audience cheered. She made a very pretty speech, saying she had come to view the town of Swansea as her resting place and home and was happy to see a new temple of music and drama opening in the town of her adoption, and she was quite unworthy of the honour of christening it. Her lovely, natural modesty and her great charm made the audience cry out in protest at this. She was thanked by two gentlemen, who were the owners of the new theatre. My Papa was convinced that one of these gentlemen was inebriated."

The end of the century

The opening season was a magnificent selection of the best modern theatre had to offer. The long history of entertainment at the Grand began with The Geisha, the musical hit from Daly's Theatre in London. The show, just one year old, was still running in the West End and the production in Swansea was one of several touring versions. Most of the major West End successes would be recreated for touring, generally with two distinct companies. There would be what was considered a Number One Tour, playing the major theatres and employing well-known and established star names and then a Number Two Tour, a trimmed-down version, playing the smaller theatres and employing less well-known performers. The Grand quickly established itself as a Number One Tour venue.

The hit songs from The Geisha included Chin Chin Chinaman, The Amorous Goldfish and Chon Kina. The story told how Molly Seamore, visiting the Teahouse of Ten Thousand Joys, tries on a geisha costume and is mistaken for the real thing. It is only through the efforts of Reginald Fairfax, an officer aboard HMS Turtle, and Mimosa San, a real geisha, that Molly is saved from marrying a Japanese marquis.

Audiences roared with laughter at The Geisha in George Edwardes' production at Daly's. But one or two voices in Swansea were raised in protest. For all its oriental flummery, a house of geishas was thought to be close to a house of easy virtue. Some Swansea protestors questioned whether this was the low level of morality that could be expected from future productions at the theatre. Despite this, the Geisha was a sell out success.

The following week saw the arrival of Albert Chevalier and his London Company in a new musical comedy. Chevalier was the first of the 'cross-over' artists, and had just returned from a successful tour of America. Equally at home in opera and straight theatre, he had become an enormously popular music-hall star – mainly due to his dramatic song My Old Dutch – sung in front of a backcloth of a workhouse, an establishment where men and women had to enter through separate doors and live in separate quarters. Chevalier would sing 'We've been together now for 40 years, and it don't seem a day too much' as a protest against being separated from his beloved Dutch. This was his duchess, a term of endearment for his wife drawn from the cockney rhyming slang Duchess of Fife meaning wife. This musical production naturally included My Old Dutch – Swansea audiences would have insisted!

Other shows in the opening season included tours from several London theatres, including the Princess and the St James. There were also well received visits from the D'Oyly Carte and Arthur Rousbey Opera companies. The season included plays by the H H Morell and F Mouillot Company. The pair would frequently mount their own productions to tour their own circuit of theatres. These proved to be an excellent source of filler shows when the major London companies might not have anything attractive on offer. The first season actually ended on a high note with one of these, a spectacular pantomime production of Robinson Crusoe.

The year 1898 brought with it a series of 'repertoire weeks', where a company would arrive and perform a different play each night. In March Mrs Badman-Palmer's company offered a most eclectic mix: Schiller's

Mary Stuart; Sheridan's School for Scandal; the melodrama East Lynne; Leah, the Jewish Maiden and Shakespeare's Hamlet – all in the same week. If that wasn't challenging enough, Mrs Badman-Palmer herself played the role of Hamlet. A three week season in June offered a feast of Shakespeare, and another Hamlet, this time played by Hermann Vezin. The Shakespeare season was served up by the Morell and Mouillot company and the leading lady was the former Gertrude Davidson, now billed as Getrude Mouillot. During this season she played Desdemona, Ophelia and Portia. Other visitors in 1898 included W S Penley in A Little Ray of Sunshine. Penley was a big name, forever associated with the title role in Charley's Aunt and touring companies headed by the likes of Louis Calvert, Cyril Maude, George Alexander and Charles Macdona, all leading names in the realms of popular late Victorian theatre.

The final year of the 19th Century saw more star names including Herbert Beerbohm Tree, Frank Curzon, Ben Greet and Robert Courtneidge. Famous actor-cellist August Van Biene performed his hit play The Broken Melody and at the end of each performance gave a special cello recital and asked the audience to throw money on the stage for the South African War Appeal.

The following year, 1899 also included historical plays including The Only Way – a version of Dickens' Tale of Two Cities and A Royal Divorce, the story of Napoleon and Josephine, best remembered for the catchphrase 'Not tonight, Josephine'. The big hits were the musicals: a return visit of The Geisha; The Greek Slave, and The Runaway Girl which on August 26 was the subject of an open-air matinee performance at Langland Bay. There were two separate visits from The Belle of New York featuring 17 year old Gabrielle Ray, later to be acclaimed as one of the great beauties of the Edwardian era. The second visit of The Belle of New York was so popular, it was staged as the Christmas and New Year attraction, replacing the traditional pantomime that year.

Into the 20th Century

The first year of the new century saw visits from the Carl Rosa and D'Oyly Carte Opera Companies at either end of the year, a seven week repertory season from

The play A Royal Divorce, about Napoleon and his two wives, proved very popular with audiences at the Grand and as a result was staged there on countless occasions. This was the poster used to promote a performance in 1915.

T Morton Powell's Company, visits from companies run by Frank Curzon, Ben Greet and the celebrated Miss Beatrice Homers. The Grand also saw its fair share of musicals including yet another return of The Belle of New York. An interesting feature of 1900 was two separate weeks performed by Walter Melville's company – The Great World of London and On Her Majesty's Service. The Melville Family were the owners of Swansea's rival theatre – The Star in Wind Street – and during these two weeks they would have been in competition with themselves for audiences and box office takings. However, there was no competition as far as pantomime was concerned. The Melvilles had the field to themselves at the Star, for the Grand staged a three-week Christmas run of the hugely successful religious play, Quo Vadis. Just three weeks into the new year this was followed by another religious play, The Sign of the Cross.

The death of Queen Victoria

On Monday, January 21, 1901 Queen Victoria died. It took longer for such news to filter through to the nation then and so it was that the following day, just before curtain-up on The Sign of the Cross, the manager of the Grand, Frank Boyce, stepped in front of the curtain to announce the sad news. He added that, as a mark of respect, the theatre would remain closed and future performances would depend on the instructions of the Lord Chamberlain. At the end of his announcement the orchestra played the Dead March, and the audience stood throughout in total silence, after which they quietly dispersed. Although many theatres throughout the country were closed for the rest of the week, it was felt that the theme and the message of The Sign of the Cross would bring comfort to local people. Performances resumed on Wednesday. However, a Thursday matinee charity performance featuring My Turn Next, Petticoat Perfidy and Chisseling was cancelled. A state funeral was held two weeks later, on Saturday, February 2. The Grand, along with every theatre in the country, was closed as part of the national mourning process and the performances of Davy Garrick by Edward Compton's Comedy Company were cancelled.

The Edwardian era

Shortly after the accession of King Edward VII, Swansea had a three-day visit from major London stars, Mr and Mrs Kendall, in The Elder Miss Blossom and The Likeness of the Night. Later in the year Tyrone Power – whose similarly named son became a Hollywood heart-throb – appeared with Kennedy Miller's Irish Comedy Players. Old favourites like East Lynne, and novelties like Did You Ever Send Your Wife to Mumbles? continued to attract sell-out houses and, as always, visits from the Carl Rosa Opera Company and major West End musicals were guaranteed to fill the theatre.

During the week commencing July 24, 1901 the Grand was hired by a new local company. The production of Gilbert & Sullivan's Iolanthe was by the Swansea Amateur Operatic Society. It was the first in what was to be a long series of amateur musicals that has entertained

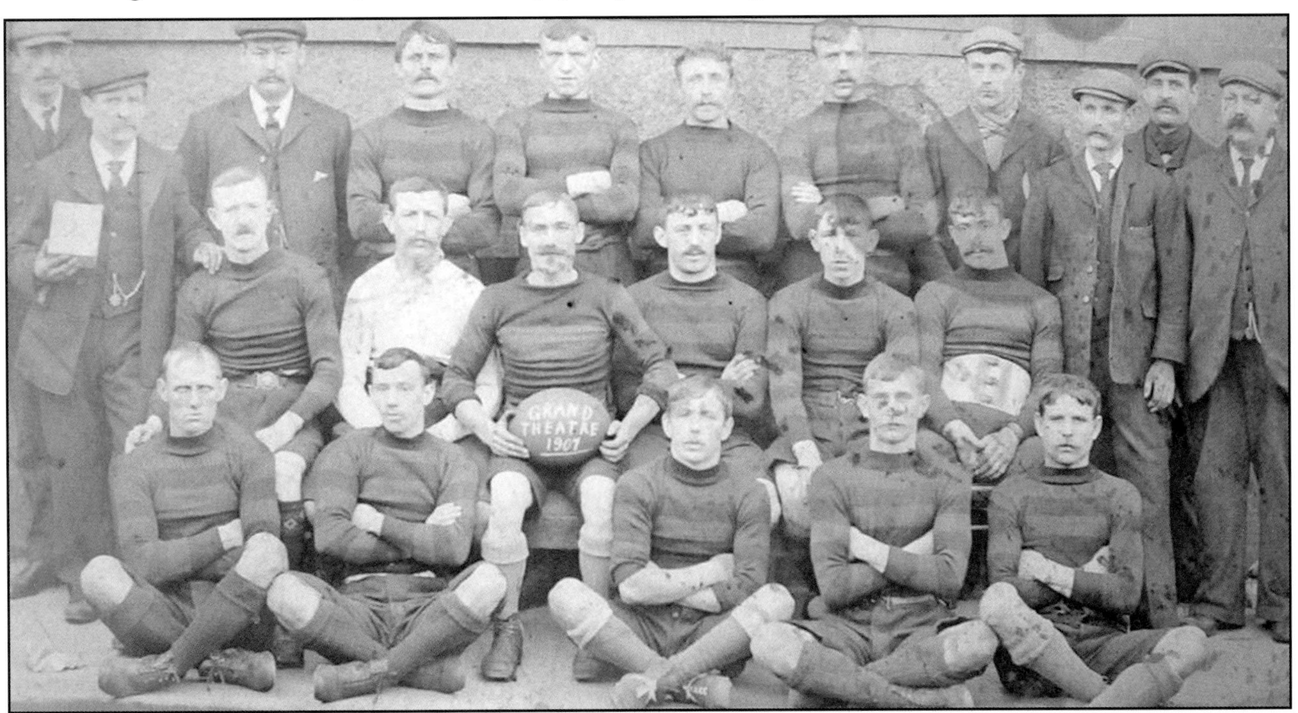

Performances of a different kind were served up by these members of the Grand Theatre soccer team, seen in 1907.

The legendary actress Sarah Bernhardt who delighted audiences at the Grand on a number of occassions.

Herbert Beerbohm Tree, the grandfather of hell raiser Oliver Reed was another who appeared at the Grand.

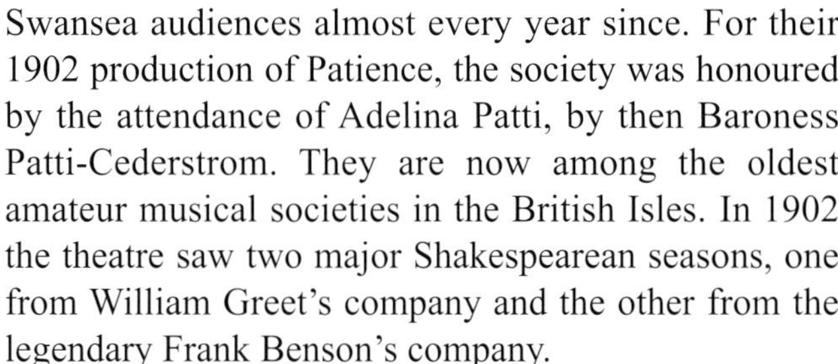

Swansea audiences almost every year since. For their 1902 production of Patience, the society was honoured by the attendance of Adelina Patti, by then Baroness Patti-Cederstrom. They are now among the oldest amateur musical societies in the British Isles. In 1902 the theatre saw two major Shakespearean seasons, one from William Greet's company and the other from the legendary Frank Benson's company.

Frank Benson was a cricket fanatic. It was said that actors in his company were not only expected to be able to act, they had to be good at cricket as well. In between performances such as Hamlet, The Merchant of Venice and Richard III, he would challenge the local stagehands to form a cricket team and compete against the actors. Woe betide his actors if they failed to win! The Grand was frequently home to productions from the several touring companies of the proprietors, Mouillot and Morell, and star name touring shows, with performers like Forbes Robertson, Fred Powell and Hilda Beverley. The final show of the year opened on Boxing Day and was the play Sweet Nell of Old Drury. This starred Julia Neilson and Fred Terry – at this time the most famous husband and wife team in the world of theatre. In February 1903 the legendary Sir Henry Irving made his first visit to Swansea. It was a brief, three-day visit, during which he appeared in his much-acclaimed role as Mathias in The Bells and as Shylock and Napoleon. He returned in October 1904 as part of his farewell tour, and his last performance in Swansea was a repeat of his Shylock in The Merchant of Venice. Irving's manager was Bram Stoker, author of the Gothic horror Dracula and in his biography, Life of Henry Irving, Stoker was complimentary in describing this farewell tour of Wales:

> ***"All was ready, and on September 19 we began at Cardiff our series of farewell visits. The Welsh people are by nature affectionate and emotional. The last night at Cardiff was a touching farewell. This was repeated at Swansea with a strange addition. When the play was over and the calls finished the audience sat still in their places and seemingly with one impulse began to sing. They are all fine part-singers in those regions and it was a strange and touching effect when the strains of Newman's beautiful hymn Lead Kindly Light filled the theatre. Then followed their own national song Hen fwlad fen Hadne*** (Stoker's own brave attempt at the Welsh spelling) – ***Land of my Fathers. Irving was much touched. He had come out before the curtain to listen when the singing began and when after the final cheering of the audience he went back to his dressing room the tears were still on his cheeks."***

The following year the Irving tour moved to Bradford and it was there that he collapsed and died. For the last quarter of the 19th Century the most famous theatre partnership had been that of Henry Irving and his leading lady, Ellen Terry. The partnership had ended in the late 1890s and as a result Swansea never saw the pair perform together.

The Grand itself suffered a great loss when Frank Boyce, the manager and lessee died suddenly at the age of 47. The theatre was forced to close for some weeks until new managers – Oswald Brooks and J W Woodbridge – were appointed. It re-opened on Boxing Day with a three-week season from the Moody Manners Opera Company. Early in February a new, iron fireproof curtain was installed and the theatre continued to generate excellent business with its programme of touring plays, Shakespeare seasons, musicals and visits by the D'Oyly Carte Opera Company. However, the biggest event of the year was the appearance on Saturday June 17, 1905 of the legendary Sarah Bernhardt. She took to the stage as part of a six-week season of historical costume dramas, and a one-night only performance of her legendary portrayal of La Dame aux Camelias. This was performed in French and the Grand was packed to the rafters. She was cheered on her entrance and given many resounding curtain calls at the end. However, the following week she was not so popular when the local press reported she had described Swansea as a dirty town.

Visits from the great touring companies of the age came in 1906 – George Dance, the Kendals, Herbert Beerbohm Tree, William Greet, Charles Frohman, and George Alexander – though in most cases these legendary producers did not appear themselves. It was the Herbert Beerbohm Tree Company, but Beerbohm Tree himself was actually packing them in the West End. This was very much in line with the later theatrical joke that when Laurence Olivier acted it was a tour-de-force, and when Donald Wolfit acted, he was forced to tour! In the middle of the year the Grand devoted six nights to a film show of the full 18 rounds of the World Lightweight Boxing Championship fight between Oscar Nelson and Jimmy Britt and filled the auditorium on every one of them. However, the end of the year saw the visit of some real stars of the day. Junius Booth, nephew of John Wilkes Booth the assassin of American president Abraham Lincoln, appeared in Monte Cristo, and Fred Karno and Company appeared with guest star William E Matthews in His Majesty's Guest.

Ivor Novello caused hysteria at the Grand in The Rat in 1924.

Henry Ainley, one of many actors who appeared at the Grand in the 1920s.

Over the next two years it was very much business as usual with all the major touring plays and musicals doing the rounds. In the summer of 1907 there were successive productions of Oscar Wilde's Importance of Being Earnest and Lady Windermere's Fan. These were the first productions of his works since the major scandal of his jailing for homosexual offences 12 years earlier. Even at the time of his death in 1900 it was said that his plays would never again be presented in any respectable theatre. During a Grand Sacred Concert on Sunday January 26, 1908 given by the 1st Glamorgan Royal Garrison Artillery Band the programme was interrupted when the bandmaster, George Hanney, collapsed in front of the audience. Sadly, he never recovered and died a week after. Later that year E Oswald Brookes became the sole lessee of the Grand Theatre.

The Merry Widow was one of the successes of the 1910 season, along with The Little Duke starring the hugely popular, 23 year old, Zena Dare. She was the most photographed girl of the time; thousands of sepia-toned postcards were sold bearing her image. The following year she married Viscount Esher and retired from the stage, then made a comeback in the 1930s for Ivor Novello. In 1958, aged 71, she played Mrs Higgins in the Drury Lane show My Fair Lady opposite Julie Andrews and Rex Harrison. The production ran for more than five and a half years and she was the only member of cast to stay for the complete run. She finally retired at the age of 77 having spent 65 years on the stage.

The show goes on

King Edward VII died on May 6, 1910 and the Grand closed for the week of his State Funeral. At the same time the management of E Oswald Brooks came to an end. His lease was not renewed, and the owners of the building, the Frederick Mouillot organisation once again took control. Their very first production was On His Majesty's Service, starring none other than Swansea's very own Andrew Melville II, the son of the much-loved Andrew Emm, the youngest of the Melvilles, a family for so long associated with Swansea's Star Theatre. Less than a year later Andrew's elder brother, Walter Melville produced The Sins of London at the Grand.

In 1911 another theatrical family – the Courtneidges – appeared in the musical hit The Arcadians. Robert Courtneidge was the star of this show, which also featured his 18-year-old daughter, Cicely. Cicely later became a major attraction in West End musicals and a TV star when she played Reg Varney's mother in the first series of the popular comedy hit On the Buses. By co-incidence Cicely

One of the original main stairways at the Grand with the swing doors to the box office alongside.

AMUSEMENTS.

GRAND THEATRE, SWANSEA.

COMMENCING APRIL 28th,
For Six Nights at 7.30.
Grand Attraction.
W. W. KELLY presents the celebrated Actress, Miss Violet Ellicott (as Josephine),
M. Juan Buonaparte (great grandson of Napoleon the First, as Napoleon)
In the most Successful Historical Play of the Century—

A ROYAL DIVORCE

Friday Evening, May 2nd, Grand Complimentary Joint Benefit to Miss Violet Ellicott and M. Juan Buonaparte (under distinguished patronage).

Box Office Now Open at GWYNNE H. BRADER'S, 17, Heathfield-street, Swansea.

Week Following:
THE EASIEST WAY.

A cutting from the Daily Post newspaper in mid-April, 1913, advertising two forthcoming plays at the Grand.

Courtneidge returned to the Grand 58 years later. She was the star of Agatha Christie's Spider's Web – the play that reopened the establishment when it became a civic theatre in 1969.

Under the management of Frank Bertram, a series of seven plays was performed over consecutive weeks in 1911. This has to be considered as the first true repertory season at the Grand. However, the most significant event during this year occurred on August 4, when theatre in general and Swansea's in particular suffered a great shock. Frederick Mouillot suffered a heart attack and died. He was just 47 and considered to be one of the leading names in British theatre. Frederick's actress-wife, Gertrude, survived another 50 years, dying in 1961 at the age of 91. She never remarried.

As a mark of respect, the Grand closed on the day of Frederick's funeral, but otherwise his widow stuck to the old maxim of 'the show must go on'. The season continued with a return visit of A Royal Divorce, W W Kelly's tour of the story of Napoleon and Josephine. The role of Napoleon was taken by Juan Bonaparte, billed as being Napoleon's Great Grandson, though the Spanish branch of the Bonaparte's seems to have been very many times removed! This successful play returned in 1913 with Violet Ellicott in the role of Josephine. Some 55 years later one of her descendants, Vivyan Ellacott, became the manager at the Grand.

Actor Laurence Irving who appeared at the Grand with his wife, Mabel Lucy Hackney in the early 1900s.

In May 1912 Cavaliere Casteliano's Italian Opera Company paid a week's visit. The programme included two scheduled evening performances of Gounod's Faust – the opera in which Adelina Patti had scored her greatest successes. From her castle at Craig-y-Nos she contacted the manager and indicated that she would like to attend the Saturday matinee performance. Unfortunately, the advertised programme had I Pagliacci and Cavalleria Rusticana scheduled for the matinee. However, such was Patti's power that this was instantly changed. She and her husband, Baron Cederstrom, duly attended and watched the proceedings from the Grand circle box. Baron Cederstrom it seems was embarrassed when a docker from his homeland, knocked the door of the Box and insisted on shaking his hand. On seeing this, Adelina was heard to say:

"I'm glad he didn't want to shake my hand."

At the end of 1913 Laurence Irving and Mabel Lucy Hackney's Company played a week of repertoire including the play version of The Barber of Seville. The company returned the following year with a production of The Typhoon. Laurence Irving was the younger son of the great Sir Henry Irving. During their stay in Swansea, Mabel became friendly with Harriet Jones, a local girl who occasionally worked at the Grand as a dresser. Mabel told Harriet how much she enjoyed visiting her home town of Swansea, and how she hoped that one-day she and her husband could retire from theatre. She said that if ever they stopped touring she would love to return to Swansea and live there.

Six months later, on May 24, 1914, Laurence Irving, Mabel Lucy Hackney and 1,010 other people were drowned when the ship the Empress of Ireland collided with another vessel in the early morning mist on the St Lawrence River in Canada. This was the worst maritime disaster in the country's history. Not long after people began reporting strange occurrences at the Grand. Doors would suddenly open and close of their own accord, curtains would move, gaslights would lower, and there would be sudden very noticeable changes of temperature in parts of the building. These incidents became more frequent and much stronger as years went by. Shortly after Adelina Patti died in 1919 these strange events were happening often, and the suggestion was that Patti's ghost was responsible. Harriet Jones remained convinced, however, that it was the spirit of Mabel Lucy Hackney returning to the town she loved and the theatre where she had been so happy.

GRAND THEATRE, SWANSEA

MONDAY, APRIL 21st, 1913. For Six Nights at 7.30

MATINEE SATURDAY at 2.30

Mr. PHILIP MICHAEL FARADAY'S PRODUCTION

The Pink Lady

A Musical Comedy

By the Author of "The Belle of New York" C. M. S. McLELLAN

Music by IVAN CARYLL

Full London Company including Mr. FRED WRIGHT, Junr.

Mr. FRED WRIGHT, Junr.

Miss HILDA VINING

A typical Grand Theatre playbill from the early 1900s. This one was for the musical comedy, The Pink Lady.

Act 3

Battling on in wartime years

As with all theatres and entertainment venues each day brings fresh battles to tackle and survive. Success and failure can see-saw through the best laid plans and life at the Grand in the early days was no different. Its spectacular launch was soon overtaken by a struggle for survival, one that became even more acute when the country itself was faced with the even greater challenges presented by the First World War.

The months immediately before the outbreak of hostilities with Germany saw business as usual at the theatre and to most the gathering storm clouds of the horrific conflict that was to follow were of little concern. Highlights included a visit from Fred Terry and Julia Nielson in one of the most successful touring shows of its time, The Scarlet Pimpernel. There was also a week of drama from a company called the Welsh National Drama Movement, the first of many subsequent attempts to create a National Theatre for Wales. For the public however, the most significant production of the year appears to have been a second visit from the legendary Sarah Bernhardt. This was, again, just for one night – Friday July 10, 1914 – and the play was Nana, another of her celebrated roles. Sadly just a year later Bernhardt, who for many years had struggled with a knee injury, sustained on stage in 1905, suffered gangrene in the affected leg and it was amputated.

Within a few weeks, Britain and Germany were at war. Initially this did not have much effect on theatre business. The touring shows continued, and the more successful ones exploited the wave of patriotism that gradually swept the nation.

By the end of the year several matinees and the occasional evening at the Grand were given over to films showing footage of the war. The only real inconvenience was due to the Government's Early Closing Order, which required all public houses and bars, including theatre bars, to close at 9pm. This was different and it had a considerable impact on theatre profits.

Swansea audiences were duly shocked when Bernard Shaw's Pygmalion was performed at the Grand in January 1915. Never before had the phrase 'Not bloody likely' been uttered on a public stage, and naturally this led to a flood of outraged letters to the local press and also the council's watch committee. There was also a great deal of condemnation from various religious bodies, and as a result of course absolutely packed houses for the whole of the run. Later in the year audiences flocked to Frank Benson's Shakespeare season, and there were mighty cheers for the patriotic speeches in Henry V. The need for entertainment at this time was such that the Grand even introduced a short season of twice-nightly plays to accommodate the demand for tickets. Shows like It's a Long Way to Tipperary were performed alongside old favourites such as revivals of Florodora and a lavish production of The Spanish Main featuring Oscar Ashe and his wife, Lily

The impressive facade of the Grand Theatre as it would have greeted patrons in 1932.

Brayton. The Grand acquired yet another new manager in 1916. This was Thomas Garret Byrne, who was to remain in the job for 23 years. Byrne had to deal with a whole new set of problems caused by the war. A minor irritation was the extension of the Early Closing Order to include all shops, banning the sale of goods after 8pm. This meant that now sweets, chocolates and tobacco could not be sold in theatres after 8pm, effectively throughout the whole performance time. This meant a further drop in profits. However, the major impact came with the introduction of an Amusements Tax to raise money to meet the costs of fighting the war. An emergency Bill was rushed through Parliament and the new tax took immediate effect. It meant a penny on tickets priced between threepence and eleven pence; twopence on one shilling tickets; Threepence on one shilling and sixpence tickets, rising to sixpence on 10 shilling and sixpence tickets.

Theatre managers throughout the country were up in arms over this. The position was made worse when cinema proprietors nationally announced they would absorb the tax and not increase ticket prices. It was estimated that 750 million tickets were sold each year for moving pictures, and an extra penny on cinema tickets alone would produce £3.5 million. Things were different for theatres however. Profits from bars and other sales had already disappeared. The introduction of compulsory military service also meant many managers were having difficulty finding actors for their shows. The theatre industry was suffering throughout the country, and Swansea theatres were no exception.

In 1917 the Government renamed the Amusements Tax as the Entertainments Tax and increased it, in some cases, by as much as 200 per cent. The Home Office also required all theatres to shorten their performances by 30 minutes in order to save electricity and help the War Effort. At the beginning of 1918 yet another restriction came into force. This was the Lighting Heating and Power Order which prohibited the consumption of gas or electric current in theatres between 10.30pm and 1pm the following day except for necessary cleaning, watching or rehearsal. The Sale of Sweetmeats (Restriction) Order of 1918 imposed a total ban on the sale of all chocolates and sweets in theatres. The Paper Controller ordered all theatres to use only moderate quality paper for the production of printed programmes and posters. All coated or art paper was banned and no theatre programme could contain more than four pages of demi-quarto size.

The Grand was struggling. It was getting harder to fill all the weeks as the number of touring productions decreased. The old stalwart companies were still touring, but their performers were getting older and the staple fare of lavish musicals seemed to be less attractive as the war news became grimmer. The theatre was home to occasional more modern and challenging dramas like Ibsen's Ghosts or T W Robertson's Caste. The latter starred Albert Chevalier, in his first return visit to the Grand since it opened 20 years earlier. The theatre would also occasionally be used as a cinema for the more up-market film, like D.W. Griffith's Birth of a Nation and Intolerance. As business worsened, the Grand closed for six weeks in the summer. Officially this was to carry out some renovation work. In reality it was because the theatre simply couldn't find enough of the type of productions that would attract audiences. It seemed there was no let up in the hurdles that theatres were forced to overcome at this time. The last quarter of the year was marked with a disastrous outbreak of Spanish 'flu. The resulting death toll in London alone during the week of October 21 was 2,225 and half the West End theatres were forced to close. In Swansea, the authorities advised people to avoid going to theatres or cinemas and to keep away from all public gatherings. Business dropped disastrously. The Royal Carl Rosa Opera Company performing that same week in Swansea played to its lowest ever audiences. The only good news was the Armistice announced on November 11, 1918. The Great War was finally over. Britain had suffered three million casualties, one million dead, and had accumulated war debts amounting to £7,100 million. Although the war had

Looking along Singleton Street towards the Grand in 1935. The cottages later became part of the theatre.

ended, it was clear it would be a long time, if ever, before things would return to normal.

A brave new world

The post-war 'brave new world fit for heroes' was not an immediately happy place, particularly for theatres. The Actors Association, the forerunner of the actors' union, Equity, was formed and demanded a standard contract with an agreed minimum wage of £2.10s per week. The National Association of Theatrical Employees also demanded a maximum working week of 44 hours. Even fewer touring companies remained in operation.

As well as the usual fare of major touring musicals, comedies and opera, the Grand occasionally hosted a revue or a variety show. The Albert Chevalier Company in My Old Dutch and Randolph Sutton in All Aboard were examples of this new kind of show. On Saturday September 27, 1919 an eight-day national rail strike began. Arthur Bourchier's Company was due to open a play called Scandal at the Grand on the Monday, but the company and its scenery were marooned in Llandudno.

The enigmatic Rex Harrison who appeared in the play A Cup Of Kindness, at the Grand in 1930.

It was a similar situation all over the country. The Association of Touring Theatre Managers came to special arrangements with lorry drivers and private transport companies in a bid to transport actors and scenery around the country, and in some cases arranged to transfer productions to adjacent theatres which might otherwise have been vacant. Since the strike covered two weekends there was considerable disruption throughout the theatre world. Scandal managed to get to Swansea on the back of a lorry by Tuesday night and opened a day late. Similar problems hit the following week, but the Oswald Gray Company production of The Plaything of an Hour did, at least, manage to open on the Monday as planned. Audiences for both weeks were very poor since there was no rail transport to bring people from the outlying districts.

The major event of 1920 was a production of Joseph Parry's opera, Blodwen. Parry, who had spent some time living in Swansea and was therefore considered to be a local, had written this first ever opera in Welsh in 1878 and it had been a huge success. This was a major 'in house' production by the Grand's own manager, Thomas Byrne, and it was performed for six nights. There were three performances in English and three in Welsh. By popular demand Parry's all-time favourite love song Myfanwy was sung as an encore at the end of each evening – Ryan Davies would have enormous success over 50 years later with the song, which became his signature tune. Just six weeks later the Grand held its own Shakespeare Festival with The Merchant of Venice (Monday), Hamlet (Tuesday and Saturday evening), Twelfth Night (Wednesday), Taming of the Shrew (Thursday), The Tempest (Friday) and a matinee performance of Julius Caesar on Saturday. A month later the Joseph O'Mara Opera Company similarly presented seven different operas on six successive days, followed in the autumn by Charles Doran and his Shakespeare Company performing six different Shakespearean plays in one week. Then the Royal Carl Rosa Opera performed seven different operas in six days, and, to crown it all, during the week commencing December 13, Frederick G Lloyd's company presented four different full-scale musicals in one week: Dorothy on Monday and Friday, Les Cloches de Corneville on Tuesday, Thursday and Saturday evening, Tom Jones on Wednesday and a Saturday matinee performance of Merrie England. No wonder the stagehands' union was calling for a maximum 44-hour working week!

The early 1920s saw visits from famous names like Forbes Robertson in The Passing of the Third Floor Back; Sara Allgood in The White Headed Boy; Henry Ainley in Uncle Ned – Henry was the father of Anthony Ainley who played the second Master in Doctor Who; Bransby Williams in David Copperfield; Matheson Lang in The Wandering Jew; Tom Walls and Lesley Henson in Tons of Money; Jack Buchanan in Battling Butler; Phyllis Neilson Terry in Bella Donna and the legendary Mrs Pat Campbell in The Second Mrs Tanqueray. Although some of these personalities are now forgotten, they were, at that time, among the very top names in the theatre world. The Grand Theatre was a Number One date on the touring circuit, and known for its loyal, enthusiastic and crowded audiences.

There was a strong local performance element too at this time. The Welsh Drama Week and the Swansea Welsh Drama Society Week were established annual features. Swansea Amateur Operatic Society had now made their home at the Grand and the Cymric Amateur Operatic Society was establishing itself as a local favourite. The Swansea Amateur Players was another company making an occasional appearance.

The Grand also achieved a loyal following for its occasional seasons of repertory theatre. There were visits by the Birmingham Repertory Company and the Langley-Howard Players were resident for a four month season in the summer of 1924. However, most of the playgoers of that time recalled the all-time highlight and most memorable production of the era as the week of February 18, 1924 when Ivor Novello, Madelaine Seymour and Hannah Jones appeared in the touring production of The Rat. Novello was already a famous name as a film star and as the composer of the wartime song Till The Boys Come Home, better known perhaps by the later title, Keep the Home Fires Burning. In this play he appeared as Pierre Boucherou, a Parisian apache dancer torn between the influences of a poor, but good, woman and a rich and beautiful adventuress. Pierre, a minor criminal, is nicknamed the Rat, by his colleagues. When the evil Baron Stetz threatens the honour of an innocent girl, the Rat attacks and kills him, but the girl herself assumes the blame to save her hero. This melodramatic tale of the Parisian underworld was written by David l'Estrange, later revealed to be a nom-de-plume for Novello himself, writing in partnership with Constance Collier. The theatre was packed night after night. For the first time in the Grand's history there were young women fainting with excitement at the sight of the handsome leading man. He simply had to turn his famous profile to the audience to create squeals of admiration from a new phenomenon in the audience – several rows of 'flappers' – young women in short dresses and bobbed hair. They had booked the front row seats and returned night after night.

Welsh actor Hugh Griffith, remembered for his highly acclaimed interpretation of King Lear in 1949.

The General Strike

The industrial unrest which had simmered over the previous years finally exploded into Britain's first-ever, week-long General Strike, on Wednesday May 5, 1926. The J Bannister Howard Company ended its run of It Pays to Advertise on the Saturday night and was due to play Cardiff the following week. The strike meant it was unable to move. Meanwhile the Brandon Thomas Company was due to transfer from Newport to Swansea at the same time and the variety company at the Swansea Empire was due to exchange with that at the Cardiff Empire. All of them would normally have moved by train on Sunday May 9 as at this time most scenery was still transported by rail. Because of the strike, there were no trains nor any working haulage companies.

To help solve the problem local supporters in Swansea provided 17 cars at just the cost of petrol, and drove the performers at the Swansea Grand and Empire to Cardiff and Newport, before returning with the performers from theatres there for the following week's shows. Both Swansea theatres, helped by local amateur companies, found stock scenery and props to replace the original scenery, which in most cases was left behind.

The strike continued in the mining valleys for several months until hardship forced most of the miners back to work by the end of the year. However, the effects of debt and lost income in the workforce on the outskirts of Swansea had a direct effect on attendances at its theatres. Despite big attractions like the Drury Lane production of Rose Marie, Jack Buchanan in the West End tour of Sunny, and productions of plays like Dracula and the thriller Alibi by the new young writer, Agatha Christie, business was in decline. To add to the misery, 1927 suffered the wettest summer for 48 years. Week after week the town experienced driving rain, deterring all but the most hardy from attending the theatre. On the other hand, cinema business was booming. Speaking pictures, later called Talkies, were beginning to make an impact and soon revolutionised the entertainment business. There were also rapid developments in the BBC's wireless service, bringing its wonders to more and more homes.

At the end of the 1920s, audiences at the Grand were treated to shows that included big touring musicals like The Desert Song and Hit the Deck with star names like Gladys Cooper in The Sacred Flame, but it was becoming difficult for those responsible for the theatre's day-to-day running to make ends meet.

Into the depression

There was a brave enough beginning to 1930 with a production of Peter Pan, followed by the play A Cup of Kindness starring Laurence Caird and a young Rex Harrison. Harrison's only other visit to the Grand was nearly 40 years later when he sat in the audience to watch Rachel Roberts, who was his wife at the time, in a successful production of Who's Afraid of Virginia Woolf? The MacDona Players did a week of Bernard Shaw plays – a different play each night – Julia Neilson and Fred Terry appeared once more in Sweet Nell of Old Drury.

In the autumn Sir Frank Benson made a farewell tour with his Shakespeare Company, while the Christmas attractions were A Midsummer Night's Dream running up to Christmas Eve and the musical play, Simba, opening on Boxing Day. The following year saw a major change in the policy of the Grand. Following a few weeks of touring shows at the start of the year the theatre became a full-time repertory venue. Its first major rep season opened on April 13, with Alfred Denville's Premier Company. The season stretched for the next 14 months until June 25, 1932. During this time the theatre staged 60 different productions, ranging from Oscar Wilde's Lady Windermere's Fan to The Barretts of Wimpole Street, and from The Cat and the Canary to The Maid of Cefn Ydfa. Charles Denville, the son of Alfred, appeared in My Old Dutch from October 24, 1932. The company had just two free weeks in all of this time. The first of these was when the Grand closed for for redecoration, and the second was to make way for the popular annual Welsh Drama Week.

In the middle of 1932 the Denville Players took a six week break. The Grand was occupied for this time by the Joseph O'Mara Opera Company. It sustained a six week opera season there, the longest operatic run in its entire history. Between June 27 and August 6 the company gave 37 performances of 14 different operas, including Maritana, Lily of Killarney, The Bohemian Girl as well as traditional favourites such as Carmen, La Traviata and Rigoletto. A new Denville Players rep season began on August 9 and ran for 15 weeks, ending in the middle of November.

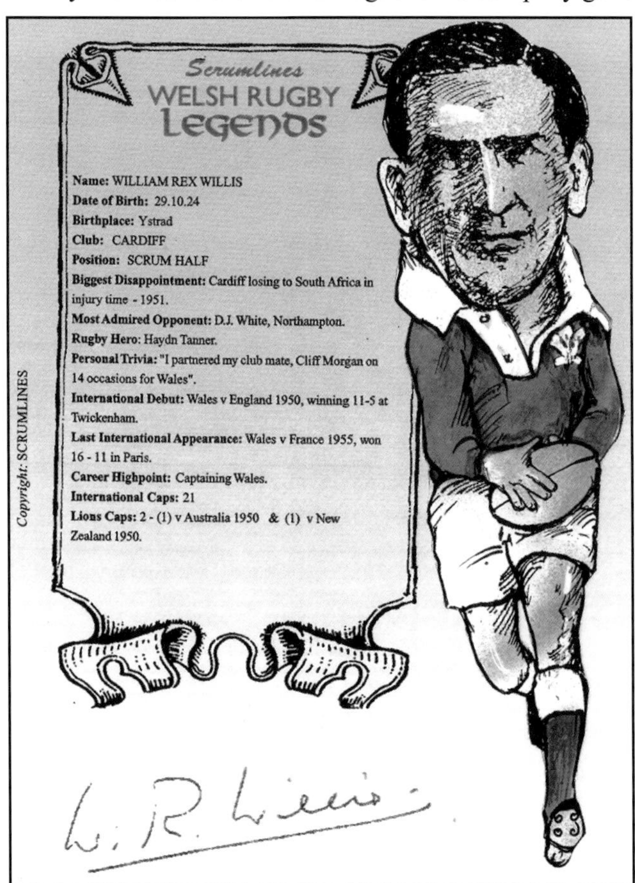

A caricature of Wales rugby international and British Lion Rex Willis who owned The Grand until it was taken over by Swansea City Council.

All was not well however. Audiences had severely declined and although there was regular and loyal support for the rep company it was not enough to cover costs. The theatre returned to its policy of post West-End touring productions for the next five weeks, but these also failed to attract sufficient customers. Business at local cinemas, meantime, was the best ever. A new rep company headed by the actor Clive Brooks took over on Boxing Day with the musical attraction Lilac Time, followed by two plays, Michael and Mary and Blackmail. The third play, Almost a Honeymoon, was cancelled. On January 26, the Grand closed with immediate effect because of a 'flu epidemic. This was nothing like the disastrous one of 1918 and the Grand was the only theatre or cinema in Swansea to close completely because of it. Surprisingly, it remained closed until the end of May, except for one week in April – the Welsh Drama Week. This four-month closure indicated not so much a fear of spreading influenza as worries about its serious financial difficulties. The theatre eventually reopened on May 29, 1933 with a new company – the Jack O'Shea and George Laurence Repertory Company and its star attraction, the actress Zillah Bateman.

The new season was announced as a 'Shilling Theatre' season, with all tickets priced at one shilling so that everyone could afford to attend. Six weeks later the season was abruptly terminated, and the company disbanded. On August 14, the Grand re-opened as a cine-variety venue, showing films with one or two variety acts performing live between them. The first film was East of Fifth Avenue, and the evening included some dancers and a conjurer. The cine-variety season continued until Christmas when the theatre returned to a fully live pantomime, Babes in the Wood which ran from December 23 to January 12, 1934. Then, tragically the curtain fell. After more than 36 years of live theatre the Grand closed.

Act 4

The lost years of live theatre

The closure of the Grand may not have ended live theatre in Swansea, but it was a blow lamented by its loyal supporters. It was not however the end of entertainment in the building as a cinema company moved in and refurbished the building for the showing of films. The popularity of the silver screen at this time may have been frowned upon by some, but it at least ensured its future as an entertainment venue.

The company involved in this temporary transition was Willis (Cinemas) Ltd. It was gradually acquiring a chain of cinemas across the South Wales valleys. Heading it up was one Captain WE Willis, a formidable, hard-nosed businessman. Willis was renowned for never being happy unless he had negotiated any deal down to the last penny and was always cutting costs where possible. His company acquired a lease on the Grand Theatre and eventually reopened it as the New Grand Cinema.

In July 1947 Willis bought the building outright. He often told a tale of how, as a young man, he had sat in the gallery of the Grand watching a performance and had accidentally dropped a gold sovereign which disappeared into a crack in the flooring and was impossible to retrieve. He said that when he heard the Grand was up for sale, he decided at once to buy it, just so that he could tear up the gallery floor and retrieve his sovereign.

The New Grand Cinema opened its doors on March 26, 1934. Fortunately, the stage and its equipment were kept in working order, and each spring the curtain would go up on a week of live performances – the Welsh Drama Week. However, even this one flickering brave attempt at live theatre came to an end after the 1940 session, when the demands of the Second World War made it impossible for the company to continue. The cinema years saw the death of King George V, the Abdication of King Edward VIII, the Coronation of King George VI and the beginning and end of the Second World War. Despite the enormous destruction caused by the German aerial bombardment of Swansea, particularly in the Three Nights' Blitz of February 1941, the town's theatre buildings survived relatively unscathed. In a stroke of ironic coincidence, during the height of the bombing, the New Grand Cinema was showing Charlie Chaplin's portrayal of Hitler in the The Great Dictator.

A grand awakening

At the end of 1947 the Willis Family decided to re-open the Grand as a theatre. It was a move in which Captain Willis's wife had a most influential part. She was a gracious, elegant and old-fashioned lady who secretly felt that her family's involvement in the cinema business was rather vulgar. She believed that having at least one live theatre under their control gave them some degree of respectability. Her two grown up children agreed with her. The son, Rex, (who later became a well-known Welsh rugby player) liked the idea of being the second in

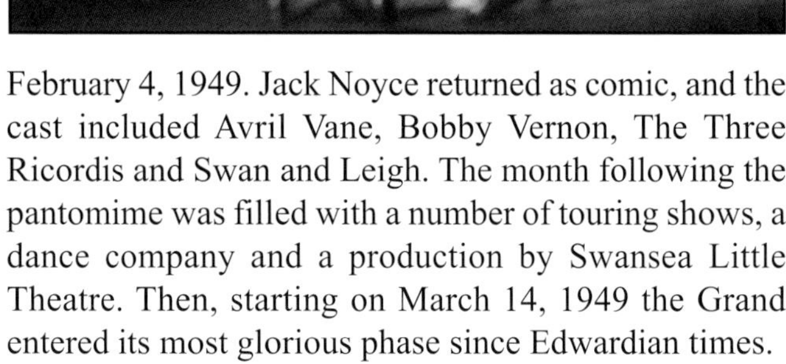

A song sheet from Mother Goose, the 1952/53 pantomime at the Grand, which starred Maudie Edwards and Ossie Morris. Alongside, Maudie engages with the audience during one of her memorable performances.

command of a theatre, with pretty actresses and chorus girls. Daughter, Jill, was especially interested in costume design and relished the opportunity of getting involved in a practical way.

Their first 'live' performance was the pantomime Babes In The Wood, starring Joyce Randall, Gus Elton, Zoe Mansel, Jack Noyce, Irene Marshall and the amazing Jimmy Currie's Waterfalls which involved the use of 15 tons of equipment and 2,000 gallons of water every minute when operational. The pantomime was a roaring success, opening on December 18 and running until March 6 the following year – an amazing 11 weeks. Because of this, the Willis's were more than happy to negotiate a repertory season with the Harry Hansen Court Players and the Grand once again became a 'proper' theatre. Hansen was one of the biggest names in repertory at the time – with companies performing all over the UK. His 1948 season in Swansea consisted of 39 consecutive weeks, and included popular successes by Emlyn Williams, Noel Coward and Agatha Christie as well as more challenging works by Eugene O'Neill, Somerset Maugham and Bernard Shaw.

The Grand had completed one full year as a live theatre and business was booming. Before long it was pantomime season again, and this time the subject was Dick Whittington, running from December 18, 1948 to February 4, 1949. Jack Noyce returned as comic, and the cast included Avril Vane, Bobby Vernon, The Three Ricordis and Swan and Leigh. The month following the pantomime was filled with a number of touring shows, a dance company and a production by Swansea Little Theatre. Then, starting on March 14, 1949 the Grand entered its most glorious phase since Edwardian times.

The Arts Council years

The Swansea Theatre Company was a creation of the newly-formed Arts Council, set up to bring art and culture to all parts of the country, and given Government funding to achieve this. Swansea was earmarked as an area likely to benefit from such investment in theatre arts, and under a series of directors including Clifford Evans and Lionel Harris, the theatre began its second era of success.

The first Arts Council season ran from March to December 1949 and consisted of 38 plays. The opening play, The Last of Mrs Cheyney, was preceded by a press conference at Swansea Guildhall where emphasis was placed on the need for both the town's council and its people, to support this brave new venture. The programme of plays was controversial however. In order to attract the widest range of audiences, it included popular hits like Miranda, Storm in a Teacup and Duet for Two Hands, but these were interspersed with the verse play Winterset, and Cocteau's The Eagle Has Two Heads. The artistic highlights of this first season included Eugene O'Neill's Desire Under the Elms with Beatrix Lehman and Wilfrid Brambell. She repeated her success later that year in Ibsen's Ghosts, and he with Goodbye Mr Chips. It was, however, a production of King Lear, staged as part of the newly created Swansea Festival of Music and the Arts which went down in theatrical legend. Hugh Griffith played Lear and Wilfrid Brambell, the Fool – and it is still spoken of as one of the greatest ever interpretations of this play.

The year 1949 brought an extremely hot summer and as a result audiences were seduced by other pleasures. By the end of the year, the Swansea Theatre Company was in financial difficulty. The Arts Council's Welsh Committee decided it would only support a second season if Swansea Council provided a financial contribution to support the venture. Eventually, a guarantee of £2,000 was offered and following a four week run of the pantomime Aladdin with Wilfrid Brambell, Eleanor Drew, Antonia Pemberton and local favourite, Harry Davies, the second Swansea Theatre Company season opened on January 23, 1950.

The 1950 season was in two sections. The first ran for 19 weeks from January to June, with a week's break for the Welsh Drama Week which made a triumphant return to the Grand after an absence of 10 years. This first half of the year offered the same kind of programme as before: a mix of the popular and the 'arty'. Chief among the latter were productions of Jean-Paul Sartre's The Respectable Prostitute and Ibsen's Enemy of the People, while the former offered Born Yesterday, Murder at the Vicarage and See How They Run. The company then took a seven week break during which the Grand played host to touring productions that included a Ballet Company, a production of Shaw's Pygmalion with Jessie Matthews as Eliza Doolittle; Mary Jerrold in The Sacred Flame, The Adventures of Tommy Trouble and the post West-End tour of Reluctant Heroes with Brian Rix, Dermot Walsh and Colin Morris.

Many years later Brian Rix recalled this visit in a letter to the Grand Theatre Club and hinted that it had not been entirely incident free. He said:

"We arrived at the Grand on Monday July 17, 1950. Apparently the electrician had drunk more than was good for him on the previous Saturday night and had been sacked. He proceeded to avenge himself by smashing up the switchboard with a five-pound hammer. So there we were, two sets, 11 actors and actresses, a few advance bookings, but no lights. However, as always seemed to happen in those days, a Good Samaritan was there to give us a hand – this time in the person of Archie Pipe. He'd looked after the lighting for a number of amateur shows and offered his services, which were gratefully received. He slaved away all day trying to create some order out of the chaos and at 7.30pm up went the curtain on a stage lit, in what can best be described as Stygian gloom. But that Swansea audience is one of the warmest in Britain. They peered through the murk and laughed and laughed. Perhaps they were all miners and found our lighting positively dazzling!"

This couldn't have bothered Archie Pipe and he remained in the business, eventually making his presence felt on the production side of religious programmes in the United States, one of which was aptly named Lead, Kindly Light.

During this period many stars of the future were to learn the ropes at the Grand and for the second half of the 1950 season the acting company was joined by newcomers Kenneth Williams and Rachel Roberts. For a week of Chekhov's play The Seagull at the end of August, the cast of Kenneth Williams, Wilfrid Brambell and Clifford Evans was joined by a young and almost unknown name, none other than Richard Burton.

To improve the artistic standard, the 11 plays in the second half of the year ran for two weeks each which signalled the end of weekly rep. Plays like Noel Coward's Blithe Spirit and the hit drama Bonaventure, managed to attract respectable audiences spread over each fortnight, but many other shows such as Shaw's Saint Joan, Jean-Paul Sartre's Crime Passionnel and even Shakespeare's Twelfth Night, were poorly supported. However, audiences did flock to the 1950-1951 pantomime, Red Riding Hood, with Maudie Edwards, Stan Stennett and Ossie Morris. Its excellent 10-week run convinced the directors of the Swansea Theatre Company, Clifford Evans and Lionel Harris and the Arts Council itself that they were wasting their time. Clifford Evans took to the stage of the Grand and announced:

"The people of Swansea are not interested in theatre, only in choral singing."

The fabulous fifties

It was left to Ballet Rambert to open the 1951 season followed by other touring shows that included The Student Prince, a touring revue entitled Shw'mae Heno with stars from Welsh Rarebit, a popular wartime radio programme which was broadcast to a weekly audience of 10 million; Ossie Morris in his own touring show, I Must Have Hush, the Welsh Drama Week and a return by Swansea Little Theatre. In the intervening six months

The theatre's hard working stage crew take a break from their labours duringn the 1960/61 pantomime Mother Goose with its star, Welsh comedian and entertainer, Stan Stennett.

Maudie Edwards had negotiated terms to stage her own repertory season at the Grand – which she accomplished successfully for the following two years. The nature of the financial deal between her and Captain Willis was later to cause a rift between them. Initially, she received a percentage of the takings. She didn't perform in the productions herself, except for the occasional guest appearance, which was certain to boost takings. The first season of the Maudie Edwards Players started in June and consisted of 26 plays. All were aimed at the popular market, and culminated in a production of The Late Christopher Bean by Emlyn Williams, with Maudie herself playing the pivotal role of Gwenny.

The Grand appeared to have struck a chord with audiences and it completed its most successful year since re-opening as a live theatre. The rep attendance had been excellent and the 1951-1952 pantomime Cinderella with Gladys Morgan and family had added greatly to this success. Swansea-born Gladys with husband, Frank Laurie and daughter, Joan, together with Wyn Calvin ensured that this was a truly 'local' panto.

Once the panto ended it was back into the second repertory season of the Maudie Edwards Players, with Salvin Stewart, Joanne Hilliard and Glyn Davys as members of the company. This season ran for 43 weeks and ended in the first week of December with Johnny Belinda. Maudie Edwards and her company had become extremely popular with Swansea theatregoers and had built up a strong and loyal following. The Willis family was instrumental in ensuring that Maudie herself had the leading role in the 1952-1953 pantomime, Mother Goose. Also on stage were Ossie Morris, and Vera Cody with her live horses!

Unfortunately, it wasn't long before things began to go wrong. Captain Willis decided against renewing Maudie Edwards' contract for the 1953 season and instead invited Terence Dudley to form a company and take over at the theatre. Dudley had been the assistant producer in Maudie's team and she was convinced he had done a secret deal with Willis to accept a lower percentage of the takings. She took legal action against them both – suing Willis for breach of contract and Dudley for improper business practice. She lost both cases, but was determined to continue the fight in her own way. In a classic and very theatrical piece of revenge, she opened a rival repertory company at Swansea's 'other' theatre The Palace. She even managed to open on January 26 – one clear week before the Grand's rep season – with a production of Charley's Aunt.

The Terence Dudley Company presented 45 plays during 1953. In mid-June the company was joined by an unknown actress for the role of Tondelayo in White Cargo. She was Mollie Sugden who remained for the rest of the year, becoming a favourite with local audiences. She later become a favourite with audiences throughout the country in the role of Mrs Slocombe in TV's Are You Being Served. Dudley himself became a top TV director associated with the early Dr Who productions and Colditz. The 1953-54 pantomime, Goldilocks and the Three

Members of a repertory company from the early 1950s take time out to celebrate a birthday. Among them, second from the right in the centre row, is a young Mollie Sugden.

Bears, was staged by Cyril Dowler, with himself, Rhoda Rogers, Marcia Owen, Hilda Heath and Norman McGlenn taking part. The production featured three live Norwegian bears. While the bears were being transported from Dover to Swansea their special mobile cage broke an axle, and there was a possibility they would not arrive in time for the first performance on Boxing Day. Luckily keepers at London Zoo were able to provide alternative transport and the bears – James, Bessa and Strike – made it just in time.

The panto ran for eight weeks, and was followed by Terence Dudley's second season. The 1954 rep season included 44 plays and welcomed back Mollie Sugden for her second season at Swansea. However, once again, winning audiences became a struggle. The Maudie Edwards Players meanwhile, continued in opposition at the Palace and though neither company would admit it, they were effectively dividing potential audiences between them. As a result, neither was covering its costs. In May 1954 in a 'double or quit' move Maudie Edwards opened a second repertory company at the Town Hall, Pontypridd, where she planned to alternate her two companies, the same play being performed for a week in each venue. Unfortunately for her the experiment was unsuccessful and short-lived.

The arrival of 1955 heralded crunch time all round. For the Grand it started well. Drawing on the popularity of the animal antics provided by the previous year's three bears, the theatre's pantomime, once more staged by Cyril Dowler and Rhoda Rogers, introduced three live sheep – Julia, Nellie and Billy – under the watchful eye of Little Bo Peep. This produced packed houses through a two-month run, and was supposed to be followed by the opening of the third Terence Dudley season. Something went wrong, however, and it was announced that the rep season would open a week later than planned. As a stopgap the Grand staged a touring production of Pin Ups from Paris.

Both Terence Dudley and Maudie Edwards struggled on for the following months with neither prepared to admit defeat. However, halfway through the year Maudie announced that due to her other professional commitments she was unable to devote herself full time to the rep company at the Palace. Rather than allow the standards to fall, she said she felt it best, though reluctantly, to close her Swansea Company, and wished to express her gratitude to her loyal Swansea audiences. Terence Dudley was delighted. At last he had a clear field. With renewed energy he staged a series of new plays by Swansea authors including The Swansea Theatre Scandal by the improbably named Howard Bromley-Chapman, and The Dark Horse by Swansea author, Michael Davies.

With a young Tom Bell joining the company that autumn, things seemed to get better and better at the Grand. There were queues for the production of I Am a Camera and Oscar Wilde's Lord Arthur Saville's Crime. It looked as if business was booming. However, the

The exterior of the Grand Theatre as it looked in 1962.

reality was that the cost of staging that season was constantly exceeding the income. Dudley too, decided to call it a day. He had the perfect excuse – the threatened closure of the Grand as part of a road-widening scheme. Theatre manager, Gordon Douglas, announced that Swansea Council had approved plans to widen Singleton Street as part of a town centre re-development. The extra 15ft width on the road and the expansion of the central bus station would involve the demolition of the Grand. In the light of this uncertain future Dudley announced he would not be returning after the pantomime. In the event, the proposed demolition of the Grand was rejected leaving the Willis family to secure fresh means of filling their theatre. The 1955-56 pantomime was presented again by Cyril Dowler and Rhoda Rogers. The Old Woman Who Lived in a Shoe once again looked to animals for its success. This time it was Ida Rosaire's Perky Pekes and Scotts' Sea Lions who drew the audiences.

Over the course of the next year no fewer than three repertory companies tried to make a go of it at the Grand. It seemed that television was now playing a part in keeping audiences away. In July 1956 Harry Davies announced the opening of yet another season using the name Swansea Repertory Company. Harry had been a very popular member of earlier rep companies and had a strong local following. But even he could only struggle on until Christmas. In the meantime, much earlier in the year, a show called Call Girl had been booked into the Swansea Empire for a week which included Good Friday. Because of this the council's Watch Committee had refused permission for it to play on such a holy day. The Grand meanwhile, was staging Widow's Mite. The committee thought that this was much more acceptable and allowed it to go ahead. Several of the cast members of Call Girl decided to spend their night off checking out the opposition. And so it was that Norwich-born actor John Chilvers made his first visit to the Grand. During the interval he chatted to Rex Willis, the son of the theatre's owner. They politely exchanged business cards, little knowing that this chance meeting would have the most important consequences for the future of theatre in Swansea.

Harry Davies's rep season ended with The Moon is Blue in December and was followed by Cyril Dowler's Sleeping Beauty, with Joe O'Gorman and Angela Scott. It was clear early on that advance bookings for this pantomime were not very good, and a decision was made to restrict the run to just five weeks. Shortly before the pantomime opened Rex Willis wrote to John Chilvers and invited him to provide a six-week, fill-in rep season starting on February 4, 1957.

Act 5

Man with the magic touch

The immediate thoughts of John Chilvers when he received a letter inviting him to conjure up a short, stop-gap rep season at the Grand are unclear, but what is known is that the actor grasped the opportunity with both hands. His efforts could have gone the way of others in the years before, but they didn't. Chilvers struck a vein of luck that saw his choice of plays boost attendances on previous bids to revitalise repertory at the theatre.

When the season ended on March 16, 1957 the Grand's owner Rex Willis suggested to Chilvers that he might like to stay on as temporary manager for the following 10 weeks and resume a rep season on May 27. Chilvers was encouraged by the response to his efforts and having considered matters decided once again to rise to the challenge. He chose six popular plays for the season. They were Ivor Novello's We Proudly Present, Ten Little Niggers, Trespass, No Escape, The Facts of Life and No Trees in the Street. The company that performed them included Tom Bell, Rosamonde Hartley, Elaine Mitchell, Daphne Wetton, James Beattie, Gordon Rawlings and Freddie Lees.

Chilvers decision was to mark the beginning of a 25 year link with the Grand. The quarter of a century that followed would bring 504 shows that he personally directed, 20 pantomimes, a series of amateur shows with the Scout and Guide movement, and eight summer seasons with top name variety stars. During his reign at the Grand he acted, directed, wrote pantomimes, auditioned performers, sold tickets, balanced the books, handled publicity, opened up in the morning, closed up at night, inspired all around him and on a few occasions even cleaned the toilets!

After a short break for visiting shows and a Swansea Amateur Operatic Society production, rep resumed at the end of May in that first year, with Agatha Christie's Murder on the Nile. This season ran right through to Christmas that year except for a week's visit from Welsh National Opera. After that Chilvers was invited to arrange a further season. The first two years were very successful. In all, 74 different plays, the usual visits from the Welsh Drama Week, the Welsh National Opera and Swansea Amateur Operatic Society, all worked well for him and the theatre, along with successful outside pantomime productions. The 1957-58 pantomime was Cinderella with Des O'Connor and Jackie Farrell while the following year it was the turn of Aladdin with Ossie Morris and Alan Wells. Both were successful, but there were signs that once again the tide was turning.

The early part of 1959 was not as successful and brought with it a temporary interruption to live theatre. The Grand became a cinema for the best part of four months showing X-rated films such as Abductress, El Bruto and The Streets of Shame, interspersed with an amateur production of The Dancing Years and a visit from the Welsh National Opera. A shortened rep season opened in May, running for just 25 weeks, and then the Grand reverted to film shows until the arrival of the pantomime, Mother Goose with Stan Stennett and Sylvia Norman. By the end of 1959 John Chilvers had been appointed successor to manager Mr E T Evers, and now held the title of manager and artistic director.

A further four-month film season launched the Grand into 1960, followed by a 28 week rep season sandwiched between films that included The Ten Commandments, Dolls of Vice, The Film of the Royal Ballet and Sins of Youth. It ended on a far different note with Wyn Calvin and George Bolton in Jack and the Beanstalk. Ironically it was the same show with which Calvin had closed the Swansea Empire just four years before – the same pantomime, the same sets, costumes, script and all!

Chilvers was nothing if not doggedly determined and 1961 marked something of a turning point that in many ways must be attributed to this. The theatre was used for films for just a few weeks, and the rep season was extended to 37 weeks. These seasons were entertaining but immensely gruelling. He would start the process in London, auditioning scores of actors and actresses. He would pick a core team who would then all move to Swansea. Then he would cast a few Welsh actors to whom Swansea theatregoers could relate. The plays would enjoy week long runs, with the cast rehearsing the following week's offering in the afternoons throughout.

Looking up at the two distinctive towers of the Grand Theatre building in 1973. They were a familiar part of the city's skyline.

By sheer effort Chilvers had raised the artistic standards and level of interest in the Grand and his hard work began to pay off. Audience support was strong, but despite this an application to the Welsh Arts Council for financial support was rejected. The drama director of the Arts Council refused to assist, stating:

"Based on our own experience in Swansea, there is no need for live theatre."

The 1961-62 pantomime, Babes in the Wood with Ossie Morris, Kenneth Earle, Malcolm Vaughan, Howell Evans and Pat Kane was the last to be presented by an outside company. For the remainder of the John Chilvers years they would be 'in-house' affairs, produced and directed by Chilvers himself, with all the profits being used to support to the Grand. The ever-growing profits from these pantomimes subsidised any losses on the rep seasons, and the next five years were very successful.

Between 1962 and 1967 Chilvers directed no fewer than 169 different plays including 14 world premieres. He created an excellent repertory company and was earning admiration and respect from the profession. The Grand was now firmly established as the only producing theatre in Wales. It also remained unsubsidised, relying almost totally on pantomime profits to make ends meet.

Since the re-opening of the theatre in 1947 pantomimes at the Grand had been staged by outside production companies which would take the major share of the profits. Chilvers raised this matter with Rex Willis who challenged him to produce his own if he wasn't happy with the arrangement. Once again he decided to give it his best shot and put together his first pantomime. It was Dick Whittington and ran from December 22, 1962 through until February 16, 1963. His idea once again was to bring in Welsh talent so the audience would feel it was their own special panto. The formula was a success with sell-out performances. Chilvers had an excellent ability to attract the kind of star-names that appealed to Swansea audiences. Dick Whittington for example starred Johnny Stewart and Ted Gatty. Subsequent stars included Johnny de Little, Sian Hopkins and Grande and Mars in Cinderella (1963), Vince Eager, Duggie Clark and Alan Wells in Aladdin (1964), Jess Conrad and Keith Harris in Puss in Boots, (1965), Marty Wilde, Ivor Owen, Danny O'Dea and George Truzzi in Robin Hood (1966) and Johnny de Little and Peter Kaye in Dick Whittington (1967).

The pantomime profits, large as they were, did not quite cover the final costs of running the theatre in 1966. At this point Swansea Council stepped in and offered a

John Chilvers surveys the majestic sweep of the Grand Theatre auditorium. In all its history he was one of the most successful and adept at filling it with patrons.

£2,000 guarantee against loss for the 1967 season. It began with a series of visiting shows, including Dorothy Squires, Sandy Powell and the Charlie Cairoli Company, before continuing with a 25 week rep season which was remarkable for its range and artistic achievement. It opened with Shaw's Arms and the Man and included Pinter's The Homecoming, Wilde's Importance of Being Earnest and epic productions of Goodbye Mr Chips and The Adventures of Tom Jones, as well as popular successes by Noel Coward and Agatha Christie. There was a vitality and enthusiasm buzzing through the theatre and its audiences. In his first 10 years John Chilvers had created a repertory theatre of national renown. And then, once again, in the manner that seems to be regularly associated with show business and theatres – it all began to go wrong.

At the start of 1968 there was little hint of what was to come. The year had started well enough: a visiting ballet, the Diana Dors Show; A Swansea Amateurs production of Oklahoma and a brilliant Welsh National Opera season. The operas included a stunning Carmen with Joyce Blackham and David Hughes, Pauline Tinsley at the peak of her career in Nabucco, and Delme Bryn Jones as Rigoletto. All seemed fair sailing for the opening of a 32-week rep season. But the new company attracted a string of bad reviews in the South Wales Evening Post and the rot set in. Week after week a new young critic attacked the choice of plays and the standard of performance. This led to a vociferous campaign from loyal patrons claiming the paper was prejudiced and the critic 'too trendy and avant-garde' to be in tune with Swansea audiences. Worse followed. A scorching summer saw audiences stay outdoors and finally the nation as a whole began to feel the effects of serious inflation. In 1968 the Grand made a loss of £5,000. The 1968-69 pantomime Jack and the Beanstalk with Wayne Fontana, Sian Hopkins and Trevor Moreton made a profit of just £3,000. The Willis family decided they'd had enough and announced their intention to close the theatre and convert it into a bingo hall to capitalise on the craze that was sweeping the nation. This would take effect from March 30, 1969, after the last performance of My Fair Lady by Swansea Amateur Operatic Society.

The numbers game

John Chilvers was invited to stay on to supervise the conversion of the theatre into a bingo hall. It was an offer that was of little interest to him, but he was privately urged to stay on by senior council officials, most notably

Members of one of the repertory companies brought together by John Chilvers in 1965.

Neil Rees, the town clerk. Then in February 1969 the council turned down an application for planning permission for change of use of the Grand from theatre to bingo. Soon after the authority made inquiries about buying the theatre, but the Willis Family made it clear they were not interested in selling. They intended instead to demolish the building and sell the site for redevelopment which they felt would be a far more profitable venture than simply selling the building.

For the following two months things were on a knife edge. It looked as if the theatre would be demolished. On May 19 the council announced it had struck a deal with the Willis family. It had taken a 10 year lease at a rent of £5,000 a year for the first seven years, and then £6,000 for the remaining three years. The council would also bear the cost of renovating and upgrading the building.

A major renovation

Over the previous 20 years hardly any money at all had been spent on repairs, maintenance or re-decoration. The Grand was very shabby and technically out of date. Certain seats could not be sold because of the springs sticking out of them while damp patches and water stains were visible throughout the building. In earlier years two cottages alongside the theatre had been bought and the adjoining walls knocked down to create extra dressing rooms and working space backstage. The different floor levels and dubious electric wiring made the backstage area hazardous to anyone unfamiliar with the layout.

The council knew it had to give the Grand a facelift before it could be re-opened. The work, which included some remodelling of the foyer and a new canopy over the front doors also included seating, carpeting, floor covering, reupholstery and redecoration of the dressing rooms. Eventually £35,000 was spent on the renovation, with a further £5,000 on new lighting and sound equipment. The work was carried out under the direction of the borough architect, R B Padmore and was completed in time for a grand civic re-opening on September 22, 1969. The first show to be staged was Agatha Christie's Spider's Web starring Cicely

A lighter moment during a read through for one of the repertory productions staged at the Grand during the mid-1960s.

Courtneidge and her husband, Jack Hulbert. The reception to the revamped and revitalised theatre was tremendous. Every seat was sold for the whole week, and on Friday and Saturday nights even the 'Gods' as the upper level of the theatre was known, were opened, for the first time in years. The renewed Grand played its first season of touring shows with star names like Rachel Roberts in Who's Afraid of Virginia Woolf, Miriam Karlin and a young Dennis Waterman. The season included visits from the Welsh National Opera, and John Quentin as Hamlet in a production by the Welsh Theatre Company. The 1969-70 pantomime, Robinson Crusoe with Stan Stennett as its star, was also hugely successful.

The early 1970s established a pattern which the remainder of the John Chilvers era comfortably settled into. The year consisted of a spring season of touring shows and star names, followed by a summer repertory season. The late autumn saw a further series of visiting shows before the year ended with a pantomime. The visiting shows of 1970 included such familiar names as Shirley Anne Field, Bill Maynard, Valentine Dyall, Dave King, Peter Adamson, Ian McKellen – in The Recruiting Officer and Chips with Everything – and Sir Bernard Miles as Long John Silver in Treasure Island. The summer rep season spanned 19 weeks and included plays by Tennessee Williams, Alan Bennett, Joe Orton and a revival of the classic Beggar's Opera by John Gay. A regular member of the company was Jean Fergusson who later became a regular cast member of TV's popular long-running series Last of the Summer Wine.

The 1970 rep company employed a larger than usual number of performers and was effectively two companies. Each play was rehearsed for two weeks, but performed for just one week. This meant that John Chilvers was, for the first time in his career at Swansea, sharing the direction duties. For this first season his co-director was James Jordan.

The two-company experiment proved to be very expensive, and, as a consequence, it was decided to change the following repertory season to fortnightly productions. Each play would rehearse for two weeks

Panto pulling power: three posters used to draw audiences to the annual favourite of thousands during the mid-1960s.

and then play for two weeks. This also enabled a more adventurous choice of play, and the next two rep seasons, 1971 and 1972, were felt to have achieved the highest ever standards. They brought a great deal of praise to the Grand and to John Chilvers himself. Productions in these two years included Hadrian VII, Brecht's Mother Courage, Oh What a Lovely War, Shakespeare's Romeo and Juliet, A Streetcar Named Desire, The Entertainer and a stage version of Dylan Thomas's Adventures in the Skin Trade. One of the great successes was a riotous production of Charley's Aunt starring Freddie Lees.

Among performers in the two seasons were local favourites Gilly Adams, Gareth Armstrong, Eleanor Thomas, Islwyn Morris and Myfanwy Talog. There was also a guest appearance from celebrated actress, Freda Jackson. The 1972 season also included Stephen Mallatratt who went on to become a well-known writer for TV and the theatre. He penned many episodes of Coronation Street and was responsible for the stage adaptation of the long-running West End thriller The Woman in Black. Sadly, Mallatratt died in 2004 aged just 57. Visiting stars during this period included Gwen Watford, Alexandra Bastedo, Peter Adamson, David Jason, Davy Jones of The Monkees pop group, Michael Denison and Dulcie Gray.

The 1971-72 pantomime was Aladdin, starring Reg Dixon. It was so successful that it was extended to an 11-week run. It was the 1972-73 pantomime, Cinderella, however, which began a legendary five-year run of Christmas successes, often referred to as the Golden Age of Swansea pantos. This was the first panto to star Ryan Davies and his partner Ronnie Williams. The amazing duo performed two years running with Dick Whittington following Cinderella. Sadly, ill health forced Ronnie to withdraw from subsequent productions. For his first pantomime as a solo act in 1974-75 Ryan played dame in Mother Goose. This was his first and only attempt at such a role. Despite the success of the inimitable 'Mam' character he had created in his TV series which he had managed to fit into the occasional pantomime, Ryan felt uncomfortable and restricted in the role of dame. He returned to his standard role of the main comic working as the character of Ryan for Jack and the Beanstalk (1975-76) and Babes in the Wood (1976-1977). During these five years the Swansea pantomimes, directed by John Chilvers and starring Ryan, had become the longest running in the country and a not-to-be-missed part of the Swansea calendar. Babes in the Wood became the longest running pantomime in the history of the Grand. Sadly it also turned out to be the last for Ryan. Shortly after it ended, the much-loved performer died of a heart attack while on holiday in the United States. Wales was left to mourn the man who had become the nation's Clown Prince.

But if the pantomimes had enjoyed ever growing runs, there were signs that the days of the old-style repertory theatre were coming to an end. Gradually, down the years, the length of each season was reduced. As the decade moved on, they shrank to an average of just six or seven plays. The mid-summer weeks were replaced with variety bills, headlined by top names to attract Swansea's holidaymakers. The amount of touring productions also increased at this time bringing with them stars such as

Marty Wilde and Joyce Baker, parents of 1980s pop star Kim Wilde, during the pantomime Robin Hood.

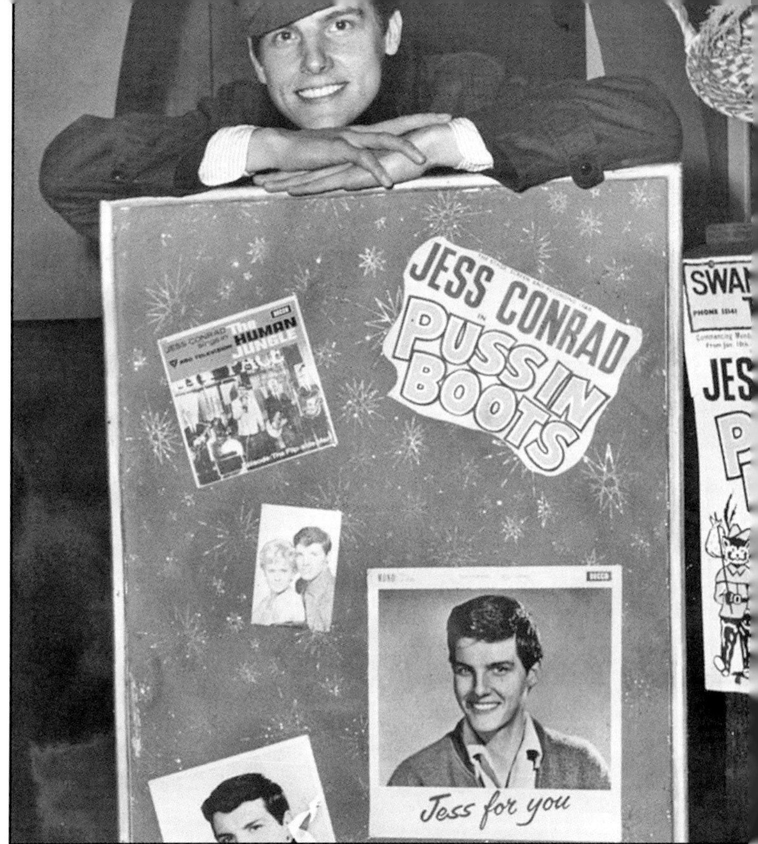

Jess Conrad in the Grand foyer at a press call before the first night of the panto Puss in Boots in 1965/66.

Pat Phoenix, Carmel McSharry, Nicky Henson, and Hywel Bennett while summer season performers included Dickie Henderson and a glorious old time music hall bill with legendary names such as Elsie and Doris Waters, Sandy Powell and Cavan O'Connor. Hylda Baker was booked to appear for one week, but because of illness she was replaced at the last minute by Russ Conway.

This mix of touring productions, star-name variety weeks, home-produced repertory plays and highly popular pantomimes meant that the Grand was now appealing to its widest ever range of audience. Business was booming as the pattern continued for the remainder of the 1970s. Touring production performers included Edward Fox, Robert Stephens, David Jason, Kate O'Mara, Eunice Gayson, Henry McGee, and Sian Hopkins. The variety shows meanwhile brought, among others, David Nixon, Freddie and the Dreamers, Max Boyce, Charlie Drake, Cilla Black, Harry Worth, Jimmy Tarbuck, Frankie Vaughan, Frankie Howerd, Leslie Crowther, Arthur Askey, and Faith Brown.

Throughout the 1970s the Grand also received annual visits from various ballet companies. Perhaps this was not surprising as ballet had always been a mode of the arts close to John Chilvers' heart. Generally there were guaranteed sell-out visits from the Welsh National Opera in spring and autumn too. Swansea was treated to performances from singers who would later become great names in international circles. They were treated to the vocal delights of Josephine Barstow, Geraint Evans, Thomas Allen, Margaret Price and Rita Hunter. There was too an unforgettable performance of Falstaff

The playbill for one of the popular plays staged in the Grand's first season as a civic theatre. Its star was Wilfrid Brambell, a favourite with Swansea audiences.

The cast of the final Ryan Davies pantomime Babes in the Wood, which ended in March 1977. Just a few weeks later Wales mourned the tragic loss of Ryan after his death while on holiday in America.

Freddie Lees, for many years, a favourite with Swansea repertory audiences.

from Tito Gobbi. As the end of the 1970s approached, and with it the end of the Council's 10-year lease on the building, it was clear that the Grand Theatre was a jewel in Swansea's crown. The successful results of the efforts of John Chilvers in its days of struggle coupled with his energy, talent and enthusiasm in the theatre's first civic decade, made it unthinkable that the lease would not be renewed. Swansea City Council did more than just renew the lease however. Instead it decided the time had come to buy the Grand from the Willis family and to enlarge and redevelop it into one of the most important theatres in the country.

Swansea's own civic theatre

The council's decision to take the final step and buy the Grand in 1976 was to launch the theatre into a further fresh and exciting phase of redecoration and building. The property had a price tag of £100,000, towards which the Welsh Arts Council contributed a special grant of £40,000. Designers and planners immediately started looking at long-term plans for enlargement and

Ryan and Ronnie two of Wales' most memorable performers who made audiences laugh in their thousands. Their unforgettable pantomimes were the most popular in the history of the Grand Theatre.

redevelopment of the theatre. In the short term further redecoration was carried out in 1978 at a cost of £20,000.

The Grand began the 1980s with the mix very much as before. There was a seven-week rep season surrounded by touring shows which brought with them popular names such as Eric Sykes, Jimmy Edwards, Lorraine Chase and Robin Askwith plus a variety season which featured, among others, Patti Boulaye and Don McLean. Performers in the rep season included Roy Barraclough, Freddie Lees and Desmond Barritt. In August the National Eisteddfod was held in Swansea and as part of that the Grand hosted a major Festival of Welsh Drama. As ever the year was brought to a close with a pantomime. This time it was Puss in Boots with Davy Jones, Kenny Smiles and Freddie Lees generating the laughs from a typically enthusiastic audience.

At its start, no one would have suspected that 1981 would turn out to be the last of the John Chilvers' years. There was the usual series of touring and variety shows, including a week with Tommy Steele. During each performance the popular entertainer would invite a young girl from the audience to come up on stage and dance with him. Then he would say to her:

> ***"When you tell your friends at school tomorrow that you danced with Tommy Steele, they probably won't believe you."***

At one of these performances the child in question was a local schoolgirl named Catherine Zeta Jones. Little did anyone in the auditorium that night realise just how big a star that little girl would become in the years that were to follow.

The rep season that year consisted of six productions: Loot, The Dresser, with Freddie Lees and David King, Once a Catholic, and Peril at End House with Desmond Barritt which were followed by a fortnight of variety shows with Iris Williams and Bob Monkhouse before the season resumed with two musicals, The Boyfriend and The Rocky Horror Show. The remainder of the season saw the usual Welsh National Opera, Welsh Drama Festival, and other touring and amateur shows, all leading up to rehearsals for the annual pantomime which was Dick Whittington.

An unusual view of the Grand circle after the seating was taken out to make way for the new developments at the theatre in 1986. Plush new seating was installed in its place.

A view across the auditorium seating at the Grand in 2010.

Rachel Roberts, who cut her acting teeth at the Grand with a debut there in 1950 alongside Kenneth Williams. She returned nearly two decades later to star alongside her ex-husband Alan Dobie in Who's Afraid of Virginia Woolf?

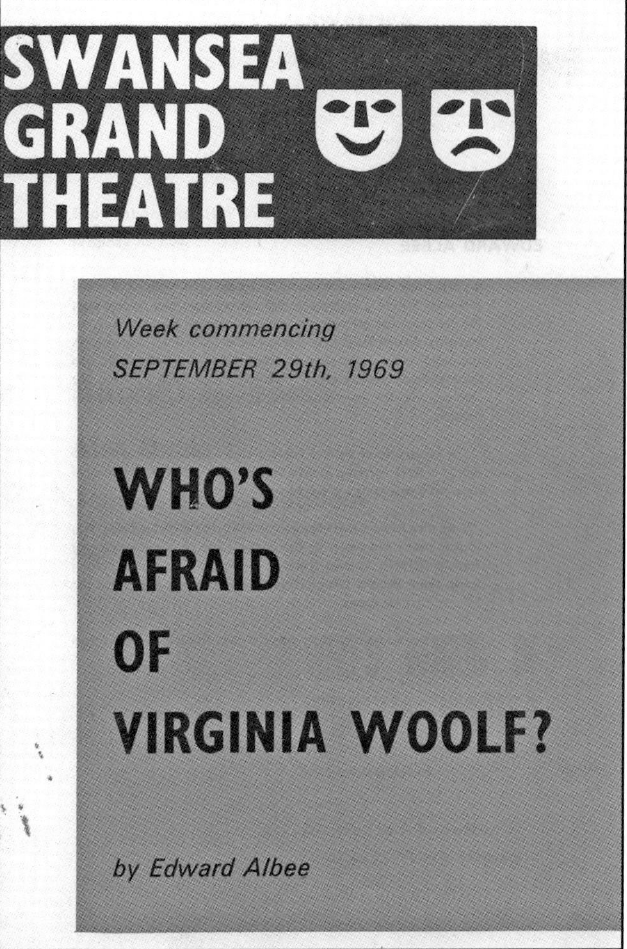
SWANSEA GRAND THEATRE

Week commencing
SEPTEMBER 29th, 1969

WHO'S AFRAID OF VIRGINIA WOOLF?

by Edward Albee

Just two days into the rehearsals John Chilvers was rushed to hospital with severe chest pains. The cast, which included Harry H Corbett, Mike Holloway and Desmond Barritt, did their best to put the show together without a director, working alongside the choreographer, Cherry Willoughby, a stalwart of Swansea pantomimes for many years.

From his hospital bed John sent an urgent message to Vivyan Ellacott at the Kenneth More Theatre in Ilford, Essex, asking if it was possible for him to come to Swansea and supervise the last few days of the technical and dress rehearsals. Vivyan wasted no time in agreeing to this, making several visits to the hospital to reassure Chilvers that everything was perfectly in order. At this point it was decided he would not be well enough to continue as administrator and artistic director of the Grand and it was eventually agreed he would take an early retirement.

On Sunday February 14, 1982 a packed house attended A Tribute to John Chilvers – 25 years. Appearing on stage were actors, dancers, singers, entertainers, musicians and opera stars from the world of theatre, and representatives of the amateur operatic and dramatic societies and the Swansea Scout and Guide Association with whom John had been closely involved. In the audience were hundreds of loyal patrons, councillors, civic dignitaries, members of the Grand Theatre Supporters Club, and representatives from dozens of local and national organisations. Every one of them leapt to his or her feet to give a standing ovation as soon as John Chilvers entered the emotion-packed theatre. This

John Chilvers, or JC as he was affectionately known, keeps an eagle eye on rehearsals for one of the theatre's popular repertory productions.

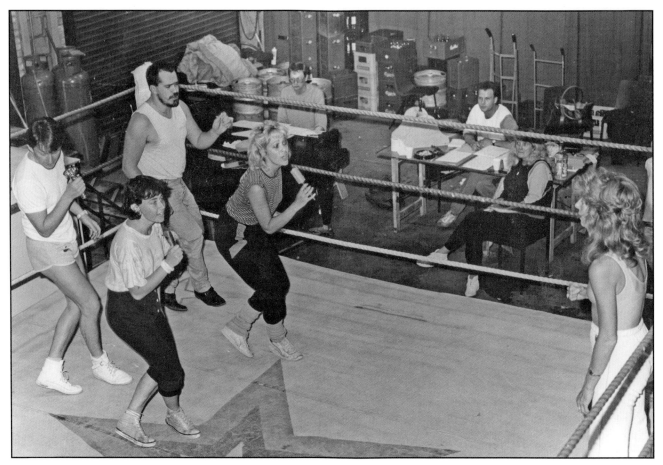

A scene from Trafford Tanzi in 1986. Well-known female wrestler Mitzi Mueller who is seated looking on choreographed the play's wrestling scenes. One of its stars was actress Denise Welch.

Theatre manager Paul Dayson on the stage during redevelopment work in 1986. Temporary seating was provided for a reduced repertory season. The audience had their backs to the curtain, which was hiding the work going on at the time.

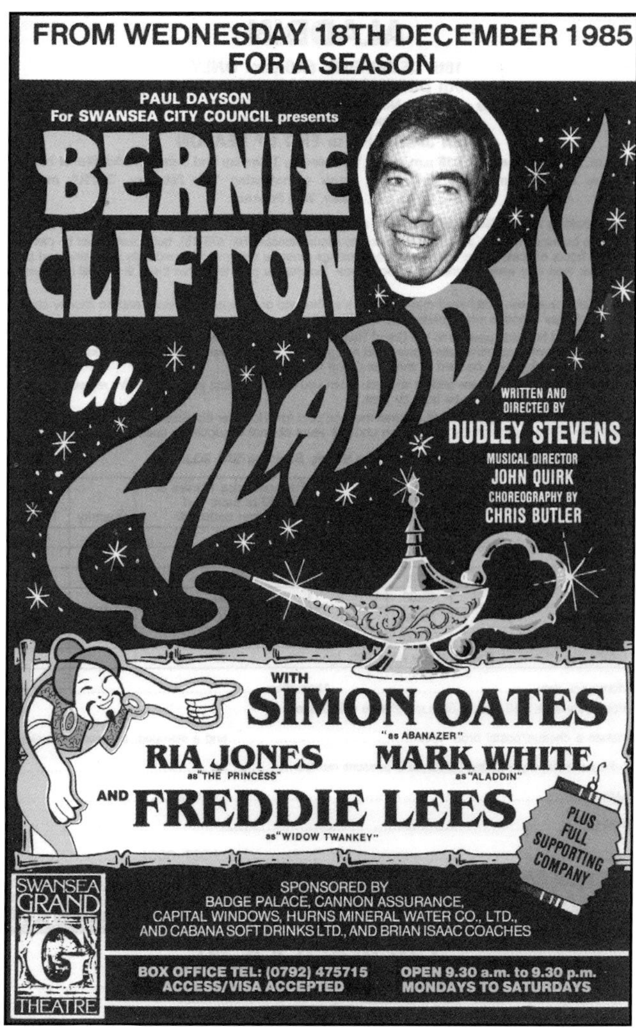

The 1985/86 pantomime Aladdin was the only one staged at the Grand to have had two different playbills. The first, left, was withdrawn because it suggested that the production was presented by manager Paul Dayson with no mention of Swansea City Council, the theatre owners. A replacement, right, was hurriedly designed to replace it.

tribute was, without doubt, a fitting end to an incomparable era.

Sadly, Chilvers, who was awarded the MBE for services to the theatre died on March 10, 2008 after a short illness. He clearly loved the Grand Theatre. For him it was not simply a job, it was a vocation. That the theatre still exists is due in no small measure to his hard work, drive and enthusiasm.

Time for rebuilding

The year following John Chilvers' retirement saw the usual mix of star names – Des O'Connor, Cilla Black, Simon Cadell, Melvyn Hayes, and a reduced repertory season. One of the rep plays was in fact, directed by Chilvers himself, whose occasional and welcome comeback was as a guest director in no way connected with the management. The end of year pantomime, Jack and the Beanstalk with Don McClean and Freddie Lees was yet another of his successful guest productions.

On February 22, 1983, following its last night, the Grand Theatre closed for major building work. This was carried out in three phases. The initial reconstruction was partly financed with a £600,000 grant from the Arts Council of Great Britain. It involved complete closure until Boxing Day the following year when the theatre reopened with Windsor Davies and Melvyn Hayes in Babes in the Wood. During the summer a seven-play rep season was organised at the Dylan Thomas Theatre in Gloucester Place. The Grand was back in business by the end of the year with a new stage, fly tower and an enlarged and hydraulic orchestra pit. Much of the rest of the building, the dressing room areas, front of house bars and foyers remained hidden behind rough wooden boards, but the auditorium itself hadn't been altered. Towards the end of 1983 Swansea City Council received a grant of £2.7 million pounds from the European Economic Community as an acknowledgement of the importance of the theatre to the city's tourist industry. This first phase of rebuilding cost a total of £3 million. The remaining phases were

A scene from the pantomime Mother Goose staged at the Grand in 1986/87. Starring Les Dennis, Christopher Biggins and Julie Paton, it was one of the few to lose money.

A playbill advertising 1980s-style summer entertainment at the Grand. This kind of show broke up the rep seasons.

carried out over the following three years, with the theatre remaining open for most of that time. During the final phase, carried out through the summer and autumn of 1986, the theatre gave a whole season of 'Studio' performances, with the actors playing with their backs to the safety curtain, and a limited audience of up to 300 sitting at the back of the new stage area. During this time the auditorium itself was completely renovated. The original ceiling and proscenium arch were raised and the 'gods' fitted with proper tip-up upholstered seating.

Throughout this three year rebuilding programme visiting stars included Frankie Vaughan, Ken Dodd, Max Boyce, Ruth Madoc, Norman Vaughan, Matthew Kelly, Leonard Sachs, Frankie Howerd, Val Doonican, and Georgie Fame. The 1984-85 panto was Cinderella, a version with Paul Henry and Roy Barraclough, while the 1985-86 production of Aladdin starred Bernie Clifton, Freddie Lees and local favourite, Ria Jones.

Finally, on December 17 1986, after a £5 million investment, the Swansea's new Grand Theatre opened with the pantomime Mother Goose, starring Christopher Biggins and Les Dennis.

Act 6

The new theatre with old problems

At last Swansea had it's magnificent new theatre, superbly restored and with the prospect of a glorious future. Everything should have been perfect. But it wasn't. There was one significant, over-riding problem. A financial one. And it was serious. In August 1986 it was revealed that the bill for staging shows at the Grand theatre was over budget by a staggering £130,000. It was a figure that shocked many.

Such a worrying start led to close scrutiny of the theatre's accounts, and in December of the same year, theatre administrator Paul Dayson was sacked for what was said to be gross misconduct and financial impropriety.

Dayson had started at the Grand in 1978 as house manager under John Chilvers and had been appointed his successor in 1984. The impact of the sacking was not only felt in Swansea, but also the theatre world at large. While the lawyers were preparing for a High Court hearing, the Grand played its opening season in the newly refurbished building. Star names like Peter Gilmore, Bobby Davro, Fenella Fielding, Keith Harris and Orville appeared in various plays and revues. Keith Harris made a triumphant return to the Grand 20 years after his previous appearance, in the pantomime Puss In Boots in 1965/66. The Welsh National Opera staged a number of productions, demonstrating how much better these could now be, with the enlarged stage space and vastly improved technical facilities. One of the major differences was that it was no longer necessary to hire St Phillip's Church Hall as extra dressing room space for the chorus of the Welsh National Opera as everyone could now fit comfortably into the enlarged Grand Theatre.

One of the earliest touring shows to visit and play the new Swansea Grand Theatre was The Rocky Horror Show which toured through the 1980s, directed by Vivyan Ellacott. For him it was a return to the very theatre in which he had started his professional career 20 years earlier, one where he had worked for five years in rep and also management. Vivyan recalls sitting in the back of the once beautiful, but by then seedy and shabby Grand, and wishing he could win the football pools and have enough money to restore the theatre to its former splendour. From the moment he entered the new building he was bowled over with emotion. The auditorium was superbly restored, as magnificent as it could ever have been; the stage and its equipment was of the most modern and highest standards, the backstage facilities superb. The old Grand had been transformed into a brilliant, modern theatre and yet had retained its Victorian magnificence. For him, and many of the 'old' actors and technicians who visited, it was a moving experience. The Grand had always earned the affection of those who regularly worked there. The new look theatre opened with the pantomime Mother Goose starring Christopher Biggins and Les Dennis on December 17, 1986. The first season offered some

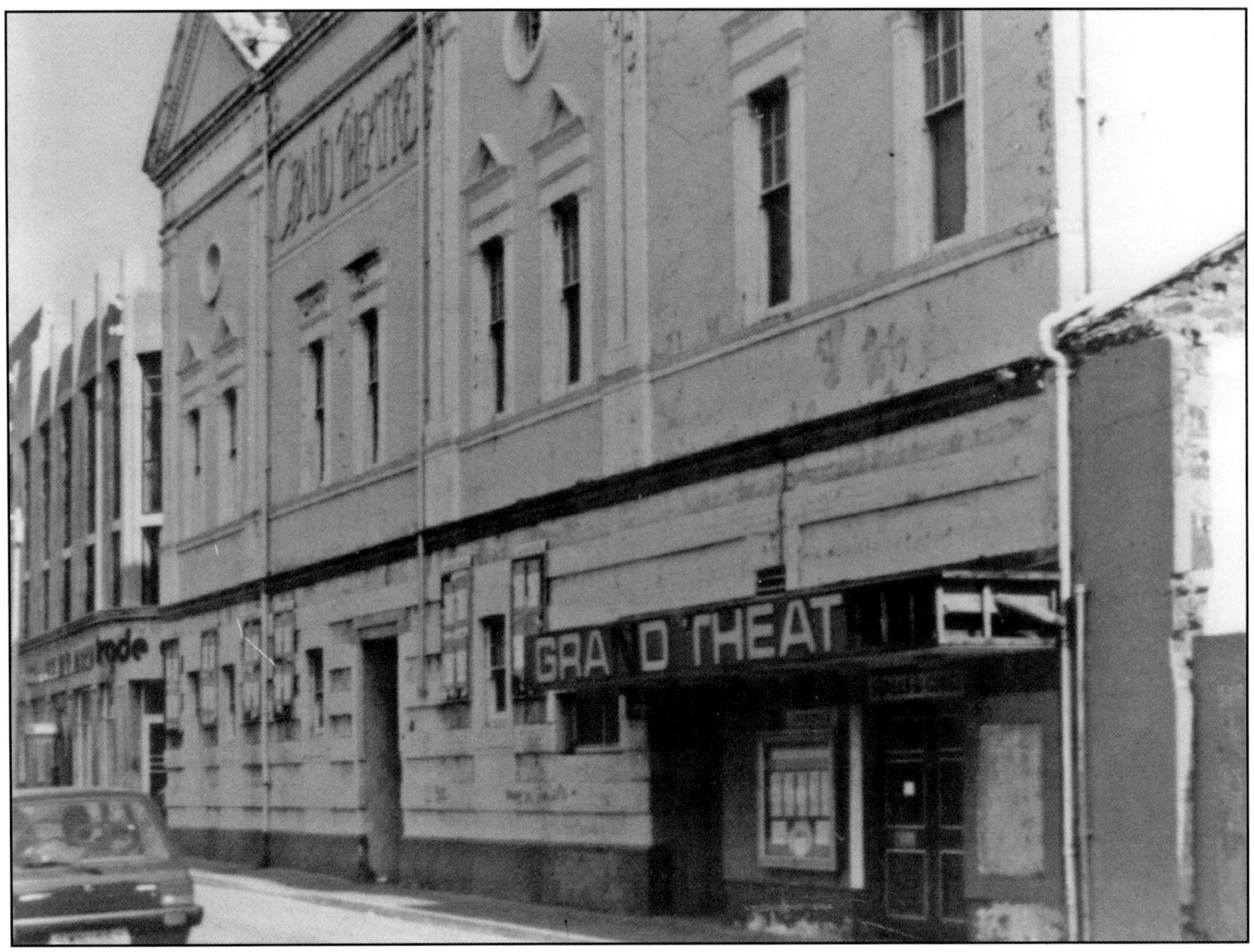

The Singleton Street facade of a tired and weary Grand Theatre shortly before it was remodelled.

splendid attractions: Rachel Thomas and Harriet Lewis in Arsenic and Old Lace, Margaret John in The Man and Sion Probert, Neil West and Joanna Field in Boeing Boeing. Sadly however there was one vital ingredient missing – the audience. They just did not come and with average attendances of just 170, things were once again looking dire. So much so that there was even talk of Swansea Council leasing the theatre to The Apollo Leisure Group which specialised in taking over failing theatres and turning their fortunes around. Fortunately, however, the city council's nerve held steady.

A special performance took place on Sunday, February 7, 1988. It was a show in memory of Con Murphy, the late stage manager of the Grand, and was organised by Anthony Lyn. Everyone who was anyone in the history of the theatre wanted to be part of it – Ruth Madoc, Bobby Crush, Stan Stennett, David Ian, Catherine Zeta Jones, Ria Jones, Nigel and Vivyan Ellacott. The highlight of the show was provided by Arwyn Davies, aged 20, the son of the inimitable Ryan who recreated a comedy scene with his father's former partner, Ronnie Williams. The year continued with visits from Frankie Vaughan, Kiki Dee, Alvin Stardust, and a season of plays with old favourites like Freddie Lees and Jean Fergusson and a return visit from The Rocky Horror Show.

Then in July at the High Court, Paul Dayson was cleared of all charges against him. To the surprise and embarrassment of the council, one of its high-ranking members appeared as a character witness for him. The council was criticised amid claims that it was split over the theatre, and Paul Dayson announced he would be suing for loss of earnings, unfair dismissal and defamation of character. He also demanded reinstatement to his former job. Meanwhile, the year continued – Julian Clary, Ken Dodd and Victor Spinetti were some who took to the stage along with established opera and ballet companies. At this point there were three local amateur operatic societies performing annually at the theatre – Swansea Amateurs, The Abbey Players and Gendros Catholic Amateur Operatic Society. Each one provided a fantastic breeding ground for local talent and it is no coincidence that Swansea has produced so many West End performers. The Grand also attracted visits from major touring companies and finished the year with a very successful pantomime, Goldilocks And The Three Bears, starring John Inman, Susan Maughan and Terry

Sir Harry Secombe in the role of Pickwick which he recreated at The Grand in 1995. The production also starred Ruth Madoc and Glyn Houston.

Hall and Lenny The Lion. On the Dayson front all was quiet and whatever settlement was or was not agreed was kept private. He was not reappointed and later became a theatre manager in Tunbridge Wells, Kent.

The 1980s proved to be a disjointed time for the Grand Theatre as its extensive redevelopment took place. The pantomimes had lost a little of their sparkle since the Chilvers days and the unthinkable happened when two consecutive pantos, Aladdin and Mother Goose, lost money. These were once again challenging times for the council as the renovations were now complete and the cost exceeded £6.5 million. Questions were asked as to why the repertory seasons were not being attended, thus incurring significant losses and eventually, the decision was taken to end the tradition of in-house repertory seasons at the theatre. Brian Sullivan then reversed the downward pantomime trend when he directed the next three: Dick Whittington in 1987/88; Goldilocks in 1988/89 and the following year's Babes In The Wood, all of which showed a healthy profit. Brian was an experienced director with a knack of knowing who to cast in which play to maximum effect. Indeed he had verbally secured the services of Danny La Rue, Brian Conley, Jack Douglas and Anita Harris for the following Grand Theatre pantomime. It would probably have been an enormous success, given Brian Conley's popularity at the time. Sadly there appeared to be a power struggle going on behind the scenes and eventually it was decided to go with Linda Lusardi, Stu Francis and Neil Morrisey in Snow White and the Seven Dwarfs. Brian Sullivan then moved on to become head of leisure in Port Talbot Borough Council and during his time there he brought The Everly Brothers, Tom Jones and Shirley Bassey to the now fire-ravaged and derelict Afan Lido on Aberavon seafront.

A very young Catherine Zeta Jones beams with delight after winning a Swansea talent contest.

Budding local stars to come through the ranks at this time included Catherine Zeta Jones, Ria Jones, Ceri Dupree, Anthony Lyn, Menna Trussler, Richard Mylan, Steve Balsamo, Leo Andrew, Claire Louise Hammacott, Steffan Rhodri, Julie Paton, Melanie Walters and Kevin Johns, to name a few.

In 1989 the former title of administrator was dropped and a new manager appointed. This marked the arrival of Gary Iles, the 36-year-old former assistant manager of the Derngate Theatre, Northampton, who remains at the helm to this day. He had his work cut out restoring the damaged reputation of the theatre, but slowly and surely he succeeded. He brought a great deal of optimism to the theatre and eventually the Grand's patronage began to grow again. It gradually become a true variety theatre. Its seasons started to cater for all tastes and included regular one-night performances by national comedians, tribute shows and full blooded West End showstoppers. Frank Vickery, a playwright from the Rhondda Valley, also staged week-long productions of his own comedy plays, which began in 1989 and soon developed a cult following. In just over 20 years he racked up more than 40 visits. Regular appearances from The Welsh National Opera, touring ballet companies and touring Shakespearian companies also satisfied the theatre purists. Sadly in 1992 Rose Marie highlighted the harsh

The Grand Theatre auditorium after refurbishment. The stage is set for a scene from Suspects which starred former newsreader Gordon Honeycombe, in 1989.

Gary Iles, administrator of the Grand Theatre from 1989 until the present day.

reality of using a professional theatre. It was the last production by Gendros Catholic Amateur Operatic Society who after 30 years were forced to disband due to the rising costs of staging an amateur show. Among their members was Catherine Zeta Jones who appeared for them at the Grand in 1982 and 1984.

The 1990s saw the theatre settle into a regular pattern of children's shows, amateur productions, major touring shows on the Number One circuit, an emphasis on local companies and a whole series of one-night star name shows. Susannah York, Alan Dobie, Richard Todd, Peggy Mount and Glyn Houston headed the 'straight' theatre productions. Guy Mitchell, Freddie Starr, Shani Wallis, Mike Berry, Rick Wakeman and Frankie Vaughan meanwhile, provided some of the light entertainment. For the rest of the decade the pattern remained very much the same. Star names included Humphrey Lyttleton, Acker Bilk, Barbara Dickson, Gene Pitney, Frankie Howerd, Harry Secombe, Jack Jones, David Essex, Tammy Wynette, Ken Dodd, Adam Faith, Max Boyce, Elkie brooks, Danny La Rue, Lily Savage, and Tommy Steele. Swansea theatre had seen nothing like this since the good old days of the Empire. In addition to such a magnificent miscellany of light entertainment there were superb offerings from the English Shakespeare Company, The Doyly Carte Opera Company, the BBC Concert Orchestra, The London City Ballet, The Northern Ballet Company and The Moscow City Ballet.

Throughout this period the Welsh National Opera played regular seasons, its repertoire growing ever more ambitious, and its audience ever more enthusiastic. The major West End touring productions became regular visitors to the Grand, among them Run For Your Wife, with Les Dawson; Evita, Driving Miss Daisy with Stephanie Cole; The Cherry Orchard with Maria Aitken; Elvis The Musical, Buddy, Return To The Forbidden Planet, Pickwick with local favourites Harry Secombe, Glyn Houston and Ruth Madoc; Blood Brothers and an almost annual visit of Joseph And His Amazing Technicolor Dreamcoat and The Rocky Horror Show. One of the rowdier attractions was the 1991 musical Home And Away with members of the original Australian TV soap cast. It was at the height of the show's popularity and the theatre witnessed scenes of amazing hysteria at every performance, which spilled over into a meet and greet session where tickets were given out to meet the cast backstage on the last night. Unfortunately the cast left the theatre earlier than expected. Crowds of expectant fans at the stage door were left disappointed and angry scenes ensued, which had to be handled by shell-shocked theatre staff.

The cost of running the theatre at this time was proving to be very expensive. During the financial year 1995-96 the budgeted loss was estimated at £571,000 – working out at more than £10,000 for every week the theatre was open. This meant that over a 10-year period the Grand lost an estimated £5 million. Things were not totally gloomy though, for during the same 10-year period the annual box office income had more than doubled. It had risen from £1 million in 1989 to £2 million in 1996. The number of tickets sold in 1995 was 178,000 and by the following year this figure had jumped to 237,000.

Gary Iles had reason to be optimistic for the future of the theatre as it approached its centenary. The annual pantomimes, now handled by outside production companies became consistently good and regularly sold out, enjoying outstanding success from 1992 onwards when Joe Pasquale became a firm favourite with Swansea audiences appearing in three consecutive pantomimes, all fantastically successful. This, coupled with the emergence of locally produced pantomime favourites Owen Money, Mike Doyle and Kevin Johns kept the audiences, and the box office takings, rolling in.

In 1997 the theatre celebrated its centenary, and was honoured with a visit from Princess Margaret. Amazingly this was the first Royal visit in its history. A special week of celebrations began in July culminating in a Grand Centenary Concert on July 26 to mark the centenary of the actual opening date. It starred Ria Jones, Mike Sterling, Lee Honey-Jones, Glyn Houston, Menna

This street level exterior view shows off some of the pleasing architectural aspects of the Grand Theatre. It is a building which holds many memories for the people of Swansea and beyond who can count themselves among its patrons.

Trussler, Ruth Madoc, Jason Howard, Dame Gwyneth Jones and Dennis O'Neill. It was a truly glittering occasion and a fitting tribute. In 1897 Dame Adelina Patti had attended the theatre's civic opening and 100 years later the opera singer Dame Gwyneth Jones did exactly the same.

In 1999 the Grand and Swansea Council were responsible for an innovative and exciting pioneering decision, which added to the prestige of the city's arts life and the status of the theatre. The theatre became the permanent home of The Swansea Ballet Russe. This dynamic young ballet troupe is made up of professional dancers most of whom trained in Russia at the Bolshoi and Kirov Academies. The political and economic changes in Eastern Europe and the dissolution of the Soviet Union caused severe problems. Artistes who had been employed by the state had lost their incomes and their outlook was bleak. In 1998 a group of dancers arrived in Britain seeking better opportunities. The company began its life in Bristol under the leadership of Mikhail Vorona, a former lead dancer himself, but rapidly had to learn new skills as a company director. In September of 1999, thanks to the vision and generosity of the City & County of Swansea, the company took up residence in the Grand Theatre. In the years since it, has established a significant reputation.

The Arts Wing

In the summer of 1999 a new arts wing was added to the Grand's facilities – taking up 2,000 square metres of what was the former neighbouring bus station to create an attractive, modern building that would assist the theatre's transition into the 21st Century.

This gave the theatre a state-of-the-art box office, a studio theatre seating up to 170 people which can also be used as a dance studio, exhibition area, meeting and rehearsal rooms plus a rooftop café bar and terrace. The arts wing also acts as home to Swansea Ballet Russe. It increased access to the entire building as it provided a lift to all floors and is completely integrated with the main building. The studio space benefits from being flat floored and having retractable seating which means that the theatre has a flexible space, ideal for a multitude of

Princess Margaret arrives at the Grand on June 4, 1997, its first Royal visit in the theatre's history.

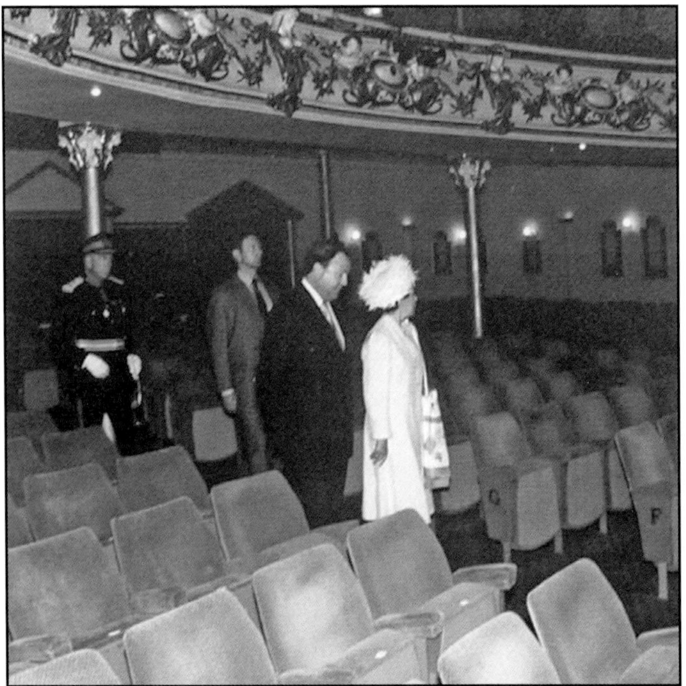

Grand Theatre manager Gary Iles, escorts Princess Margaret through the stalls of the theatre during her centenary visit.

uses to support its main role. The new facilities allowed more adventurous, experimental and avant-garde productions to be programmed into The Grand's calendar, plus a wide range of regular events such as a comedy club, magic club, poetry group, wine appreciation nights and other classes of various kinds. Apart from being popular in their own right, these events have allowed the theatre to develop new audiences and re-engage with some others. The studio also allowed for more intimate gatherings to take place such as galas or supper cabaret evenings and gave the theatre a diverse, new lease of life by encouraging people over its threshold for a multitude of different reasons.

Iconic Welsh entertainers Sian Phillips and Victor Spinetti are just two who have scored spectacular success using the facilities offered by this far-sighted extension. Its space also allows a platform for emerging local talent. It can be used by local theatre companies, small scale touring companies, or for encouraging engagement with schools for whose pupils this may be a first theatrical experience. Regular features of the studio theatre include drama, contemporary and classic dance,

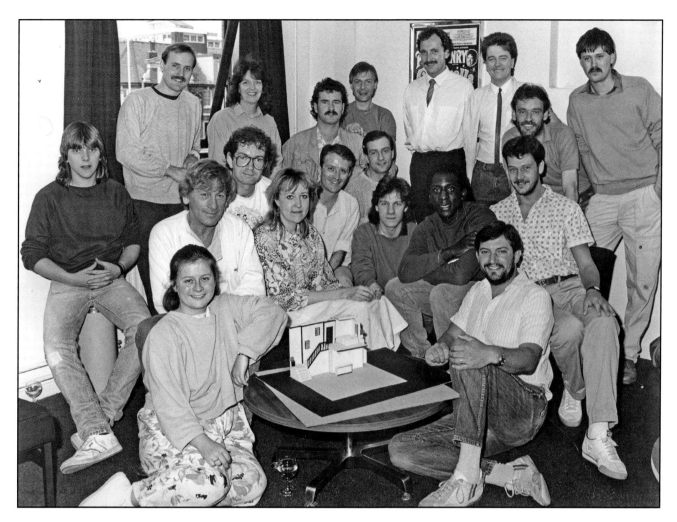

The cast and crew from the repertory season of 1986.

children's presentations and workshops, comedy, social events and demonstrations, while the exhibition spaces have seen shows of local, national and international repute being presented annually. It has also become a popular and unique venue for wedding ceremonies and family celebrations.

The studio has given theatre audiences some brilliant nights of entertainment. It has provided a stimulating and creative environment for many workshops, demonstrations, meetings and seminars, allowed artists to show off their creative skills in many different media and importantly, it has encouraged many young people to engage with cultural events from both sides of the limelight. Initially, the arts wing was financed by The City & County of Swansea; matched funding from David McLean Developments; and an arts lottery award of half a million pounds.

Dawn of the 21st Century

As the Grand entered its second century it seemed that the old days were back. All the big names from British entertainment came to the theatre. Performances from the likes of Shane Ritchie, Ken Dodd, Tommy Steele,

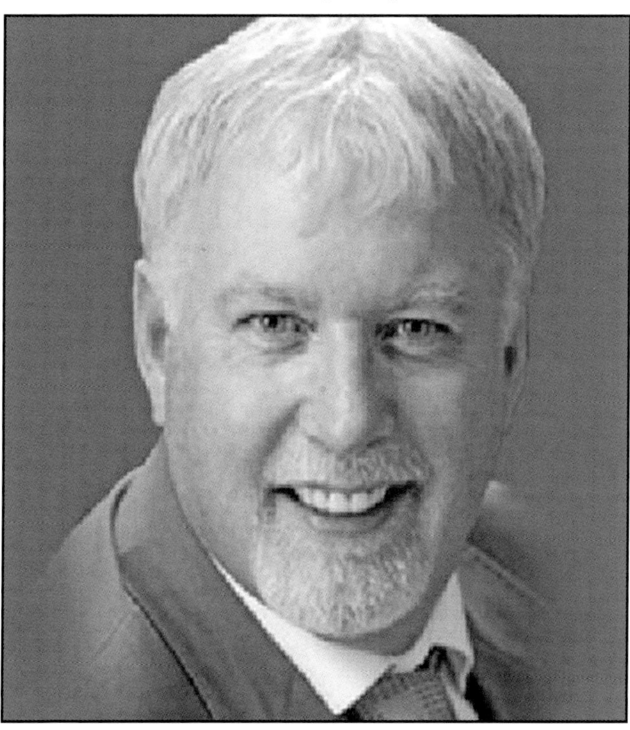

Playwright Frank Vickery who brought his first production, One o'clock From The House, to The Grand in 1989. Since then he has staged more than 40 productions there.

Sir Harry Secombe surrounded by members of the Grand Theatre Club when he officially opened the refurbished dressing rooms in the early 1990s. He is seen, right, cutting a ribbon to allow access to the new facility.

Jason Donovan, Paul Nicholas and Michael Barrymore. Touring productions with established performers like Stephanie Beacham, Wendy Craig, Prunella Scales, Trevor Bannister, Letitia Dean, Carmen Silvera. Major ballet and opera companies; one night variety shows and concerts; educational events and children's shows. A great deal of community and local amateur involvement all contributed to a growth in the theatre's reputation into the new millennium. The Swansea Amateur Operatic Society and The Abbey Players continued to put on accomplished shows and Alex Frith's annual charity show The Best Is Yet To Come highlighted the wealth of young talent coming through.

In 2000 the great Sian Phillips made her first appearance at the theatre, and other legendary names including Honor Blackman, Sylvia Syms, Jenny Agutter, and Britt Ekland came too. Changing theatre patterns in the 21st Century meant more and more of the touring shows were for one-night only. The old system of Monday to Saturday with mid-week and Saturday matinees gradually disappeared. This obviously created a vastly increased workload for theatre management as they had to negotiate and publicise several different shows each week. It also led to the end of the regular patrons or permanent bookings where people would always attend on the same night of the week and sit in the same seats — sandwiches, flasks of tea and all! The availability of so many one or two night productions did however lead to a huge range of shows at the Grand. Opera companies from Eastern Europe could tour with a large entourage and bring productions like Aida to Swansea for just one night, something unheard of in earlier days. During the old days the first three months following the pantomime would have offered 12 different plays, each one playing a week at a time. The same 12 week period at the Grand in 2001 saw no fewer than 41 different shows. These were mainly one-nighters, including vast undertakings like a performance of Jesus Christ Superstar in Welsh; a one-night performance of Gershwin's Porgy And Bess and a full length performance of the enigmatic ballet Swan Lake. The standard one-week run of a touring play now became the exception rather than the rule. The early years of the new century also saw a dramatic rise in tribute acts, probably due to the success of TV 's Stars In Their Eyes with no fewer than 17 acts in 2000, and 19 in 2001. They continue to be very successful as fillers in the theatre calendar as they are normally very well attended, cheaper than the originals and yet can still provide a great night's entertainment. They also serve to bring people to the theatre who perhaps would not generally visit. In 1997 the Grand returned to the kind of repertory seasons that were such a staple of the theatre during the John Chilvers years. This came about when Ian Dickens Productions was engaged to provide four or five plays each summer starring familiar theatre and television names. This arrangement continues to the present day.

The difference between John Chilvers' days and today's productions is that the repertory seasons involved a group of actors in a season of different plays. The Dickens' productions on the other hand involve different casts with touring productions.

Highlights from 2002 were The Lavender Hill Mob, starring Victor Spinetti and Clive Francis, My Beautiful Laundrette and Blood Brothers with Denise Nolan. Des O'Connor also made a return visit to the theatre that he

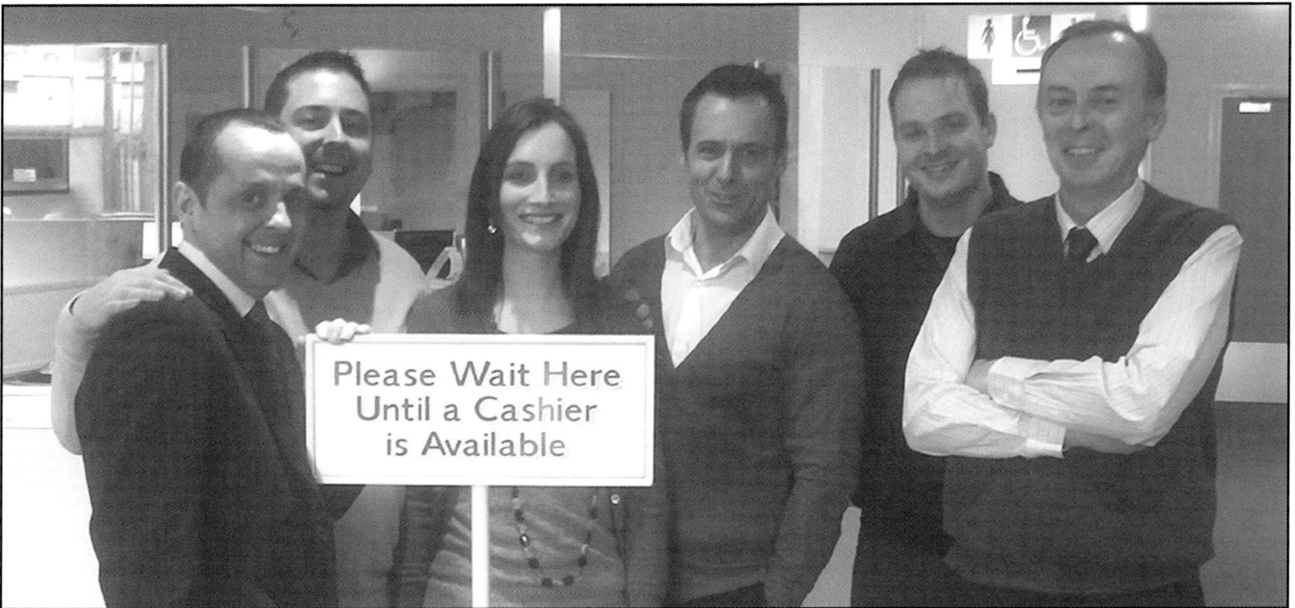

The Grand Theatre box office staff in 2010. They are, from the left: Andrew Hughes, Curtis Evans, Rhian Wolfe, Rob David, Barry Evans and Nigel Waters.

first visited in pantomime in 1957/58. The 2003 seasons included superb productions of The Buddy Holly Story and Summer Holiday with Suzanne Shaw. Oddities included An Audience with Ann Widdicombe MP and An Evening With Christine Hamilton. Rob Brydon appeared at his home town theatre in The Marion and Geoff Tour and comedic one nighters included Max Boyce, Jethro, Roy Chubby Brown, Julian Clary, Kevin Bloody Wilson and Ed Byrne.

In October 2003, the 50th anniversary of Dylan Thomas' death was celebrated with a performance of Under Milk Wood starring future Hollywood star Matthew Rhys. The year ended with an emotional one-night show with Joe Longthorne. The following year, 2004, began strongly with Joseph and The Amazing Technicolor Dreamcoat and a wonderful performance of The Woman In Black adapted by Stephen Mallatratt who made a welcome return to the Grand where he had appeared in the rep season of 1972. Swansea Amateurs performed Jesus Christ Superstar a production acknowledged as one of their best for many years. Swansea's own Spencer Davis appeared with his band in June and Derren Brown and Derek Acora performed their unusual shows, a throwback to the type of show, which would appear at Swansea's Empire in the early 1900s. It would have been interesting to discover what Oswald Stoll's thoughts would have been about the staging of Puppetry of the Penis at the Grand in 2001.

In 2005 large scale productions included Sleeping Beauty, Jekyll and Hyde starring Paul Nicholas, Annie with Ruth Madoc and The Life of Ryan and Ronnie. Ellen Kent and Opera International continued their association with the theatre with a rousing Carmen and Swansea Ballet Russe and Swansea City Opera, along with The Welsh National Opera satisfied the local enthusiasts of their genre. In March 2006, Connie Fisher won the Young Singer Of The Year final at the theatre. She later achieved further fame by winning BBC TV's How Do You Solve A Problem Like Maria competition. An Evening with Joan Collins accompanied by Four Poofs and a Piano came in April and in the same month the play Beyond Reasonable Doubt brought Alexandra Bastedo back for the first time since 1971. A highlight of 2006 was A Christmas Carol with Ron Moody in the leading role. In 2006/2007 the Grand Theatre box office takings exceeded £3 million for the first time, with over 260,000 patrons passing through its doors in one year.

The beginning of the Grand's 110th year brought a locally written play, Toshack Or Me to the theatre starring local favourite Kevin Johns in the role of Vicar Joe. Very funny and well written by Peter Read, it was followed by a remarkable Peter Pan On Ice. In April Contender written by Mal Pope and starring Mike Doyle as boxer Tommy Farr opened to critical acclaim and was a notable diversion from Mike's normal roles, which he carried off effortlessly. Other highlights from this year were The Billie Holiday Story starring Rain Prior, the daughter of American comedy legend Richard Prior; Frank Vickery's A Night On The Tiles starring Ian H Watkins and veteran Stan Stennett who had first performed at the theatre in 1950. The year ended with another locally written play Swansea Girls starring Menna Trussler and written by Lynne Mackay. Running a 21st Century theatre was very different from the Grand's early days. The one thing that

Two views of some of the Grand's original 1897 ornate plasterwork that can still be seen in the theatre's circle. Below is a close-up of the intricate figurework.

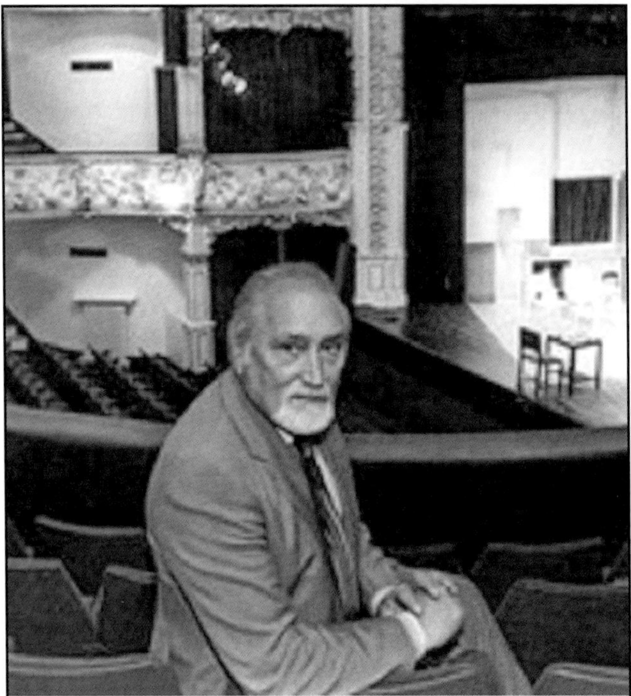

John Chilvers in the auditorium he called home for 25 years until his enforced retirement through ill health in 1981. Sadly, John died in March, 2008.

held true, however, was the annual pantomime. The great traditions of the John Chilvers era were maintained, with local performers like Owen Money, Mike Doyle and especially Kevin Johns enrolling themselves into that special hall of fame reserved for panto comics, such as Ryan Davies, Stan Stennett and Ossie Morris. Other traditions that survive are the regular seasons of Welsh National Opera, where its Swansea following remains as passionate, loyal and supportive as ever, and the annual performances from the Abbey Players and Swansea Amateur Operatic Society.

On March 10, 2008 John Chilvers died, aged 88, at his home in London. It was 20 years since he had last been involved with a production at the Grand, but his importance in the theatre's history was recognised. The management provided a coach to take past and present staff and audience members to his funeral in London. A large Swansea contingent joined an equally large gathering from the theatre world to celebrate the life of the man who had made possible the magnificent Swansea Grand that is so widely known and recognised today. In his modesty John always pointed to those Swansea councillors who took the bold step of creating and funding a civic theatre, but, as someone said at the well attended funeral:

> ***"If you're looking for a memorial to John Chilvers, it stands there in Singleton Street, Swansea."***

There is no doubt that the Grand Theatre is a memorial of which John Chilvers would be justifiably proud.

Act 7

Spreading the theatre message

Before the birth of the Grand there were a number of other theatres in and around Swansea, but audiences were also able to attend performances in less permanent structures referred to as fit-up or portable theatres. There are similarities between the two – and occasionally historians have confused them – but in reality they are quite different. What they shared is a role in spreading the news about theatre.

They may have been less permanent structures but in a way they are just as important to the history of entertainment in general and theatre in particular in the Swansea Bay area. The chief difference between them is that the portable theatre was complete in itself while the fit-up company needed to find a suitable venue. This might have been a town hall, assembly rooms or even a countryside barn. The company would then move in with their scenery and props and stage a performance.

The portable theatre company on the other hand would tour with its own building. This was usually a collection of wide wooden slats cleated together with a canvas roof to form a rectangular tent-like structure. The stage and set would then be built inside. Portable theatres travelled with their own bench seating and could be erected on any suitable patch of ground. They were designed to be easily dismantled and transported from one place to another on carts or railway wagons. Some of the largest could hold as many as 2000 people and accommodate lavish spectacles to rival the smaller permanent theatres. Their overheads were lower and as a result so was the price of admission. They avoided towns where stock companies played and sought audiences in the villages and townships of the new industrialised areas. The main feature of the portable theatre was that it moved from place to place. In a way it was taking the theatre to the people rather than the other way around. A portable theatre might stay for a few weeks or a few months in one town before moving from place to place in a fixed circuit or tour.

Portables became common in Wales after the passing of The Theatres Act of 1843, which excluded booth and tent structures from the licensing requirements. The owners were nominally under control of local magistrates but were free to give their entertainments without restriction during agricultural fairs or race meetings. The earliest recorded travelling theatre in the Swansea Bay area was in Neath and pre-dates the Theatres Act by two years. In 1841 a performance of The Cobblers Hut was given at Charlesville Place, location of one of the current entrances to Neath General Market. It starred Charles Sanders and Maria Tyrer who was principal actress at the Theatre Royal in Bath. Mr Sanders apparently doubled as a scene painter when he wasn't on stage performing. He later settled in Neath and did a large number of paintings in the district, chiefly armorial bearings. Some of these survive today and can be seen at Llantwit Church on the north eastern outskirts of the town.

Victoria Gardens, Neath. For more than 20 years the site played host to John Hord's annual visit with his portable theatre. The performances were immensely popular and would regularly attract hundreds of patrons.

The Cambrian Theatre, Neath

Among notable portable theatres was John Hord's Cambrian Theatre which played a South Wales circuit between 1856 and 1875. He was based at Merthyr for around six months of the year before moving to other towns. In 1858 he played a successful season at Neath, regularly attracting capacity audiences. However when he tried to return in 1859 he was refused permission by the town's magistrates. It was said his shows were pandering to the vitiated tastes of the uneducated. But Hord was nothing if not determined and he tried again in 1861. This time a change of heart allowed him to return and thereafter his company attracted large crowds to his theatre which regularly played to audiences in Victoria Gardens for the following 20 years. An actor himself, Hord enjoyed enormous popularity. Favourite amongst his roles was that of Mathias in The Bells. Some of his fans in the area claimed his portrayal was a better performance than Henry Irving's at the Lyceum in London. In an area bounded by Pembroke Dock in the west and by Abergavenny in the east, his company performed in more than 15 centres.

The Star Theatre, Neath

The Jennings Company, managed by two brothers of that name also played regular seasons at Neath between 1869 and 1877. Their portable went by the name of the Star Theatre and travelled a circuit that included Merthyr, Neath, Llanelli and Carmarthen, originally staying up to three months in each town. In 1875 the Star Theatre, treated audiences at Neath to the unusual spectacle of a female Hamlet, portrayed by Julia Jennings. The main thrust of the Jennings Company however was the comic and clown, John Noakes, who later took over the circuit when the Jennings brothers moved out of Wales.

From 1877 the Star Theatre, by then under the management of John E Noakes, created a smaller circuit consisting of Carmarthen, Llanelli and Neath and playing three or four months in each town. For its Christmas season in 1883 the Star Theatre, was erected opposite the station in Neath and the generous Noakes arranged for all the residents of the town's cottage homes, the workhouse and reformatory to have free admission as a festive treat. During one three month season in Neath, from August to October 1889, almost 50 different plays were performed, giving an indication of the extent of the Star Theatre's extensive repertoire. Eventually Noakes withdrew from the touring circuit and settled at Llanelli, where he built a permanent theatre, the Royalty, which could accomodate audiences of up to 1,500. Noakes retained an interest in it until he died in 1910.

The Castle Theatre, Neath

The Haggar family of Aberdare was another family immersed in the portable theatre business. William Haggar, born the illegitimate son of an Essex housemaid in 1851, ran away from home at the age of 18 to join a troupe of travelling players. In 1871 he married Sarah Walton, an actress, and spent the following 20 years touring the West Country and south and west Wales with his portable Castle Theatre Circuit. The circuit included regular seasons at Neath, Tonypandy, Ferndale and Ebbw Vale. William and Sarah had 11 children, eight of them surviving into adulthood, and all of them involved in the family business of running of the portable at some point. They were recognised as kind and generous employers.

Will Haggar Junior was in charge of The Castle Theatre, Tonypandy in 1901 when Queen Victoria died. He was one of the few managers across the country who paid full wages to his performers during the time the theatre was closed for her funeral. In March 1907 James Haggar placed an advertisement in The Stage, thanking the company at the Castle Theatre, Neath, for their farewell present to him and his wife upon the termination of their engagement there. He also thanked his brother W Haggar Junior for a most comfortable engagement, which he was relinquishing in order to assist in the management of his father, William Haggar Senior's New Mammoth Bioscope Exhibition. In December 1908 Will Haggar Junior placed a further advertisement thanking the company and staff of the Castle Theatre, Neath, for their magnificent birthday present of a wine cabinet. The Castle Theatre would spend three or four months in each town while at the same time the Haggars ran a 'fit-up' company, which would play smaller venues around South Wales. On one occasion while preparing to open in Neath, Haggar's portable theatre was destroyed by fire. The company bought the necessary timber locally and rebuilt it entirely within four days in readiness for their planned opening performance.

As time moved on William Haggar Senior became a pioneer in the cinema business. From 1898 to 1901 he had been staging his bioscope show at various fairgrounds and agricultural shows. Because of a shortage of suitable material to screen he become a film producer himself. Using actors from within the family, he made a few initial films which were shot inside his Castle Theatre. In 1902 he hit the jackpot with a six-minute version of The Maid Of Cefn Ydfa. His son, Will Haggar Junior played the main character Will Hopkins, while his daughter-in-law Jenny Lindon played the maid. The film was a massive success and earned him substantial box office takings. He went on to make a 50-minute version of it in 1914.

From 1907 the Castle Theatre more or less became a permanent fixture in Neath. Will Haggar Junior bought Castle House, Gnoll Park Road, Neath, to live in and at the same time began to gather a permanent staff and company for his theatre. He advertised for a

> **"First Low Comedian, must be young and well up in modern stock business and farces. Preferences given to those doing a turn between. Good money for a good man."**

He also said he was looking for the rights to short dramas, sketches and fit-up companies looking for two-night engagements. As further evidence that the Haggars were seeking permanent roots rather than the portable and the fairground circuit, in June 1910 William Haggar Senior bought the Royalty Theatre in Llanelli. The newspapers reported:

> **"The theatre will be carried on along the usual lines with the addition of frequent picture shows and variety, and in future it will be known as Haggar's Theatre."**

The Castle continued to be run successfully by William Haggar Junior. Mr Haggar Senior was one of the first to recognise the growing popularity of moving pictures and his bioscope show was one of the finest travelling.

Just seven years later he sold the Llanelli theatre on the grounds of ill health and his sons being embroiled in the First World War. Like many of the other portable theatres, The Castle at Neath seemed to have closed towards the end of the First World War. All the Haggar venues were being used as cinemas. Some of the family took over management of the various venues and Will Haggar Junior and his wife continued as performers, working mostly for other managements, though occasionally venturing out with companies of their own. After the death of Sarah in 1909 William Senior decided to settle down and open a chain of cinemas in the south Wales valleys. He based himself in Aberdare where he opened the Coliseum and Electric Palace. His most luxurious venue was the Kosy Kinema, which opened in August, 1915. After his death in 1925 this was sold to Captain W E Willis of Pentre. Interestingly while some theatre owners were turning to the cinema, Willis was heading in the opposite direction and later became owner of the Grand Theatre itself.

The Royal Pavilion

In November 1868 Swansea was given the opportunity to witness the excitement and entertainment offered by a different kind of portable. Joseph Tayleur, 24, and his partner, a Mr Hutchinson were equestrians and circus proprietors, who ran The Great American Circus from 1868 onwards. On November 6, 1868 they were given a licence by Swansea magistrates permitting them to stage a winter season of circus and equestrian displays. The circus opened three days later in a large specially erected building. This was the Royal Pavilion. The main entrance was in Wind Street, with another to the gallery and other areas in York Street. The performances started at 7.30pm with admission at two shillings for a chair in the boxes, one shilling in the pit or one shilling to mingle in the comfortable and commodious lounge. Children were admitted at half price. The performers were reported to be unequalled in the provinces, while 'the well known reputation of the proprietors is a sufficient guarantee that the whole arrangement will be constructed with the greatest order and decorum.' Along with the large equestrian troupe of male and female artists that included champion riders, vaulters, acrobats, and marvellous gymnasts attached to the establishment. Visiting performers included Henry Brown, the clown and jester, Little Bob and Ned Hall, a renowned funny, black-faced act from Burtons Christy Minstrels, Signor Parzini on the flying rope who, at the age of 64, was said to still be as nimble as a squirrel, funny Bob Anderson and the final appearance of the daring Niblo, prior to his departure for the United States.

After a successful season which ended in March 1869, Hutchinson and Tayleure took the circus on a tour of South Wales and some of the principal towns and cities of the United Kingdom. In May 1871 Hutchinson and Tayleure's Circus, now amalgamated with Howe and Cushing's American Circus, returned to Swansea performing in a tent on Walter Road. The following year, on August 12, 1872, they were back at the Amphitheatre in Wind Street. Their 1873 visit saw performances at a portable theatre in Walter Road, while in 1874 the visit was advertised as 'The Great American Circus' at Mumbles Road.

In December 1881 a review in The Stage newspaper for the Royal Pavilion, Swansea proclaimed:

> **"Messrs Tayleure's Company have fairly established themselves in the favour of Swansea circus goers by their first class performance last week. This week an entire change of programme proves no less interesting. Tonight, Friday, a special performance will be given in aid of the Hospital."**

It is likely the Royal Pavilion was some kind of portable theatre erected for the winter season. However two years later, in November 1883 The Stage reported:

> **"Tayleure's Circus took up its quarters in Swansea last week, and will remain for the season. The proprietor, Mr Joseph Tayleure, has rendered the interior of the building most attractive and comfortable, and his catering for the public amusement has been rewarded by liberal patronage. He intends making still further improvements shortly."**

The chief attraction of the 1883 season was Dr Carl, The Demon Marksman, and Poole's Diorama of The World, was highly popular for the Christmas week. Tayleure's season lasted until Easter and his annual visits continued until 1888.

End of the portables

By this time however, the times were changing. Gradually the smaller towns, the lifeblood of both portables and fit-ups, were increasing in size and attracting the construction of permanent theatres. Methodism and notions of delicacy were also coming to the fore. The managers of portables now had two courses open to them, either to settle down in one of the towns on their circuit and set up a permanent theatre or retreat to the smaller towns and villages, as yet unvisited by the touring companies.

In 1889 the Gwyn Hall, a modern, comfortable, elegant performance space aimed at the growing middle-classes was built in Neath. By 1897 Morriston had its own Opera House. The 'rough and ready' approach of the old portables was now out-dated. Instead, audiences preferred the sophistication of the new, permanent and vastly more comfortable theatres.

The Prince of Wales Theatre, Morriston

One of the last of the portable theatres was the Prince of Wales Theatre managed by John Johnson. By 1885 his main base was in Morriston, though he often played short seasons at nearby towns and was a regular feature of the annual September Fair at Neath. It seems that the Prince of Wales, Morriston, was more or less a permanent building also used as a store for a portable which could occasionally be taken to other venues.

The Prince of Wales survived at least 12 years, and frequently placed advertisements in The Stage looking for performers and attractions. In April 1887, from these advertisements, it is clear that it was a more or less permanent theatre, playing throughout the year. It always advertised itself as the Prince of Wales, Morriston, thus implying it was a 'proper' theatre and not a portable. However, in 1891 it staged a series of shows at Neath's September Fair, including a highly successful production of The Bleeding Nun. Johnny Johnson as he was popularly known, later moved away from the theatre business, continued to travel with fairgrounds and became a well-known showman.

The last of the big portables disappeared with the outbreak of the First World War though, incredibly, some of the smaller ones survived well into the 1950s in more rural communities.

Act 8

Rivalry of the other venues

The Grand may claim that it is the last surviving theatre in Wales' most popular seaside city. What it cannot lay claim to however is that it was the first purpose built theatre in Swansea. There were others before. They had some eye-catching names: there was the Theatre Royal; The Star and The Pavilion. And like The Grand, they too, all had their moments, often generated by the intense rivalry that existed between them.

The Theatre Royal was built in Bank Street, later called Temple Street, more recently the site, until April 2007, of the David Evans department store. This was a serious venture. If all the seats in the theatre were sold, each performance would take £80. The investors found themselves a top manager in Andrew Cherry. Attracting him to Swansea was quite a coup. He was a star of London theatre. His Shylock at Drury Lane had been widely acclaimed. He was also a playwright, well known for his hit The Soldier's Daughter. Indeed the Theatre Royal was due to open with the play. Unfortunately the scenery – coming by ship from Bristol – didn't arrive in time because of bad weather so the opening night, on July 6, 1807, was hastily re-arranged as a gala concert.

Like most provincial theatres of the time, the Theatre Royal was not originally a full-time operation. Cherry ran a season of plays from July to October, performing three nights a week with occasional extra shows if demand warranted. He would then lead his company for seasons at other theatres in the region – Carmarthen, Haverfordwest, Brecon, Abergavenny and Cardiff were all, at various times, part of the circuit. During the winter and spring the Theatre Royal would generally be closed with only occasional short seasons by visiting touring companies, such as the Bath Company of Comedians. For his 1809 season Cherry employed unknown actor Edmund Kean. He paid him 25 shillings a week and extra if Mrs Kean appeared as well. Kean was short and had the wild air of a Gypsy, but he made a great impression on audiences. To take up his job in Swansea, he and his wife travelled from Birmingham. For the last part of the journey they walked for more than 50 miles from Newport to Swansea – because they had no money. Kean made his Swansea debut as Hamlet on June 21, 1809. He was a great success. Kean played two seasons at Swansea and then left to better himself, something he succeeded in doing. For by the time he died 22 years later, he was the biggest name in British theatre, a legend on both sides of the Atlantic and acknowledged as one of the greatest actors of all time.

Andrew Cherry had a knack of spotting rising young talent. Another of his employees was Sheridan Knowles, who later became one of the most popular playwrights of the time. However, much as he wanted to encourage unknown talent, Cherry was wise enough to know that the Swansea public liked star names and in 1811 with this in mind, he engaged John Bannister, the first comedian of Drury Lane for a short season. Under

A drawing depicting the view up Temple Street in the 1850s. The Theatre Royal is the building on the left.

A view up Temple Street from Oxford Street, this one captured on camera. The Theatre Royal is on the left but at this time was mostly unused.

The end of the road for the Theatre Royal as it lays almost derelict and ready for demolition in the late 1890s.

Cherry's management the Theatre Royal prospered. He wrote the successful Jubilee in Honour of the King, to mark the Jubilee of King George III and when business was beginning to wane he wrote his own hit play, Angeline, or Who's the Murderer? and saved the day. Ironically, 150 years later the Grand Theatre's manager, John Chilvers, similarly turned to plays with the word 'murder' in the title whenever business took a downturn.

Following Andrew Cherry's death in 1812 – just before an opening night in Monmouth – the Theatre Royal's fortunes dipped. It had ceased to produce any of its own shows, and was reliant on short seasons from the visiting Bristol or Bath companies. Henry Bengough organised these seasons for the next four years, and then from 1816-1818 it seems there were no visiting seasons at all. The theatre was mostly unused, except for occasional private hire.

In July 1820 William M'Cready became manager and introduced regular nights for the gentry along with pantomimes like Cinderella and Dick Whittington and his Cat. He also staged non-theatrical attractions including a diorama and a Chinese air balloon floating inside the theatre. However, William M'Cready's best attraction was his own son. W C Macready – a Drury Lane star and famous actor in his own right – who was a close friend of Charles Dickens. The young Macready was happy to pay the occasional visit to his father's theatre to help boost the business. M'Cready even managed to persuade Edmund Kean – by then a famous name in the theatre world – to return to Swansea. Kean opened with Othello and was paid £136 for eight performances. Just 12 years earlier his wages had been £1.5s per week. Another star who appeared at the time was Master Burke, who was described as a five year old infant phenomenon. His appearance caused a sensation with all the box seats sold to adoring ladies. However, audiences were falling and in 1826 there was no theatre season at all. The following year M'Cready introduced Grand Opera – Der Freischutz – and the occasional ballet to improve matters. He even staged a lavish production of Goethe's Faust with fireworks and all manner of other effects. But not even this succeeded in boosting attendance. Matters were not helped by the fact that Swansea was gradually losing its image as a fashionable resort. Increasing industrialisation was changing the image of the town. The end of the French wars now made it possible for the well to do to visit European towns and cities for their cultural and fashionable holidays. After M'Cready's death in 1829 a few managers, including a man named Brunton, tried to revive interest in the Theatre Royal, but nothing seemed to work. In 1833 Swansea was hit by a severe outbreak of cholera. The theatre closed, and for a while it looked as if it might not reopen. However when the cholera epidemic subsided, James Woulds, or Jemmy as

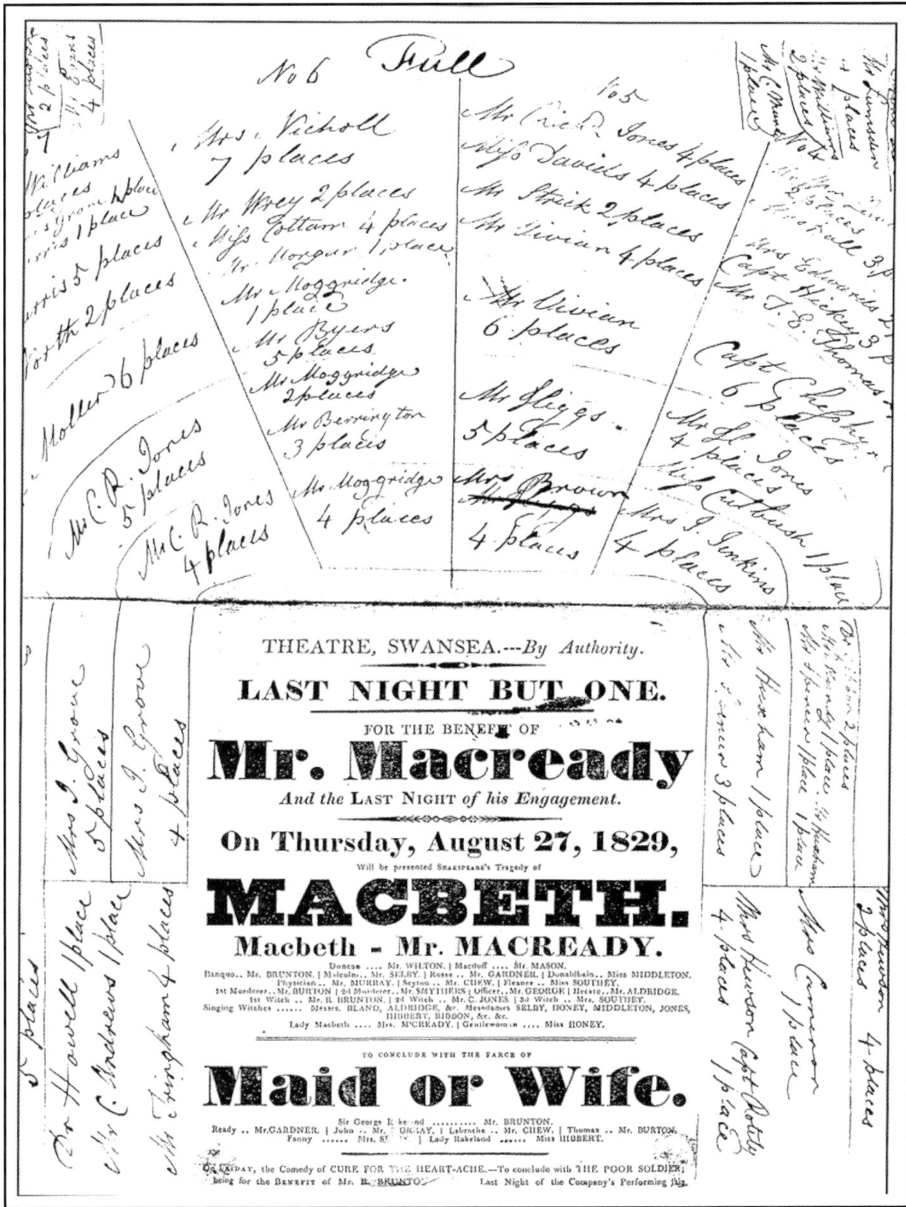

THEATRE, SWANSEA.---*By Authority.*

LAST NIGHT BUT ONE.

FOR THE BENEFIT OF

Mr. Macready

And the LAST NIGHT *of his Engagement.*

On Thursday, August 27, 1829,

Will be presented SHAKSPEARE'S Tragedy of

MACBETH.

Macbeth - Mr. MACREADY.

Duncan .... Mr. WILTON. | Macduff .... Mr. MASON.
Banquo.. Mr. BRUNTON. | Malcolm.. Mr. SELBY. | Rosse .. Mr. GARDNER. | Donalbain.. Miss MIDDLETON.
Physician.. Mr. MURRAY. | Seyton .. Mr. CHEW. | Fleance .. Miss SOUTHEY.
1st Murderer.. Mr. BURTON | 2d Murderer.. Mr. SMYTHERS | Officer.. Mr. GEORGE | Hecate.. Mr. ALDRIDGE.
1st Witch .. Mr. R. BRUNTON. | 2d Witch .. Mr. C. JONES. | 3d Witch .. Mrs. SOUTHEY.
Singing Witches ...... Messrs. BLAND, ALDRIDGE, &c. Mesdames SELBY, HONEY, MIDDLETON, JONES, HIBBERT, RIDDON, &c. &c.
Lady Macbeth .... Mrs. M'CREADY. | Gentlewoman .... Miss HONEY.

TO CONCLUDE WITH THE FARCE OF

Maid or Wife.

Sir George R[illegible] .... Mr. BRUNTON.
Ready .. Mr. GARDNER. | John .. Mr. [illegible] | Labreche .. Mr. CHEW. | Thomas .. Mr. BURTON.
Fanny ...... Mrs. [illegible] | Lady Rakeland ...... Miss HIBBERT.

On FRIDAY, the Comedy of CURE FOR THE HEART-ACHE.—To conclude with THE POOR SOLDIER; being for the BENEFIT of Mr. R. BRUNTON. Last Night of the Company's Performing [illegible]

A seating plan for the Theatre Royal for a benefit production of Macbeth staged for William Charles Macready. The layout plan shows that the house was divided into individual boxes in a typical Georgian theatre style. The role of Lady Macbeth was played by Mrs McReady, and the spelling suggests that this was not WC Macready's wife, but his mother.

he was popularly known, decided to give it one more try. He abandoned the 'fashionable' nights, brought back star names and worked hard to attract ordinary people and the growing middle classes. Even W C Macready returned for an occasional performance while Sheridan Knowles also came back for a few shows. This helped business since Swansea audiences were loyal supporters of their favourite performers. They were however, still very small in number.

In 1833 W C Macready returned for a four night engagement. On Monday August 26, he played Iago to what his diary recorded as 'a very loud and bold' Othello. His diary also noted that the audience was 'small and indifferent' while on Tuesday he 'acted particularly well' in the role of William Tell. On Wednesday he appeared as Hamlet. His diary records:

> ***"Acted Hamlet very unsatisfactorily. Having rehearsed it very well I anticipated a good performance, but I did not begin well, and Horatio quite threw me off my balance."***

On Thursday he appeared for the first time in his career in the role of King Lear. This was later to become one of his most acclaimed roles, and he was the most praised Lear of his era. Of his first attempt he recorded:

> ***"Acted Lear. How? I scarcely know. Certainly not well – not so well as I rehearsed it; crude, fictitious voice, no point; in short, a failure! To succeed in it I must strain every nerve of thought, or triumph is hopeless. Woulds called and paid me; not a very profitable engagement, but I am seldom discontented."***

Among the new names Jemmy Woulds brought to Swansea was the famous T P Cooke, who acted in nautical dramas, and was famous for his role as Roderick Dhu in Thomas Dibdin's The Lady Of The Lake, and among his series of sell-out Swansea performances he played this and the equally successful Fate Of

THEATRE ROYAL, SWANSEA.

LESSEE - - - - - - MR. WYBERT REEVE, 22, BRUNSWICK STREET.
Licensed to Play the Dramatic Authors' Society's Pieces.

GREAT SUCCESS OF THE NEW COMPANY

Acknowledged to be the best which has visited Swansea for many years.

The Theatre Beautifully Re-decorated!

OPINIONS OF THE PRESS.

"In a word, it has been completely metamorphosed from a dirty, dingy building, to a light, elegant, and beautiful Temple of the Drama, one which can bear comparison with any in the provinces . . We have no hesitation in stating that the Swansea Theatre is now a credit to the town, whilst the *corps dramatique* is one of the best which has visited us for many years, and as such we hope Mr. Reeve will receive that public support and patronage he so richly deserves. — *Vide Bristol Daily Post*, June 18.

"This Theatre has been newly and handsomely decorated. The performances were of a very superior description, the audience bearing testimony thereto by frequent bursts of applause. Nothing has been left undone to insure a successful Season." — *Cambria Daily Leader*, June 16.

"The decorations of the Theatre were the theme of general admiration, and the company is the best which has visited us for many years. — *Cambrian*, June 19.

LADY AUDLEY'S SECRET!

With New Scenery! and New Effects!

The Liverpool Press, speaking of Miss Vaughan's performance says:—LADY AUDLEY'S SECRET has been the means of introducing to the playgoers of Liverpool Miss Bella Vaughan, a lady in every respect suited for this part, possessing, as she does a commanding figure, which at the same time is graceful and juvenile in appearance. This, together with the power she has of alternating between simple girlishness and the sternness of an incessant woman of the world, give her the power of truthfully rendering one of the most difficult of female stage characters.

The *Daily Post* of May 12th, says:—LADY AUDLEY'S SECRET has introduced into Liverpool an Actress of considerable power and remarkable promise in Miss Bella Vaughan. She has completely mastered all the niceties of the character, and while performing the colloquial parts with the greatest ease, portrayed with the utmost vividness the various shades of Lady Audley's terrific and criminal experience."

Monday & Tuesday, June 22 and 23,

Will be produced for the first time in Swansea a New Drama, with new Scenery, Dresses, and Appointments, &c., founded on Miss Braddon's popular Novel of the same name, entitled (and now played in London with immense success)

LADY AUDLEY'S SECRET

AUDLEY COURT.—"It lay down in a hollow, rich with fine old timber and luxuriant pastures, and you came upon it through an avenue of limes; at the end of the avenue there was an old arch, and a clock tower, with a stupid bewildering clock, which had only one hand, and which jumped from one hour to the next, and was therefore always in extremes. The house faced the arch, and occupied three sides of a quadrangle; it was very old—very irregular—and rambling—great piles of chimneys rose up here and there behind the painted gables, and seemed as if they were broken down by age and long service that they must have fallen but the straggling Ivy, which, crawling up the walls, wound itself about and supported them. A glorious old place, inside and out—a noble place!"

Sir Michael Audley, Bart., of Audley Court, Essex .... Mr. WALTER WILLIAMS
Robert Audley, his Nephew, a young Barrister .... MR. WYBERT REEVE
George Talboys .... Mr. G. W. HARRIS | Luke Marks, under Gamekeeper at Audley Court .... Mr. JAMES CRAIG
Slip .... Miss WILLIAMS | Smithers .... Mr. MARSTON   Servants Countrymen, &c.
Lady Audley, Sir Michael's second Wife .... Miss BELLA VAUGHAN
Alice Audley, Sir Michael's Daughter .... Miss F. CHAPMAN
Phœbe Marks, Lady Audley's waiting maid .... Miss FANNY PITT

ROBERT AUDLEY'S APARTMENTS IN THE "TEMPLE."

George Talboy's Return   A strange History.   The *Times*—"On the 20th inst., at Ventnor, Isle of White, Ellen Talboys, aged 2[illegible]."

AUDLEY COURT!

Robert's Arrival---The Cousins---George induced to take a peep at the Hall.---THE PICTURE.

MEETING OF LADY AUDLEY & GEORGE TALBOYS--THE HIDDEN WITNESS

A playbill from the time when Wybert Reeve leased and redecorated the Theatre Royal in 1861. During the following five years he brought a number of worthy plays to the town.

A group of people pose for a photograph outside the Theatre Royal. Its days as a theatre were over by this time and it was demolished in 1898.

Frankenstein based on the popular Gothic novel by Mary Shelley. He also introduced amateur nights, encouraging local people to perform. The 1834 season was especially successful. It opened on July 14 and closed on October 22 having given 56 performances of 45 different plays. This success encouraged Woulds to expand, and he began a series of exchange productions with the Theatre Royal in Bath. As soon as a show finished in Swansea, he would take it for a run at Bath, while the Bath Company would move to Swansea. In 1840 however, following a disastrous season at Bath, Jemmy Woulds was declared bankrupt. The Swansea theatre was taken into joint management by two actors from the Bath company – J R Newcombe and Paul Bedford, though they did employ Jemmy Woulds as their stage manager at Swansea. They struggled for six years, during which they staged operas by Bellini and Donizetti; plays by local authors and even Vaudeville nights. In 1843 Newcombe and Bedford declared they could no longer sustain regular annual losses of around £200 and as a result, the Theatre Royal closed its doors.

The 1840s were economically bad years for the whole country, and especially for industrialised South Wales. This was the time of the Rebecca Riots as well as one when the religious movements in Wales were strengthening. People who valued their good name were no longer prepared to be seen to attend theatres. The early Victorians were gradually turning away from theatre. Ordinary working men were turning more and more to music hall entertainment – songs and monologues performed in rooms attached to public houses were now getting an audience. The additional attraction here was that they could eat and drink at the same time as being entertained. The middle and upper classes were also looking elsewhere; to the more refined delights of home and saloon entertainment. A piano in the home became the 'must have' item of the day. The theatre business was struggling.

Between 1847 and 1854 no fewer than eight managers attempted to revive the Theatre Royal. They all failed. Mrs Lowe (1847), D F Rogers (1849), E W Gomersal (1850), Mr Macarthy (1852), W Rignold (1852-53), Mr Brandon (1854), F Lloyd (1854) and T R Cobham (1854) were all forced to admit defeat.

In 1855 the next manager, John Chute formerly of the Bristol Theatre, managed to partially reverse the downward trend. He engaged The English National Opera Company for performances of Acis and Galatea and Il Trovatore. He also decided to open the theatre on

The original site of The Star Theatre in Wind Street.

The marble plate laid by the architects after the rebuild of the Star Theatre in 1902. It is preserved and on display in Swansea Museum.

a regular basis and not just for fixed short seasons. He staged large spectacular productions based on contemporary events such as the Great Indian Mutiny. He also encouraged star names from London to make guest appearances at Swansea. Mr and Mrs Charles Kean came with a production of Hamlet. In July 1857 one of the biggest names Chute brought to the Theatre Royal was also the smallest – General Tom Thumb. He was a tiny man who stood just 30 inches tall; his fame had spread far and wide as a main attraction with P T Barnum's Circus. Barnum even paid a flying visit to Swansea to watch Thumb on his last night. Despite enjoying moderately better success, even John Chute finally withdrew from the challenge of running the Theatre Royal in 1861.

The next manager was Wybert Reeve, who held the reins from 1861 to 1866. During his five years in charge he presented a number of worthy plays. When he wrote his autobiography in 1892 he recalled his Swansea years with pleasure, particularly one week in 1863 when he presented the famous actor Charles Pitt and his Company playing Hamlet, Othello and Macbeth. This was to coincide with the holding of the National Eisteddfod in Swansea. Business remained barely adequate. At the same time however, a company from Her Majesty's Theatre in London was performing Gounod's opera Faust in a pavilion at the Eisteddfod. They sold every ticket. This led Wybert Reeve to hope opera could save the theatre's fortunes. After all, he thought, it had a much better image than plays. Opera was respectable and Welsh people were known for their love of music. The Lyric Opera Company from Covent Garden came to Swansea with La Traviata, a new opera by Verdi. But audiences did not like new and unknown operas performed in modern dress! So, the company then staged the established favourite, The Quaker – but even that didn't work. Then, in 1864, The Swansea Music Hall opened in Cradock Street, it was a splendid and elegant new building and served to emphasise that the 57 year old Theatre Royal was now outdated and shabby. Wybert Reeve had frequently complained to the owners – The Tontine – but they had refused to spend any money on updating and improving the theatre, claiming that annual profits were low, often non-existent, and they could not afford to renovate the building. Wybert Reeve finally gave up in 1867. Surprisingly his resignation shocked the owners into doing something about the state of the theatre. The new manager, Mrs Charles Pitt, made it a condition of her leasing the building, that major renovation was carried out. She had her way. For the first few months of 1867 the theatre was closed for this work to go ahead. The floor of the stage and the pit were lowered by five feet and taken under the boxes. The proscenium was moved back six feet, thus increasing the seating capacity of the pit by 200. Separate entrances were created for the pit, the gallery and the more expensive boxes. The boxes received a splendid new entrance in front of the building; the gallery door was moved to the side of the building in Goat Street. A new stage and grooves were erected, so that the height of the scenery was increased to 17 feet instead of the former 13 feet. The interior was also completely and lavishly redecorated.

Mrs Pitt proudly reopened her splendidly renovated theatre in June 1867 with Dion Boucicault's hit play The Streets Of London – suitably adapted into The Streets Of Swansea. This was a good start to a successful few months, culminating in a sell-out pantomime. Things however fell away in the New Year. Mrs Pitt left to manage the Surrey Theatre in London, and a series of temporary managers struggled to keep the theatre open.

In 1869 the Theatre Royal had a new tenant – George

Melville, a 55-year-old tragedian who had already established himself as a theatre manager in Cardiff and was planning to branch out into the world of music hall and variety. He intended building a new music hall in Swansea and running both a legitimate and a variety theatre alongside one another. His first shows at the Theatre Royal included the pantomime Dick Whittington with Jessie Melville as Dick, and a summer season which included various plays of local interest, including The Collier's Life.

Within a few years George had taken over the old Amphitheatre in Wind Street and had rebuilt it as a music hall and variety house. The day to day running of the new Star Amphitheatre was in the hands of George's son, Andrew. The rival attractions of circuses, clowns, rope-spinners, minstrel groups and comedians at the Star, and plays, operas, high tragedies and melodrama at the Theatre Royal were now all in the hands of one family – the Melville's. Frequently the Theatre Royal would be closed for several weeks at a time. George claimed this was to enable him to transfer Swansea productions to his Cardiff theatre, but others believed he was deliberately running the Theatre Royal down to benefit the Star. From 1881 onwards, the closure periods became even more frequent. It was available for private hire, amateur companies and the occasional charity show. In March 1884 the Temple Glee and Dramatic Society presented a one-night concert there for local good causes. Three months later the St David's Amateur Players (who in 1901 renamed themselves Swansea Amateur Operatic Society) staged a one-night charity show and announced that Mr Melville had kindly permitted use of the theatre free of charge. The two theatres occasionally complemented one another through the following years, especially during the holiday season and Christmas time. During the pantomime season at the Star, by now known as the New Theatre, Melville would re-open the Theatre Royal for the presentation of straight plays. In January 1886 he secured the engagement of W T Richardson's Proof company and the following January also offered a dramatic alternative. However the theatre was closed through the greater part of the 1880s. In 1893 it seems that a special effort was made to get it back into full time operation. Throughout the autumn the Theatre Royal ran a weekly advertisement in The Stage offering the venue for hire or for sharing terms. However, the old theatre was no longer attractive to touring companies. It gradually ceased to stage any theatrical productions and towards the end was used only rarely for the occasional choral evening or religious meeting. The Melville family expanded their theatre ownership to other towns. Although their theatres were flourishing all over the country, the Theatre Royal was slowly fading away. This was partly a deliberate move on Melville's part, and partly due to the opening of rival theatres. By the early 1890s the Theatre Royal had effectively ceased to be used as a theatre. It stood almost derelict for the next few years until the opening of The Grand and the New Empire made it clear the town had no further need for it. As the 20th Century began, so the Theatre Royal was demolished.

The Star Theatre

The origins of the Star Theatre probably stretch as far back as the late 1850s or early 1860s, when it is recorded that Henry Clare built a wooden amphitheatre in Wind Street, on the site of the old Star Inn. He used it to put on equestrian shows which at that time were popular. The building was sometimes promoted as the Swansea

A tram rumbles down a busy Wind Street, just about to pass the Star Theatre in 1902. Later the Star became The Rialto cinema which was demolished in 1968. Today the La Tasca restaurant, pictured right, occupies the same site.

Circus, but was generally called the Prince of Wales Amphitheatre. Before the end of its life the building and its reincarnations assumed a number of other names including the New Theatre, the Theatre Royal, Royal Theatre and finally the Rialto Cinema. It appears to have been a ramshackle place, and in October 1869 as if to prove this, the local magistrates refused to give it a licence on safety grounds.

It was originally a wooden structure and after the loss of the licence work began immediately to erect a more permanent building. It is believed the rebuilt theatre opened around 1870, but nothing more is known until 1872, when something of a scandal erupted. The Cambrian newspaper started a campaign to ban Ernest Boulton, a female impersonator, from appearing at the Swansea Circus in Wind Street. The Cambrian felt that the prospect of a man dressed in women's clothing was deeply offensive and should not be permitted in a respectable town like Swansea. The campaign must have struck a chord in the community for an advertisement in the Cambrian on July 24, 1874 announced that the lease of the Circus, Wind Street, was for sale. The lease was taken over by the Melville family, and after considerable rebuilding, a theatre licence for the Amphitheatre was granted to Andrew Melville on November 12, 1875 and it was renamed the Star. Andrew was the elder son of George Melville Robbins. George had dropped his surname when he became a showman and entertainment producer in Cardiff. In 1869 the family moved to Singleton Street, Swansea. The 45-year-old George had already become the tenant of Swansea's Theatre Royal and now, five years later, had taken over the dilapidated premises in Swansea's Wind Street and rebuilt it as the Star Theatre. George had several daughters and four sons. His first, Andrew, was heavily involved with the new theatre from the very beginning. Initially the Melvilles planned to run the Theatre Royal as a house of drama and the Star as a house of variety. The Star would be a direct competitor with the Swansea Music Hall and their own Theatre Royal.

After their first season they discovered that when they staged a straight play at the Star, it did better business than a similar play at the Theatre Royal. This was perhaps because the new theatre was modern, better equipped, more comfortable and more attractive than the old Theatre Royal. Gradually, the Star expanded into producing its own plays and acting as a receiving house for touring companies as well as staging regular variety productions. Within the first two years the Melvilles were successful enough to concentrate their efforts on the Star and allow the Theatre Royal to serve as an overflow theatre and a venue available for outsiders to rent for all manner of purposes.

The father and son team had set off on what became a 25-year stint running Swansea's most successful theatre. Their mix of musical acts, comedies, tragedies and their hallmark thrilling melodramas – many of them written by members of their own family – turned the Star into a well supported and money-making venture. Among their most successful ideas was involving local performers and the growing amateur theatrical movement. They would regularly stage concerts by groups they had discovered – the Landore Linnets and Cwmbwrla Cuckoos among them – and always encouraged local talent to appear.

With popular and financial support, the Melvilles did well. George started to expand the family business. As the years passed, Andrew married a Swansea girl, Alice Bullock, and moved to Christina Street. The couple had four daughters and four sons. Eventually all of them were involved in the family business as performers or managers. In the 1880s the Melvilles started to expand further afield. They took over the Standard and Shoreditch theatres in London and the Grand in Birmingham. George moved to London while Andrew became sole manager of the Star. At this point he carried out some further renovation and renamed it the New Theatre. As so often happened, however, Swansea people didn't take to the new name and affectionately continued to refer to it as the Star.

Andrew Melville's growing theatrical empire meant he was now mostly living away from Swansea. He appointed a succession of managers to run the New Theatre, Swansea including the remarkable J K Murray. Murray had eloped with Ada Amelia Ponder and the couple had fled to America to avoid parental conflict. They were caught up in the American Civil War and performed for both opposing armies before returning to England in 1870. Managing and performing in a theatre in Swansea must have been a lot easier than performing in the war-torn United States.

The pattern of shows at the New Theatre was a mixture of visiting touring productions, and then a short season of stock productions, with a resident company filling the gaps between tours. Andrew Melville himself was a favourite performer with Swansea audiences, and he would occasionally appear in a show under his stage name of Andrew Emm. His father, George, was also much loved by local theatregoers. While Andrew was the man for comedy and not to be missed in pantomime, his father George was the 'serious' actor, whose roles included Hamlet, Othello, Ruy Blas, and Don Caesar de Bazan. Running a theatre in the 1880s was a demanding business: a whole week's run was most unusual, and generally there were two or three different productions each week. In the fortnight prior to the 1881 pantomime,

Babes in the Wood, the New Theatre staged The Castaway on a Monday and Tuesday, Leah on Wednesday and Thursday, East Lynne on Friday and Saturday, then Ruy Blas on Monday, Don Caesar de Bazan on Tuesday and Wednesday, Othello on Thursday before closing on Friday and Saturday for pantomime rehearsals. To add to the pressure, at this time the Melvilles were running both the old Theatre Royal and the New Theatre.

While Babes in the Wood was in its final week at the New Theatre, the Royal was offering the William Duck Company's Married in Haste, The Money Spinner and Our Boys, playing just two nights of each show. Our Boys was a total sell-out, with hundreds of people being turned away. Not to miss an opportunity and with a quick rearrangement of their schedules, the Melvilles moved Our Boys from the Royal to the New Theatre to play two extra performances on the following Monday and Tuesday. To do this they rearranged a planned D'Oyly Carte season to fit into four nights instead of six and all this while both father and son were appearing on stage in different shows each night!

Another example of the volume and turnover at the New Theatre can be gleaned from a newspaper report published during June 1882:

> **"Henry Hampton will appear as the Waif in Forsaken on Monday. During the week the company will appear in The Gamester, Virginius and Hamlet, finishing on Saturday night with the usual two or three five-act dramas and a couple of farces to complete the programme."**

The range of shows presented at the theatre was vast. The autumn season of 1883 included the Compton Shakespeare Company, the D'Oyly Carte Opera with Iolanthe, Sam Hague's Minstrel Show, and Professor Johnson and his Two Daughters who it was proclaimed at the time exhibited some really remarkable swimming and diving feats. The season culminated in the pantomime Little Red Riding Hood. The annual pantomimes were great attractions, opening on Boxing Day and running until the end of January. Successive years offered Cinderella with Miss Kate Bertram and Mr J F Locke as the sisters and with the Great Little Alfred Gravonelli as the clown in the Harlequinade. Other pantos included Aladdin, The Forty Thieves, Robinson Crusoe and Bluebeard.

In April 1894 Andrew Melville's most publicised performance was not in the theatre, but the local courtrooms. An actress named Miss Eden, touring in Maid Marian at the New Theatre, suffered an accident while dancing. She blamed this on an improperly secured drugget, a cloth stretched on the stage floor, representing the forest floor, and claimed damages from Andrew Melville. He denied liability stating that the floor covering was part of the scenery and therefore the responsibility of the visiting manager. The visiting manager claimed it had been supplied by the theatre and was therefore part of Mr Melville's responsibility. Mr Melville counter-claimed that the drugget had been secured by employees of the visiting manager and was not the responsibility of the New Theatre. Judgement was reserved. Andrew Melville seems to have been a frequent plaintiff in the courts. During these years he is recorded as suing people for stealing his copyright, libelling him, or breaking contracts. Between 1893 and 1895 he was involved in at least five different court actions.

Swansea audiences enjoyed novelty and spectacle. In June 1884 the Frank L Frayne Company appeared in Murdo, which according to one newspaper report:

> **"Bristled with thrilling situations, including plenty of shooting, two conflagrations and a dynamite explosion as well as the introduction of real wild beasts."**

Despite all of this, business was poor. For Easter 1885 Lionel Ellis and Company appeared with Light in the Dark. One newspaper reported:

> **"The introduction of a real baby perhaps rendered the scene more realistic but was in questionable taste and the audience exhibited some dissatisfaction especially when the child began to cry."**

In July of that year Frayne began to advertise the venue as the New Theatre and Star Opera House. Perhaps he added the word opera in an attempt to enhance the image of the theatre.

Apart from his visits to Swansea in connection with acting performances, Andrew Melville spent much time out of Wales, looking after the other family theatres. He made regular visits to Swansea to oversee the affairs of the theatre, but he was by now approaching middle age, and happy to see the next generation of Melvilles getting ready to make their mark on the family business. His daughters regularly performed at the family's theatres – Edith had particular success as Cinderella in the 1892 pantomime at the Star. Two of Andrew's sons – Walter and Frederick Melville were being groomed for the business. A third son, Andrew Jnr, was also waiting in the wings.

By early 1891 the Melville family was no longer in control of the old Theatre Royal. It appears George Melville had originally taken a 21 year lease on the Royal, and either he decided not to renew it, or the landowners decided to offer it to a rival company.

The new management at the Theatre Royal was headed by a Mr Alex Stacey, whose main company was based in Sheffield. In July 1891 he took a series of

One of the most popular musical hall artistes of her day, Marie Lloyd was a frequent visitor to the Swansea Empire both at High Street and Oxford Street.

advertisements in the trade and local press announcing the re-opening of the extensively improved Swansea Theatre Royal, claiming it was the 'prettiest theatre in the provinces.'

Andrew Melville immediately retaliated with an even larger advert claiming the New Theatre was 'the largest theatre in Wales.' His advertisement read:

> **"Vacant dates for first-class travelling companies. Sole proprietor and manager: Andrew Melville."**

The advertisement gave the main address for the Melville family business as the Grand Theatre, Birmingham, and pointed out that the company also owned, or leased, the Grand Theatre, Derby, the Bristol Theatre Royal, the St George's Theatre, Walsall and the Standard in London.

Over the next few years there was serious rivalry between Swansea's three principal theatres: the Theatre Royal run by Alex Stacey, the Swansea Pavilion, shortly to become Oswald Stoll's Empire Theatre and the New Theatre and Star Opera House run by the Melvilles. If that wasn't enough, occasionally the Albert Hall would stage a major attraction in competition with them. They were lively times.

In December 1895 Andrew Melville collapsed while rehearsing the pantomime Forty Thieves at the Grand Birmingham. The family rallied round. His son Walter, aged 20, took over that show. His other son, Frederick, 18, took over producing Andrew's pantomime at the Star, Swansea. It was a great blow when Andrew died just a few weeks later, aged just 43. The shock of losing his first-born son had a profound effect on George Melville. He never recovered from the event and he too died within two years, aged 74. The family was clearly struggling with so many ventures spread over so many different parts of the country. In March 1897 they announced that the New Theatre, Swansea and the Queen's Theatre, Battersea, were up for sale by private treaty. However, it seems that they remained unsold. The New Theatre closed and was unused for the next three years. Andrew Melville was buried in Oystermouth cemetry where his grave can still be seen.

At the turn of the century the Melvilles decided to revive their efforts to sell the premises. An advertisement appeared in The Stage in June 1900. It stated:

> **"Those desirous of investing in theatrical property should take note that the New Theatre, Swansea, for many years in the possession of the late Andrew Melville will be offered for sale on June 12."**

Again, it seems that no one was interested in an outright purchase, so the theatre was taken on a three year lease by the T Morton Powell Company, which already operated the Grand Opera House, Liverpool and the Queen's Theatre, Farnworth, Bolton. With the temporary disposal of the Star, the Melvilles had severed their links with Swansea.

By the spring of 1902 T Morton Powell had decided to turn his lease into an outright purchase. He invested a large sum of money in renovating the premises, and approached William Coutts from the Lyceum Birmingham to be his acting manager and potential partner. Coutts was already established as a successful theatre proprietor and touring manager, and had earned a great deal of money from his ongoing tour of Hands Across the Sea. In April 1902 he sold his interest in the Birmingham theatre and moved to Swansea.

The next phase in the history of the Wind Street premises came in October 1902 when T Morton Powell announced:

> **"The reconstructed New Star Theatre opens on October 27, with The Belle of Cairo starring Miss Ada Blanch."**

A week later he placed an advert in The Stage reporting the enormous success of the opening:

> **"As pronounced by the Press, describing a most charming theatre, magnificently furnished with a full band and staff. Everything has been done to ensure the success and comfort of travelling companies. The Shilling Pit has been beautifully upholstered and the Star claims to have the finest stage in Wales. Mr Morton Powell takes this**

opportunity of thanking his numerous friends and well-wishers for their kind and encouraging letters and telegrams numbering considerably over 200. The generous expressions of goodwill contained therein will be ever most heartily appreciated."

The New Star carried on with a mix of variety, melodrama, touring shows and pantomime until, in July 1905, William Coutts successfully bought out Powell's share in the building, and thus became the sole proprietor. Finally, just four months later, Coutts increased his business interest by buying the lease on the Palace Theatre in High Street.

Despite William Coutts's expansion into the cinema world, the Star remained a live theatre throughout, and several of his premises occasionally staged live shows, sometimes following or preceding a week at the Star. Curiously he made a sudden decision to change the name of the Star Theatre. The attraction during the week commencing December 31, 1912 was A Girl Without Conscience. Towards the end of that week an advertisement for the following show appeared inviting:

"All playgoers in Swansea and District to attend the opening of the Theatre Royal, Swansea on Monday, January 6, 1913 at 7.30pm when Hall Caine's successful play The Christian will be presented by Marcus Draper and Co."

Without explanation, the Star Theatre had changed its name overnight to the Theatre Royal, reviving a name that had last been present in Swansea 17 years earlier. A few more weeks of productions were performed at the newly named Theatre Royal and then in March, the theatre closed briefly for refurbishment.

At the reopening William Coutts declared:

"This newly reconstructed, redecorated and refurnished theatre is now open for staging the very best productions on the road."

Shortly after he took out another advertisement seeking operas, plays and musical attractions for the New Theatre Royal, claiming a capacity of 2,000. In November 1913 the theatre hosted a week-long tour of a play called Driven from Home, ironically starring Andrew Melville, Jnr – back at the theatre where he had spent his childhood. It is not known what he thought of the refurbishment or the new name.

Over the Easter holiday in 1914 the Theatre Royal presented an out-of-season pantomime, Boy Blue and Little Goody Two Shoes with a cast of over 40, under the management of a Mr Codman. This was enormously successful, breaking all box office records. A profitable rep season followed, and then, in August of that year, the country was at war. All manner of wartime restrictions were placed on theatres: no alcohol could be sold after 9pm; the sale of sweets and chocolates was banned after 8pm and an Amusements Tax was introduced, forcing a significant ticket price increase. Shows were urged to save electricity by reducing their running times, all display lighting was banned and power supplies to tramways and electric railways were rationed. It was becoming harder and harder to make a profit out of running a theatre.

Despite all this, 1915 started well enough: in February the Theatre Royal did record business with the Percy Brown Company's tour of Remember Belgium. However, at the same time William Coutts was advertising for 'money-making attractions for the Theatre Royal, Swansea' and was obviously having difficulty finding suitable shows to attract the crowds.

For much of 1915 the Theatre Royal was unused, and then on Boxing Day it reopened as a 'high-class picture house' called the Royal Theatre. The Coutts circuit was now almost exclusively a cinema business, with hardly any live theatre activity. In 1920 the Royal Theatre briefly returned to live theatre with a season from the H Evans Gibbon Repertory Company, but just as quickly appears to have gone back to being a cinema. Then in August 1922 the Coutts organisation seems to have suffered a major crisis. His cinemas closed and the Royal Theatre was taken over.

The new management reverted to the name Theatre Royal – a sensible move since in any case no one seems to have adopted the Royal Theatre name – and within a short while the theatre was once more being used for live shows. In 1924 it offered attractions varying from Chester and Lee's Marionettes to full-scale variety bills, and in September that year was advertising for 'dramas, revues and star combinations' with respondents asked to apply to 'the manager' – his name was not given.

The following year the Theatre Royal continued to offer touring plays and variety shows, this time advertising the manager's name as Marcus Solomon. However, in the trade directories from 1925 onwards, the Theatre Royal is no longer listed as a touring theatre and appears under the picture house classification.

Even so, the theatre still presented the occasional week of live entertainment, sandwiched between its film weeks. At the end of 1929 it celebrated the holiday season with live acts including Miss Betty and Partner – The Riskits – and Una Corda, 'a brilliant musical act.'

In 1931 the Theatre Royal along with other theatres in the town, succumbed to the 'talkies' craze. It was rebuilt, adapted for sound and reopened as the Rialto Cinema. It continued as such until the early 1960s. By then however, it had become something of a fleapit, finally being demolished in 1968. The building didn't quite make its centenary. After that its site was redeveloped and occupied by retail premises before becoming part of Swansea's bustling nightlife, surrounded by bars, restaurants and cafes.

The Pavilion

The Swansea Pavilion opened on Christmas Eve, 1888 as a purpose built music hall and variety theatre at a cost of £10,000. It was created as a joint venture between a tramway company and a local businessman, Mr Almond. Built on a small triangular site that was previously occupied by the Ancient Briton public house, it originally had a capacity of 900 with excellent sightlines because of the new cantilever-beam style that was employed in its construction.

This was another entertainment venue that suffered from a frequent change of name that at one point might have confused some. After the Pavilion it became the New Empire and then the Palace Theatre. The building still stands though in a state of some disrepair.

At the corner of each dressing room of this innovative new theatre, was a triangular trap door under which a ladder went down to the next dressing room. This was the fire escape for the performers. The architect was Alfred Bucknall who had already designed parts of Craig-y-Nos Castle and its Summer Pavilion for Madame Adelina Patti, as well as the much-praised Ben Evans store in Swansea.

The Pavilion was only four years old when Mr Almond decided theatre management wasn't for him. He leased it to a mother and son who were already running a music hall in Cardiff. As a result, Swansea had its first meeting with Oswald Stoll, the man who was to become a legend in the history of British theatre. In April 1892 the trade press reported:

> **"Great improvements have been made in the Empire, Swansea which was reopened on Easter Monday, April 16, under the management of Oswald Stoll, whose successful music hall catering in Cardiff and Newport promises to be repeated in Swansea. The greater portion of the pit, from the orchestra to the pillars beneath the balcony, has been transformed into luxurious stalls seated in crimson plush; large gilded mirrors are ranged entirely around the walls. The floor has been covered with noiseless cork carpeting. The lighting has been rearranged and improved and the whole house has been repainted and redecorated. The old boxes have been removed from the balcony, which has been furnished with long, semi-circular cushioned loungers also in crimson plush. Massive mirrors adorn the balcony walls and new scenery has been painted."**

That opening night performance starred Bonnie Kate Harvey – The Queen Of Serio-Comedy and a young George Robey. There was an unusual but very spectacular way to mark the end of the first performance each night with a very public pyrotechnic display of rockets from the roof of the theatre, lighting the High Street sky with a red glow, which could be seen for miles. The Stoll's ran the theatre for eight years. During this time the New Empire was the premier variety house in Swansea. Treorchy Male Voice Choir sang out from the small stage in April 1898 and there was also a bagpipe performance there in the same year by piper George Findlater who, just a few months earlier, had received the Victoria Cross for his exploits during the attack on the Dargai Heights in the Indian Mutiny. After being shot through both feet and unable to stand, Findlater propped himself against a boulder and continued playing a rousing tune under heavy fire in October 1897.

Oswald Stoll was a man of some standing in the entertainment world and able to draw many of the great music hall performers. During one memorable season in 1899 composer and performer Harry Champion appeared there. Many of Champion's songs are still familiar today. They include Any Old Iron, Boiled Beef And Carrots and his signature tune I'm 'Enery The Eighth, I Am. He was followed a week later by George Robey, a famous singer and actor who was knighted in 1954. Robey, a keen footballer, was once offered an amateur contract and also scored during his only appearance for Chelsea Football Club. He was definitely a popular and successful artiste and went on to record the first version of If You Were The Only Girl In The World in 1916 with Violet Lorraine, a copy of which still exists.

George Lashwood, The Brothers Poluski, Harry Tate, Horne Troupe, Lillie Langtry, J W Rowley, Edwin Boyde, Albert Christian and Sisters Geretti all appeared during this season, which was a huge success for Stoll and The Empire, High Street. A future Hollywood star also arrived in June 1899, as part of a troupe called The Eight Lancashire Lads. It was a 10-year-old Charlie Chaplin. Chaplin's daughter, award-winning actress Geraldine Chaplin stayed in Swansea during the filming of Heidi in 2004 more than 100 years after her father had played the New Empire.

Many more famous performers of the age appeared at the New Empire in High Street, including Marie Lloyd who first appeared there for two weeks (at £50 a week) in June 1892. Dan Leno, Vesta Victoria and Little Tich were other star names of the time that appeared there. The theatre also offered many unknown and long

An early 1900s view down High Street, with the theatre which was by this time a fully-fledged cinema called the Palace Bioscope, on the left.

forgotten performers including Little Flossie, The American Child Marvel, the greatest juvenile artiste of the day; Miss Emilie Sells, The Boneless Lady, Fritz Young, The World-Famous Clown and Miss Mari Tyler, England's greatest versatile comedienne.

In 1896 the New Empire even hosted Swansea's first cinema show. During the Stolls' final six months at the theatre in 1899 they delighted Swansea audiences with stars like George Lashwood, famous for In The Twi-Twi-Twilight and Hetty King of All The Nice Girls Love A Sailor fame.

The Palace Theatre of Varieties

By 1900 Oswald Stoll realised that he had outgrown the New Empire in High Street and built a new, luxurious Empire theatre in Oxford Street. The whole operation then moved to the new premises and a new company moved in to the old. Since Oswald Stoll insisted on retaining the name Empire, the new company was obliged to find another name. They decided on the Palace Theatre of Varieties. The years that followed were very difficult for the Palace. All the great variety performers were under contract to Stoll at his Empire, and the newly built theatre in Oxford Street was the last word in elegance, making the Palace appear a little shabby. All the popular melodramas and smaller London tours were the province of the Melville's at the Star in Wind Street, and the bigger and more prestigious London tours were engaged by the newly opened Grand Theatre. The Palace was struggling – and it was only 12 years old. Appearing at the theatre in November 1902 was Belle Elmore, who later married the infamous Dr Crippen and was subsequently murdered by him, in 1910.

In 1905 things changed. William Coutts, the popular manager who had taken over running the Star theatre, raised funds to take over the Palace. Under joint management, the Star and Palace were no longer competitors, but partners. Coutts carefully booked his attractions so that there were no clashes, and he arranged the programme to give audiences the widest possible choice. In the August 2, 1906 edition of The Stage he placed an advertisement for The Palace Theatre Swansea which read:

"Wanted: First class dramatic companies for September 3, onwards. Will managers please note that this beautiful theatre will be opened as a drama house on September 3 and being situated in the vicinity nearest the great tin and copper works should prove a veritable goldmine appealing as it will to an industrial population of 100,000. The Palace Theatre has cost upwards of £20,000 and is

An artist's impression of Oswald Stoll's Empire Theatre at High Street in 1892. Its best years as a theatre spanned the period from 1892 – 1900, when the twice nightly variety shows drew large and appreciative audiences.

replete with every modern appliance and convenience. It holds about 1,000 persons and is, perhaps, the most charming bijou playhouse in the provinces. Manager: Samuel Powell."

The 1906 autumn season of dramas offered Dora Drench and full company in The Rich And Poor Of London and A Rogue's Daughter with Madge Devereaux – but the business was not good and the Palace quickly returned to variety. However, given a choice, it appears that much of the Palace's audience showed a strong preference for the new-fangled cinema.

For a while the Palace was renamed the Palace Bioscope, and by 1912, it was called the Popular Picture Hall. By this time it ceased to stage live shows. Coutts later took over the Picturedrome in Morriston and with his assistant, Larry Warner – later the manager of the Globe, Clydach and the Patti Pavilion – became the most prominent of Swansea's impresarios.

For another 10 years or so the Palace operated as a cinema, but by 1923 Swansea was home to several purpose built cinemas. The Palace meanwhile had not been designed for cinema shows and the new premises offered a better view of the screen and greater comfort. So once again the Palace returned to live entertainment and its former name the Palace Theatre of Varieties. In 1924 a revival of Casey's Court, a mad-cap knockabout show with Mrs Casey and her gang of children, played to full houses. This was followed by a series of popular touring revues. By 1928 the management of The Palace had changed hands. The lessees were now Reeve and Russell Ltd under the general management of J Rowland Sales and with Will Scotton as the resident manager. It was proudly announced that:

"This theatre is being repainted throughout, decorated and brought up to date and run on first class lines under the personal management of Reeve and Russell Ltd."

Later that year The Palace was host to the famous Dr Walford Bodie. Dr Bodie was known as the Electrical Wizard Of The North. To some he was a master showman, to others, a conman. His act utilized comedy, magic, hypnotism, sleight of hand, telepathy, clairvoyance, ventriloquism and the use of electricity. He would pass electrical currents of tens of thousands of volts through his body, to light lamps and bulbs which he would hold in his hands. He also used electricity to heal medical complaints of members of his audience. His assistant was nicknamed La Belle Electra. He called the force of electric the Bodic Force. He would often invite the audience to inspect his apparatus and pass electric through the body of a volunteer. By 1928 he had extended these tricks in an act he called Bodie Electric Drug Company in which he would cure the lame and the sick with his bloodless surgery using hypnotism and electricity through the use of what he titled Electric Liniment, Bodie's Health Spa and Electric Life Pills. What the audience did not know is that Walford Bodie used static electricity which would appear showy and produce lots of spark – but was totally harmless and it is alleged that the sick and infirm were healthy people paid by Bodie. Nevertheless, the act was a huge success in Swansea and after the opening night J Rowland Sales wrote to Bodie stating:

Neath born actress and entertainer Maudie Edwards who re-opened the Palace Theatre in 1953.

"I am delighted to tell you that we played to a record Monday last night. I have never seen an audience so carried away with enthusiasm as they were last night and I am looking forward to doing a big week to our mutual benefit."

However in spite of Bodie's drawing power, in May of the following year, The Palace changed hands once again. This time the proprietors were The Palace (Wales) Ltd and the theatre was run by the Cambrian Agency in Mansel Street, Swansea.

The next 12 years saw a series of live shows, followed by films and then periods of closure. The Palace was definitely the shabbier of Swansea's two live theatres and it was struggling. Only the Empire and the Palace could be counted as 'live' theatres at this time. The Grand had been taken over by a cinema company and was used exclusively for the screening of films. During the infamous Three Nights Blitz of late February, 1941 the Palace was used as a temporary morgue to house the scores of casualties of the wartime German bombings.

In 1942 the Palace announced it would shortly reopen under new management, controlled by Mr S M Lipman as a combination of cinema and cine-variety, and it advertised for a chief projection operator and a scenic artist exempt from military service. In 1943 it also advertised for some second hand scenery, but by the following year the theatre succumbed to full-time cinema, with new RCA equipment. The Palace continued as a cinema until 1949 when a fire broke out during a film show. It suffered serious fire damage mostly confined to the back stage area and part of the roof above the stage which collapsed. Some remedial work was carried out to make the building water tight and safe, but it then remained unused for a considerable time.

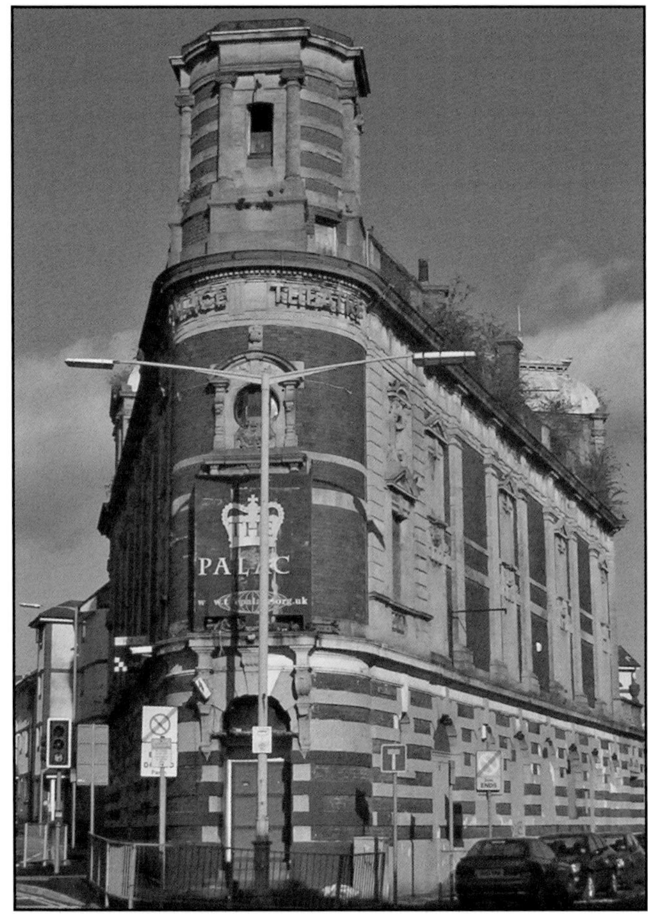

The almost derelict Palace Theatre, thankfully preserved as a listed building. Its future is unclear.

The Maudie Edwards seasons

On January 26, 1953 the Palace reopened as a theatre becoming home to the Maudie Edwards Repertory Company. This resulted from a major quarrel at the Grand Theatre. Maudie Edwards, a well-known, Neath-born actress, had accepted an invitation to stage a repertory season at the Grand in June 1951 as a replacement for the Arts Council Company, which had withdrawn. She did two successful seasons under an arrangement where she and the Grand's owners shared the box office takings on a percentage basis. Just before the beginning of her third season there a dispute arose over this while Maudie was appearing in the pantomime Mother Goose. It remained unresolved and as a result her contract was not renewed. Instead it was offered to and accepted by her assistant, actor Terence Dudley who formed a new company under his own name and took over. Maudie was furious. She immediately sued the Grand Theatre's proprietors for breach of contract. She lost the case, but soon hatched a revenge scheme. She raised enough money to renovate and reopen the Palace Theatre. This was a mammoth task given the short time that she had to get things ready, as she needed to open her season before the Terence Dudley group opened theirs at the Grand and bearing in mind she was still appearing in pantomime there until February 7. Relations with the Grand management were extremely strained, but being a true professional, she still delivered a perfect performance each time to an unsuspecting audience. The Palace was in a sorry state after the fire in 1949 and it is amazing that everything was completed in just four weeks, ready for the opening night of Dear Evelyn on January 26, 1953. Patrons queued around the theatre in pouring rain until it was officially opened by Councillor W T Mainwairing-Hughes. Maudie had taken the balance of her loyal company and also many of her loyal audience to the theatre she had opened in opposition to the Grand. At the end of that first night, Maudie rushed across town after the pantomime curtain call and delivered a rousing speech, in which she thanked the builders for completing their work on time, and finished with a call to the audience:

> ***"Whether we keep the theatre or not is up to you. Without you we cannot do a thing, this is theatre in Wales and I want you to think of it as your theatre."***

The Grand Theatre repertory season opened two weeks later with a production of Charley's Aunt.

Swansea, struggling to support just one repertory company, now had two. Neither, of course, could have hoped to succeed. Maudie had the power to draw guest actors including Glyn Houston and Philip Griffith for her seasons. Even that however, was not enough to secure her survival and her link with the Palace came to an end during December 1955. For Maudie it was long enough to accept that she had at least got her revenge on the Grand. A few months later the Terence Dudley Company also gave up its battle for survival.

An atmospheric glimpse from the circle of the Palace Theatre captured by Erich Talbot. The last theatre show performed on its stage was Follies in 2002. After that the building has been empty and continues to decay with time.

Maudie Edwards had a long and successful career in films, theatre and early television but was a very special radio favourite during and after the Second World War. In 1950 she supported Frank Sinatra at the London Palladium for two weeks. On her weekly radio programmes she had her own theme song introduction where the announcer would croon:

> ***"I bring you the voice of the people, from over the hills and dales, and the voice of the people is brought to you, by a voice that comes from Wales."***

The Swansea Little Theatre era

By 1956 the Palace was again facing closure. This time the saviours were a group of long established amateur actors known as Swansea Little Theatre. Originally based in Southend, Mumbles, they had frequently hired both the Empire and the Grand for their productions. Now they took the opportunity to secure their own theatre. They paid an annual rent for the Palace and were responsible for its upkeep. They used it as a regular base for their own productions, hired it out to other amateur companies, and they brought in occasional professional companies. Their efforts kept the theatre intact, and provided the occasional excellent piece of live theatre. The people running Swansea Little Theatre had certain things in common with those who had created the original theatre. They were local and prepared to invest considerable sums of money into it. Whereas in the early days these people had been the local aristocrats and gentry, the later benefactors were from the business and commercial world. Among them names such as Mrs Sidney Heath, wife of the clothing store owner and D L Davies 'The Bon', so called after his Bon-Marche fashion stores, were prominent among the Little Theatre benefactors. Some of them were excellent amateur performers in their own right, including Ruby Graham, a Swansea dress shop owner; Evelyn Burman-Jones and Eileen Llewellyn-Jones, the wife of the principal of Swansea University College. The amateur management of the Palace Theatre thrived for several years. In 1960 Swansea Little Theatre hosted a professional production of Have a Cigarette, the play in which Sir Anthony Hopkins made his professional debut. By 1961 the cost of running the theatre was escalating and eventually proved to be beyond the means of an amateur company despite its generous local backing. Although Swansea Little Theatre wanted to continue, the owners of the

The Palace as it looked after going the way of many theatres around the country during the 1970s and 80s and became a bingo hall.

theatre were keen to demolish it so that they could sell the land for redevelopment. Sadly Swansea Little Theatre was forced to move out and the Palace ceased to be used as a theatre.

In the many years since then, it has been dark as a theatre except for the very rare, special event, including the first professional engagement of Ceri Dupree on September 9, 1983. There was also a fascinating production of Stephen Sondheim's musical Follies in 2002. It was used as a bingo hall for a long time, and then became Jingles disco. In 2005 there was an attempt to save the building and reopen it as a live entertainment venue, although this was fraught with problems, particularly lack of funding, and it still faces an uncertain future.

On February 29, 2008 I was fortunate to be allowed access to the almost derelict Palace Theatre. There was no electricity and the only light was provided by a crew filming and taking photographs of the interior to use as a backdrop for a play about the venue at the Taliesin Arts Centre in May that year. This was directed by Mark Rees an actor from Alltwen, Pontardawe. The lighting was very dim and I was left to find my way around with the aid of a torch, which ironically I had bought that day from the shop in Oxford Street that stands on the site of the old Empire Theatre.

Seeing the Palace in this sorry state was sad, although at the same time my imagination ran riot, transporting me, back to the golden age of music hall and variety when the Empire as it was called then, was flourishing in the 1890s. It still had the original bench seats from 1888 in the gods and as I climbed up on the stage I could almost hear the clog dancing of Charlie Chaplin and the rest of the Eight Lancashire Lads who appeared at the very point where I was standing in 1899. When the crew went for lunch they left me taking photographs. It suddenly dawned on me that I was alone in a building steeped in theatrical history. As I turned to face the 'audience' I imagined what it must have been like for performers such as Marie Lloyd, Dan Leno, George Robey and Harry Champion to entertain a noisy audience, one that would let you know readily if they liked you or not. The stage was very small and I found it hard to imagine how a strong man act made up of three brothers called the Milon Marvels, whose showstopper was to have one of the brothers walk a tightrope held between the teeth of the other pair while carrying weights, would have had the room to perform such a feat. But they did in 1895. As I guided my torch beam around the stalls area, empty of seating and covered by pigeon feathers and droppings, the sound of dripping water from the holes in the roof brought me back to reality. The steady plip, plop reminded me that the Palace had probably seen its last performance, and was unlikely to be restored. Its place in the history of theatre in general and Swansea theatre in particular must however, never be forgotten.

Act 9

Half a century of hope and glory

The Grand had one major rival as the best theatre in Swansea. It was the showpiece Empire that opened in Oxford Street on December 10, 1900 at what was then a staggering cost of £40,000. It was a replacement for Adelaide and Oswald Stoll's smaller New Empire Theatre in High Street and the latest part of the growing Moss Empire circuit, destined to become the country's major theatre chain in the first half of the 20th Century.

The Empire was built in the Italian Renaissance style, with much polished brass, crystal chandeliers and red plush seating. It was easily the most illustrious and majestic theatre ever built in Swansea and for 57 years the Empire was the premier entertainment venue in Swansea. Week after week it delivered quality turn after quality turn with a few novelty acts thrown in for good measure. The Moss Empire Circuit frequently toured popular straight plays, and was not always a variety house. In the 1940s and early 50s plays were regularly a feature of the Empire's programme. As always in a Stoll theatre, the audience was assured that nothing in poor taste would be allowed and every member of the family could safely be brought to the Empire without risk of being offended.

The Empire was often home to some of the biggest star names of the time, though sadly many have long been forgotten. The opening night at the theatre proudly boasted a star attraction, the famous songstress Ida Rene, though her fame has almost completely faded now. More enduring names from the Empire's early years include Harry Tate, George Robey, Fred Harcourt the Magician, Eugene Stratton and Ventriloquist Fred Russell with Coster Joe his puppet. Interestingly Fred's son was Val Parnell who later became managing director of Moss Empires.

Top of the bill in 1904 was Paul Cinquevalli, a juggler and acrobat unrivalled for his skill and invention. He used everyday objects in his acts on the basis that people could try his tricks at home. He spent hundreds of hours rehearsing and a new trick might take anything from two to five years of daily practice before being ready to perform in public. In one of his acts he juggled a cigar, a bowler hat, a coin, and a cane. Suddenly the hat would plop onto his head, the cigar would land in his mouth and the coin on his toe. He would then flick his foot sending the coin up into the air and it would land flat in his eye like an eyeglass.

Frequently the Empire offered more unusual acts. In 1905 audiences were offered instruction in 'Cake-walking' from famous Negro Cakewalkers, Charles E Johnson and Dora Dean. The pair, billed as 'A merry pair who make things hustle' featured in a show called 'Cause I'se in Society Now. In 1908 Bransby Williams appeared with his famous interpretations of Dickens' characters. The programme also included Ted and Mary Hopkins in a comedy sketch called A Welsh Courtship. On July 10,

Oswald Stoll's Empire Theatre in Oxford Street, built in 1900 at a cost of £40,000. It was the most lavish theatre ever to grace Swansea.

Legendary Swansea Empire commissionaire Alf Penny cuts a regal presence outside the theatre he loved.

1910, two future screen legends, Stanley Jefferson who became better known as Stan Laurel and Charlie Chaplin appeared at the Empire in the same show. Charlie Chaplin played the title role of Jimmy The Fearless and Stan Laurel was further down the cast in a touring Fred Karno comedy. Shortly after this the tour went to America where they both became silver screen legends.

There was other news hitting the headlines in 1910 however. This was the business split between Oswald Stoll and Edward Moss. Their joint 'empires' would in future be known as the Moss-Empire circuit, though Stoll would remain a major shareholder. He would run an independent Stoll Theatre Circuit and there would be a parent organisation known as Stoll Moss Ltd. These linked organisations were to become the biggest theatre organisations in Europe.

The following year saw Clarice Mayne, G H Elliott, who was known as The Chocolate Coloured Coon, and the world-famous escapologist Houdini make their appearances at the Empire. Houdini brought his unique brand of showmanship to the theatre during the week commencing May 5, 1911. He was challenged by a group of local carpenters: Christopher Hodge, John Goodwin and Benjamin B Davies, employees of T W Thomas and Company to escape from a rough timber wooden packing case that they would construct for him. He accepted the challenge on the condition that the box was not airtight. It took place during the second house on the Friday night. With the theatre full and the tension mounting, Houdini escaped with ease and was cheered loudly by an appreciative audience.

Oswald Stoll demanded very high standards of behaviour on and off stage from his performers and he required the same good behaviour from his audiences. On one occasion in 1913 he had a man ejected from the theatre for hissing. The aggrieved customer decided to sue for wrongful ejection and the subsequent legal judgement found in his favour. He was awarded £50 costs.

Stars at the Empire in 1913 included Gertie Gitana singer of There's an Old Mill by the Stream Nellie Dean, Will Hay and Little Ena Dayne, a child star who had been such a hit at the Neath Hippodrome the previous year. She was billed as the future Marie Lloyd. One of the more bizarre, attractions to appear at the Empire came in 1914 when Fred Dyer, the Welsh baritone-boxer sang a selection of songs – popular, operatic and religious – before fighting exhibition bouts with volunteers from the audience. In May 1914 Fred Barnes and Lily Leman appeared in a comedy called Alice Up Too Late. Shortly after Fred Barnes' successful career ended when it was revealed that he was a homosexual. He was hooted off the stage with cries of Get you Freda, and his life was ruined. How things were to change when openly camp performers like Larry Grayson, Paul O'Grady and Julian Clary would become much-loved performers in the years to come.

Just as the First World War was about to engulf Europe, performers like Mona Vivian, Harry Weldon and G S Melvin were packing them in to the Empire. Melvin was a famous Dame comedian who later drowned in the River Thames. On Friday April 17, 1915, the 25th anniversary of the opening of the Empire was celebrated at both performances. The existing building was only 15 years old, so presumably this anniversary incorporated the 'old' Empire in High Street. Even this was strange because The Pavilion had opened in 1888 which was actually 27 years earlier, but it had been bought by Oswald Stoll and renamed the Empire in 1892. This was therefore, actually the 23rd anniversary of Stoll's first Swansea Empire.

Visitors at each of the two performances that night were able to buy a souvenir booklet written and compiled by George H Richardson. This booklet provided details of how the old Empire grew and contained other features such as the reminiscences of an old patron. It also had a list of the dates of the first appearances there of several well known artists. Every penny derived from the sale of the booklet was donated to the Swansea Hospital.

The early war years saw theatres, music halls and cinemas doing their best ever business. Music hall stars like Whit Cunliffe (She Sells Sea-Shells by the Sea Shore), George Lashwood (In the Twi Twi Twi-light) and Billy Merson (The Spaniard who Blighted My Life) were great attractions in Swansea, and one much talked-of week saw the Empire packed for the play The Frenchwoman starring Lily Langtry, well known as the mistress of the late King Edward VII.

Marie Lloyd, whose previous local appearances had been at the old Empire in High Street returned to Swansea in December 1916, again in February 1920 and for the last

Hollywood screen legend Charlie Chaplin appeared in the title roll of Jimmy The Fearless which came to Swansea Empire in 1910, just before Chaplin left for America.

Stan Laurel, then Stanley Jefferson, who appeared at Swansea Empire in 1910. The comedian returned in 1952 with his partner Oliver Hardy.

In 1922 George Formby junior who, at just 18, fulfilled a booking his late father had made at Swansea Empire.

George Formby was a very droll comedian who was a frequent and very popular visitor to The Empire.

time on February 11, 1922. Sadly, she died in October of the same year three days after collapsing on stage at the Edmonton Empire. A special tribute was paid to her in October 1933 when her sisters, Alice, Rosie, June and Daisy Wood, along with her daughter Marie Lloyd Junior, performed together at the Swansea Empire. A further tribute came in the form of a one-off BBC TV drama of her life, Miss Marie Lloyd – Queen of The Music Hall, in 2007. Lloyd was portrayed by EastEnders actress Jessie Wallace.

George Formby topped the bill at the Empire many times between 1904 and 1920 – his was a very droll and lugubrious comic act, complete with a genuine hacking cough. His catchphrase was: 'Eee, coughing better toneet!' In 1921, aged just 45, he died of a lung disease. George was extremley popular and when he died, his diary had bookings for the following seven years and he left £21,000 in his will. Almost immediately his fresh-faced 18-year-old son took over the act. When George Formby Junior appeared at the Swansea Empire in 1922 he performed a carbon copy of his father's act, even wearing his father's costumes. The local paper reported:

> **"George Formby Junior is a very promising young comedian. One member of the audience at least, thought it was his late lamented father who was on the stage."**

Despite this Formby Junior soon dropped his father's act and reinvented himself as Gormless George and his ukulele. He adopted the catchphrase 'Turned out nice again' and became the highest-paid British film star of pre-Second World War years.

The 1920s brought many great variety artists including some destined for later fame in films and early television. Among these were Harry Champion (Boiled Beef and Carrots), Max Miller (There'll Never be Another), Max Wall, Kitty Mcshane (pre-Old Mother Riley), Dick Henderson (the father of Dickie) Leslie Crowther Senior (father of Leslie Crowther) Stan Lupino (father of Ida Lupino), Nellie Wallace and Doris Hare. In 1924 Gracie Fields was a success in Swansea when she came with her first husband Archie Pitt in the hit West End Show, The Tower Of London. Maudie Edwards also made her Swansea Empire debut as a 21 year old in 1927.

The 1930s was the decade of the Big Bands and the Empire presented almost all of them. Roy Fox, Henry Hall – who famously recorded Teddy Bears Picnic in 1932 and which subsequently sold a million copies – and Harry Roy and his band all drew the masses to the Empire. In 1937 Dorothy Squires made her debut there with the Billy Reid Orchestra. Jazz and Swing were extremely popular genres of music at the time and the Empire was perfectly suited to them. At the end of the performances, Oxford Street would be awash with very happy patrons dancing and singing their way home.

The 1930s also brought Flanagan and Allen, Jewel and Warris and also Jimmy Jewel's future TV sit-com partner, Hylda Baker. Star names included the jazz legends Louis Armstrong and Larry Adler, Elsie and

Oxford Street in gentler times when the well to do would be driven to a night at the Empire in horse drawn carriages. Others however might well have arrived on a tram like the one seen here.

Doris Waters (billed as Gert and Daisy and the real-life sisters of Jack Warner, later to become TV's Dixon Of Dock Green), Ted Ray, Stanley Holloway, Tommy Handley and Tommy Trinder. A curiosity from 1935 was the first appearance of the 15-year-old Hughie Green who went on to become Mr Opportunity Knocks. He was later revealed as being the father of the late TV presenter Paula Yates, and his granddaughters are Fifi, Peaches and Pixie Geldof from her marriage to Bob Geldof and Tiger Lily from her relationship with Michael Hutchence.

Bebe Daniels and Ben Lyon were top of the bill for the week beginning May 24, 1937. At this time Lyon was a famous American star from the days of silent films, and had appeared opposite stars like Pola Negri, Gloria Swanson, and, most famously, Jean Harlow, with whom he appeared in the hugely successful film Hell's Angels. The attraction of this bill was the chance to see a big American film-star in the flesh. Only later would he and his family become great British comedy favourites with their radio series, Life with the Lyons. Ben Lyon went on to discover a young actress, renamed her and turned her into the legend that was Marilyn Monroe. He also earned himself a 'star' on the Hollywood Walk of Fame for his contribution to motion pictures.

In September 1939 all theatres were closed by Government order after the declaration of war with Germany, though this decision was reversed shortly afterwards. Early in 1940 the entertainer Brian Michie was presenting his Youth Takes a Bow talent show at the Swansea Empire. Two young lads, were invited to appear with their separate acts. They met for the first time at the Monday band call. That meeting would eventually lead to the formation of one of Britain's best-loved double acts – Eric Morecambe and Ernie Wise. At the end of August 1940 Ivor Novello returned to Swansea – he had appeared at the Grand in The Rat in 1924 – this time in the play I Lived With You. Throughout the Second World War the shows at the Empire were morale-boosters for the beleaguered townspeople. During February 1941 Swansea town centre was almost destroyed during the Three Night's Blitz. Playing at the Empire on the first night of the aerial bombardment, February 19, was the show Eve On Leave with Nat Mills and Bobby and The Ganjou Brothers with Juanita. The show finished and all patrons had left before the bombing began. Swansea Market took a direct hit and was destroyed. The market was less than 100 yards away from the Empire, which remained completely intact as did the Grand Theatre and the Palace. Ironically playing at the Grand, which was a fully-fledged cinema at this point, was The Great Dictator starring Charlie Chaplin. No matter how much Hitler's Luftwaffe tried to bomb Swansea into submission, it was still possible to defy them, and be entertained at Swansea Empire. It remained closed for eight weeks until April 14, however because of bomb-damaged buildings nearby and the rubble-strewn roads surrounding it. It re-opened with the play Smilin' Through produced by Harry Hansen and George Black.

Popular Empire Theatre variety artists of the day included Flanagan and Allen whose hit song Underneath The Arches is still remembered today.

The glorious auditorium of Swansea Empire just after it opened in 1900. The theatre cost £40,000 to build, which was considered a huge sum at the time.

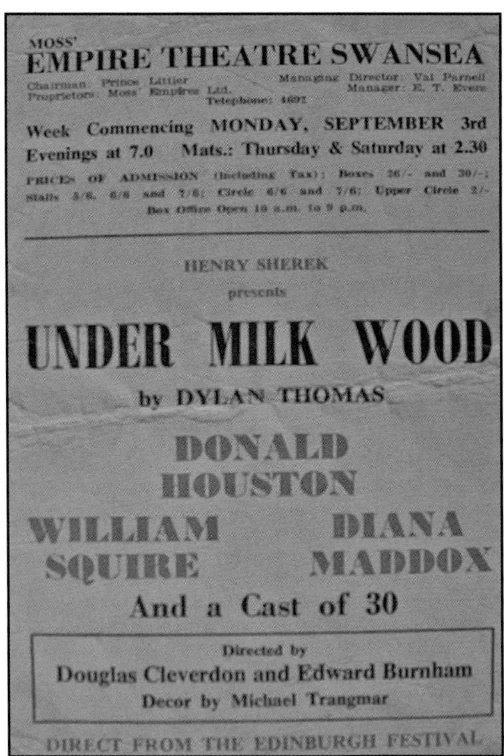

A poster advertising the first performance of Under Milk Wood in Swansea in 1956 prior to going to the West End. The play has since been performed many times on almost every stage in the city.

Moss Empires Limited celebrated 50 years of success in 1949. This view of the Swansea Empire in Oxford Street, is from a jubilee booklet the organisation produced to celebrate the event.

In June, 1941 Swansea theatregoers were treated to a performance at The Empire by Tommy Farr, the former boxer who also had a short-lived career as an entertainer.

The big variety names of the time came week after week: Issy Bonn, Hutch, Two-Ton Tessie O'Shea, Billy Cotton and his 'Wakey-Wakey' Band, Sandy Powell, Sid Field, Wilson, Keppel and Betty, and the amazing acrobatic elegance of the Dresden Clock as performed by the Ganjou Brothers and Juanita.

A typical Empire programme of the era would include one or two big names, supported by lesser-known novelty acts. A standard week from 1941 offered G S Melvin and Elsie & Doris Waters as the 'tops', while the 'wines and spirits' (the smaller names on the programme) included Ted Andrews and Barbara (accompanied by their six year old daughter, Julie Andrews – the future star of The sound of Music, and Mary Poppins), Maloney and his Dog, and the Roller-Skating Desardo Duo.

The Andrews family was back a year later in a show called Venus Comes to Town featuring the brilliant acrobatic act, Gaston and Andree, though the biggest attraction of the year was a show called Radio Funfare, reflecting the great power of the wireless and its entertainers in those days.

The post-war austerity – with rationing even stricter than during the war itself – was cheered by the continuing arrival of well established performers like Old Mother Riley, Max Miller, George Formby and the young Vera Lynn. A typical bill from November 1948 offered Wee Georgie Wood and Dolly Harmer, Wilson Keppel and Betty, The Peters Sisters, La Petite Poupee, Bill Waddington and his Little Dog Comics, Paul Beray the Juggler and Reg Dixon, whose catchphrase was 'I'm proper poorly' and whose signature tune was Confidentially. This Reg Dixon of course should not be confused with Reginald Dixon, the Blackpool Tower organist.

By the early 1950s Transatlantic travel was once more possible, and as a result legendary American stars were again able to visit the UK. Laurel and Hardy's British tour came to Swansea on just one occasion, the week of September 22, 1952. It was the penultimate week of their visit, and there were queues the like of which the Empire had never seen. During their week they stayed at the

Mackworth Hotel in High Street, now the site of Alexandra House. The Mackworth had a balcony overlooking High Street and during the daytime they would often sit out on this and wave to the passers by. They shared the bill with the Sisters Lorraine, The Aerial Kenways, Archie Elray and Co, The Great Cingalee, Jimmie Elliot, and Mackenzie Reid & Dorothy. Stan and Ollie were last on the bill and would perform a slapstick 20-minute routine assisted by Leslie Spurling and Kenneth Henry.

Their second British tour was in 1954. They revealed that they had been overwhelmed by the warmth of Swansea audiences and were delighted that the final week was to be back at the Empire. Sadly this was not to be. Oliver Hardy was taken ill the previous week at Plymouth, and the tour ended there. They cancelled the Swansea week and went back to America, never to return. As a last minute replacement Gladys Morgan and her company stepped in to fill the week, alongside Harry Worth who had toured with Laurel and Hardy previously.

Transatlantic travel was not all one-way however. In November 1950 the Empire proudly announced Swansea's own Radcliffe and Ray, on their return from a triumphant tour of the United States. They were brothers who had a wide following on radio and through their many records.

Pantomime was not a strong feature of the Empire programme until the end of the Second World War. The majority of the Moss Empires in the circuit would play standard variety bills over Christmas and the New Year. Occasionally the London-based management would engage a touring pantomime and have it play one or two weeks at several of their venues. In 1933 Cinderella played two weeks at Swansea, followed by two weeks at Cardiff and Newport Empires. In 1937 Babes in the Wood played the middle two weeks in January following Newport and Cardiff.

After the death of Oswald Stoll and the end of the Second World War the Empire Circuit opened its theatres to managements like Prince and Emile Littler, John D. Roberton and S H Newsome, and began to stage long-running pantomimes at many of its venues. Those at the Swansea Empire were big favourites: Cinderella with Ford and Sheen as the ugly sisters in 1944/5, followed by Robinson Crusoe, Humpty Dumpty, and Mother Goose with Bertram Tyrell as Priscilla the Goose in 1947/8. His costume was said to be made of 1,700 white feathers that all came from French turkeys.

Christmas 1948 saw the opening of an 11-week run of Goody Two Shoes with Sonny Jenks as the dame and –low down on the bill – a nostalgic return for the unknown double-act Morecambe and Wise, playing characters known as Late and Early. During an interview in the 1980s

Morecambe and Wise had a great love for Swansea and appeared in two long running pantos there, Goody Two Shoes in 1948/49 and Babes In The Wood in 1955/56.

the pair spoke of their soft spot for Swansea, especially Langland Bay, and its pubs. They also remembered the difference in wages: they were paid £6 each for the week in 1940 with Brian Michie, and this had increased to an impressive £33 each for the panto eight years later. Hollywood favourite Allan Jones was a top attraction in 1950. His son Jack Jones became a popular singer in the 1970s and 80s when he brought his show to the Brangwyn Hall and also played a one night show at the Grand Theatre on October 6, 1991.

In 1950 Max Wall played Billy Crusoe and in 1952/3 the young Harry Secombe stole the show in Puss in Boots. Two years later another young Welsh comic, Stan Stennett, had great success as Silly Billy in Babes in the Wood. Much lower on the same bill in the roles of Marmaduke and Horace were a couple of comics making yet another sentimental return to Swansea Empire – they were Morecambe and Wise.

Things were changing in the variety world though. The pantomimes were still packing them in, but

Vera Lynn, Gracie Fields and Dorothy Squires were just three of the star names that commanded top billing at Swansea Empire whenever they appeared there.

attendances during the rest of the year were very poor. Television had by now taken over as the nation's favourite source of entertainment. Cinemas too, were doing badly, in spite of fighting back with Cinemascope, 3D films and great epic movies. Theatres had nothing to fall back on. Some of them tried adult shows, with nudes. Swansea Empire even offered the striptease artiste, Phyllis Dixey. Such an act would have been unthinkable in a Stoll-Moss Empire theatre in the days when Oswald Stoll was alive. Perhaps he was right, because shows like this, and controversial adult only plays like No Trees in the Street did not appeal to Swansea audiences. Business was very poor and rumours abounded. In June 1955 a spokesman for Val Parnell, managing director of Moss Empires, said:

"In connection with the building development at Swansea there have been several offers to buy the Empire. We have done nothing about these offers and will continue to run the theatre as normal. There are no plans to close down the Empire, despite rumours to the contrary."

Just a year later in August 1956 Moss Empires it seems had a change of heart. Confirmation of closure came when Swansea Amateur Operatic Society applied to hire the theatre for their annual spring production in March 1957. They were told that the Empire would close at the end of the pantomime run in February. It was revealed that Swansea Corporation had accepted in principle a scheme for the development of the block of buildings in which the Empire was situated. This would include a super food-store being built on the site. The news was out, but it did not have a great impact on the people of Swansea. The Stage newspaper commented that:

"One of the most disheartening features of the affair is that hardly a voice has been raised in the chambers of the local council against the closure of such a beautiful theatre."

Swansea Empire closed with the last night of the 1956-1957 pantomime, Jack and the Beanstalk. It was the first major closure in the Moss Empire circuit. A joke going around variety artists at the time was: Moss are closing the Swansea Empire – and if it's a success they'll shut all the others as well. The star of the last panto was the much-loved Port Talbot born Welsh comedian, Ossie

Jack And The Beanstalk starring Port Talbot comedian Ossie Morris was the last show staged at the Swansea Empire. Its emotionally charged last night was on February 16, 1957.

Old Mother Riley and Kitty appeared at Swansea Empire during the week of February 10, 1941 shortly before the wartime bombing blitz of the town centre.

Stan Laurel made a return visit to Swansea Empire with Oliver Hardy in 1952. They topped the bill performing a 20-minute slapstick sketch to full houses all week.

Morris. His catchphrase was 'Hush! I must 'ave 'ush' preceded by an ear-piercing whistle. The cast also included Wyn Calvin as second comic, Devine and King, Gulliver's Seven Giants and the Sherman Fisher Young Ladies. Wyn remembers vividly that emotional last night:

"The last night will remain engraved on my memory for ever. It was such an emotional occasion. We'd had a long pantomime there running well into February, a very successful production. Ossie Morris was the top of the bill; Ossie on the last night was almost uncontrollable emotionally. The theatre was packed, of course, it was more than packed because everybody wanted to come to the last night. Now you know how we in Wales love a good funeral, and this was going to be a good funeral – the death of the Empire. The boxes used to hold four or six people, if you crammed them in. There were as many as 14 and 16 people in each of the boxes that night. Every time there was a laugh the atmosphere was electric. For every time there was a laugh and Ossie heard it, he would look up and he'd say 'It's a damn shame, it's a damn shame.' And he was getting so emotional about this, while we were trying to be disciplined about the production, about doing Jack and The Beanstalk for the last time, the last production in the theatre. But theatres have living souls and Ossie felt so terrible that the theatre was being allowed to be converted into something else. But we kept going, we stuck to the pantomime as much as possible. We were throwing in adlibs of course and I did a rock and roll scene, a send up of the rock that was developing. I had a ponytail wig and teenage gear and I remember saying 'You've heard of the first dame of the British Empire, I'm the last dame of the Swansea Empire.' Somehow that caught the imagination – it was a throwaway, but the laugh and the applause from that went on and on and on. That was the sort of atmosphere on that last night. That was how people were feeling this, tremendously personally, as they sat there on the last night thinking of all the times they had been there before of all the memories they had of music hall performers of musicals. We came to the end of the pantomime... finale... flowers... some speeches, the mayor then made a

Hollywood film star Allan Jones came to Swansea in 1950. His son, popular singer Jack Jones performed at the Brangwyn Hall and The Grand in the 1980s.

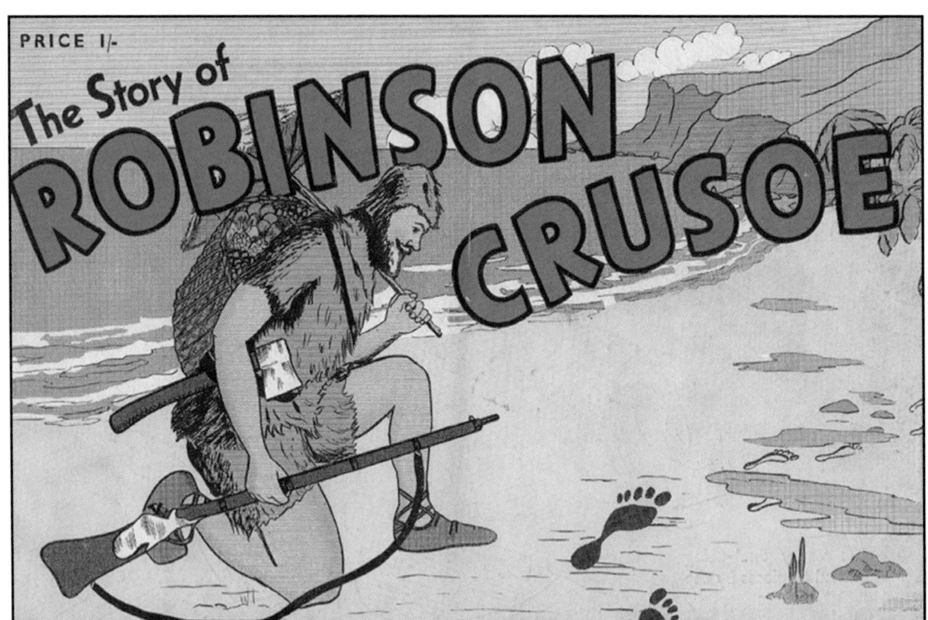

The programme for Robinson Crusoe starring Max Wall in 1950/51. The front cover was universal with all Empire Theatre productions of this pantomime. Just the centre pages would be unique to whichever theatre it played at.

Max Wall was the star of the pantomime Robinson Crusoe in 1950/51. The pantomimes at the Empire ran for many weeks in direct opposition to the Grand at this time.

A fresh-faced Harry Secombe wowed his hometown audience with his performances in the pantomime Puss In Boots at Swansea Empire in 1952/53.

The auditorium of the Empire. It was the premier entertainment venue in Swansea for 57 years.

speech, the theatre chaplain made a speech. Then into the first music that had ever been played in the Swansea Empire back at its opening all those years before – Mae Hen Wlad Fy Nhadau, the Welsh national anthem. And I don't know who was on the tabs on the front curtains when we did that, but he was inspired, as we all were and when he brought the curtain down he started right at the beginning of the national anthem and slowly inch by inch the tabs came in. They didn't drop with a swoop, they came in very, very slowly and we who had been quite controlled, when we became aware that the curtain was coming down at that speed, just inch by inch for the last time, we had to stop singing as there was something else in our throats that wasn't a song."

As well as the many thousands of artists who appeared at the Empire in its 57 years, there were many great characters amongst the staff. In the box office were Milly Bevan and Phyllis Morris who took great pride in announcing on sell-out nights: 'Sorry all seats are gone. There's not even standing room in the gods. You should have booked in advance.'

There was always hope, however, thanks to the immaculately dressed commissionaire, Alf Penny. He must have made a small fortune out of those who did not book in advance, since he always kept either up his sleeve or in his white gloves a dozen or so spare tickets, which could be secured for a tanner tip. A 'tanner' as many will remember was slang for a sixpenny piece.

The Empire's last manager was Ewert Evers who was about to leave to manage the Brighton Hippodrome, but briefly managed the Grand Theatre before he went. As soon as the curtain came down on that Saturday night, February 16, 1957 a team of volunteers moved in to unscrew all the seats. Under the rules of the time, as soon as the seats were removed, the owners, Moss Empire, would not have to pay any rates on the building. The seats had been advertised for sale and had been sold to Pentremalwed Church in Swansea and another church in Llanelli. The last of the seats left the theatre on the Wednesday morning. It was then, finally, that stage-doorkeeper and watchman, Harry Holmes, said a last farewell to his beloved theatre.

Harry Holmes was himself a famous local character in his own right, an unpaid trick cyclist known as Cyclino he was often seen performing on the streets of Swansea on his monocycle. At the age of 77 he accepted and won a bet of £100 pounds by peddling up the incredibly steep Constitution Hill on his bicycle. In his younger days in 1934 he won local fame by cycling from Mumbles pier to Porthcawl pier. He had constructed a wooden raft with empty oil drums at each corner, instead of a back wheel he made paddles, which were powered by the chain of his bike which was bolted to the raft. He did a trial run first from Mumbles Pier to Swansea's West Pier watched by thousands. It was a great success so the following week he embarked on his epic journey to Porthcawl; it took him six hours and forty minutes. He is affectionately

The site of the Empire just after the theatre's demolition in 1961. This left the Grand as the only active major theatre in Swansea.

remembered by many of the cheeky Swansea teenagers of the time, who would try and sneak in to the theatre to watch the shows for free and often get a clip around the ear from Cyclino for their troubles.

On February 20, 1957, 56 years and two months after the Empire opened, the doors closed on a significant piece of Swansea's theatrical past. The Stoll-Moss Company, after many changes of owners, is now in the hands of Lord Andrew Lloyd Webber who purchased it in 2000 for £87.5 million pounds. Many of Swansea's older residents feel that the wrong theatre was demolished.

The Empire was grander in all but name than the Grand Theatre. The rates paid on the Empire were roughly twice the amount of its smaller rival. It had a superb interior design and a much bigger stage area than the Grand. The theatre did have one final swansong when a live tribute show was televised by the BBC from its stage, with temporary seating brought in for the event. It was presented by Alun Williams and featured a typical variety evening, ending with Alun on the stage giving a eulogy to the theatre. As the credits rolled he dropped a handful of former playbills onto the empty stage. The old building remained for a few more years, but by the first week of February 1961, there was a gaping hole in Swansea's fast-changing Oxford Street. On February 1, that year, the demolition contractors officially handed the site over to the builders. At the same time they carried out an unofficial handover. They presented the last remaining brick of the structure to Harry Holmes, the night watchman and fireman at the Empire for 40 years.

A new, rather unattractive building housing a supermarket was erected on the site. It is now a retail outlet. Ironically its next door neighbour, Waterstone's bookstore, is on the site of the old Carlton Cinema. It was built after the Empire and is now preserved as a listed building. The Empire however, even with its wonderful heritage was condemned to being just a fading memory.

The Empire site in 2010. The once beautiful building has been replaced by a functional retail outlet.

Act 10

Guessing games over the ghosts

Like many other historic buildings with interesting backgrounds, theatres can often lay claim to ghostly goings on. Whether large or small these buildings frequently experience strange goings on that allow their owners to revel in the antics of their own special apparition. The Grand Theatre is no exception and tales abound of mysterious sightings down the years, tales which can sometimes appear exaggerated, but then again can occasionally stand up to much closer investigation.

So does the Grand Theatre come complete with its own resident ghost or ghosts? That will always be a matter for conjecture. Reports and accounts of unexplained happenings are plenty. These ghostly sightings have, over the years, generated many different theories. One in particular relates to a sighting of a female performer. Some believe that this could be the singer Jenny Lind, dubbed the Swedish Nightingale. Jenny supposedly sang at the Grand Theatre before setting sail on the ill-fated Transatlantic liner, Titanic and, as it sank in icy waters after hitting an iceberg, became one of its tragic victims. This is a remarkable story, but Jenny never performed at the Grand and actually died on November 2, 1887 at Malvern in Worcestershire. Records confirm that this was a good 10 years before the Grand Theatre even opened its doors.

Another popular story that has been in circulation for some time concerns a wardrobe mistress who met and fell in love with a touring American actor at the theatre. On his return to America he sent a ticket back to Swansea for her to join him in New York. It is said that the ticket was dated April 14, 1912 and the vessel was the ill-fated ocean-going leviathan, SS Titanic.

The opera diva Adelina Patti is another of the much-favoured suggestions. She after all had a soft spot for the Grand Theatre and sang at its opening. More than that her favourite flowers were said to have been violets. That interests many people because a common theme which runs through ghostly experiences at the Grand is the smell of violets.

But many people have regularly questioned why Patti would choose to haunt the Grand. After all, they say, she only ever performed at the theatre once – to open it. Not only that, but she had her own theatre at Craig-y-Nos and perhaps more importantly her legendary successes had been in major opera houses around the world, so why would her ghost choose to haunt the Grand?

Vivyan Ellacott, a former manager at the theatre is among many who have a story to tell when conversation turns to ghostly goings on in the Singleton Street theatre. He is quite clear about the experience and his recollection is nothing if not convincing.

It happened on Saturday, April 20, 1968 when he had stayed very late at the theatre helping the stage manager

Mabel Lucy Hackney, the wife of Laurence Irving who appeared at the Grand Theatre in the early 1900s. There is some speculation that Mabel may be the fabled ghost claimed to visit the theatre from time to time.

Philip Ormond with the fit-up for a following production. Vivyan recalls:

> ***"There was a very intense storm going on outside. Around 2am, as we came to lock up, I noticed one gaslight still on at the back of the dress circle. Philip stayed on stage while I went up the back stairs and into the very dimly lit circle to turn the light off. Philip was shouting jokingly 'Watch the ghost doesn't get you.' As I put my hand out towards the gaslight, I saw the lever move without me touching it. I swear it turned itself off! For a brief moment I felt someone behind me. I thought it was Philip – though how he could have made it from the stage to the Dress Circle in just seconds didn't occur to me. I also smelt a perfume, a brief but distinct lavender-like smell. I shot across the back and down to the stage very quickly. At first I didn't say anything to Philip. Rationally, I was trying to persuade myself I was imagining things, and didn't want to make a fool of myself. But I noticed Philip looked a bit shaken too. When we were sitting safely in the car outside, he asked me what had happened. He listened intently as I explained what I had experienced and then surprised me when he said that for a very brief moment he thought he saw someone appear behind me. It disappeared so quickly that he, too, thought he had imagined it."***

So, what was going on in the theatre on that stormy night? All Vivyan will say is that for him at least it was a very strange experience.

Another story has evolved from occurrences during a visit to the Grand by Laurence Irving – the son of Sir Henry Irving – and his wife Mabel Lucy Hackney. These took place during October 1911, November 1912 and then again in October 1913 and generated what many regard as a rather fanciful piece of Grand Theatre ghost lore.

The story says everyone has got it wrong. The Grand Theatre apparition is not that of Adelina Patti, but Mabel Lucy Hackney. Swansea born, she had first performed at the theatre as part of Sir Henry Irving's farewell tours and later appeared at Swansea Empire, then again at The Grand alongside her husband Laurence. At the end of her last performance there in October, 1913 she told her dresser that she had enjoyed the week enormously. She had been so well looked after and thought that she would definitely return. She is alleged to have remarked:

> ***"When my performing days are over, I want to come back to this lovely town, and spend my evenings on the other side of the curtain, watching other people act.***

She is also reputed to have said to her dresser that she would definitely come back to see her. It was not very long afterwards, according to the tale, that the dresser was in the theatre late one night when Mabel Lucy Hackney suddenly walked in.

"I told you I would return, but I can't really stay long," she said to the surprised dresser. And, just as quickly, she walked out of the room. The date was May 29, 1914. The following morning, May 30, the dresser read in the newspapers that Mabel Lucy Hackney, along with her husband and a thousand others, had drowned in the Empress of Ireland shipping disaster. The accident had happened the night before, at the very moment when Mabel is claimed to have appeared in the dressing room of the Grand. So, according to the story, Mabel Lucy Hackney had done exactly what she'd said and now her performing career was over, she had returned to Swansea Grand. In the years to come she fulfilled her promise, and

British character actor Anthony Bate next to the piano that caused possible paranormal activity during the play Masterclass in October 1984.

she spent (and continues to spend?) her evenings on the other side of the curtain watching other people perform.

It's an entertaining story and perhaps more logical than that of the ghost of Adelina Patti lingering at the theatre. The first sighting was a mere seven months after their last performance at the Grand and they were booked to appear there again in 1914. So is Mabel the ghost that people claim they have seen at the Grand?

By an amazing coincidence Laurence Irving's London neighbour, Paul Compton, died in the sinking of The Lusitania a year after Laurence and Mabel.

Another fascinating tale comes from Kerry Wilcox a veteran of Swansea Little Theatre and who has acted since 1948. Kerry remembers a time in the early 1950s when he was helping Ruby Graham set up some props for a play at the Grand. She asked him to go up to the gods to get something. It was late into the evening and there were only about four or five people on the stage helping out. He climbed the stairs, went through the door of the grand circle, picked up what he needed and was about to come back down when he noticed a lady sitting on the opposite side of the circle. Thinking nothing of it he ran back down the stairs and asked Ruby why she had sent him up when there was already someone up there. She simply laughed and remarked that it must be the ghost. He looked back up and sure enough there was not a soul to be seen.

Another intriguing story from the theatre's 'ghost files' concerns Simon Moss, who has worked at the theatre since the 1980s. Simon is known to be an extremely rational and credible person. His story relates to an incident one afternoon in the theatre:

> ***"I was working in the grand circle when I was aware of a colleague showing a visitor around. Suddenly the hairs on the back of my neck stood up and I immediately felt very cold. This feeling lasted until the visitor had left the circle. Later, I spoke to my colleague and asked who the visitor was. She informed me that it was psychic healer Debbie Rye. She had worked with John Sparkes on the Ghost Story series on ITV. One episode of which was broadcast in 2006 and***

Madame Adelina Patti who some believe is the lady behind the ghostly events at the Grand.

featured the Grand. Was she perhaps attracting attention from one of the Grand's ghosts?"

Swansea Actress Eleanor Thomas is another person who can lay claim to an odd experience while in the theatre:

"It was during a performance of A Streetcar Named Desire in 1972 that I saw a white figure in the circle that didn't go away," recounted Eleanor.

"I met a strange old gentleman some weeks later who told me that I had actually seen his mother who had worked at the Grand and had lost her life, along with the rest of the company when sailing to perform in Ireland.

"Some people say it's Madame Patti – but it isn't. When they brought in a medium for a TV show some years later he stood in the very spot where I had seen her and said that there was something there."

Popular British character actor, Anthony Bate tells a very strange story of possible paranormal activity at The Grand during a touring production of the play Masterclass in October, 1984 during which Anthony portrayed Stalin. The play had been touring for a few months and it had a very tight knit cast. Anthony admits to having a great love of classical music and painting and describes himself as a total sceptic to the idea of ghostly happenings.

The play, a satire based on the Soviet attitude towards freedom of expression in the arts, had gone well in rehearsal. In one scene Anthony, as Stalin, is seen lecturing Shostakovich and Prokoviev and criticising their efforts, when he sits at the piano and with one finger he picks out a rather banal tune, My Lonely Heart is a Caravan. Anthony knew the notes very well after playing many, many performances elsewhere, but on opening night at the Grand, the eighth and ninth notes of the piece the same E above Middle C, failed to play. He told the stage manager who had it checked out for the following evening. Anthony could play the note out of character, but as soon as he donned his Stalin guise, it failed to play the same notes on the second evening as well. Anthony suffered a restless night's sleep that night with growing whisperings of a ghostly interference among the cast. This strange phenomenon continued right up until the very final performance when the piano — or the ghost — relented and allowed the note to be played. He has no rational explanation for what happened and the rest of the tour went by without incident. Even though it is over 20 years ago he still remembers the experience vividly and with puzzlement.

Another with an interesting ghostly anecdote to relate and so add further colour to the mystery of whether there is or isn't one or more apparitions at the Grand is actress Wendy Weaver. She recalls having an odd experience during the pantomime Babes In The Wood in 1983/84. She was playing fairy godmother and while waiting in the wings to make her entrance felt a hand on her shoulder with a very cold touch. Wendy got the shivers, but all that happened was that the hand seemed to pull her and her wand onto the stage to meet her cue. Other cast members also reported some strange backstage happenings during the run of the panto.

Act 11

Out of tune with the music halls

As well as other theatres clamouring for audiences and the income they provided the Grand was faced with competition from a growing number of music halls whose tradition was based as much on food and drink as entertainment. And though initially they tended to attract what was described as the working class elements of society, while theatres were the target of the gentry, as time went by, all this began to change.

The Music Hall, which opened in Craddock Street in 1864, aimed to be a particularly high class example of the rapidly developing music hall scene of the time. It featured a wide variety of attractions. The first music halls were specially built rooms above or alongside pubs. In many cases the entertainment was provided free of charge as long as the customer bought sufficient food and drink. From the beginning therefore, music halls were considered more suitable for the lower classes and not respectable enough for the gentry. Gradually they gave way to the more family-friendly variety theatres. The Swansea Music Hall acquired a major business rival within five years, when a new, proper variety theatre opened. However in the early 1870s the Swansea Music Hall, still a new building, saw its business collapse through lack of support. Obviously, some major changes were needed. Eventually it relaunched itself as a more serious musical venue. Staging classical concerts, choral events, religious meetings and musical evenings. In 1874 the Music Hall was host to the Fisk Jubilee Singers, was a group of black Americans raising money for the Fisk University, Nashville, Tennessee. The Fisk University was established after the American Civil War to provide university education for freed black slaves. Over 1,500 people attended the Swansea concert, making it one of the most successful of a UK tour. Swansea citizens were highly praised for their generosity and support. It soon created its own specialised market. In 1881 it underwent some refurbishment and re-opened with a new name: the Albert Hall. It was intended that this new name – echoing the name of the 11-year-old national concert hall, built in Kensington as a memorial to the Queen's Consort – would emphasise the respectability of the premises and disassociate it from its earlier few years. On August 14, 1884 The Stage reported:

> **"Madame Adelina Patti, assisted by Madamoiselle Castellan, violin; Signor Nicolini, Signor Bonetti, Signor Tito Mattei and Mr Josiah Pitman gave a morning performance at the Albert Hall to raise funds on behalf of Swansea Hospital. This is the second time, within a comparatively short period, that Adelina Patti and her friends have come forward in a similar manner to assist this deserving institution, and this fact has endeared her to the townspeople of Swansea, who accorded her a hearty welcome by an ample display of bunting on the route from the railway station to the concert hall, which, it need hardly be added, was crowded with a delighted and enthusiastic audience. At the**

An illustration of The Music Hall in Craddock Street just after opening in 1864. It was later renamed The Albert Hall, a title it retained right up to its closure in 2007.

> **conclusion of the entertainment the fair cantatrice was warmly thanked in person by Sir H Vivian Hussey for the generosity displayed by herself and friends, and she returned to the station en-route for her Welsh residence, Craig-y-Nos, loudly cheered by the crowds assembled to do her honour."**

Another great moment of respectability came on August 3, 1899, when the legendary Adelina Patti gave a one-night charity concert at the Albert Hall. She sang The Nightingale's Trill, The Jewel Song, Quand Tu Chantes and Home Sweet Home. She was received by the Mayor and Corporation at the railway station and escorted to the venue. Other performers were Richard Green and Hirwin Jones and Marianna and Clara Eissler. The concert raised over £600. The Albert Hall survived into the 20th Century. Its role as a concert hall for Swansea was replaced when the Brangwyn Hall – a purpose built concert auditorium opened in 1934. However, before that the Albert Hall had become a cinema – firstly a home for the 'silents' and then the 'Talkies'. Like so many theatres and cinemas, the Albert Hall hit hard times in the last quarter of the 20th Century – the age of television – and became a bingo club. The building still exists – happily with a preservation order – as one of the hidden gems of Swansea's historical past. Unfortunately the Albert Hall closed as a bingo venue in April 2007 – a casualty of the smoking ban in public places – its future is uncertain, but hopefully the building has not seen the last of its entertainment days.

The Albert Hall during its silent movie years.

The Foxhole Music Hall

The Foxhole Music Hall is shrouded in some mystery associated with the very powerful Grenfell family. The Grenfells were immensely wealthy industrialists. They had made a fortune in the copper industry and were known for their charitable and philanthropic work in the Swansea area. According to the Grenfell family records, among their vast property holdings in Swansea, much of Wales and even a series of head offices and properties in London, they had built and owned The Foxhole Music Hall on Swansea's Eastside. In October 1892 the Grenfell Companies went into voluntary liquidation. The news hit Swansea like a bombshell; nearly 600 men were thrown out of work. Most of their Swansea and even some of their London property was put up for sale. However, they did retain some of their Swansea buildings, including schools, cottages and The Foxhole Music Hall. However, by 1892 there doesn't seem to be a building called The Foxhole Music Hall anywhere in Swansea. There is also an unanswered question. It is why would a very respectable, deeply religious and philanthropic family build and own a music hall in the first place? Music halls were especially frowned upon, by all church groups at that time. The mystery deepens. In the early 1870s George Melville took over the dilapidated wooden Circus in Wind Street and rebuilt it as the Star Theatre. The Melville family papers contain an old photograph of this site and written on the back of this photo are the words: 'site formerly called the Foxhole Music Hall.' This might be considered evidence enough, but the writing is much more recent, perhaps from the 1960s, and appears to have been written in ballpoint pen. Grenfell legal papers from 1892 used the original name and the property referred to, had subsequently been leased to the Melvilles and given a new name. It is more likely that the Foxhole Music Hall was a completely different building and site than where the name suggests.

Fletcher's Music Hall

In January 1885 a newspaper review stated that Fletcher's Music Hall in Swansea had been doing such good business that the management had announced their intention to enlarge the premises. Again in April that year it was reported:

> **"Fletcher's Music Hall (manager Arthur Dashwood) is a place of amusement in Swansea which has**

recently been doing good business. It wishes to announce a gigantic programme for Eastertide."

The Gloster Music Hall

The Gloster Music Hall (proprietor Mr R Russell) is listed in an 1880 directory of Swansea businesses. An advertisement in The Stage in August 1884 was seeking actors and actresses for a season at The Theatre Royal, Barnstaple. Applicants were asked to write to a Mr C Haynes at the Gloster Music Hall, Swansea.

Corporation Music Hall

The Corporation Music Hall is listed in The Stage in December 1880, where its ownership was credited to W Jenkins.

The Drill Hall/ Prince of Wales Hall

The Drill Hall occupied the site in Singleton Street, which eventually became the Grand Theatre. When its military days were over, the hall was used for entertainment purposes and often these included the presentation of 'proper' theatre. In November 1883 the old Drill Hall underwent major renovation and remodelling and was renamed The Prince Of Wales Hall. An advertisement stated:

> **"This new hall is situated in the centre of the town and is especially adapted for evening entertainments, with ante-rooms and other necessary offices. Licenced for dramatic performance. The principle floor is 68 by 62, stage 45 by 19, balcony extra. Will seat 300 persons. Minor hall 20 by 28, quite separate approach. For terms apply to the secretary, Singleton Street, Swansea."**

It became a popular venue for local amateur companies. On April 3, 1883 the hall staged the premiere of a 'new and original agricultural comic opera' called The Rustic composed by W F Hulley, who had already established himself as an opera composer with The Coastguard. Hulley later became musical director at The Grand Theatre when it opened. The Coastguard was chosen as the opera to open Adelina Patti's Craig-y-Nos theatre seven years later. The Rustic was very well received. The leading role of Simon Daw, a miserly Englishman, was sung by Mr A E Siedle who also wrote the Libretto; the hero, Reuben, a foundling was sung by Mr W J Murphy and the heroine, Margie Daw was Miss Ellen Flynn. There was a rousing chorus of flunkeys headed by Mr H Siedle who was clearly some kind of relative of the leading man/librettist. Several of the songs proved to be very popular. The first performance was to a crowded house on the Tuesday evening. Word of mouth was such that for the second performance on Thursday the hall was completely sold out and a large number of people were turned away, disappointed. In January 1887, the hall presented the touring production of Hazel Kirk performed by Miss Kate Berresford and her Capital Company. The proprietor and manager was Mr W Pike. On June 22, 1888 Jem Smith the champion Pugilist of England fought at the hall. Then later that year Charles Dickens's son, Charles Dickens Junior went on a nationwide tour of Britain. He came to Swansea on October 26, 1888, and appeared at the hall, reading excerpts from his father's works. This must have been an unmitigated success as he was to return again on November 29 of the following year. Mr Pike eventually sold the site to Frederick Mouillot to enable The Grand Theatre to be built. The hall was demolished in 1896 and became part of the site of the new Grand Theatre. During its 13 years as an entertainment venue it seems to have been advertised sometimes as the Prince Of Wales Hall and at other times as the Drill Hall.

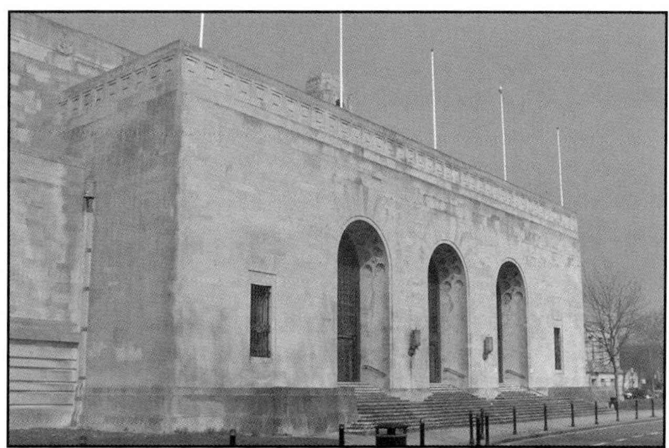

The Brangwyn Hall which opened in 1934 and was named after famous artist Sir Frank Brangwyn whose magnificent Empire Panels line its interior walls.

The Brangwyn Hall

Primarily a concert hall built in 1934 inside a new Swansea Civic Centre, the Brangwyn Hall seats more than 1,000 and the walls are lined with the magnificent Empire Panels. These were originally created by the artist Sir Frank Brangwyn for the refurbished Houses Of Parliament, but were considered unsuitable for Westminster and ended up in Swansea. The hall can be used for a multitude of purposes and is frequently used for radio and TV broadcasts as well as symphony concerts. It has also been used for semi-staged opera and choral performances. Past performers include an unlikely mix of Bruce Forsythe, Jack Jones, Katherine Jenkins, Freddie Starr, Rory Bremner, Slade, Queen, Mott The Hoople, The Bay City Rollers and cage fighting.

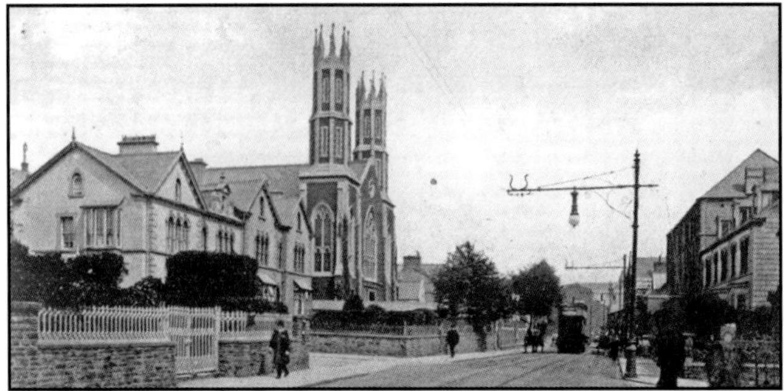

The Shaftesbury Hall was the headquarters of theatre and cinema impresario William Coutts' Swansea operation.

Dylan Thomas Theatre

This was converted from a garage and car showroom operated by the Oscar Chess group in Gloucester Place in the Maritime Quarter in 1979. It is an intimate theatre with an open stage and raked seating for 156 people. It is the permanent home of Swansea Little Theatre. There is also a smaller 100-seat studio named the Ruby Graham Room. Ruby Graham, a former president of the Little Theatre, was a prominent amateur actress in Swansea during the 1930s and 1970s. During the renovation of the Grand Theatre in 1983 several of its repertory productions were staged there.

The Llewellyn Hall

This is a flat floor auditorium with a balcony and proscenium arch inside the YMCA building in the Kingsway, Swansea. It was used regularly by the Uplands Arts Group, The Abbey Players and The Swansea Youth Theatre for many years. It even housed the occasional touring professional show – once – notably, Emlyn Williams performing his one-man Dylan Thomas show. Dylan Thomas himself also appeared at the Llewellyn Hall as a performer in a youth production.

The statue of Dylan Thomas sits proudly outside the theatre named after him. The Dylan Thomas Theatre is the home of Swansea Little Theatre.

The Taliesin Theatre which opened in 1984 is the regular venue for a number of Swansea amateur companies.

Shaftesbury Hall

The Shaftesbury Hall is listed as a performance venue in the theatre guides of 1908 right through to 1951. In 1908 the manager is listed as Mr A Williamson. The venue, situated in St Helen's Road was later used as a head office for William Coutts' Swansea Cinema business. In the 1920s it was regularly used to stage boxing matches. The hall was demolished and the site is now occupied by the Swan House apartments.

Ty Llen Theatre/Dylan Thomas Centre

This 111-seat theatre is situated within the Dylan Thomas Centre, which was created out of the former Swansea Guildhall and was opened in 1995 by US President Jimmy Carter. It is used for plays and lectures.

The Little Theatre, Mumbles

The early home of Swansea Little Theatre was a small hall in Southend, Mumbles. It was originally the National School, then the Motor Boat & Fishing Club and is now Patrick's with Rooms. It is noteworthy because Dylan Thomas himself appeared in several shows there.

Penyrheol Theatre

Built in 1982 and attached to the Penyrheol Community Leisure Centre, this is a 600-seat flat floor auditorium used for a mix of amateur and professional shows. The theatre suffered serious damage when the adjacent school burned down in March 2006.

Taliesin Theatre

This purpose-built arts centre opened in March 1984 on the University College Campus. The main theatre has 330 seats with an adaptable end stage. It is used for university and visiting productions, and annually by Uplands Arts, Penyrheol Light Amateur Operatic Society and Cockett Amateur Operatic Society.

Act 12

A launch pad for impresarios

Swansea has without doubt provided the launch pad for countless actors and performers who have cut their teeth on its stages on their way to becoming top names in the entertainment world. At the same time many of those owning or running the theatres that gave those same stars their earliest opportunity were themselves taking their first tentative steps to becoming some of the UK's best-known impresarios.

Among these successful and often innovative businessmen were Oswald Stoll, Andrew Melville, William Coutts and Alfred Denville, who almost certainly started the first professional repertory company in the country at a theatre called the New Opera House in Woodfield Street, Morriston, in 1899.

The New Opera House had opened in the third week of August, 1897 and claimed to have the largest stage area in Wales. It measured 50 feet by 25, there was overhead lighting, footlights, a fly-tower for drop scenery, and a seating capacity of 1,100. Written above the proscenium arch were the Welsh words Chwaraefwrdd Yw'r Byd which translates as All the world's a stage. It is not known if the Opera House was built on the site of the former Prince of Wales portable theatre, but it seems that the earlier theatre disappeared from the records shortly before it was built. The publicity for the opening emphasised the word 'new' – it is the 'New' Opera House – which suggests the management were at pains to point out it was a completely new building.

The opening performance was the hit play of the day, Ingomar. It featured William Calvert and Clara Cowper, who ran an established touring company, in the leading roles. The opening publicity announced a forthcoming autumn season which would include the Calvert-Cowper touring productions of The Lady of Lyons, Black Ey'd Susan, A Wife's Secret and Life and Honour. At this time the theatre was under the management of Mr H A Chappell.

It was soon advertising for suitable touring productions and offering either a rental or sharing deal. Towards the end of 1899 the owners employed a talented young man to serve as their manager. He was the 23-year-old actor Alfred Denville.

Denville created a 'stock' company – a very early form of repertory – and began producing shows of his own as well as renting the theatre to touring productions. One of the earliest plays under his management was A Royal Divorce, the hugely popular story of Napoleon and Josephine. It also happened that W W Kelly's touring company was due to perform the same play at the Grand, Swansea just a few weeks later. On realising that Denville had got in first, the management of the Grand immediately printed posters which read:

> **"Grand Theatre, Swansea. The management of the above beg to announce that the company appearing at Morriston is not the company that will shortly appear at the above theatre."**

Denville was not dismayed. A few hours later handbills flooded the town, proclaiming:

> **"Opera House, Morriston. Mr Denville begs to inform the public that the notice issued by the management of the Grand, Swansea is quite correct. The company appearing at the above theatre is not the same company that is visiting Swansea. It is much better."**

As a result, A Royal Divorce proved a sell-out, the Opera House had to retain the production for a second week and was firmly established as a rival to the Swansea theatres.

A year later, in November 1900, it was announced that Alfred Denville had taken a long lease on the Morriston Opera House and the new management would commence its reign on December 22. The plays would be presented in repertory, with the same actors appearing successive weeks in different attractions.

Alfred Denville as he was pictured in a programme in 1932. He described himself as 'The Guvnor' of the Denville Players.

Initially this new and unusual kind of performance company met with great success. Audiences flocked to the theatre and soon developed their own particular favourites among the players. Just a few weeks into the new season The Stage reported:

> **"Success follows the management of Mr Alfred Denville. Owing to the death of the Queen, Tuesday evening's performance was stopped. Mr Denville made special reference to the death of Her Majesty. No performance was given on Wednesday night also, but a crowded house witnessed The Slave Hunt on Thursday evening. Tom Trunnion, the chief role, was vividly portrayed by Mr Arthur Gilroy, who was enthusiastically received. As Diego, Mr Fritz Russell made a favourable impression. The Sam Shiddery of Mr Alfred Denville created roars of laughter. Messrs Fred Hart (Gus, the Black Boy), James J. Belverstone (Manuel), Claude Merton (Senor Corderillo), Will Collins (Palmedo), Mrs Fritz Russell (Signoria Riccio), Miss Daventry (Naretta) and Mrs Collins (Bugler Wilson) did their allotted parts well. Monday evening opened with The Flower Girl, Mrs Alfred Denville making her first appearance. She undertook the role of Jane, and the pathos and dramatic effect were most real. Mr Arthur Gilroy as Jack Pryor made a signal success. The other characters were well acted."**

The following month it was reported that business was enormous, increasing every week, with hundreds turned away nightly. The occasional visiting productions also achieved excellent business. When the H V Woods Company brought its musical Florodora to Morriston in April, 1901, the Opera House was regularly filled to capacity.

Denville's first season came to an end in June with a production of The Avenging Hand. On the last night he was presented with a silver-mounted pipe and case by theatre staff as a token of their respect at the end of the season. It was announced that the Morriston Opera House was to close for the summer season for extensive alterations and renovation of the stage and auditorium. It reopened with a new season on August Bank Holiday, by which time it claimed to be one of the best equipped places of amusement across the whole of South Wales.

The second season ran from August 1901 to February 1902 and included such attractions as The Reign of Terror and Rip Van Winkle. These were the farewell performances of local favourite William Macready who was leaving the stock company for an engagement in London. In November 1901 Alfred Denville staged a production of The Death of General Gordon or the Fall of Khartoum, the biggest success at that point witnessed at the Opera House.

George Burt played Gordon and Mr Wal J Edwards played Mahmoud. Denville himself played the role of Terry O'Halloram. A noteable feature was the attendance of the 1st Glamorgan Voluntary Artillery and the fine band of the regiment, which assisted in the entry of Lord Kitchener (Tom Wilson) into Khartoum. This spectacle was hugely admired and a cause of much patriotic cheering from the audience.

One of Denville's Christmas attractions was a Welsh pantomime entitled Llewellyn E'en Llyw Olaf. He was tapping a completely new audience since none of the other theatres in the area had staged a Welsh language production. He was much praised for his energetic and pioneering approach to theatre management, for his personal abilities as an actor and for his commitment to Welsh culture. Yet despite this something went wrong. The season ended abruptly on February 8, 1902. Several of the actors and actresses in his stock company took advertisements in The Stage and the Era thanking him most sincerely for their six month engagement at the Opera House, Morriston and at the same time advertising their own immediate availability. Mr and Mrs Denville (she was known professionally as Miss Kate Saville) themselves placed advertisements stating they were disengaged and were available for employment.

It is not known what caused the abrupt departure of the Denvilles. Had they run of out money? Was the competition from the Swansea theatres proving too great? There are few clues to help solve that riddle, but what is known is that the Denvilles were unemployed for a month or so after leaving Morriston.

The Opera House however immediately began a new season under the management of Mrs Edwin Clarke as lessee, and Edwin Clarke, as general manager. The Clarke's season included productions of Rollicking Robinson Crusoe and the premiere of a new play, Sins In The City, but within six months they were advertising for staff familiar with the operation of cinema-type equipment. This suggests that the regular production of plays and musicals was now interspersed with some variety shows. The number of straight plays at the Opera House was declining and more and more musicals were being staged. In September 1902 they appointed a new musical director, Mr F G Prosser, who had spent the previous eight years at the Metropole in Abertillery. By the beginning of 1903 Mr and Mrs Clarke had moved out of Morriston and were based at the Lyceum Theatre, Pentre. When Edwin Clarke left, he was presented with a gold-mounted walking stick, inscribed by staff of the Opera House as recognition of his service to the theatre. He was still nominally in charge of the Opera House and continued to advertise for suitable touring shows, then just two months later the building was unexpectedly put up for sale. On March 19, 1903 the following appeared in the press:

> **"Notice to theatre proprietors, managers etc. To be sold: cheap scenery, consisting of cloths, sky borders, wings, flats, etc. also rollers, stage screws, check boxes and other accessories. Must be sold by 25th inst. Full particulars may be obtained of or inspection made by appointment with the secretary, DJ Thomas, New Opera House, Morriston."**

That it seems was the end of live theatre at Morriston. Little is known about the use of the building for the next seven years, however in 1910 William Coutts, the Swansea theatre and cinema impresario announced the opening of his Bioscope Hall in Morriston. This was advertised as a cine-variety hall seating over 1,000 people. It is likely that the Bioscope Hall was a new name and conversion of the old Opera House. It was part of the Coutts circuit, which included the Palace and Star Theatres in Swansea and cinemas in Ystalyfera, Pontardawe, Morriston and Cwmbwrla.

In later years the Bioscope Hall was renamed the Picturedrome and was used exclusively as a cinema. Later still it changed its name to the Regal Cinema. The last film was shown on August 4, 1962. The building was a familiar landmark in the town, boasting a prominent figure of Mercury on the top of its dome, until it was demolished in 1965.

After his departure from Morriston in 1902 Denville eventually opened a stock company at The Coronet Theatre in Jarrow, and later at the Theatre Royal in Dipton. In 1904 he opened another theatre in Durham and by that time was well on his way to becoming a leading name in the new repertory movement, going on to become one of the most important men in the world of theatre. He had been born into a show business family, travelling with his parents in their portable theatre company. When the company was out of work, he worked as a miner, quarryman, factory hand and for a while he earned a living as a professional footballer. He was just 24 years old when he went into theatre management at Morriston and created the first repertory company. After his mysterious setback in Morriston, he went on to organise and send out touring companies throughout the country. At one point he had 22 of them on the road at the same time.

Denville's spat with the Grand was forgotten when he returned to Swansea with a show called The Miracle at the theatre on May 12, 1913. By 1925 Denville was both wealthy and successful when his eldest son Jack suddenly died at the age of 26. He decided to create a rest home for elderly or sick actors in memory of Jack. That same year he bought Northwood Hall, a mansion in Middlesex and a year later it opened as Denville Hall which became a charity in 1925. It still exists today as the major charitable home for elderly members of the acting profession. In 1931 Alfred was elected MP for Newcastle Central. He became known as the actors' MP and remained in the seat until he retired in 1945. He continued his theatrical business alongside his service as an MP and in 1940 he built the Coliseum, Harrow which was opened by Queen Mary. His second son, Charles, eventually took over the family business and was a major name in repertory theatre throughout the 1920s, 30s and 40s. The Denville players performed at the Grand during the 1930s.

In 1948 Alfred Denville celebrated 50 years in the theatre. At that time the actor Wal J.Richards who had played Mahmoud at the Morriston Opera House 50 years earlier wrote the following letter to The Stage:

Alfred Denville established what were probably the country's first repertory seasons at Morriston Opera House in 1900. The building it occupied can clearly be seen on the left .

Woodfield Street, Morriston in 2010. Any signs of the Opera House are just a distant memory.

"The story as I knew it, having joined him in 1898 and served under his banner for 20 years, is as follows: there were no stock companies of any description except portable theatres when Mr Denville opened at The Opera House in Morriston, Swansea, and where we played stock for a matter of two or three years. Amongst the visitors to come out of curiosity was a little lady named Madame Patti. She visited the company several times and then she brought along a lady with her on two occasions, and the latter spent a considerable time with the Guv'nor. After this she watched the performance on several occasions and was so enthralled that she was persuaded to take an interest in the theatre. With that object in view she took over the Gaiety in Manchester. This was Stock Number Two. Her name was Miss Horniman. It is quite possible that but for these two – Alfred Denville and Miss Horniman – stock might have died and never been revived. It was jeered at and scorned. I have often been jeered at when I told friends that I was playing in stock. I have heard Mr Denville mention in front of curtain that he has played something like 350 stock performances. Once when I was with him he had 23 companies running at the same time. Some of those people that laughed at the idea of Stock realised that perhaps there was something in it after all."

Alfred Denville died in 1955.

The Melville family

Triumph out of adversity seem to have been the watchwords of other entreprenerial families involved with theatre in Swansea in their early days. The Melville family is another classic example. George Melville, a 55-year-old tragedian who had already established himself as a theatre manager in Cardiff and was planning to branch out into the world of music hall and variety had intended to build a new music hall in Swansea, but instead he became the new tenant of the Theatre Royal in 1869.

Within a few years George had also taken over the old Amphitheatre in Wind Street and had rebuilt it as a music hall and variety house. The day to day running of the new Star Amphitheatre was in the capable hands of George's son, Andrew. The rival attractions of circuses, clowns, rope-spinners, minstrel groups and comedians at the Star, and plays, operas, high tragedies and melodrama at the Theatre Royal were now all in the hands of one family – the Melville's. They appear to have possessed a recipe for success and as a result did extremely well. This led to the expansion of their theatre ownership to other towns. As the years passed, Andrew married Alice Bullock, a Swansea girl, and moved to Christina Street. The couple had four daughters and four sons all of whom became involved in the family business as performers or managers. In the 1880s the Melvilles started to expand their empire further afield. They took over the Standard and Shoreditch theatres in London and the Grand in Birmingham. George moved to London while Andrew became sole manager of the Star.

Sadly, Andrew Melville collapsed while rehearsing the pantomime Forty Thieves at the Grand, Birmingham, in December 1895. He died a few weeks later, aged just 43 and was buried in Oystermouth Cemetry. The shock of losing his first-born son had a profound effect on George Melville who never recovered from the event and he too, died within two years, aged 74. By then the family owned provincial theatres in Derby, Glasgow, Manchester, Bristol, Newport and two in Birmingham as well as two London theatres, the Standard in Shoreditch and the Queen's in Battersea. When George died he left £90,000 – a huge amount of money for that time.

Initially the remaining Melvilles tried to share the management of their various theatres: Walter looking after London, Frederick, Birmingham, and Andrew, Jnr – aged just 17 – looking after Swansea. The formal recording of the management of the New Theatre as Mr A Melville, remained for a while, but it was clear that he should return to his studies. The manager was then advertised as Mrs A Melville, Andrew senior's wife.

The Oystermouth Cemetery gravestone of Andrew Melville Robbins, one of Swansea theatre's guiding lights.

The family was clearly struggling with so many ventures spread over different parts of the country. In March 1897 they announced that the New Theatre, Swansea and the Queen's Theatre, Battersea were being offered for sale by private treaty. However, it seems that no sale took place, and the New Theatre closed and remained dark and unused for the next three years.

The family gradually began to consolidate their interests in London. They leased or bought several London Theatres: the Metropole, the Terris Theatre, Rotherhithe (1901) and the Brixton Theatre (1907). Frederick Melville ran the Brixton Theatre for 30 years. After his death it was renamed the Melville Theatre in his memory, but was destroyed by a bomb in 1940. In 1909 the family took over the Lyceum and then in 1911 built the Princes Theatre, later renamed the Shaftesbury Theatre.

In the first 30 years of the 20th Century, the Melville brothers, now based in London, became famous for their melodramas, popular touring productions and lavish Lyceum pantomimes. Many of their successes were written by one or other of them. From their humble beginnings in Swansea they had risen to become a major force in British Theatre.

William Coutts

Williams Coutts was another for whom the road to success began in Swansea. He had been lured to the seaport in the spring of 1902 by the promise of a role as acting manager and potential partner for T Morton Powell, who by then had bought the New Theatre after leasing it for a short time. When Coutts agreed to come to Swansea from Birmingham little did he realise that before long he would be on his way to replacing the Melvilles as Swansea's 'Mr Theatre' and also becoming a national tour de force.

Things moved quickly. By July 1905 Coutts had bought out T Morton Powell's share in the building and became sole proprietor. Finally, just four months later, he increased his business interests by taking a lease on the Palace Theatre in High Street. Later, he brought classical ballet and even the Castellano Opera Company to his theatre in Wind Street.

Times were changing however and Coutts was quick to recognise that he needed to move with them. Theatres everywhere were closing and being converted into cinemas so he converted the Palace Theatre into the Popular Picture Hall and thereafter began to accumulate other cinemas in the area, earning himself the title of Swansea's Mr Cinema. In May 1912 the Coutts' organisation was advertised as the largest entertainment enterprise in South Wales, and announced that it controlled, the Star Theatre, Shaftesbury Theatre, Palace Theatre, The Picture House, The Tivoli, all in Swansea along with The Picturedrome, Morriston, The Coliseum, Ystalyfera, The Globe, Clydach, The Pavilion, Pontardawe and The Playhouse, Ystalyfera.

Coutts was proud that he had a permanent staff of 200, and that, worked once nightly, his houses would generate £250 a night and accommodate 11,500 persons. Every night his picture houses showed 38,000ft of film. Hugely ambitious he was always anxious to hire or buy films and was also keen to hear from any varieties or specialities, including comedy artists, sketch artists, duettists, vocalists, dancers, instrumentalists, acrobats, animal turns and any good novelties that would, in his eyes, draw the masses.

After the First World War Coutts moved to Cardiff where he became manager of the Cardiff Playhouse and the Kings Theatre as well as an adviser to a number of other companies. He died, aged 84, on New Year's Day, 1953.

An obituary for Coutts in The Stage on January 15 that year referred to him as a well-known and respected figure in the theatrical life of Swansea. It also highlighted his Sunday night concerts and his 'Street Robins Brigade,' something they said would be recalled by his old patrons to whom his name was a household word.

An article in the South Wales Evening Post on January 5, 1953, also celebrated his contribution to Swansea. It told of how he brought W F Cody to the Star in a wild west show, and how Colonel Cody flew outside the theatre in a man-lifting kite he had invented.

The Post report continued:

> **"Coutts also brought a foreign ballet company to the Star, even though ballet in London theatres was a rarity at the time. He had some success by bringing the Castellano Opera Company to Swansea. In 1912 he ran a Kinema colour film reel of the 1911 Delhi Durbar. Charles Urban's greatest achievement was the Kinemacolor record of this spectacular ceremony held in Delhi, India, to recognise the newly crowned King George V as Emperor of India and Coutts brought it to The Star in Swansea in 1912."**

Coutts was a larger than life character, a deeply religious man; he held a series of winter Sunday sermons at The Star, in Wind Street. He would present these with a series of lantern slides and they would finish with a singalong of hymns, the words appearing on the cinema screen. The proceeds of these sermons bought tobacco for the old men of the Tawe Lodge workhouse in Mount Pleasant, snuff for the women and sweets for the children, and would also help finance the Street Robins Brigade whose headquarters was at the Palace Theatre. They also helped support soup kitchens during times of distress.

Sir Oswald Stoll

Of all of the impresarios associated with Swansea perhaps Oswald Stoll stands out most. Born in Melbourne, Australia, his real name was Oswald Gray, but he was just a year old when his father died and his mother and younger brother moved back to England.

Mrs Adelaide Gray moved to her native Liverpool, where, in 1875, she married John G Stoll, a Danish waxwork show proprietor. Oswald and his brother, Roderick, assumed the same name as their stepfather. In 1880 John Stoll died suddenly and 14-year-old Oswald left school to take over the family business – the Parthenon Music Hall, Liverpool. It had started as a waxworks and had added live performers later. It was a 'beer and sawdust' hall with very cheap prices. The theatre boxes were locked during the performances to prevent anyone tickling the legs of the dancers. In 1890, at the age of 23, Oswald and his mother moved to Cardiff and took over the Levino music hall, immediately changing its name to the Cardiff Empire. Once again adversity played its hand with the budding impresario. It was an auspicious start and on the first night the box office takings totalled just 25 shillings. Stoll himself painted large posters bearing the slogan: Support the Empire. He was nothing if not fearless and on one occasion, because an audience at the Cardiff Empire were very rowdy he turned a fire hose on them from the front of the stage.

Stoll introduced a policy of twice-nightly shows, and insisted the Empire would only stage respectable family entertainment. He was obsessed with the idea that music hall shows should be akin to drawing room entertainment. His staff were instructed to report any expletives used, nothing beyond a mild 'damn' was tolerated and nothing offensive was allowed on stage. In 1892, at the age of 25, he married a Welsh girl, Harriet Lewis. They made their home in the fashionable Newport Road area where their daughter was born. In the same year Stoll and his mother took over the Swansea Pavilion and changed its name to the New Empire. He discovered Vesta Tilley in 1899 and he wrote many songs for her.

Three years later the Stolls bought The Parrot Music Hall in Newport, and redeveloped it as the Newport Empire. In 1896 Stoll noticed the Theatre Royal in Nottingham was up for sale. He announced he would be bidding and turning it into a music hall. The local citizens were heavily opposed to their lovely established theatre becoming a music hall. So Stoll decided to ignore the Theatre Royal and instead to build a brand new variety theatre on an adjacent site. He engaged brilliant theatre architect, Frank Matcham, and set about designing a proposed Nottingham Empire. This led to the conference between Edward Moss and Oswald Stoll. Moss, a Scotsman, had his own chain of theatres called Empires – 10 in all. And a rival chain with the same name was not in Moss's interest. The two came to a famous working agreement. Oswald Stoll became managing director of the Nottingham Palace (not an Empire) which opened in February 1898. Further negotiations took place and a year later, Stoll and Moss merged their companies. Oswald Stoll became managing director, and Edward Moss the chairman of the new company, Moss Empires Limited. The company had a combined capital of well over £1,000,000 – an absolute fortune at the time.

The three Stoll theatres in South Wales, including the New Empire, Swansea, were incorporated in the new set up, but Stoll insisted upon a clause, which left him free to build and operate his own music halls, providing that these interests did not clash with the Moss syndicate. His early theatres, the Empires at Cardiff, Swansea and Newport, were all rebuilt on the same or nearby sites by Moss Empires in the early years of the Century. Thus the New Empire, Swansea in High Street, was replaced with the larger and more luxurious Swansea Empire in 1900. In time Moss Empires was to become the most important variety theatre group in the country, controlling 33 music halls. Within five years almost every sizeable town in Great Britain had an Empire Theatre, run by Stoll, many of them newly constructed and designed by Frank Matcham. In his own right, Stoll built the magnificent London Coliseum, and in partnership with Moss, the London Palladium. He was noted for his charitable work – especially for disabled and homeless ex-servicemen. He was knighted in 1919 and died on January 9, 1942, ironically in the same week that the Newport Empire was destroyed by a fire. Moss Empires started selling off their variety theatres in 1957 and by 1960 they had withdrawn from the provinces completely due to the growing competition from other entertainment media.

The company continues as Really Useful Theatres, formed from the merger of the Stoll Moss Group with RUG theatres, a company with which Lord Andrew Lloyd-Webber is involved. They continue to manage seven theatres: the London Palladium, Theatre Royal, Drury Lane, the Palace, the New London, the Adelphi, Her Majesty's and the Cambridge Theatre.

Frederick Mouillot

Born in Dublin in 1864 Frederick Mouillot was another who built up an amazing portfolio of theatres. He began his career as an actor in stock companies. His first visit to Swansea was in a touring play in the 1880s entitled The Dark Continent. He went on to forge a successful career as an actor, manager and proprietor of a large number of theatres and music halls.

By the time of his death Mouillot, was manager or proprietor of 20 theatres and music halls, around the UK including the Gaiety, Dublin; Theatre Royal, Jersey; Theatre Royal, Bournemouth; Boscombe, Margate, and Southampton Hippodromes; The Theatre Royal, Dublin as well as The Grand Theatre, Swansea which was in fact built for him and business partner H H Morell.

Leon Vint

So far, most of the theatre moguls mentioned have had direct links with Swansea and at times operated out of the town, as it was in their day. However, there is one worthy of mention who came to the fore after establishing himself in the neighbouring town of Neath.

Leon Vint had a background as interesting as his theatres and though at times appearing to be anything but the easiest man to deal with, did go on to become something of an entertainment impresario in his own right.

His real name was Edward Preston and he was a one-time variety performer with a conjuring act. In 1894 he was touring the variety halls as Dr Vint, the world's greatest mesmerist. Three years later he and his wife formed Dr and Madam Vint's Globe Choir Opera and Scenorama. This unique show boasted 30 artists, singers, musicians and speciality music acts, together with special effect dioramas and scenic effects. Popular with audiences it proved to be very successful, financially.

During the early years of the 20th Century he began to invest his money into property, buying a series of smaller theatres around the country. By 1910 he owned eight of them, some of which were operating as cinemas. These were Barry Dock Palace, Long Eaton Picturedrome, Loughborough Hippodrome, Neath Hippodrome, Neath Palace and Rugby Palace. In 1911 he added three more: the Aberavon Palace, Ilkeston Picturedrome and Llanelli Palace. Two years later he added a further three: Carmarthen Palace, Nuneaton Picturedrome and the Nuneaton Prince Of Wales. He also built the Port Talbot Hippodrome. Half his venues were used as cinemas and the others for touring or variety shows. The weekly listings of performers in his theatres suggest they were very much part of the Number Two or second class circuit. Apart from the occasional star names like Charles Coburn (famous for The Man Who Broke The Bank At Monte Carlo and Two Lovely Black Eyes) his performers included some long forgotten acts like the Hungaria Trio, The Bouncing Dillon's, Ben Mohamed's Sousa Arabs, and Chard's Dogs. By the outbreak of the First World War it was clear that Vint had clearly overstretched himself and was in financial difficulty. On September 12, 1914, he announced that he had sold six of his theatres (two each in Rugby, Nuneaton and Loughborough) to United Electrical Theatres Ltd. This wasn't enough to solve his problems however, and in 1915 he was declared bankrupt. Somehow he managed to keep hold of The Palace in Neath and one or two of the smaller venues and by 1917 he had bounced back.

Leon Vint, an impressario who had a background as interesting as his theatres.

He secured the film rights to The Life Of Lord Kitchener and had great success placing it in theatres all over the country. He also obtained the touring rights of Elinor Glyn's romantic play Three Weeks and was able to tour this for over four years, playing to capacity houses almost everywhere. It enabled him to gradually restore his fortunes, and by 1920 he was the owner or proprietor of five theatres. These were The Grand Derby, The Palace, Barry Dock, Vint's Palace Neath, The Palais De Danse and The Coliseum Picture Theatre in Edinburgh. His main office by then was at Long Acre in London's West End.

There will, no doubt, have been others whose business efforts made an impact on the entertainment world, but those here were certainly among the most highly visible of their time.

Act 13

Memories are made of this

The Grand has generated countless fascinating stories during its long and often difficult, struggle for survival. But there is also a human side to its day to day operation that is just as interesting. Many of those who have had links with the theatre down the years, from staff to celebrities, patrons to performers, have memories that can provide an important extra dimension when chronicling the theatre's history.

One of my most cherished memories is of my first experience of the Grand Theatre's magical appeal. It was in 1972 when my father took me to the pantomime, Cinderella, starring Ryan and Ronnie. From the opening bars of the orchestra, through all the comedy slapstick and musical interludes, I was spellbound and left the theatre mesmerised.

I vividly remember later trying to recreate some of the scenes in our front room, pretending I was Ryan Davies, telling jokes and singing. One joke I remember still makes me laugh, though today it may be regarded as corny, but that's pantomime for you. It featured Ryan, dressed, I believe, as Shirley Bassey talking to Ronnie:

Ryan: "I went to the Top Rank the other night and the Doorman asked me for my ticket, I said my face is my ticket"

Ronnie: "What happened next"?

Ryan: "He punched it".

Not exactly sidesplitting by today's standards, but to a seven year old it was enough to ignite a love for the theatre that I retain to this day.

What follows is a random selection from the many memories that have surfaced as this salute to the Grand Theatre has progressed. They are all fascinating in their own individual way and show just how vibrant the theatre has been in making its special contribution to the world of entertainment in Swansea and beyond.

Eleanor Thomas:

"I had the pleasure of working in many of the Grand Theatre repertory seasons from 1970 onwards. They were of course directed by John Chilvers who was a master of his craft. We usually ran for almost 20 weeks, doing a different play each fortnight and so, because of the intensity of the work, we became a very tight knit community. On Friday evenings JC would announce the cast for the next show and then on the Monday we would begin rehearsals during the day while playing the other show in the night. My first season included The Prime of Miss Jean Brodie with Jean Fergusson, of Last of the Summer Wine playing Miss Brodie. In the next season we had Freda Jackson starring as Mother Courage and she had to pluck a ghastly rubber chicken in each performance. The stage crew stuck the feathers back on each night and by the end of the run it was utterly fetid. The following show was Oh! What a Lovely War and on the first night, during the shooting party scene, down from the flies, thrown by an unknown stage hand, came the rubber chicken. There were

many occasions when jokes and tricks peppered the performances, but our wonderful stage manager, Con Murphy would always reprimand us and remind us that people had paid good money to see us. Then there were the rats! Before the renovations the Grand was plagued with rats and we could often see them gambolling in the aisles as we rehearsed. JC swore they didn't exist but when the cast list of the next show went up a new actor was mysteriously added: And Ratty will play himself. Outside the stage door you could always hear the buses and next to that was The Volunteer Arms where we would go for some after show refreshment. They were happy days! I became the wardrobe mistress after the theatre was re-opened and that was full of incident too."

Owen Money: He appeared at the Grand in 1980 as part of the comedy band Tomfoolery in the panto Robinson Crusoe. Tensions in the band came to a head and Owen was asked to leave. He was however, allowed to choose his replacement. He made a phone call to a young comedian/singer from London, booked him into a guest house on Oystermouth Road, met with him and offered him the job and he finished the run in Owen's place. His name was Brian Conley.

Vivyan Ellacott:

"My mother and father ran the nearest grocery store to both the Grand and the Empire. When food rationing was in force during and just after the Second World War any artists visiting either theatre would have to sign a temporary register at our shop. They would usually come in at about 4pm – after their band calls and I would usually be there having just finished school and would meet all the stars. We'd get free tickets to the shows, but I'd also be able to go backstage at the Empire. I became a kind of 'mascot' – the cute kid who'd sit in the wings watching the acts. Because of this, I started taking singing and dancing lessons. Later I achieved my ambition of appearing on the stage of the Empire as one of the juveniles in panto. I played the Swansea Empire several times as a child. I also got to play in rep at the Palace during more than one week when they needed a child performer. As a teenager I did some productions with the Swansea Little Theatre at the Palace, but I never got to play the Grand. I went to University in the early 1960s and began to play odd roles in the London suburbs, to work in a few West End theatres and even do some small bits on TV and film. I would frequently come back to Swansea for weekends or holidays and would regularly go to see the rep productions and pantos at the Grand. Then in 1966 I was offered a job as Assistant Manager at the Swansea Grand. I was due to start with the panto rehearsals in the middle of December. Just one week before I was due to start, I got a panicky phone call from the Swansea Little Theatre. They were doing their annual play at the Grand and their juvenile lead had dropped out. Could I help out as a last minute replacement. I stepped in and, by the strangest of circumstances, I made my acting debut at the Grand, just one week before I was to start work there in a management role. I stayed at the Grand for two years until we were told the theatre would be closing at the end of the pantomime in 1969. I got another job and left. However, a group of us began the campaign to keep the Grand open and Swansea Council stepped in with its ten-year lease and a £30,000 renovation. In September 1969 I came back to the Grand as theatre manager, (John Chilvers had been promoted to administrator and artistic director) and we were both now Council employees. In January 1973 I was offered the job as design consultant and manager of the planned Kenneth More Theatre in Ilford – and I left the Grand. Altogether I had worked there for six years. Over the ensuing years I was invited back to direct a couple of shows in the repertory seasons. I directed a number of UK touring productions in the 1970s and 80s, two of which – Hair and The Rocky Horror Show – played at the Grand as part of their tour."

Peter Sandeman:

"I came to the Grand as general manager from Cardiff's New Theatre on January 8, 1973 the day before my 21st birthday, and left around about May 1978 to work at Theatre Clwyd in Mold. I very much enjoyed Swansea and remember fondly my time at the Grand. There were a great number of characters on the staff there. Among them Con Murphy, the stage manager; Gladys Westwood, the box office manager together with attendants Stan and Hildegard, who controlled the filling of the benches in the unreserved gallery. I have great memories of actors in the various rep seasons, some of which have subsequently gone on to bigger things. Among them Jean Fergusson, who later appeared in Last of the Summer Wine and Swansea's Menna Trussler later seen in Little Britain. I also remember with fondness the amazing 12-week pantomimes, starring Ryan and Ronnie. In my days at the Grand we shared very cramped office accommodation behind the sweet kiosk with John Chilvers. I remember an unfortunate incident when I had changed from stocking Kia Ora orange squash carton drinks to another product. During an Easter holiday break the contents of these orange juice cartons fermented and exploded in the stock room adjacent to the office. We arrived after the holiday to a flood of this fermenting liquid. Then there was the time that a fire hose reel perished in the balcony and overnight the mains water that supplied it gushed down and seeped

through the various levels until it arrived in the stalls. That was a major clear up operation."

Frank Vickery: He remembers when one of his plays had to be shortened due to its many laughs which stretched the show's run time to three hours. This caused a major problem on the Saturday when there were two shows, one at 5pm and one at 8pm. The problem was that there were 700 people at the matinee, which finished at 7.55 pm and there were 800 people waiting to come in for the second performance. Chaos ensued. Frank also recalls a dilemma he faced when A Kiss On The Bottom was staged at the Grand. One of the actresses, Jennifer Hill, suffered a fall at home during the run, which resulted in a serious fracture and she was forced to pull out for the last few nights, Frank didn't have an understudy lined up and decided to play the part, that of a woman in a hospital bed, himself. He suffered a close shave in both respects that time, but it was well received by the appreciative audience.

Max Boyce: He remembers his first appearance at The Grand in 1976 when to his amazement people queued around the building to see each show.

Menna Trussler: She remembers an unfortunate incident in a bedroom farce with Roy Barraclough when during a scene where she had to strip and throw away her underwear, it inadvertently landed high up onto the stage lights, out of her reach. She looked across to Roy for some help, but he was in bed under the covers giggling uncontrollably. She also recalls an embarrassing incident at a dress rehearsal in a repertory play with John Chilvers directing. Her character was in bed, and as John was explaining some re-writes to the rest of the cast, Menna who had been at the theatre since early that morning drifted off to sleep and had to be gently woken by John. She has done three pantomimes at the Grand and particularly remembers an ageing speciality act called Duval, who was employed as part of a deal with Harry H Corbett. The act involved live birds, rabbits and magic, which got progressively worse during the run, with instances of dead birds, nasty rabbits, and petrified magic assistants.

Mike Evans: In the early 1970s some pantomimes were block booked by local works and factories. During a matinee of one starring Ryan, British Steel at trotter, Llanelli, he recalled, had done just this. However there was a bomb scare in Loughor and the roads were closed delaying many coachloads of would-be audience members by over an hour. Ryan and the cast performed to an empty theatre except for the staff filling the first few rows. When they finally arrived he stopped the show, did a 10-minute recourse on what the audience had missed and then carried on.

Stan Stennett: His final pantomime at the Grand was in the 1969/70 production of Robinson Crusoe. Stan truly was the star as he entertained the audience with talent and charisma, breaking the theatre's panto box office records. It was also the longest running at that point. He remembers a particularly hilarious moment when the stage door, which in those days went straight out into the street, opened during a matinee performance one afternoon and a coal deliveryman, who also worked backstage, came in through the stage door. Instead of turning right as he usually would he turned left, walked straight across the front of the stage nodded to Stan before walking off the other side. The audience fell about laughing thinking it was part of the show.

Warren Mitchell: He'll always remember Swansea. He appeared at the Grand in his one-man show The Thoughts of Chairman Alf, on August 8, 1977. He aired his views – albeit as Alf Garnett, his character from the television hit Till Death Us Do Part – amazingly someone on the night took offence to some of them and started heckling from the stalls, then soon after got up to leave. 'Alf Garnet' seizing the opportunity, carried on his tirade singling out the man and his wife for further abuse as they left. This crossed the line and the man jumped on the stage and attacked the actor. This made national news.

Margaret John: tells a story from the 1950s when she was dining out with her mother at the Burlington restaurant in The Kingsway, when the manager of the Grand, John Salmon, ran into the restaurant looking for her. He rushed up to her table and asked if she could fill in as a last minute replacement in a play at the Grand as a leading member of the cast had been taken ill. Margaret agreed, and was whisked off straight away to the theatre to rehearse, but remembers being really upset at not being able to finish her mushrooms, which she loved!

Stephen Wischhusen:

"I joined the Grand in late 1965 as assistant manager. It is interesting to note that in its pantomime publicity, which went all over South Wales, the Grand used the style: Swansea Grand Theatre and not Grand Theatre Swansea. Rex Willis, director of Willis Cinemas Ltd the owners, thought the emphasis should be on Swansea. Structurally the theatre was in poor shape when I arrived and interior decoration was poor. The photo frames within the foyer were all of 1930s cinema origin and the outside signs over the entrance doors were in pieces and didn't light up. I did get some work done on these, but the costs were high and it was some weeks before John Chilvers felt able to submit the bill to head office for payment. The theatre also owned a cottage next door which at one time had been lived in by a previous manager named Gordon

Douglas, but in my time was used as extra dressing rooms for the visits by Welsh National Opera. That the theatre was still open was due in no uncertain terms to the unstinting work of John Chilvers. In those days the panto opened on Boxing Day and was still running in March. Prices of admission were four and five shillings and on Mondays all seats were two shillings and sixpence. Every effort was made to save money. Mondays and Saturdays were busy days and tickets properly printed for all seats for the nights. Other nights could be thin, and blank tickets were used for booked seats (there was little advance booking) and we wrote the seat numbers and row letters on them as they were booked, using roll tickets when the doors opened each night. The usherettes came in early to put 'reserved' cards on those seats, which had been booked. This was a valid point. Unused tickets were money wasted, why throw money away? We had a day-man called Tom who did maintenance and kept the coke-fired boiler going in winter, except that Tom liked a drink on Friday nights and didn't always get up on time. Sometimes I had to send a taxi for him or light the boiler myself. Secondary lighting was gas. I also had to light the gas brackets each night before the performance. Our scenic artist was Edward J Mann, who worked away at the back of the stage during daytime rehearsals. Willis still owned the semi derelict Theatre Royal in Tonypandy which was used as a scene store, and pantomime cloths going back years were stored there and brought down to Swansea for touching up when needed. Edward did that too. Frank Ellis was our leading man, Anita Morgan leading lady and John Velasco was assistant stage manager. He now runs a TV shopping channel. Islwyn Morris was a local actor who came in to play when we needed extra cast – and I sometimes went on too, on one occasion as a Chinese servant in Maugham's The Letter.

Marty Wilde:

"The Grand Theatre played a big part in one of my biggest song writing hits, Abergavenny. While driving with Joyce my wife to the theatre for the Robin Hood Pantomime in 1966/67 we passed a sign for Abergavenny. I can remember saying to Joyce what a fantastic name it was and the resulting song was partly written while we were in the pantomime. The song is still played around the world and hopefully pays tribute to yet another beautiful part of Wales. Another abiding memory I have of the Grand is while performing in Robin Hood. At one matinee Maid Marian who was played by my wife Joyce had a big row with Robin Hood – me! When I went out on stage with my arms outstretched to sing her tender words of love she probably amused the audience of the day by refusing to hold my hand and refusing to look at me!"

Duggie Chapman: The internationally renowned producer organised old time musical shows in the early 1960s. These were extremely popular and toured every major theatre in the UK.

"I played with my music hall many times at the Grand for John Chilvers. At the time I was Britain's youngest Impresario. I used Marie Lloyd Jnr, the daughter of music hall legend Marie Lloyd as a guest star on many of my programmes in the early 1960s and we played the Grand with her. I also had Dorothy Squires as a guest star when she was making a comeback. She complained about the scruffy dressing room at the Grand, but it was my favourite theatre from all our 60s tours and I will always remember how very kind and helpful JC was to me at the time."

Juliet Ace: The successful writer who worked on scripts for early EastEnders episodes, before it was cast, has memories of times as an assistant stage manager at the Grand during the Repertory seasons of 1963.

"One of my jobs as an assistant stage manager was to source props for the various plays," she said. "One in particular needed a consulting couch. I rang the local mental hospital to ask if they would lend me one. A doctor there was convinced that I had some emotional problems, and that the request for the couch was a smoke screen. He questioned me rather suspiciously: "Bach, you can tell me your problems," he said.

Brian Sullivan:

"At a meeting to discuss some content in the pantomime Goldilocks and The Three Bears which I directed in 1988/89, most of the cast were present. They included John Inman, Susan Maughan, David Copperfield, Terry Hall and myself. Each of them was putting their point across and things were getting a little heated. Suddenly Terry's puppet Lenny piped up and explained how he wanted things to be. Everyone stopped, looked and listened to the Lion, when suddenly John Inman boomed 'I refuse to take direction from a puppet.' There was silence for a moment and then everyone fell about laughing."

Anthony Lyn:

"During the pantomime Dick Whittington in 1987/88 Andrew Ryan was understudy to Nigel Pivaro, never thinking for one moment that he would have a chance to perform. Over that Christmas Nigel went home to Manchester and was delayed from returning in time for one performance. Hastily and at extremely short notice Andrew had to go on as his replacement to play King Rat. This was nothing if not confusing for the audience as Pivaro

was the current baddie in Coronation Street and each time he came on, the TV soap's theme tune would be played."

John Chilvers: The first Panto John directed at the Grand was Dick Whittington in 1962/63. This panto made the local press for the allegedly blue material in the script, which was leaked. Sales shot up after this. When interviewed JC defended it, explaining that pantomimes needed to cater for all ages. Although the material would be tame by today's standards, the Herald of Wales took the moral high ground by stating, in the same paper that it advertised the pantomime, that:

"The content in this year's pantomime, Dick Whittington, is totally inappropriate for children and that dirty jokes should be left to die in dark alleys."

Natasha Hill: At the age of 10 she appeared in the pantomime Babes In The Wood in 1983/84. It is an event she won't forget! As one of the chorus she had to hold a square board which had a letter on it, the chorus would then assemble in a line across the stage and on cue turn the board over revealing their letters and spelling out Babes In The Wood. She was fourth from the end of the line and in a fluster one night held her board upside down revealing an M instead of a W. This of course read Babes In The Mood! which gave the title a whole new meaning to the delight of the audience.

Robin Askwith: Confessions took on a different meaning for Confessions Of A Window Cleaner star Robin Askwith in December 1980 when the touring stage version of the film came to the Grand, starring Askwith himself. During one memorable performance he was pelted with bibles by a disgruntled churchgoer who took offence to the raunchy content of the show.

David W Kidd: A lighting technician at the Grand for seven years in the 1970s, I have many memories of the stars who came and went during that time and some interesting events on stage too. The scenery was on heavy cloths in those days, flown by pulley, and not counterweighted. In one panto, at the end of the first big scene, the company sang a number, held for applause before the lights went out and the first frontcloth flew in. One flyman, taking the whole weight of the cloth, let the rope through the cleat a little too loosely and the cloth, with a heavy timber batten at the bottom fell too quickly. While the lights were out, the wooden batten clipped the fairy's head knocking her out and leaving her lying on the floor. When the lights came up, the cloth was in but the fairy's feet were protruding beneath it. She was dragged upstage and fanned heavily by her fellow artists. Con Murphy yelled up into the flys orderings the flyman to come down immediately. 'Look what you've done to the fairy' he shouted. 'Go over the Vols (the Volunteer Arms) and get a double brandy – quick!'

The flyman vanished and didn't reappear for about 20 minutes. On his return Con yelled again. 'Where the **** have you been?'

"I went over the Vols to get a double brandy like you told me," replied the flyman.

"Not for you, stupid " shouted Con "For the Fairy!"

My seven – and very formative – years at the Grand afforded me the chance to work with some wonderful people. I was lucky enough to be asked to light some of the variety shows scheduled by John Chilvers.

Mike Evans:

"In 1975 Ryan was taken ill while rehearsing Jack and The Beanstalk, his penultimate pantomime at the Grand. Ryan had been away from the pantomime for 10 days and the audience had become accustomed to the pre-performance announcement: The part of Simple Simon will be played by Gordon Peters. On the tenth night, no such announcement was made and the performance began with the audience unsure of whether Ryan had returned or not. A few minutes into the performance and it was the lead up to Ryan's normal entry, the stage was clear and a figure stepped from the back of the set. The audience recognised the figure as he walked to the front of the stage and immediately a deafening cheer rang out and the applause began. Ryan stood there smiling as the applause went on… and on…and on. If Ryan had not raised his hand they would probably still be cheering. It was both a moving and memorable moment that reflected the public's deep affection for Ryan."

The Box Office staff: They have their share of memories too. Since the council take-over they have kept a book of silly sayings compiled from customer inquiries. They call it their book of little treasurers. The book gains an entry every time someone makes a strange request to the box office. Former employee Maureen Jones and current box office manager Nigel Waters dipped into the world of the Grand theatre box office book. From hundreds of entries they have shared those below:

- Is the ballet in Welsh?
- How much is it in the gallery? - £1
How much would two cost?
- **Is that the Grand Theatre?
Yes. This is the Grand Theatre.
Can I speak to someone who works there?
Well, I work here.
Oh! yes so you do.**
- Have you two seats for tomorrow at 5 o'clock?
We will be two pensioners. One unemployed and one filthy rich.
- **What time does the 6 o'clock show start tonight?**
- Are you paying by credit card?
Yes. I can do

Which card are you using?
Mine.

• Are you on our mailing list
No. I've only just moved here, but my son can speak Welsh and my wife is going to Singapore on Friday

• Any seats left for the panto?
Only single seats or restricted.
Any singles together.

• Can you tell me what's on in the middle of April?
We have the opera here with the Coronation of Poppea and Tosca and on Sunday we have Ken Dodd.
Who wrote that opera then?

• Customer: Can you tell me if you do block bookings for pantomime?
Cashier: Yes we do. Do you have a date in mind?
Customer:Well yes, sometime when the panto is on.

• Customer: I'd like to return two tickets for Beyond the Barricade.
Cashier: Ok. Where are you actually sitting?
Customer: On a sofa in Abergwili

• Have you got any plays about the Orient? Only my girlfriend is from Hong Kong and she's homesick.

• I'd like to book tickets for the comedy club.
I haven't been out for 22 years and I need a laugh.

• Have you got concussions for Godspell?

• On the leaflet for Elkie Brooks it says returns only. Does that mean that only people who have seen her before can go?

The Phippen family: This family will surely have had their share of memories. They had links with the Grand theatre spanning an amazing seven decades.

Shortly after the theatre opened, Gilbert Phippen of Fleet Street, Swansea, was employed as general handyman, bill-poster, and manager of the gallery bar. He had his own pony and trap, and would regularly travel as far as Llanelli putting up posters.

In those days the theatre had a large staff, all fitted out in resplendent uniforms.Gilbert had three daughters – Emily, Nellie and Edith. As soon as they left school, all three girls started work at the Grand. Emily was there for eight years and Nellie for 18. But the record was held by Edith, She married one of the 'Chocolate Boys' at the theatre and as Edith Llewellyn stayed at the Grand for an incredible 41 years, eventually as housekeeper, responsible for keeping the theatre clean and in good order. Edie, as she was affectionately known, was there through the Grand's heyday with visiting stars, opera companies, and glamorous nights when horse-drawn carriages would pull up outside the theatre to take their passengers home. She was also there when the theatre hit lean times and became a cinema. Edie could remember weeks when the management would tell the staff there wasn't enough money to pay them. In the 1950s she retired, but the family tradition continued when her daughter, Joyce, started to work at the Grand and eventually became the head usherette. Joyce was still in charge when the theatre reached its 75th birthday in 1972. This meant that at least one member of Gilbert Phippen's family had been working at the theatre for more than 70 years. The tradition was to continue a little longer since Joyce's daughter, Paula, worked temporarily at the theatre during her school holidays – becoming a fourth generation of the same family working front-of-house at the Grand.

Three employees of the Grand in 1976. They are, from the left: David W Kidd, Mike Griffiths and Con Murphy.

And finally: I started so I'll finish, as they say! I took my mother to see Tony Christie at the Grand in 2005 as a birthday treat. She was then 69 years old. Now my mum will talk to anyone no matter where she is and she won't mind me saying that she is a little hard of hearing. As we made our way to our seats she was telling all and sundry how she was looking forward to the show. I just tagged along smiling. As we took our seats and waited for the show to start she was asking me all sorts of questions, which I tried to answer as quietly as I could. Just as the lights dimmed to signal the start of the performance I could hear her talking to a couple to her left saying: "I have been looking forward to seeing Tony Christie for ages" I then sank into my seat as I heard her mention garlic bread and Rola Cola. It dawned on me then that she thought she was coming to see Peter Kay!

Act 14

Panto power saves the day

Pantomime occupies its own very unique and very special place in the history of theatre in general and that of the Grand Theatre in particular. Anyone who disagrees and throws up a noisy 'Oh no it doesn't!' is likely to be drowned out by a resounding 'Oh yes it does' from the countless thousands who have witnessed some amazing annual fun and frolics that has emerged from the genre there down many years.

From the very first pantomime to be staged at the Grand, a production of Robinson Crusoe well over a century ago in 1897, to the most recent, they are almost guaranteed to attract audiences of all ages and are a delightful way of introducing youngsters to the delights of the theatre.

They have come in all shapes and sizes and included Cinderella, Puss in Boots, Babes in the Wood, Jack and the Beanstalk, Aladdin, Sleeping Beauty, Mother Goose and countless others. They have all taken their audiences on a journey of escapism and they have all shared a final watchword: laughter. For more than a century, with only a few breaks between, they have occupied one of the most popular spots in Swansea's theatrical calendar.

Often they have utilised the acting prowess of the stars of the day in a totally different style. Some of the best known names from film, stage, television, radio, music hall, circus and speciality acts have been seen in the most amazing roles. In more recent years the careful selection of highly popular TV stars has been responsible for their continued success. For many patrons it is a rare opportunity to see their idol in person and at close quarters.

Sometimes these headlining performers, hired to put 'bums on seats' have a quick rise to stardom and then disappear without trace, but there are many seasoned campaigners who through talent, hard work and a love of their art, have forged fantastically successful careers in pantomime. It would be lost as an entertainment medium without them. So, no doubt, would theatres like the Grand countrywide, for the annual pantomime is a huge money spinner, bringing in much needed revenue at the box office. They often sell out quickly. Certainly the Grand Theatre would not have survived if it wasn't for the panto season which often rescued it from financial ruin. The pantomimes are important also as they are generally a child's first experience of live theatre and develop both future theatregoers and performers as well.

The first recorded pantomime in Swansea was Mother Goose and Her Golden Egg in 1809. This was staged at The Theatre Royal which occasionally hosted other pantos until it closed. In later years, as panto became more popular, the renowned Melville family took its appeal to a new level. The Empire Theatre pantomimes started just as the Grand became a cinema and were lavish productions attracting some very big star names of the day and from 1947 – 1957 Swansea theatregoers had a choice of The Grand or The Empire Theatre pantomimes as they ran in competition with each other until the closure of The Empire in 1957.

Some pantomimes have enjoyed enormously successful runs, sometimes being staged for months, while others have been and gone in just a week.

Grand Theatre pantomimes

1897/98 – Robinson Crusoe

December 27, 1897 – January 15 1898: Tom Fancourt, Alice Dewent, Alice Percival, Maude Bowden, Ethel Netherton, A. Ouston, Jenny Ruby, Ralph Foster, Ellis Oglivie, James Russell, The Sisters Emerald, Alec Darwen, H Wright The clown

1898/99 – Bluebeard

December 26, 1898 – January 14: 1899 Performed by Messrs Dottridge and Longden's Company Flo Varley, Nellie Merton, Steve Cook, John Cooper, Miss Annie Hathaway, Will White, Mr Ryder, Mr Clare, George Rydon, Leslie Clare, Primrose Ballet Troupe, George Harker, Robert Imden, Nelli

1900 – Cinderella

January 8 – January 20: Performed by Ernest Carpenter's Company Harry Karr, Walter Kooney, Four high kicking Somersaulters, Rosina, (musical speciality), Amandus, (impressionist), Grand Transformation: The Coral Realms Of The Mighty Deep

1901 – No pantomime

1902 – Cinderella

January 27 – February 8: Milton Bodes Company, Marian Ayling, Addie Love, Tilly Vaughan, Georgina Leonard, Frank Dunlop, J.W Baxter, Arthur Godfrey, Hettie Letch, Minnie Duncan, John Tiller's Troupe Of Lady Dancers, The Eight Little Wonders, Leo Sterling's Musical Speciality Act, Abel And Welsh (Contortionist & Acrobats)

1903 – No Pantomime

1904 – Blue-bell In Fairyland

January 18 – January 23: Rosadie Jacobi, Daisy Markham, Minnie Mace, May Lawrence, Harry Herbert Robert Milstead, Harry Bruce, Harry Douglas, Julia Yivers

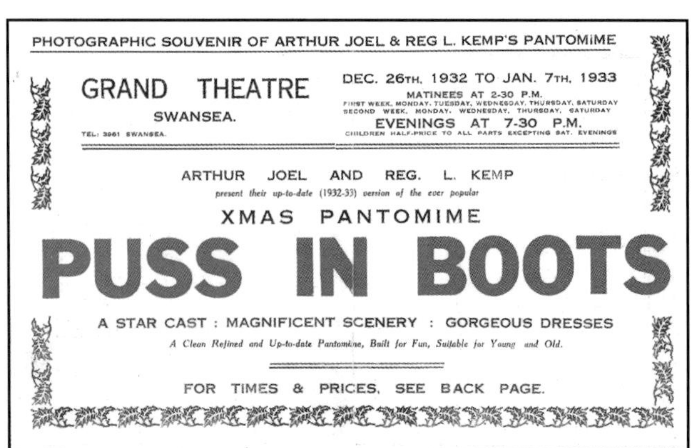

1905 – Sinbad

January 16 – January 21: Florence Dillion, Ann Brenan, Laura Humphreys, Stephen Fitzgerald, J.R.Val, A Murray, Denby And Dent (Comics), Carlyle's Spanish Whirlwind Dancers

1906 – Cinderella and The Glass Slipper

January 29 – February 10: Cissy Wade, Mary Sadie, King and Delane, Mayer and Bode, Denby and Dent, Laura Humpreys, Stephen Fitzgerald, Cissy Hilton, Frank Thatcher

1907 – Little Red Riding Hood

January 21 – February 2: John A Thompson's Company, Ella Willmer, Beatrice Varley, Fay Desmond, several unnamed comedians

1908 – Robinson Crusoe

January 20 – January 25: John A Thompson's Company, Madelaine Du Val, Maggie Allwood, John Thompson comic; Billy Bracey Gymnasts

1909 – Babes in the Wood

February 8 – February 13: Irene Damdeoa, John Richards, Turners Tropical Still Pictures

1910 – No Pantomime

1911 – Cinderella

January 23 – January 28: Barry Howard, Dorothy Clark, Kitty Douglas, Damerell, Rutland & Cinda, Maria Ault, Miss B Cadman, J W Hooper, A. Patterson, H St John

1912 – Aladdin

January 22 – February 3: Daisy Hurdle, Leonard Teel, Hettie Critchley, Iris Vaughan, Vera Lennie, Marie Gilbert

1913 – Mother Goose

January 13 – January 18: Nellie Le Breton, Gladys Johnson, Mr C Henry, Reg London, William H Wright, Nellie James, Hal Lester, Milton Brothers, The Three Jewells, The London Chorus and Ballet. Animals included a Goose, Donkey and a Horse

1914 – Babes in the Wood

January 12 – January 17: Leslie Morton and Guyton Heath's Company, Olive Sparke, Kathleen Severn, Dorothy Edwards, Lydia Williams, Alan Kennedy, Preston and Cooper (comics), Glanroy Troupe, S Holden

1915 – Aladdin

February 1 – February 6: J Bannister Howard's Company, Lillie Lassali, Billy Evelyn, Gertie Orchard, Will Judge, Mr G Stoney, Sisters Oxley, Hartley and Mellor, comic policemen

1916 – Cinderella

January 17 – January 29: F Leslie Moreton and Guyton Heath's Company, Mr B Noel, Mr H Barnett, Minnie Rayner, Maud Diamond, Mr and Mrs B Charles, The Six Merry Macs, Spectacular Fairies Boudoir, Magic Coach

1917 – Dick Whittington

January 15 – January 20: F Leslie Moreton and Guyton Heath's Company R Murray, Miss Ena Lestrange, Mr B N Alford, Mr H Talbot, Mr C Gardener, Rency and Dare (comics)

1918 – Babes in the Wood

January 14 – January 19: J Bannister Howard's Company, Miss Tina Frank, Miss May Romayne, Frank Hood, Mr H Benett, Mr G.Aspin

1919 – Humpty Dumpty

January 20 – January 25: Pauline Gilmer, Dot Eden, C Goff, Courtney And Dixon, E Kipling, D Kelsey, Cast of 30 artists, a diving bell and grottoes in the Land of Heartsease

1919 – Aladdin

January 27 – February 1: Arthur Roseberry's Merry Cheerio Victory Pantomime (presumably to celebrate the end of The Great War) with Hettie Gale, Fred Regent and Kitty Taynton

1920 – Cinderella

January 12 – January 24: Fred Clement's Company, Frank Leigh, Lorna Cherry, Evelyn Grace, Frank Johns, Pauline Rivers, Scholey and Scholey, The Blossoms

1921 – Dick Whittington

January 24 – February 5: Ada Wise, Frank Leigh

1922 – The Babes in the Wood

January 30 – February 11: Ada Wise, Willie Cave, Kenna Brothers, Little Pearl and May, The Pony Quartet, Aeroplane Stunt, Spectacular Toyland Scene

1923 – Cinderella

January 22 – February 3: Nita Larche, Lorna Sherry,

Kitty and Digger Sherry, Brock's Cyclists, Talberto and Douglas (acrobats), Jack Murray (comic), Syd Chester (comic), London Welsh Quartet

1924 – Jack and the Beanstalk

January 21 – February 2: Dorothy Brett, Miss Tomlins, Lester Holwood, Fred Hutchings

1925 – Robinson Crusoe

January 19 – January 31: Leon Salberg and George Slater's Company, Val Edwards, Madame Tardy Thomas, Linfield Troupe, Romany Singers, Lyceum Juveniles, The Hal Edwards Musical Comedy Girls

1926 – Aladdin

January 18 – January 30: Bert Symes, Gwen Highley, Jay Highley, Rosina May, Simple And Smart (acrobats), Koppah and Sloppah (clowns)

1926/27 – Dick Whittington

December 26, 1926 – January 8, 1927: Gloria Gay, Nellie Ryan, Harry Gilmour, Charles Harvard, Wal Watson, Ivy Raymond, Archie Wallen

1927/28 – Cinderella

December 26, 1927 – January 7, 1928: Eva Renee, Ray Rayson, Billy Royll, Doris Pearce, Lily Rose,

Zoe Sheld, Walter Cranbury, The Dinkie Ducklings (Clever Little Kids), The Willenors (trick cyclists)

1928/29 – Aladdin

December 26, 1928 – January 5, 1929: Renda Rudd, Bessie Evans, Zena Carol, Billy Revell, Bobbie Hall, The Ventons, (acrobats and comics), The Zeimar Brothers with educated donkey, Hector; The Chinese Chicklets

1929/30 – Cinderella

December 30, 1929 – January 11, 1930: Tom Dixon, Angela Guilberte, Broadway Girls, Doris Tilly (The Painted Girl), Nell Campbell and Roy Walters

1931 – Jack and the Beanstalk

January 5 – January 17: Edward Houghton, Maisie Griffiths, Hazel Glenn, Archie Wallen, Betty Millar, Gene Durham, Smarte Bothers Clowns, Dame Halleybutt's Choir

1932/33 – Puss in Boots

December 26, 1932 – January 7, 1933: Billy Barr (a Charlie Chaplin double), Eileen Merrie, Betty Millar, Shaun Desmond, Pat Walcott (the cat)

1933/34 – Babes In The Wood

December 23, 1933 – January 12, 1934: Eileen Merrie, Rita Kerva, Rene and June Gray, Cecil Roche, Irene Walters, Shaun Desmond, Mary E Wilkins, Charles Stevens, Fred Weedon, Fred Sylvester and his Nephews (acrobats), The Ten Riviera Girls, The Twelve Kittens (Tiny Tots in song and dance), Arley Sisters, Rosa Langue and Proctor (baton spinners), Joe Somers and Johnny Fell (comics)

1934 – 1946

There were no pantomimes as the Grand became a cinema between these years.

1947/48 – Babes In The Wood

December 26, 1947 – March 6, 1948: Joyce Randall, Gus Elton, Zoe Mansel. Jack Noyes, Irene Marshall, Joan Macfarlane (Scottish Dancer), Jimmy Currie's Waterfalls, The John-Joyce Girls

1948/49 – Dick Whittington

December 18, 1948 – February 4, 1949: Avril Vane, Bobby Vernon, Jack Noyce, Dorothy Lorraine, Winstanley Babes (formerly The Swansea Girls), The Three Ricordis (clowns), Swan and Leigh (international gymnasts), Teddy Knox, Miss Malta and Company, Dreser and Dale, Melville Birley, Bobby Patterson, Charles Regan, Irma Hanson, Derrick Kaye, The Paramount Girls, Edward Wood, A Dale

1949/50 – Aladdin

December 24, 1949 – January 21, 1950: Eleanor Drew, Wilfrid Brambell, Jackie Lester, Pamela Reed, Antonia Pemberton, Paul Lee, Harry Davies

1950/51 – Red Riding Hood

December 26, 1950 – March 2, 1951: Maudie Edwards, Ossie Morris, Stan Stennett, Mary Sullivan, Fairies Snowflakes, Royston Smith, Frank James, Rita Page, Maurice Keary, The Welcome Singers, Marianne James, Teresa Waters, Gordon Caddy

1951/52 – Cinderella

December 15, 1951 – February 16, 1952: Gladys Morgan, Joan Laurie, Wyn Calvin, Eddie Connor, Sylvia and Doreen Stephens (accordion act), Bert Cecil (Ugly Sister), Frank Laurie

1952/53 – Mother Goose

December 26, 1952 – February 7, 1953: Maudie Edwards, Ossie Morris, Olivia Jevons, Vera Cody with her live Horses, Marionettes

1953/54 – Goldilocks and the Three Live Bears

December 26, 1953 – February 13, 1954: Cyril Dowler, Rhoda Rogers, Marcia Owen, Hilda Heath, Norman McGlenn, Roulette Dancers, Hans Peterson (trainer of The Three Bears – James, Bessa and Strike)

1954/55 – Little Bo Peep and her Live Sheep

December 26, 1954 – February 19, 1955: Cyril Dowler, Rhoda Rogers, Joy Royston, Silly and Billy (clowns), Waltzing Waters Of Fairyland; Julia, Nellie and Billy (The three live sheep)

1955/56 – The Old Woman Who Lived in a Shoe

December 26, 1955 – February 11, 1956: Cyril Dowler (Big Head), Rita Page (The Old Woman – dame role), Rhoda Rogers(Mickey Mischief), Monica Wood (Prince), Billy Shenton, Campbell and Rogerson (Novelty Dancers), Magyar Ballet, The Singing Songsters (Welsh Boys Choir), Ida Rossire's Perky Pekes, Scotts Sea Lions

1956/57 – Sleeping Beauty

December 26, 1956 – February 2, 1957: Cyril Dowler, Joe O'Gorman, Angela Scott, Phyllis Bartel, Sam Linfield. Bourne and Barbara, May Warden, La Petite Poupee, Billy Knight, Stanley Massey, Bobby Gordon's London Babes, Len Trevor, Larry Gordon's TV Toppers

1957/58 – Cinderella

December 21, 1957 – February 8, 1958: Des O'Connor, Jacqueline Farrell, Sheila Atha, Melody Scott, Ramoni Brothers, Billy Wells, Charlie Jones, The Brockways, Dale Williams, Margaret Edwards, Kathleen Grasby's Four Shetland Ponies, Corps De Ballet, 12 Swansea Babes

1958/59 – Aladdin

December 13, 1958 – February 14, 1959: Ossie Morris, Alan Wells, Lynne Hughes, Reginald Vincent, Robert Marlowe, John Cartier, Helen Du Toit, Phyllis Jones's Swansea Babes, The Robertis, Flip And Bobi Roberts, Barbara Willoughby

1959/60 – Mother Goose

December 12, 1959 – February 20, 1960: Stan Stennett, Sylvia Norman, Eddie Henderson, Tony Snape, Alan Taylor

1960/61 – Jack and the Beanstalk

December 10, 1960 – January 28,1961: Wyn Calvin, George Bolton, Rex Rashley, Haval & Byl, Alan Wells, Yvonne Marlow, Sylvia Norman, The Five Romas, Eddie Fields, Tom Kyffin, Elizabeth Richards, The Corps De Ballet, Phyllis Jones Juveniles

1961/62 – Babes in the Wood

December 16, 1961 – February 24, 1962: Ossie Morris, Kenneth Earle, Malcolm Vaughan, Karl Heinz live Chimpanzees with Barbara, Phyllis Mellor, Stan Sanders, Howell Evans, Pat Evans

1962/63 – Dick Whittington

December 22, 1962 – February 23, 1963: Johnny Stewart, Sylvia Norman, Peter Boyce, Jill Alison, Reginald Vincent, Linda Lee, Ted Gatty, Pat Somers, The Three Lesters, Trio Vitalites, The Lynvettes, Nico and Co, 12 Jack Horton Dancers, Phyllis Jones's Swansea Babes

1963/64 – Cinderella

December 14, 1963 – February 29, 1964: Johnny Stewart, Johnny De Little, Sian Hopkins, Grande and Mars, Jonathan Prince, Brian Freeman and Monty Bond (acrobats)

1964/65 – Aladdin

December 12, 1964 – February 27, 1965: Vince Eager, Duggie Clark, Alan Wells, Lynton Boys (Chinese policemen), Lesley King, Hymas and Cece, Frank Ellis, Jonathan Prince, Emerson & Jayne (flying carpet), Cherry Willoughby dancers

1965/66 – Puss in Boots

December 11, 1965 – March 5, 1966: Jess Conrad, Keith Harris (as Puss), Jennifer Creighton, Bryan Burden, Grande and Mars

1966/67 – Robin Hood

December 10, 1966 – March 4, 1967: Marty Wilde, Ivor Owen, Bud Smart & Peter Tracey, Joyce Baker, George Truzzi, Danny O'Dea, Cherry Willoughby Dancers

1967/68 – Dick Whittington

December 22, 1967 – February 24, 1968: Johnny De Little, Peter Kaye, Sandra Wells, Tommy Rose, Du-Marte & Denzar ('Skeletons Alive'), Manetti Twins, Roz Early, Berwick Kaler, Sula Cartier

1968/69 – Jack and the Beanstalk

December 26, 1968 – March 8, 1969: Wayne Fontana, Roy Lance, Sian Hopkins, Trevor Moreton, Harmon Brothers, Jonathan Prince, Jean and Peter Barbour, Sandra Wrenall

1969/70 – Robinson Crusoe

December 26, 1969 – March 7, 1970: Stan Stennett, Ronné Coyles, Iain Sinclair, The Falcons, Johnny Tudor, Angela Barclay, Johnny Worthy, Curries Waltzing Waters, Gary Allen, David Evans, Judy Fielder, Cherry Willoughby Dancers

1970/71 – Puss in Boots

December 26, 1970 – March 4, 1971: Derek Roy, Barry Hopkins, Dave Swan, Cindy Williams, Danny O'Dea, Pavlov's Puppets, Simmons Brothers, Mike Fields (Puss), Vivienne Black, George McClaren

1971/72 – Aladdin

December 27, 1971 – March 11, 1972: Reg Dixon, Noel Talbot, Eddie Caswell, Nicky Stevens, Colin Cresswell, The Fourmost, Barry Hopkins, Jonathan Blake, Anna Lou & Maria, Cherry Willoughby Dancers

1972/73 – Cinderella

December 26, 1972 – March 17, 1973: Ryan Davies, Ronnie Williams, Susanna Page, Douglas George, Grande & Mars, Jonty Miller, Selena Lauder, Stan McGowan, Ian Calvin, Desmond King, Hugo Myatt

1973/74 – Dick Whittington

December 20, 1973 – March 1, 1974: Ryan Davies, Ronnie Williams, Bryn Williams, Clifford Henry, Gaynor Williams, Terry Doogan, Fernand Monast, Paul and Danny Denver (Escapologists), Jill Fitzjohn, Barry Dean, Cherry Willoughby Dancers

1974/75 – Mother Goose

December 26, 1974 – March 15, 1975: Ryan Davies, Bryn Williams, Alita Petrof, Roger Howlett, Kevin Darby, Manoff Puppets, Calli, Alison Temple Savage, Billy James, Timothy Wales, Cherry Willoughby dancers

1975/76 – Jack and the Beanstalk

December 26, 1975 – March 13, 1976: Ryan Davies, Bryan Evans, Freddie Lees, Kay Colman, Beverley Kay, Golden Brandy, June & Paul Kidd, Cherry Willoughby Dancers

1976/77 – Babes In The Wood

December 27, 1976 – March 19, 1977: Ryan Davies, Glyn Houston, Barry Hopkins, Elaine Gibbs, Karen Williams, Golden Brandy, Cherry Willoughby Dancers. (This was Ryan's last panto: he died shortly afterwards)

1977/78 – Cinderella

December 26, 1977 – March 18, 1978: Clive Dunn, Bryn Williams, Burden and Moran (Sisters), Debbie Young, Roger Tolliday, Jingles, Frank Leighton, Ria Jones (appeared as one of the Babes), Cherry Willoughby Dancers

1978/79 – Aladdin

December 26, 1978 – March 10, 1979: Anne Aston, Ivor Emmanuel, Kenny Smiles, Chris Hamill (later known as

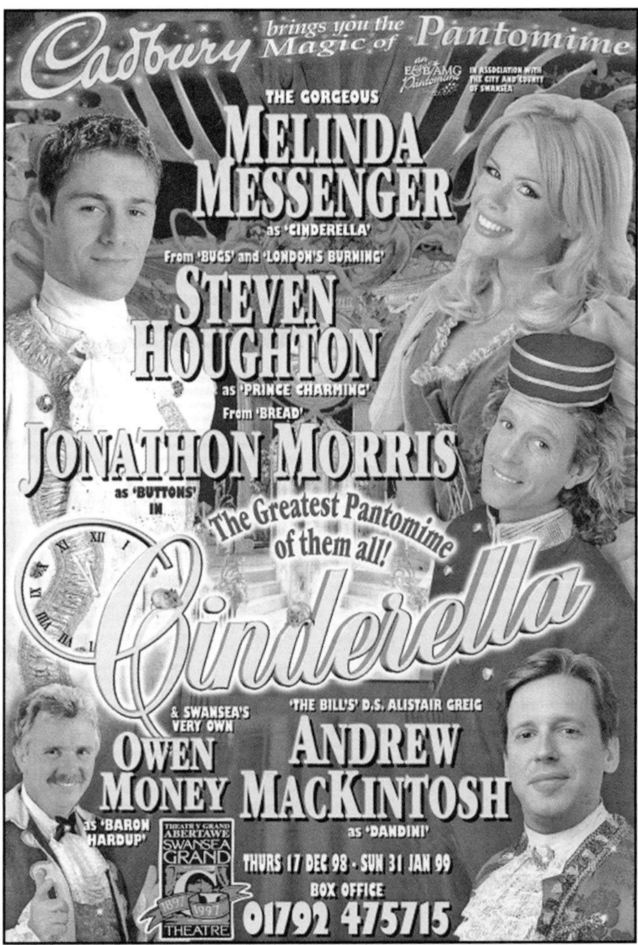

Limahl), Graham Cole, Vicky Kember, Freddie Lees, Mark White, Tim Ward, Peter Dayson, Carolyn Alexander, Nicholas and Nickleby, Cherry Willoughby Dancers

1979/80 – Robinson Crusoe

December 26, 1979 – March 9, 1980: Kenny Smiles, Philip Griffiths, Barry Howard, Maggie Ryder, Peter Holbrook, Leo Andrew, Owen Money, Brian Conley, Ben Ellison, The Star Puppets, Cherry Willoughby Dancers

1980/81 – Puss in Boots

December 26, 1980 – March 8, 1981: Davy Jones, Kenny Smiles, Peter Holbrook, Graham Cole, Freddie Lees, Menna Trussler, Katrina Tanzer, Diana Gibson, Two's Company, Jenny Alwen, Cherry Willoughby Dancers

1981/82 – Dick Whittington

December 26, 1981 – March 7, 1982: Harry H. Corbett, The Chuckle Brothers, Mike Holloway, Desmond Barrit, Peter Holbrook, Derek Holt, Menna Trussler, Duval, Wendy Smith, Wendy Weaver, Gerald Armin, Robert Hopkins, Andrew Thomas James, Andrew Swaby, Clare Cooper Jones, Debbie Bundy, Janet Ellen, Emma Myant, Tessa Pritchard, Terri James, Lynne Winslo, Jane Foxall, Richard Oriel, Colin Small, Ian Fricker, This was the last pantomime directed by John Chilvers as administrator of The Grand

1982/83 – Jack and the Beanstalk

December 27, 1982 – February 26, 1983: Don McClean, Freddie Lees, Graham Cole, Paul Keown, Steve Dewitt, Barry Holland, Jackie Marks, James Marston, Keefe and Annette, John Chilvers guest directed this pantomime

1983/84 – Babes In The Wood

December 26, 1983 – March 3, 1984: Windsor Davies, Melvyn Hayes, Desmond Barrit, Gareth Snook, Aliki, Wendy Weaver

1984/85 – Cinderella

December 19, 1984 – March 2, 1985: Paul Henry, Roy Barraclough, Caroline Berry, Mark Bond, Menna Trussler, Michael Harding, Jonathan Kiley, Robin Denys

1985/86 – Aladdin

December 18, 1985 – March 1, 1986: Bernie Clifton, Freddie Lees, Simon Oates, Ria Jones

1986/87 – Mother Goose

December 17, 1986 – February 28, 1987: Les Dennis, Christopher Biggins, Dorothy Vernon, Julie Paton, Christina Shepherd

1987/88 – Dick Whittington

December 22, 1987 – February 13, 1988: Ken Goodwin, Bobby Crush, Glyn Houston, Nigel Pivaro, Roy Lance, Lynne Winslow, Anthony Lyn, Derek Holt (Cat), Andrew Ryan

1988/89 – Goldilocks and The Three Bears

December 21, 1988 – February 11, 1989: John Inman, Susan Maughan, Susan Lee Hayward, David Copperfield, Terry Hall and Lenny the Lion, Bruce Montague

1989/90 – Babes In The Wood

December 20, 1989 – February 10, 1990: Little And Large, Paul Keown, Douglas Fielding, Patsy Ann Scott, David Hopkins, Frankie Desmond

1990/91 – Snow White And The Seven Dwarfs

December 19, 1990 – February 3, 1991: Linda Lusardi, Stu Francis, Neil Morrisey, Owen Money, Mike Holloway, Nikki Kelly

1991/92 – Cinderella

December 18, 1991 – February 1, 1992: Bobby Davro, Linda Nolan, Owen Money, Charlie Cairoli Jr

1992/93 – Robinson Crusoe

December 17, 1992 – January 31, 1993: Rod Hull and Emu, Joe Pasquale, Cheryl Baker, Mark Greenstreet, Owen Money, Karen Ashley, Dave Benson-Phillips

1993/94 – Sleeping Beauty

December 16, 1993 – January 30, 1994: Joe Pasquale, Windsor Davies, Carol Lee Scott, Paul Shane, Bruce Roberts, Suzanne Dando

1994/95 – Aladdin

December 15, 1994 – January 29, 1995: Joe Pasquale, John Altman, Adam Woodyatt, Owen Money, Jean Fergusson, Cobra

1995/96 – Jack and the Beanstalk

December 14, 1995 – February 4, 1996: The Chuckle Brothers, Dan Falzon, Vicki Michelle, Patrick Mower, Owen Money, Zoë Nicholas

1996/97 – Robin Hood

December 19, 1996 – February 2, 1997: Little and Large, Ruth Madoc, Sarah Vandenbergh, Mark Cameron, Mike Burns, Kevin Johns

1997/98 – Peter Pan

December 18, 1997 – February 1, 1998: Michaela Strachen, Norman Bowler, Deborah McAndrew, Owen Money, Warrior

1998/99 – Cinderella

December 17, 1998 – January 31, 1999: Melinda Messenger, Jonathon Morris, Steven Houghton, Andrew Mackintosh, Owen Money

1999/00 – Aladdin

December 17, 1999 – January 31, 2000: Tim Vincent, Andrew Lynford, Vikki Michelle, Barry Howard, Kevin Johns, Ria Jones, Simmon Brothers

2000/01 – Snow White And The Seven Dwarfs

December 15, 2000 – January 20, 2001: Mike Doyle, Kevin Johns, Jansen Spencer, Shaun Scott, Nikki Diamond, Poppy Tierney

2001/02 – Peter Pan

December 14, 2001 – January 20, 2002: Mike Doyle, Kevin Johns, John Challis, Dora Bryan, Jenna Lee James

2002/03 – Goldilocks and the Three Bears

December 18, 2002 – January 26, 2003: Lisa Riley, Sooty, Kevin Johns, Mark Jardine, Clive Webb and Danny Adams, Rebecca Oglesby

2003/04 – Cinderella

December 18, 2003 – January 18, 2004: Dan Paris, Mike Doyle, Kevin Johns, Geoffrey Hayes, Leanne Masterton, Michelle Potter, Quintin Young

2004/05 – Jack and the Beanstalk

December 15, 2004 – January 16, 2005: Mike Doyle, Kevin Johns, Gary Beadle, Kim Gee, Frank Vickery, Geoffrey Hayes,

2005/06 – Snow White And The Seven Dwarfs

December 22, 2005 – January 22, 2006: Kevin Johns, Gillian Taylforth, Fogwell Flax, Frank Vickery, Simon Lipkin

2006/07 – Aladdin

December 14, 2006 – January 14, 2007: Mark Little, Mike Doyle, Kevin Johns, Craig Gallivan, Gemma James, Phillip Arran, Sianad Gregory

2007/08 – Dick Whittington

December 19, 2007 – January 20, 2008: Ray Meagher, Kevin Johns, Hannah Waterman, Anne Charleston, Rik Gaynor, Hayley Gallivan, Barry Daniels, Adam Gaskin, Nia Jermin

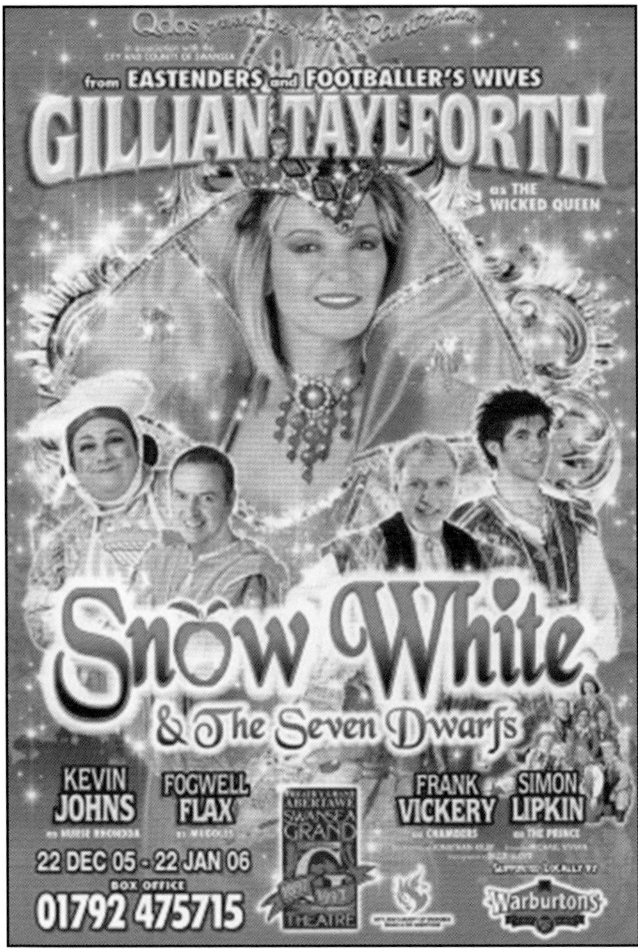

2008/09 – Cinderella

December 17, 2008 – January 18, 2009: Su Pollard, Chris Jarvis, Kevin Johns, Frank Vickery, Sarah Thomas, Nia Jermin, The Sensational Shetland Ponies

2009/10 – Sleeping Beauty

December 16, 2009 – January 17, 2010: Malandra Burrows, Andrew Agnew, Helen Fraser, Lewis Bradley, Kevin Johns and Nia Jermin

The Swansea Empire Pantomimes

1932 Red Riding Hood

Peter Fannan, Elsie Denham, Stan Annison, Eira Elma, Jenkins Brothers, Wallington Sisters, Melville Birley, Evelyn Major, Fred Cary, The Capitol Plaza Girls and Doris O'Shea's Little Rosebuds

1933 Robinson Crusoe

Walter Niblo, Emmie King, Gus Elton and full chorus

1934 No Pantomime

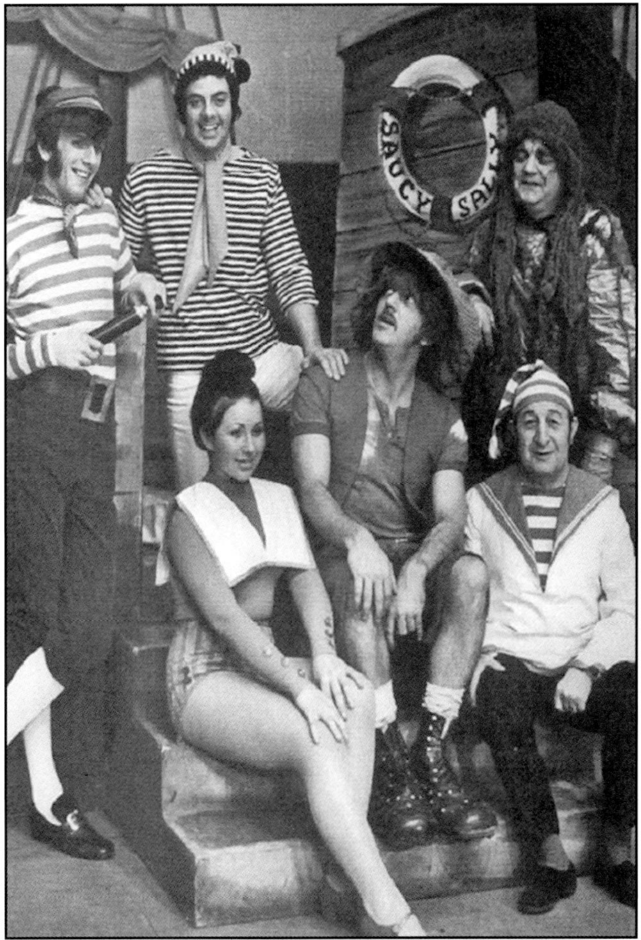

The cast of the successful 1969/70 pantomime Robinson Crusoe with top of the bill, Welsh favourite Stan Stennett.

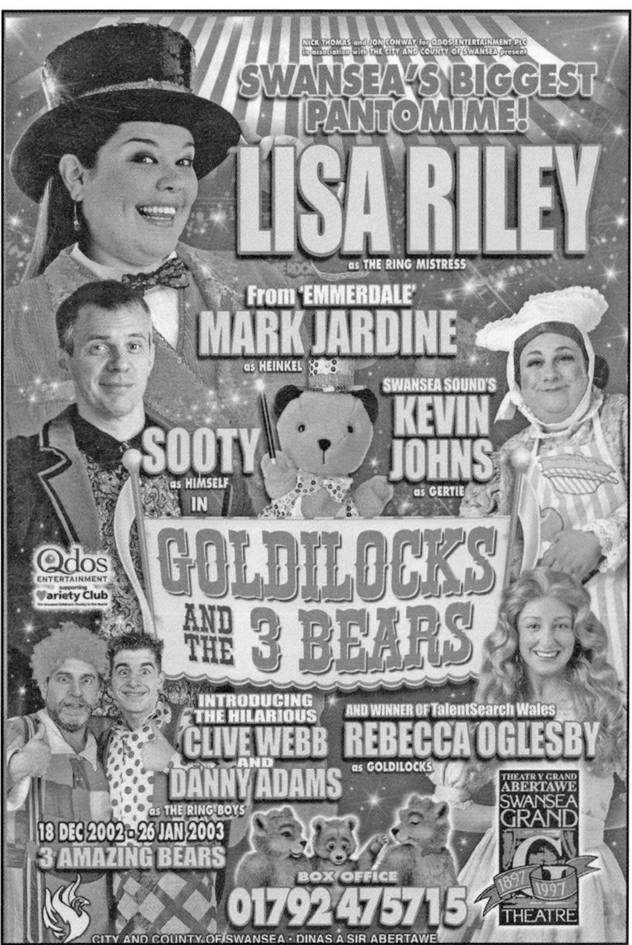

1935 Dick Whittington

Moya Dean, Fred Gwynne, Zenora, Phyllis Harrison, Gus Elton, The Willenors, Kenealy Sisters, The Henrietta Fuller Dancers, Lily Bell's 12 Rosebuds

1936 No Pantomime

1937 Babes In The Wood

Doris York, Frank Monckton, 12 Skating Babes, Ardana Sisters, Lily Bell's Six Frivols, Bob Lecarbo's Doughboys and full chorus and ballet

1938 Mother Goose

Jack Murray, Joe Arthurs, Fred Hale, Dixon And Burke, Freda Gardner, Henrietta Fuller Dancers, The Alexanders, Arthur Jeffries, Vera Finch Juveniles, Edna Moncrieff and Isobel Day

1939 Snow White And The Seven Dwarfs

Walter Niblo, Pegi Rhys, Joan Brett, Benita Lydel, Vivian Gibson, Tony Barrett, Arnold Rooke, Isobel Wan, Harry Daniel, Danny O'Dare, Sherman Fisher Girls and The Madzein Electrical Phantasy

1940 No Pantomime

1941No Pantomime

1941/42 Cinderella

December 22 for 2 weeks: Tom Moss

1942 Mother Goose

Jan 26 for 1 week: Jimmy James, Celia Kitson, Sheila Howard, Eddie Welsh, Kingsley and Forde, Jack Mayer, Doris Lester, Winstanley Babes, Alan Kitson, 12 Dancing Maids, Kathleen Stanley, Kemble Bros with Helen, Magu and Yuri, Fay Robins and Les Cygnet Four

1942/43 Mother Goose

Joe Arthur, Ivy Luck, Fred Hale, Fred Walker, Mary Carr, George Gower, Tony Vann, Audrey Dunham, Velda and Vann, Joe Heritage and Co., The Jason Girls, Grace Woottons Talented Juveniles and Leon And Niki

1943 Jack And The Beanstalk

Jan 18 1 week: Moyra Gay, Teddie Brogden, Dave Lee, Hal Jones, Gladys Watson, Zola And Mattie, Alec Pleon, Marjorie Murray, Betty Webb, Arthur Pitt, O'Reilly and Tracy, Lionel Gadsen, Jean Telfer, The Sherman Fisher Girls, Kirby's Flying Ballet

1943/44 Aladdin

December 20 – January 29: Tim McCoy and Raymond Hatton. Listed as the longest running pantomime ever in Swansea at the time

1944/45 Cinderella

Ford And Sheen, Delya, Neville Kennard, Nenee Beck,

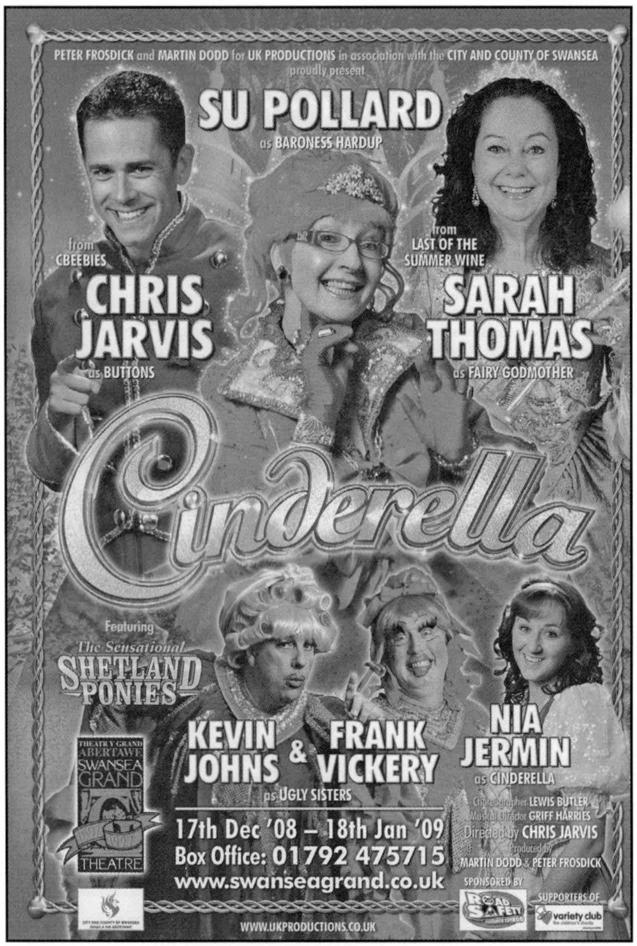

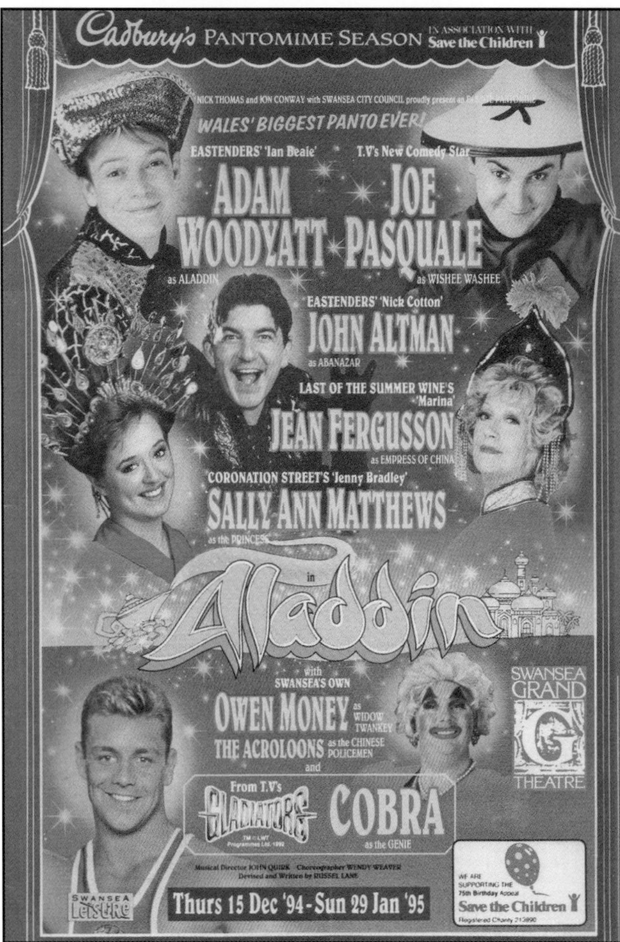

Audrey Marshall, George Bolton, Anna Marita, The Morjoy Babes, Iris Kirkwhite Dancers, Three Renowns

1945/46 Robinson Crusoe

Peggy Rowan, Ernest Maxim, Betty Felstead, Fred Gwyn, Arthur Pond & Co. Reg Kinman, Eddie Hart, Ben Whiteley, Lesley Horsman, Ray Johnson, Dorothy Anne, Eugene's Flying Ballet and Kitty Slocombe's Embassy Girls, Tom Dick and Harry

1946/47 Humpty Dumpty

Frank O'Brian, Jack And Stan Little, Joy Francis and Iris Villiers

1947/48 Mother Goose

Frank O'Brian, Dehaven And Page, Avril Lane, Janet Haley, Bonnie Downs, Cilla's Football Dogs, The Lyceum Juveniles and Bertram Tyrell

1948/49 Goody Two Shoes

Morecambe and Wise, Joy Hayden, Vic Marlowe and Sonny Jenks

1949/50 Jack And The Beanstalk

Alec Pleon, Ray Barry and Charles Harrison and Raie Copp as one of the dancers

1950/51 Robinson Crusoe

Max Wall and Sandy Lane

1951/52 Dick Whittington

Dave and Joe O'Gorman

1952/53 Puss In Boots

Harry Secombe, Shirley Hepburn, Tony Sympson, The Lynton Boys, Susan Irvin, Pauline Lucas, The Four Salvadoris, Richard Curnock, Graham Nelson Corps De Ballet, Eileen Regan Babes, The London Serenaders and Fred Kitchen Jr

1953/54 Aladdin

Nat Mills and Bobbie, Roy Jeffries, Jack E Raymond, Valerie Lawson and David Gardner

1954/55 Cinderella

Ken Roberts, Joyce Blair, Terry And Doris Kendal, Barbaur Brothers and Joan, Douglas George's White Ponies, Jane Martin, Reco And May, Peggy Thomson, Roy Jeffries, Silva Corps De Ballet and Eileen Regan Babes

1955/56 Babes In The Wood

Stan Stennett, Morecambe and Wise, Mary Miller, Gladys Joyce, Alan Curtis, Shirley Cook, Reggie And Betty, Shirley Cook Corps De Ballet, The Welcome Singers And Leslie Hatton

1956/57 Jack And The Beanstalk

Ossie Morris, Wyn Calvin, Hilda Dixon, The Two Astaires, Gerald Mordan, Mavis Hoffman and Gullivers Seven Giants.

Act 15

Big is best, but small is beautiful

As well as the larger theatres which served audiences in their thousands during the heyday of live entertainment, others in towns and districts surrounding Swansea played their part too, albeit on a smaller scale. Of these, one in particular stands apart from all the rest. Finance was never an issue during its construction and audiences didn't matter — at the box office at least. This was, and indeed still is, a very special theatre.

It is of course the theatre at Craig-y-Nos built by Adelina Patti, the most famous opera diva of her day. Madam Patti was a megastar even before the term was invented and at the height of her fame said to be the highest paid performer. Three times married and immensely wealthy, she decided to go into semi-retirement and after much searching for the ideal location decided to settle amid the solitude and stunning scenery of the upper Swansea Valley. She bought a rambling Victorian mansion at Craig-y-Nos and in 1878 set about converting it into her very own castle. As well as throwing money at her project Patti created a winter garden pavilion there, built her own waiting room at nearby Penwyllt station and even had her own private railway carriage. Some people at the time may have thought Patti extravagant but her enthusiasm for spending seems to have been balanced by her her enormous enthusiasm for supporting charity work. In the 1880s, as work progressed on her Swansea Valley wonderland she decided to forsake retirement in order to raise money to ensure it could be completed. At £1,000 a performance – around £60,000 in 2010 – a tour of the Americas brought in enough to complete her castle.

In 1890, she decided to add an extra ingredient to her already fabulous retreat. It was her own private theatre. She wanted a smaller version of La Scala in Milan, the scene of her major triumphs and appointed theatre architects, Bucklands and Jennings to create a perfect miniature replica. Patti announced that her new theatre would not be just for her own pleasure and the convenience of visitors to Craig-y-Nos, but for the purpose of occasional performances to benefit the various charitable institutions in the adjacent towns and to relieve the poor of surrounding districts. The auditorium is just 42ft by 27ft with a small gallery fixed in a curved end at the back. The coved ceiling is 22ft high supported by Corinthian columns. An ingenious device enabled the auditorium floor to be adjusted into a level position when the area was used for a ball, or raked downwards towards an orchestra pit when a performance was given on the stage. The proscenium opening is 20ft wide and the stage depth 22ft. The proscenium arch is embellished with the names of Verdi, Rossini and Mozart. The original stage scenery is still in existence, together with a spectacular backdrop depicting Patti as Rossini's Semiramide – one of her most acclaimed roles. The opening performance on Thursday, August 21, 1890, was by the St David's Operatic Company which in 1901, became Swansea Amateur Operatic Society. They gave what was reported

The stage of Adelina Patti's theatre at Craig-y-Nos in 2010, still with its original backdrop depicting Patti as Rossini's Semiramide – one of her most acclaimed roles.

An elevated view of Craig-y-Nos. The building on the bottom right was the winter gardens pavilion, later donated to the people of Swansea by Patti.

at the time as a well-received performance of W F Hulley's Coastguard or The Last Cruise Of The Vampire. Among Patti's guests for the occasion was Luigi Arditi, the conductor of Her Majesty's Opera in London and the composer of the popular song of the day, Il Bacio, or The Kiss. Signor Arditi warmly complimented Mr Hulley on the beautiful music of the opera and the general excellence of the performance. At the close Mr Hulley, on behalf of the company, presented Patti with a framed illuminated address. The whole company then enjoyed a champagne supper before leaving.

In an article written in 1961, Claude Jenkins recalled his visits to the Patti Theatre in 1904 and 1907:

> **"Madam Patti was a theatre enthusiast and used to produce three plays every year. The company was usually recruited from members of the Swansea Amateur Dramatic Society who could spare time for rehearsals at Craig-y-Nos. The baroness usually took a leading part in each of these productions. One member of the company was an expert professional piano tuner in addition to being a good amateur actor. He was able to turn his visit to good account by tuning the 14 pianos, which were distributed about the reception rooms, salons and boudoirs, as well as the magnificent concert grand piano in the theatre. Patti was an excellent actress; a quick student, she entered into rehearsals with the gusto of a young woman and played her part with aplomb. A great character at Craig-y-Nos was Patti's major-domo and Swiss butler Jacques. He was a fellow of vast importance, commanding a small army of footmen and servants. He too, loved the theatre. On the night of the performance he took over front of house. He personally welcomed every guest and escorted them to their seats with much dignity."**

After the death of Adelina Patti in 1919, Craig-y-Nos eventually became a hospital until it was bought by a private owner and converted into a hotel. The theatre was used for many years by Neath Opera Group for annual productions. The fabric of the building has been maintained to a degree , but its main use today, is for weddings where the couple are married on the stage. The mystique of Craig-y-Nos has attracted TV cameras on a number of occasions. In 2004 the Most Haunted production team came to investigate paranormal activity, and in 2006 an episode of Doctor Who (Tooth and Claw) was filmed in the courtyard. Patti's theatre is one of the most important private theatres in the United Kingdom, fortunately protected by a Grade 1 listing. It does need special care to preserve this unique and nationally important piece of theatre history.

Craig- y-nos before it was bought by by Adelina Patti. It was later developed as an extensive home, paid for by her lucrative personal appearances.

The entrance to Patti's theatre at Craig-y-Nos. She would have been pleased that Neath Opera Group used it as a home for their annual opera from 1963 – 1999.

The Patti Pavilion which was fully refurbished in 2006 courtesy of a £3 million lottery grant.

During the early years of the 20th Century, Leon Vint bought a number of theatres. Vint's Palace in Windsor Road, Neath, seen on the left here, was one of them.

The Patti Pavilion

The name perhaps uncovers the fact that this building, standing alongside Swansea's Victoria Park, has links with Adelina Patti too. Originally built at Craig-y-Nos in 1891, the Winter Pavilion as it was called was stocked with palm trees and exotic plants. It was yet another addition to Patti's lavish castle. Before her death she decided to donate it to the people of Swansea to be used for what she described as their leisure and pleasure. Unfortunately the shortage of manpower in the last year of the First World War meant it was impossible to carry out the removal immediately. Sadly Adelina Patti died in 1919, and it was a further year before the pavilion was moved by train to Swansea, then by horse and cart to its final resting place in Victoria Park. It was then named the Patti Pavilion in memory of the diva. It has indeed been used for all manner of 'leisure and pleasure' – from dog shows to beer festivals, from dancing school shows to pantomimes and from flower shows to rock concerts. Sadly, during the 1980s it became known as the 'Tatty Patti' as its décor left much to be desired. In the 1990s its plight was highlighted nationally when the TV series Challenge Anneka, with presenter Anneka Rice, refurbished it. At the end of the programme it was shown reopening with a performance by Swansea-born West End star, Ria Jones. Because of the extended community use over the past 90 years, thousands of Swansea people have attended an event there and it has become one of Swansea's best-loved landmarks. In 2006 the Patti was again overhauled, although not this time with MDF and a lick of paint as had been claimed about Anneka's brave efforts! Over £3 million was spent by the city council through a Lottery grant. It is now fully refurbished but retains the look of the old Patti.

The Palace Theatre/Vint's Palace, Neath

This was a timber building situated near the forecourt of Neath railway station. It began life as the Neath Assembly Rooms, but around 1910 it came under the control of Leon Vint. He changed its name to Vint's Palace which it retained until it was destroyed by fire in 1935. Audiences at Vint's Palace were generally offered a standard variety bill with the occasional film show. Vint, who also owned Neath's other theatre, the Hippodrome, eventually became heavily involved in the cinema business. Over time the two Neath venues settled into a routine where the Palace accommodated live shows while the Hippodrome screened films. Among those who performed at Vint's Palace was a young Maudie Edwards, a star in the making, who with her father Ned and sister May were billed as Ned Edwards and his Two Little Queenies. They would frequently give performances at 8am, timed to suit miners coming off the night shift in local collieries who would come by train into nearby Neath station. They needed some entertainment before going home for a well-earned rest. This is a pattern of performance, which although perfectly logical, does not seem to have been recorded at other theatres or music halls around the country. It does however indicate how a theatre could adapt to the community it served.

Ned Edwards and his two Little Queenies. Maudie Edwards is on the left. Both her father and sister died at a young age and are buried at Llantwit Cemetery in Neath.

The Neath Hippodrome

The Hippodrome was the second of two Neath theatres under the management of Leon Vint towards the end of the first decade of the 20th Century. Initially it was chiefly used for touring plays while his other theatre, Vint's Palace, was a variety house. It played host to a number of the smaller plays including Henry Herne and Company in Blackmail, The Chas H Lester Company in The Frontier Queen and a repertory season from Mrs Frank Bateman's Company. Occasionally the Hippodrome would be used for special events and one-night attractions. In 1912 it featured the child star Little Ena Dayne, who was billed as 'The future Marie Lloyd' and was undertaking a tour of one-night shows around the country. By 1913 it was clear that the touring plays were not attracting sufficient business at the theatre. From March to July that year the Hippodrome played the occasional week of films and variety shows. During one week in May, the resident manager, Mr Noice, reported to Vint:

> ***"The Bilfords in their cycling act, supply a good turn here; and Miss Pamela Moore's Company, including Edward Rainer, in The Bank Robbery, are well received. Cleve and Don, comedians and dancer, complete an attractive program."***

There definitely seemed to be some variety there!

By July business had dropped however, and the George Bowes' Company with Ali Baba and The Forty Thieves proved to be something of a disaster. The Hippodrome closed on July 13, 1913 and didn't reopen until October 9, the same year. The opening attraction was a play entitled The Boy Detective. After that the building was used exclusively as a cinema with the occasional variety act preceding the film, until it was severely damaged by fire in 1918. It was later bought by the owners of The Gnoll Hall, The Gnoll Picture and Variety Company Ltd. They allowed the site to remain undeveloped to reduce the competition for cinema audiences. In 1935, after Vint's Palace was also destroyed by fire, The Gnoll Picture and Variety Company was taken over by Union Cinemas, who thus ended up owning all three entertainment sites. They chose to build a completely new cinema on the site of the Hippodrome, and as a result, the Windsor Cinema opened in 1936. Along with many others it was forced to close in the 1980s, and it signed off as a cinema with the film Batman, starring Michael Keaton in 1989. After that it led a colourful life as a nightclub called Talk Of The Abbey until it again closed and the building demolished to make way for an apartment block in 2007.

The Gnoll Hall, Neath

The Gnoll Hall, Neath, managed by Mr V Aldridge, was a very early cine-variety establishment, showing a mixture of live acts and film shows. Immediately before the First World War it worked in direct opposition to the Neath Palace. During one week of variety in May of 1913 its rival attractions were The Three Merrill's smart cycling-act and comedian Billy Curzon. They were billed as the best of the week's entertainment in Neath. The building was later rechristened as The Gnoll Picture House and used exclusively for the screening of films,

The Gnoll Hall, Gnoll Park Road, Neath was used as a performance venue for Neath Amateur Operatic Society until the 1950s.

with only annual productions by Neath Amateur Operatic Society until the 1950s. The building still exists as a tyre centre and it is still possible to recognise parts of the old cine-variety and its dressing rooms there.

The Gwyn Hall, Neath

The Gwyn Hall was built in 1887 on land given to the town by local benefactor Howell Gwyn. It was designed primarily as a concert hall, with seating for 686 people. It had a flat floor and a raked balcony. It was fitted with a proscenium stage. It had a very mixed use ranging from touring productions and music hall to wrestling and amateur operatic performances. It was often used for council business until the construction of the town's civic centre in the early 1960s. A statue of Howell Gwyn was unveiled outside the Gwyn Hall on September 26, 1888. Its siting caused much controversy at the time as it was thought it would interfere with carriages pulling up outside the building. In 1967 the statue was moved to its current position in Victoria Gardens, because of a proposed road-widening scheme that never materialised. Among notable people who appeared at the Gwyn Hall were Adelina Patti and former prime minister David Lloyd George who once gave a speech there. Other highlights include a visit by Joan Hammond, the Australian opera singer in the 1950s. Among the audience on that occasion was a very young Anthony Hopkins who later became a star in his own right. Neath born singer Katherine Jenkins also appeared at The Gwyn Hall in 1990 as part of the chorus in The Briton Ferry Musical Theatre Company's production of Oliver. The Gwyn Hall received a Grade 2 listing in 1989. During a £4 million development, it was destroyed by fire on October 21, 2007. Rebuilding was finally underway in 2010 and it is hoped that eventually it will again become an entertainment venue.

The Gwyn Hall, Neath was a popular venue until its destruction by fire on October 21, 2007. Rebuilding and refurbishment work started in 2010.

Public Hall, Briton Ferry

The Public Hall at Briton Ferry was built in 1911 at a cost of £37,000, it was used as a theatre and later became a cinema before closing in 1961 shortly after achieving its biggest claim to fame – the interior was used for filming of the the Peter Seller's film Only Two Can Play. It was eventually demolished and the site became home to a garage and car sales operation.

The Public Hall, Briton Ferry. The interior was the setting for scenes in the Peter Sellers film Only Two Can Play.

The interior of Pontardawe Arts centre. It is a multi-use venue with music, films, and comedy as features.

Pontardawe Arts Centre

Pontardawe Arts Centre has gained a reputation as one of the finest cultural venues in South Wales. It hosts professional work of the highest calibre, from classical music to drama and dance, literature and children's theatre to blues and world music. The centre boasts a 450 seat theatre, dance studio, cinema, snooker hall, meeting rooms and art gallery. The original hall on the Herbert Street site occupied by the centre was built in 1908 as the then thriving town's Public Hall. It was officially opened by Adelina Patti on May 6, 1909. This fine building which consisted of an auditorium with a balcony, originally offered seating for up to 1,500 people for concerts, musical performances and recitations. The modern day building remains the focal point of Pontardawe's cultural and social activities but also attracts patrons from a much wider circle.

Early Port Talbot theatres

There were many attempts at establishing regular theatre at Port Talbot, but a long term established venue never really caught the imagination of the locality. Before the 20th Century the town was regularly visited by portable and fit up theatres. There are advertisements in The Stage for The Theatre, Port Talbot in 1885. It was described as the 'only theatre open in Port Talbot or Aberavon' by the advertiser, Sidney Williams.

In 1886 an advertisement appeared for Johnson's Theatre of Varieties while in 1888 the Prince Of Wales Theatre, Aberavon, advertised similarly, with the manager listed as John Johnson. This was possibly just a new name for Johnson's Theatre of Varieties.

On February 3, 1890 Arthur Lloyd opened the Prince Of Wales Theatre. It was described as new and commodious and capable of seating 1500. In April the theatre was advertised as Hybert's Theatre, Aberavon, but in May it had reverted to the name Prince of Wales, Aberavon, still with Mr Hybert as manager.

A Mr Beasley highlighted the New Grand Theatre, Aberavon in September 1890. This accomodated 1,500 and in October advertised itself as the New Grand Hall, Aberavon.

Probably the most popular and consistent visitor to the town was Ted Ebley's portable theatre, The Olympic, near the Railway Station, Port Talbot. It was advertised in 1884 and continued to be advertised in The Stage as the Olympic, Aberavon, up until 1902. Edward Ebley was born in Essex and with his brother William set up the Olympic Travelling Theatre in the 1880s, visiting towns in Shropshire and South Wales. Edward took over the company and settled in South Wales with his wife Blanche. Their son Robert Vernon Ebley was also involved, eventually taking over the family business. The company performed in the area until the First World War when acting was not deemed an essential occupation. Blanche Ebley took over the running of the theatre when her husband and son went to work in local collieries. By the end of the war the Government had granted permission for theatres to reopen as a morale boost for the public, recognising the country's need for entertainment and escapism. After 1918 the Ebley's set up their Olympic travelling theatre in the Jersey yard, now the Jersey Arms pub, Cwmafan. In 1927 Edward Ebley bought land that was part of the old works depot in the village and built a cinema. By the time Ebley's closed during the 1960s/70s it had become a bingo hall.

The Grand Theatre, Port Talbot

Located in High Street, Aberavon, it opened in 1905. It was the largest purpose built theatre in the town with a capacity of more than 1,200. A number of managers

The brickwork exterior of Port Talbot's Princess Royal Theatre which opened in 1989.

and lessee's tried to make a success of the theatre but after the First World War it struggled to compete with the other venues in Port Talbot and by 1924 it had become a cinema, changing its name to the Grand Cinema in the process and was leased by Swansea cinema impresario William Coutts. The theatre was demolished in 1972 to make way for town centre redevelopment.

Vint's Palace, Port Talbot

Situated in Water Street, Vint's Palace opened in 1911 and was mainly used for variety acts and as a cinema, later becoming a full time cinema. The building was demolished to make way for redevelopment of the town centre in 1972.

New Theatre/ Hippodrome

Leon Vint opened his New Theatre in Talbot Road, Port Talbot in 1912. It was a comfortable modern theatre. It had boxes, dressing rooms and a huge stage door entrance; he renamed it The Hippodrome and tried to establish this as a Number One touring circuit theatre. He achieved this between 1915 and 1918 when a series of touring productions, which had appeared on the Number One circuit in Swansea and Cardiff were attracted to the theatre. The people of Port Talbot were treated to productions of Alias Jimmy Valentine, The Christian, Eliza Comes To Stay, Grumpy, Jerry, Lucky Durham, The Passing Of The Third Floor Back, Potash and Pearlmutter, A Royal Divorce, Pygmalion, The Second Mrs Tanqueray, Sherlock Holmes and an annual Shakespearian Week with a different play offered every night. Sadly Vint was suffering financially and was no longer able to sustain the Hippodrome as a theatre and it later became the Empire Cinema, which burnt down in 1937 during the screening of Allan Jones's film The Firefly. The town then had to wait until 1989 before it would once again have a purpose built theatre.

Princess Royal Theatre, Port Talbot

The Princess Royal officially opened the theatre on September 29th 1989, though its unofficial opening as a theatre was a visit by the BBC television programme the Tom O' Connor Road Show in 1987. The theatre has held numerous and varied events including professional and amateur shows, concerts, children's shows, operas, musicals, comedy evenings, ceremonies and presentations, major conferences, seminars, exhibitions, fayres, dinner dances and weddings.

Since 2000 the Owen Money Theatre Company has performed their annual pantomime at the theatre and this is now a major highlight of the year. The multi-purpose venue has a maximum seating capacity of 798 and is situated next door to the civic centre in Port Talbot. Famous names who have performed there include Catatonia, The Stereophonics, Dave Arthur and the Fureys, Errol Brown, Shane Ritchie, Alan Carr, Reginald D Hunter, Rhod Gilbert, Freddie Starr, Paul Child, Mike Doyle, Owen Money and Peter Karrie.

Act 16

A pick 'n' mix of entertainment

It's not only the professionals who have been entertaining audiences in and around Swansea since the first barnstormers rolled into town. Amateur performers and groups have made their mark too. Producing all kinds of musical feasts and theatrical productions, they have earned their place in the community and the history of theatre in the area. They have also provided a launch pad for many an aspiring star.

These amateur societies have also been the lifeblood of their professional big brothers. For they acted as feeders of much needed talent, particularly in the formative years of theatre. Swansea gave birth to a number of groups at the turn of the 20th Century. Among these was the St David's Players in 1876, though this itself became Swansea Amateur Operatic Society in 1901, now the oldest such group surviving in the city. Indeed before the popularity of cinema and later TV, a night out at the theatre to see an amateur performance of a musical was highly desirable with frequent sell-outs and early morning queuing for tickets at the box office the norm. On occasions even society members had to draw lots for tickets. Sadly in recent times many amateur societies have failed to attract audiences in great numbers to their annual productions and some indeed are having trouble recruiting new members. Over the past 20 years many longstanding societies in the area have folded. There are however some new and innovative younger groups which concentrate on producing musical theatre shows with a deliberate move away from the normal amateur operatic offerings. There does seem to be a clear divide between the two and with their survival in mind, perhaps many of the remaining traditional amateur operatic societies should embrace and encourage change and move with the times. There is no doubt that young talent is still coming through the amateur ranks, but with an ageing membership and ageing audiences, societies should perhaps strive to be more adventurous. The same is true of amateur theatrical groups and there is no doubt that both genre are holding the future of amateur entertainment in their hands.

Swansea Little Theatre

In 1929 a group of professional and business people came together with young people from schools and colleges to form the Swansea Stage Society, whose aim was to produce classical plays, which Swansea's struggling commercial theatres could not afford to put on. The society staged plays by Shaw, Shakespeare, Barrie, Houseman and Galsworthy, and held drama workshops and play writing competitions. Their home was a church school hall in Southend, Mumbles. Later they performed at the Llewellyn Hall before taking over The Palace Theatre in 1955. Their home since 1979 has been the Dylan Thomas Theatre in the Maritime Quarter.

Swansea Little Theatre productions have been:

1924 – Leah Krishna
1925 – St Cecelia
1926 – The Thief
1928 – The Ship, If Four Walls Told
1929 – R.U.R., The Tempest, Change, Sport of Kings, Dear Brutus
1930 – Midsummer Madness, Knight of the Burning Pestle, Prunella, Love at Second Sight
1931 – Gruach, Scenes from Macbeth, Love at Second Sight, Loyalties, Cwm Glo (Welsh Drama Society), Skin Deep, The Insect Play
1932 – Change, Hay Fever, The Silver Box, Beaux Stratagem, Arms and the Man, Merchant of Venice, Clandestine Marriage, The Witch, Thirteenth Night
1931-32 – Man at Six, Captain X (Junior Players), The Way of the World, Richard II
1933 – Peter and Paul, Electra, Kingdom of God, Strange Orchestra
1934 – The Way of the World, Martine, Richard II, The Confederacy, Graft March, Conquest
1935 – School for Scandal, Pillars of Society, A Bed of Feathers, Too good to be True, Othello, The Moon in the Yellow River
1936 – The Winters Tale, Lady Precious Stream, The Voysey Inheritance, On the Rocks, The Simpleton of the Unexpected Isles, She Stoops to Conquer
1937 – The Maid of Cefn Ydfa, Mocking Bird, Richard III, Noah, The Swan, The Ascent of F6, Mark your Man
1938 – Much Ado About Nothing, Land of My Fathers, Caesar and Cleopatra, Trilby, Eden End, She Stoops to Conquer, The Tramp, Twelfth Night
1939 – Cherry Orchard, Bidden to the Feast, The Insect Play, Bidden to the Feast, The Disinherited, Influences
1940 – Rock and Fountain, He Was Born Gay
1942 – To Elizabeth
1944 – Gaslight
1945 – Uncle Vanya
1946 – The Sleeping Beauty, Time and the Conway's, Dolls House, Wishing Well, To See Ourselves, You Can Never Tell, Quality Street, A Month in the Country
1947 – John Ferguson, Alice in Wonderland, Thunder Rock, A Month in the Country, Silas Wood, Passion and Putrefaction, Midsummer Night's Dream, Mr Bofrey, Le Bourgeois Gentilhomme
1948 – Ballad of the Marie Lwyd, Tinkers Wedding, John Ferguson, All Through the Night
1949 – Barbed Wire and Bracken, Half a Loaf, King Lear, The Wishing Well, The Happy Journey from Trenton to Camden, The Bathroom Tap
1950 – Happy as Larry, In Good King Charles's Golden Days, The Glass Menagerie, Bachelor Brothers, Hedda Gabler in Welsh
1951 – A Phoenix Too Frequent, The Happy Journey from Trenton to Camden, Thor With the Angels, Asmodee or The Intruder, Sheep and the Goats, Man of the World, The Happy Journey from Trenton to Camden, Theatre Scrapbook, King of the Castle, Love in Albania, The Tempest
1952 – Asmodee, The Sheep and the Goats, Bricks Without Straw, Cocktail Party, Man with a load of Mischief, Asmodee, My Brother Tom, John Gabriel Borkman, The Lady's Not for Burning
1953 – An Evening of Music at Llewellyn Hall, The True Waters of Lethe, Queens of France, Dragon's Mouth, Bless This House, London Pride, Antigone, Bless This House
1954 – Tom Tom The Pipers Son, The Toby Chair, Confidential Clerk, Boy with a Cart, Bait, Christmas in the Market Place
1955 – The Cherry Orchard, Twelfth Night, Antigone, Druids Rest, The Rivals
1956 – Letters from Swansea, Hay Fever, The Taming of the Shrew, The Atom Doctor, The Sport of Kings, She Stoops to Conquer, The Boy with the Cart
1957 – Beauty and the Beast, Love and Lunacy, Pro Patria (performed at the St David's National Festival in the Albert Hall, Sleeping Dragons, Summer Day's Dream, Skin of our Teeth, Pygmalion, The Tempest
1958 – Lucky Strike, School for Scandal, Not this Man, Queen and the Rebels, Reluctant Heroes, Macbeth, In Good King Charles's Golden Days
1959 – Importance of Being Earnest, Ring Round the Moon, Escapade, According to the Doctor, Tobias and the Angel, Dinner with the Family
1960 – The Sacred Flame, Maria Marten, Capt. Carvallo, Merchant of Venice
1961 – Major Barbara, Little Women
1962 – Waiting for Godot, Under Milk Wood, Arms and the Man, The Caretaker, Life with Father, Frost at Midnight, Madam Patti
1963 – Midsummer Night's Dream, Point of Departure, A Party for Christmas
1964 – Death of a Salesman, As You Like It, The Birthday Party, The Kingdom of God
1965 – Juno and the Paycock, A Winter's Tale, Cheaper by the Dozen, Six Characters in Search of an Author, The Brontes
1966 – The Rivals, An Evening with Chris Fry, 1966 and All This, Albert's Bridge, Picnic on the Battlefield, Caligula, Crime Passionel, Carnal Knowledge, A Long Christmas Dinner, The Winslow Boy, Treasure Hunt
1967 – The Business of Good Government, She Stoops to Conquer, Double Bill of Albee
1968 – The Drunkard, Summer and Smoke, Tribute to Vernon Watkins, Much Ado, Lysistrata
1969 – Christmas Carol, The Daughter in Law, Letters from Swansea, Sergeant Musgrave Dance, Thwarting of Baron Bolligrew
1970 – After the Rain, A Slight Ache, A Resounding Tinkle, The Lesson, Emlyn Williams Centenary Tour, Under Milk Wood, Resounding Tinkle, Merchant of Venice, Under Milk Wood, The Flight of Princes

1971 – You Like It, Happy Haven, Lovers, Mixed Doubles, Lock up your Daughters

1972 – Comedy of Errors, Little Malcolm and his Struggles against the Eunuch, The Winslow Boy

1973 – In Celebration, The Rivals, Loot

1974 – A Delicate Balance, Twelfth Night, Under Milk Wood, Semi-Detached, Aladdin Pantomime

1975 – Relatively Speaking, Triple Bill, Swansea's Dylan, The Intricate Image Gill Adams, Dylan's Swansea, Anthology, Noel Coward Revue

1976 – Bless This House, Who's Afraid of Virginia Woolf, The Caretaker

1977 – Habeas Corpus, An Evening with Shakespeare, Blood Wedding, Lunch Hour, Mill Hill, Mother's Day, Bait, Enter Edmund Kean, Mr Melville and Mr Emm

1978 – Our Town, Playboy of the Western World, Under Milk Wood, Dylan Thomas Remembered

1979 – Arms and the Man, We have our Exits and our Entrances, The Hollow Crown, Lest Ye Be Judged, Under milk Wood

1980 – She Stoops to Conquer, In Confidence, Lest ye be Judged, Jet Set, Finvola Davies, The Corn is Green, A Tribute to Ruby Graham, Candida

1981 – Under Milk Wood, Two one act plays: A Gathering of Doves and Lunch Hour, Lest ye be judged, Zigger Zagger, When We Are Married, Young Wives Tales, Magnificence, The Food of Love, Lock Up Your Daughters, A Gala Night, Xmas in the Market Place

1982 – Magnificence, Table Manners, Six Characters in Search of an Author, Tartuffe, Beckett, Macbeth, Teachers, Harlequinade, The Dumb Waiter, Prime of Miss Jean Brodie, A Rock and Roll to Paradise, The Letters of Abelard and Heloise, Toad of Toad Hall, The Importance of Being Earnest

1983 – Mixed Doubles, Noah, The Bosses Funeral, King of the Castle, With Great Pleasure, Arsenic and Old Lace, A Rock and Roll to Paradise, Under Milk Wood (to mark official opening of theatre), Imprisonment, The Voysey Inheritance, The Would-be Gentleman, The Thwarting of Baron Bolligrew

1984 – The Olive Bullet, The Tempest, The Happiest Days of Your Life, Pal Joey, An Evening with John Betjeman, A Man for all Seasons, Laughter from Afar, Xmas Presents

1985 – Laughter from Afar, Public Eye/Private Ear, London Observed, Pride and Prejudice, Under Milk Wood, Unexpected Guest, Lysistrata, Under Milk Wood, Much Ado about Nothing, Fumed Oak, Creme due Noel, Christmas Carol

1986 – The Choice is mine, The Voysey Inheritance, Love – a celebration, Magritte and the Real Inspector Hound, A Doll's House, The Outside Edge, Henry X, Macbeth

1987 – The Aspern Papers, The Beau Stratagem, How the Other Half Loves, Victuallers Ball, Hi-fi Spy Bomb, You Can't Take it With You, Can't Pay, Won't Pay, Charlie's Aunt

1988 – Confusions, Uncle Vanya, Oh! What a Lovely War, People and Places, Whose life is it Anyway?, A Little Carnival, You Can't Take it With You, The Crucible, Winnie the Pooh

1989 – Benefactors, A Midsummer Nights Dream, Play it Again Sam, Spider's Web, Under Milk Wood, The Dresser, Caucasian Chalk Circle, Under Milk Wood, A Chorus of Disapproval

1990 – Benefactors, Rebecca, Pass the Butler, Alice, A Black Comedy, Miss Julie, Dames at Sea, Godspell, Bouncers and Shakers, Under Milk Wood, An Evening with Bernard Shaw, GB's Essence of Women, An Evening with Dylan, Intricate Image, David Copperfield

1991 – Dracula Spectacular, All the World's a Stage, Amadeus, Workshop Shakespeare, An Evening with Thomas Hardy, The Maintenance Man, A Murder is Announced, Lettuce and Lovage, Under Milk Wood – Youth Theatre, Two Contemporary One-Act Plays, See How they Run

1992 – Bedroom Farce, Valley Man, Comedy of Errors, Teachers, Relatively Speaking, The Real Inspector Hound, The Odd Couple, Jack the Ripper, Crown Matrimonial, Our Day Out, Aladdin

1993 – Rope, Thursday's Ladies, Come Blow your Horn, An Evening with Frank Vickery, See you Tomorrow Night, A Night Out, An Evening with Frank Vickery, Little Shop of Horrors, Shakespeare's Country, Dylan, Quality Street, A tribute evening

1994 – Spring and Port Wine, The Real Thing, The Hollow Crown, Shop at Sly Corner, The Rivals, 2 and 2 Make Sex, Macbeth (Youth Theatre), Blithe Spirit, Jane and the Magic Pumpkin

1995 – Love Letters, Wind of Heaven, Letters from Swansea, One o'clock From the House, Christmas Carol

1996 – Daisy Pulls it Off, Beyond a Joke, A Taste of Honey, Wildest Dreams, Death on the Nile, Under Milk Wood, Pools Paradise, Still Life and Public Eye, Wind in the Willows, Love Plays

1997 – Mort, Inspector Calls, Travels with My Aunt, Under Milk Wood (in the Grand Theatre), Dick Whittington

1998 – Abigail's Party, Honeymoon Suite, Wyrd Sisters, Under Milk Wood, Aladdin

1999 – Three one-act plays by Neville Makin – Pressures, Auditions, Sisters – When Dorothy Meets Alice, When We Are Married, Your Best Night Ever, Masquerade, Under Milk Wood, Merchant of Venice

2000 – Filumena, Silly Cow, Family Planning, Under Milk Wood at Laugharne, Twelfth Night

2001 – Educating Rita, Fatalities, Jump, Stepping Out, Dylan by Tony Layton, Carpe Jugulam, Under Milk Wood, Babes in the Wood

2002 – She Stoops to Conquer, Jakes Women, Allo! Allo!, Gold Pathway Annual, Under Milk Wood, A Tribute to DJ

2003 – Mother Goose, Hay Fever, Under Milk Wood, Are You Being Served?

2004 – The Witches, Hobson's Choice, The Constant Wife, Fallen Angels, Lords and Ladies, Not Now Darling, Return Journey, The Outing
2005 – The Diary of Ann Frank, The Importance of Being Earnest, Dads Army, Having a Ball, Under Milk Wood, Maria Marten and the Red Barn
2006 – Red Balloon, The Crucible, Shakespeare's new play, Death by Audience, War Play, Don't Dress for Dinner, Under Milk Wood, Midsummer Night's Dream
2007 – Macbeth – Youth Academy, Great Expectations, Steel Magnolias, The Truth, Deckchairs, Sleeping Beauty Panto
2008 – The Jungle Book, Of Mice And Men
2009 – Around The World In 80 Days, Who's Afraid of Virginia Woolf, Treasure Island, The Day They Kidnapped The Pope, Under Milk Wood, Puss In Boots Panto
2010 – A View From The Bridge, Ecstasy, The Canterbury Tales, Welcome To The Neighbourhood

The Abbey Players

The Abbey Players were formed in late 1960 when a small group of friends got together to do a one off show to raise money for the University Appeal. The driving force was Frank Tucker alongside Val Treharne and Adrian Howells. The first meeting and reading of The Boyfriend was at a member's house in Cwmdonkin House, Terrace Road. The first show was performed at the Llewellyn Hall in January 1961. It was such a success that the group was invited to perform at the Waterford International Festival of Light Opera in Ireland in the autumn of 1961. As some of the original cast and the producer, were unable to go to Waterford, the show was recast and David Thomas was appointed producer. The Abbey Players were named after Singleton Abbey where they first rehearsed, and they made many visits to the Waterford Festival where they won many awards over the years. The society eventually, outgrew its home at he Llewellyn Hall in the YMCA and moved to the Grand in 1978 where they have performed ever since, barring 1983 and 1986 when the Grand was being redeveloped.

Abbey Players productions:

1961 – The Boyfriend
1963 – Salad Days
1964 – Free as Air
1965 – No No Nanette
1966 – Bob's Your Uncle
1967 – Where's Charlie
1968 – Pajama Game
1969 – Half a Sixpence
1970 – Salad Days
1971 – How to Succeed in Business Without Really Trying
1972 – A Funny Thing Happened on Way to the Forum
1972 – The Boyfriend
1973 – Bye Bye Birdie
1974 – Little Me, No No Nanette
1975 – The Music Man
1976 – Guys & Dolls
1977 – Sweet Charity
1978 – How to Succeed in Business Without Really Trying (First Performance at The Grand Theatre)
1979 – Pajama Game
1980 – Charlie Girl
1981 – Little Me
1982 – The Wizard of Oz
1983 – Promises Promises
1984 – Oklahoma
1985 – Sweet Charity
1986 – Calamity Jane This was performed at the Taliesin Arts Centre due to Grand Theatre improvements
1987 – South Pacific
1988 – Mame
1989 – Annie
1990 – Guys & Dolls
1991 – The Wizard of Oz
1992 – A Funny Thing Happened on Way to the Forum
1993 – Half a Sixpence
1994 – South Pacific
1995 – Carousel
1996 – My Fair Lady
1997 – The Boyfriend. On July 21 as part of The Grand Theatre's centenary celebration The Abbey players performed a one-night show.
1997 – Camelot
1998 – Dolly
1999 – Oklahoma
2000 – Gypsy
2001 – Fiddler On The Roof
2002 – Scrooge
2003 – Annie Get Your Gun
2004 – The Scarlet Pimpernel
2005 – Guys and Dolls
2006 – The King and I
2007 – Anything Goes
2008 – Oliver
2009 – Kismet
2010 – The Scarlet Pimpernel

Gendros Catholic Operatic Society

Gendros Catholic Amateur Operatic Society was formed in 1961. It prided itself in affording opportunities to young performers and was the starting point in the careers of Catherine Zeta Jones, Julie Paton, Anthony Lyn and Richard Mylan. One of the guiding lights of the society was Swansea theatrical legend Peter L Howard. Peter was involved in amateur dramatics in the city from an early age, firstly with Gendros. He was instrumental

Peter L Howard, one of the guiding lights of Gendros Catholic Operatic Society.

in their first performance at the Grand in 1980 with Kismet, right through to their last at the theatre with Rose Marie in 1992. Peter also performed with many other societies in the area and was a great friend of Catherine Zeta Jones. He was a charismatic, imposing figure with a heart of gold. He was also a great source of theatrical knowledge. Sadly Peter died, aged 70, on April 5, 2010. His last stage appearance was a memorable one in the award winning production of Beauty and the Beast by Cockett Amateur Operatic Society just a few weeks earlier. The award was a fitting tribute to a gentleman.

Full list of productions:

1961 – The Desert Song
1962 – The Vagabond King
1963 – The New Moon
1964 – The Babes In The Wood, Good Night Vienna
1965 – Dick Whittington And His Cat, Gipsy Love
1966 – The Gipsy Baron, Little Red Riding Hood
1967 – Land Of Smiles
1968 – Jack And The Beanstalk, The Merry Widow
1969 – Robin Hood, Naughty Marietta
1970 – Aladdin, Waltz Time
1971 – Mother Goose, Pink Champagne
1972 – Dick Whittington, The Desert Song
1973 – Little Red Riding Hood, The Gipsy Princess
1974 – Tom The Piper's Son, Viva Mexico,
1975 – Goldilocks & The Three Bears, White Horse Inn
1976 – Cinderella, Waltzes From Vienna
1977 – Jack And The Beanstalk, Maritza
1978 – Goody Two Shoes, Sweethearts
1979 – Robinson Crusoe, Old Time Music Hall
1980 – Kismet
1981 – Kiss Me Kate
1982 – The Sound Of Music With a young Catherine Zeta Jones and Anthony Lyn
1983 – Old Time Music Hall
1984 – Oliver with Catherine Zeta Jones and Richard Mylan
1985 – Half A Sixpence with Richard Mylan
1986 – Silver Jubilee Celebration
1987 – Fiddler On The Roof
1988 – Camelot
1989 – Showboat
1990 – The Merry Widow
1991 – The Pirates Of Penzance
1992 – Rose Marie. The group's last production.

Swansea Amateur Operatic Society

The society was formed as the St David's Players in 1876 by W F Hulley – who later became musical director at the Grand theatre. As the St David's Players they were the first to perform at the newly-built theatre in the grounds of Adelina Patti's Craig-y-Nos home. They took the name Swansea Amateur Operatic Society during their performance of Iolanthe at the Grand theatre in July 1901. After it became a cinema in 1934 the society switched performance venues to the larger Empire, in Oxford Street, and after the closure of The Empire in 1957 switched back to the Grand with The Belle of New York. The longest standing amateur society in the area they celebrated their 80th performance at The Grand in 2010. Some of their stars have included Colin Hodges, Jean Thorley and Catherine Zeta Jones.

Full list of productions:

1901 – Iolanthe
1902 – Patience
1903 – The Marauders
1904 – The Mikado
1905 – Les Cloches De Cornville
1906 – The Yeoman Of The Guard
1907 – The Gondoliers and Trial By Jury
1908 – The Pirates Of Penzance
1909 – Dorothy
1910 – The Mikado
1911 – Iolanthe
1912 – Merrie England
1913 – Les Cloches De Cornville
1914 – The Gondoliers, 1916 – HMS Pinafore
1919 – The Yeoman Of The Guard
1920 – Princess Ida
1921 – Haddon Hall
1922 – Patience and The Mikado
1923 – Tom Jones
1924 – The Rebel Maid
1925 – Iolanthe
1927 – A Greek Slave
1928 – Young England
1928 – A Tale Of Alsatia
1929 – Princess Ida
1930 – the Duchess of Dantzic
1931 – The Arcadians
1932 – The Chocolate Soldier
1933 – Miss Hook Of Holland
1934 – The Vagabond King
1935 – The Desert Song
1936 – Rose Marie
1937 – New Moon

1938 – Showboat
1939 – The Three Musketeers
1947 – The Vagabond King
1948 – The Desert Song
1949 – New Moon
1950 – Rio Rita
1951 – Tulip Time
1952 – Masquerade
1953 – Katinka
1954 – The Quaker Girl
1955 – The Maid Of The Mountains
1956 – The Student Prince
1957 – The Belle Of New York
1958 – Oklahoma
1959 – The Dancing Years
1960 – Hit The Deck
1961 – Carousel
1962 – White Horse Inn
1963 – The Merry Widow
1964 – Annie Get Your Gun
1965 – Rose Marie
1966 – The Student Prince
1967 – Guys And Dolls
1968 – Oklahoma
1969 – My Fair Lady
1970 – Summer Song
1971 – Carousel
1972 – New Moon
1973 – Fiddler On The Roof
1974 – Camelot
1975 – Calamity Jane
1976 – Hello Dolly
1977 – Song Of Norway
1978 – Show Boat
1979 – South Pacific
1980 – Brigadoon
1981 – The King And I
1982 – My Fair Lady
1983 – The Merry Widow
1984 – Guys And Dolls
1985 – Carousel
1986 – No! No! Nanette
1987 – King's Rhapsody
1988 – Hello Dolly
1989 – Annie Get Your Gun
1990 – Kiss Me Kate
1991 – White Horse Inn
1992 – The Best Little Whorehouse In Texas
1993 – Brigadoon
1994 – The Sound Of Music
1995 – 42nd Street
1996 – Oliver
1997 – Me And My Girl
1998 – Crazy For You
1999 – The Merry Widow
2000 – Calamity Jane
2001 – My Fair Lady and Iolanthe
2002 – Mack and Mabel
2003 – Carousel
2004 – Jesus Christ Superstar
2005 – The Slipper And The Rose
2006 – Titanic
2007 – Thoroughly Modern Millie
2008 – Hello Dolly
2009 – HMS Pinafore (Australian version)
2010 – The Pirates of Penzance

Frank Vickery Productions

Playwright and actor Frank Vickery has had his own plays performed at Swansea Grand Theatre since 1989. They have proved immensely popular and developed something of a cult following among Swansea audiences. Frank who was born and still lives in the Rhondda Valley has written over 30 plays. In 1977 he won the Howard De Walden Trophy for his play, After I'm Gone. His first association with the Grand Theatre was in 1989 with One o'clock From the House, since then he has had over 40 productions staged there.

Vickery also has close links with the Parc and Dare Theatre, in Treorchy. He uses his remarkable ear for dialogue to explore the secret passions and quiet desperations of suburban and working-class life, often tackling taboo subjects. As a performer Frank has appeared three times at the Grand in pantomime and many times in his own plays. He has also written extensively for radio and TV. These are the productions he has staged at the Grand Theatre:

1989 – March 2: One O'clock From The House, June 26: One O'clock From The House, June 29: Breaking The String
1990 – March 5: Family Planning, October 15: Easy Terms
1991 – February 4: All's Fair, October 28: A Kiss On The Bottom
1992 – February 17: Triple bill of After I'm Gone, After Eight and A Night Out, July 23: Sleeping With Mickey Mouse
1993 – February 15: A Night On The Tiles, August 4: Family Planning, November 8: Trivial Pursuits
1994 – May 25: Loose Ends, September 12: Breaking The String
1995 – July 4: Roots And Wings, August 1 Family Planning, October 3: Love Forty
1996 – September 16: Easy Terms
1997 – November 3: One O'clock From The House
1998 – March 18: Family Planning, September 26: Pullin' The Wool, November 23: Loose Ends
1999 – February 22: A Kiss On The Bottom, October 5: A Night On The Tiles
2000 – February 15: Three of the Best, a series of three one act plays, September 26: All's Fair, October 31: Roots and Wings

2001 – May 1: Family Planning,
September 18: Erogenous Zones
2002 – March 26: Trivial Pursuits,
June 14: Side-By-Side by Stephen Sondheim
2003 – May 6: Spanish Lies, October 28: Tonto Evans
2004 – April 14: Side-By-Side by Stephen Sondheim
June 8: Pullin' The Wool, November 2: Love Forty
2005 – May 11: One O'clock From The House,
November 5: All Through The Night followed by Sleeping With Mickey Mouse
2006 – May 16: A Kiss On The Bottom,
November 14: Family Planning
2007 – May 15: Granny Annie,
September 25: A Night On The Tiles
2008 – May 20: Roots And Wings,
September 30: Erogenous Zones
2009 – May 5: Trivial Pursuits, Oct 27: Tonto Evans
2010 – May 4: Loose Ends, Oct 26: Barkin'

Ian Dickens Productions

Former actor turned director/producer Ian Dickens formed his own company in 1990. Initially he produced Shakespeare, which he also directed and acted in. He then moved into more commercial theatre and has produced over 180 plays, from comedies to dramas to the classics and pantomimes in over 150 theatres. He first approached Grand Theatre manager Gary Iles, to reintroduce a repertory season at the theatre in 1997. Rep was so much a staple of the successful John Chilvers era that had been missing since the late 1980s. On getting the green light from Gary, Ian assembled a group of professional stage actors and put on a season of four plays starting with Educating Rita on July 29, 1997 just a few days after the theatre's centenary. The success of the season led to another in 1998 this time with five plays, then again in 1999. Gradually the tradition of repertory theatre at Swansea was re-established. In 2010 Ian brought his 70th production there, although the format is slightly different today as each play is a touring production and will have a headlining TV name. Nevertheless it provides the opportunity to see locally, a pick and mix of drama, comedy and murder mysteries, which would otherwise only be available in London's West End. Popular performers to have appeared in Ian Dickens Productions include Leslie Grantham, Hannah Waterman, David Janson, Sabina Franklyn, David Callister, Frazer Hines, Giles Watling, Deborah Watling, Dilys Watling, Jonathan Morris, Carmen Silvera, David Griffin, Ruth Madoc, Fenella Fielding and countless others. Special mention must also go to technical director David North and productions co-ordinator and director Caroline Burnett who have been with Ian since the beginning and help keep things running like a well oiled machine. Today Ian Dickens Productions have more than seven touring productions on the road at any one time. Ian Dickens productions at the Grand:

1997 – July 29: Educating Rita, August 5: Communicating Doors, August 12: Spider's Web, September 2: The Dresser
1998 – July 21: Don't Dress For Dinner, July 28: How The Other Half Lives, August 4: Dial M For Murder, August 11: What The Butler Saw, August 18: And Then There Were None
1999 – July 27: Dangerous Obsession, August 3: Round And Round The Garden, August 10: Charley's Aunt Aug (This play was first performed at The Grand almost 100 years previously in week of October 9 1899), August 17: The Unexpected Guest, August 24: No Sex Please We're British, November 2: Abigail's Party
2000 – July 18: Spring And Port Wine, July 25: Deathtrap, August 1: Stagestruck, August 8: Wife Begins at Forty, August 15: Murder At The Vicarage
2001 – July 17: Rebecca, July 24: Table Manners, July 31: Night Must Fall, August 7: A Murder Is Announced, August 14: Run For Your Wife
2002 – May 7: Rope, July 16: When We Are Married, July 23: Living Together, July 30: The Ghost Train, August 6: One For The Road, August 13: Double Double
2003 – July 15: Sailor Beware, July 22: My Cousin Rachel, July 29: It Runs In The Family, August 5: Trap For A Lonely Man, August 12: The Importance Of Being Earnest, August 19: The Decorator
2004 – July 20: Blithe Spirit, July 27: Killing Time, August 3: Out Of Order, August 10: The Turn Of The Screw, August 17: Outside Edge
2005 – July 26: Table Manners, August 2: Present Laughter, August 9: Jane Eyre, August 16: Just Desserts, August 23: I'll Be Back Before Midnight, August 30: Caught In The Net
2006 – August 1 Bedroom Farce, August 8: Wuthering Heights, August 15: Funny Money, August 22: A Party To Murder, August 29 Star Quality
2007 – July 24 Cash On Delivery, July 31: The Decorator, August 7 The Secretary Bird, August 14: Dangerous Corner, August 21: Dead Guilty
2008 – July 22: See How They Run, July 29: The Business Of Murder, August 5: Daisy Pulls It Off, August 12: Don't Look Now (cancelled), August 19: Run For Your Wife
2009 – July 21: Strictly Murder, July 28: Rattle Of A Simple Man, August 4: The Tart and The Vicar's Wife, August 11: Write Me A Murder, August 18: Fools Paradise
2010 – July 20: The Late Edwina Black, July 27: It's Never Too Late, August 3: Inside Job, August 10: Love's A Luxury, August 17: Murdered To Death

The Wales Theatre Company

For many years South Wales lacked a theatre company specialising in large-scale projects. The Wales Theatre Company, born out of discussions with Swansea City Council and operating out of the Grand Theatre, was formed to fill that gap, with the support of The Welsh Assembly Government, The Arts Council of Wales, and Swansea City Council. Under Milk Wood, the opening production, with Matthew Rhys as first voice, marked the 50th anniversaries of both Dylan Thomas' death and the first stage/radio performances of the play. The production toured Wales, before embarking on a round of major cities and theatres throughout the UK in 2004. In May a parallel production was mounted in Hamburg and toured Germany for three months that autumn. Set up by acclaimed and award winning director Michael Bogdanov, The Welsh Theatre Company enjoyed critical acclaim with each of its productions until sadly, in 2009, the company was forced to close, blaming dwindling funding, which made future productions untenable.

Wales Theatre Company productions were:

2003 – Under Milk Wood
2004 – Under Milk Wood, Shakespeare (Cymbeline, Twelfth Night, The Merchant Of Venice)
2005 – Amazing Grace, Hamlet
2006 – A Child's Christmas In Wales, A Christmas Carol, Amazing Grace
2007 – Contender, The Servant Of Two Masters
2008 – Romeo And Juliet
2009 – The Thorn Birds A Musical

Uplands Arts – Swansea's Gilbert and Sullivan Society

The society started life in Pantygwydr Church in 1942 as the Brynmill and Uplands Youth Club. Under the guiding hand of Rev H J Flowers they provided such activities as handicrafts, gym and drama. The first show, The Gondoliers, opened on February 17, 1943 and played to enthusiastic applause for four nights, under the inspiration of the late Mrs. Reggie Morgan and Mr Jim Barlow. In 1949 the annual production was moved to the Llewellyn Hall, in the YMCA under the new name, Uplands Arts, where it remained for many years, except for a brief stay in Bryn Road Scout HQ, the Patti Pavilion became the new, larger venue for three years before the society moved to its current home, the 320 seat, amphitheatre-style Taliesin Theatre, where the intimate atmosphere and excellent facilities suit G&S and Uplands Arts ideally. Past society patrons have included Patrick Moore, OBE and the late Donald Adams, who, right up until the time of his death, took an active role in supporting the society. It was very proud of one of its current and long serving members, Bronwen Evans, when at the 1998 Buxton International G&S festival she was given the award for 'Best Female Performance of the Festival', for her portrayal of Rose Maybud in the festival production of Ruddigore. Then at the Y2K festival, she eclipsed this achievement by not only winning the same award again, but also winning the title of Best Female Voice of the Festival for the same performance, the first time this has ever been done. Former members of Uplands Arts who have performed in the West End include: Lee David Bowen and Claire Louise Hammacott. Other ex-members who have turned professional include Michael Gunney, who has toured with the English National Opera, and Laura Rogers, who appeared on TV with Pete Postlethwaite in The Sins and also series seven of Bad Girls as Sheena Williams.

Full list of productions:

1943 – The Gondoliers
1944 – The Mikado/ Trial By Jury
1945 – The Pirates Of Penzance
1946 – The Yeoman Of The Guard
1947 – Princess Ida
1948 – The Gondoliers
1949 – HMS Pinafore
1950 – The Mikado
1951 – The Yeoman Of The Guard
1952 – Iolanthe
1953 – The Gondoliers
1954 – The Mikado
1955 – Patience
1956 – The Pirates Of Penzance/Trial By Jury
1957 – Iolanthe
1958 – The Yeoman Of The Guard
1959 – The Gondoliers
1960 – The Mikado
1961 – Princess Ida
1962 – Ruddigore
1963 – HMS Pinafore/Trial By Jury
1964 – Iolanthe
1965 – The Yeoman Of The Guard
1966 – Sorcerer
1967 – The Mikado
1968 – Princess Ida
1969 – The Gondoliers
1970 – Ruddigore
1971 – Iolanthe
1972 – The Pirates Of Penzance
1973 – Sorcerer
1974 – The Mikado
1975 – The Yeoman Of The Guard
1976 – The Gondoliers
1977 – Patience
1978 – HMS Pinafore/Trial By Jury
1979 – Iolanthe
1980 – Princess Ida

1981 – The Pirates Of Penzance
1982 – The Mikado
1983 – Ruddigore
1984 – The Gondoliers
1985 – The Yeoman Of The Guard
1986 – The Sorcerer
1987 – The Mikado
1988 – The Pirates Of Penzance
1989 – Iolanthe
1990 – Ruddigore
1991 – HMS Pinafore/Trial By Jury
1992 – The Gondoliers
1993 – Patience
1994 – The Yeoman Of The Guard
1995 – The Mikado
1996 – The Sorcerer
1997 – The Pirates Of Penzance
1998 – Princess Ida
1999 – Iolanthe, 2000 – Utopia Limited
2001 – HMS Pinafore/Trial By Jury
2002 – Ruddigore
2003 – The Gondoliers
2004 – The Yeoman Of The Guard
2005 – The Mikado
2006 – The Grand Duke
2007 – The Pirates Of Penzance
2008 – Iolanthe
2009 – Patience
2010 – The Gondoliers

Cockett Amateur Operatic Society

Founded as Cockett Church Gilbert and Sullivan Society by Fred Secombe, the brother of Sir Harry Secombe in 1962 they now produce their annual show at the Taliesin Theatre, Swansea University and have moved away from the normal amateur shows towards musical theatre productions. The vibrant society is well supported and is currently directed by Kath Rice, the daughter of the late David Thomas MBE. In 2010 they became the first society in Wales to produce Beauty and the Beast.

Full list of productions:

1963 – The Pirates of Penzance
1964 – The Mikado
1965 – The Gondoliers
1966 – Utopia Ltd
1967 – Iolanthe
1968 – The Yeoman of the Guard
1969 – The Grand Duke
1970 – The Pirates of Penzance / Trial By Jury
1971 – Princess Ida
1972 – HMS Pinafore / Cox & Box
1973 – The Gondoliers
1974 – The Sorcerer
1975 – The Mikado
1976 – Ruddigore
1977 – The Yeoman of The Guard
1978 – The Pirates of Penzance
1979 – Patience
1980 – HMS Pinafore / Trial By Jury
1981 – La Belle Helene
1982 – Princess Ida
1983 – Fiddler On The Roof
1984 – The Music Man
1985 – Show Boat
1986 – Summer Song
1987 – Oklahoma
1988 – The Pajama Game
1989 – Kismet
1990 – My Fair Lady
1991 – Oliver
1992 – Fiddler On The Roof
1993 – Pickwick
1994 – Chess
1995 – Calamity Jane
1996 – Mame
1997 – Annie
1998 – Kiss Me Kate
1999 – Guys and Dolls
2000 – Anything Goes
2001 – Half A Sixpence
2002 – The New Pirates of Penzance
2003 – Me & My Girl
2004 – Hot Mikado
2005 – Honk!
2006 – Summer Holiday
2007 – Jekyll & Hyde
2008 – Oklahoma
2009 – My Fair Lady
2010 – Beauty and the Beast.

Sir Harry Secombe Trust

The trust was founded by Louise Cohen and Robert Francis-Davies in 2002 in memory of Sir Harry Secombe. It was set up with the aim of providing the youth of Swansea and surrounding districts with quality tuition in all aspects of musical theatre and the opportunity for them to further themselves in performing arts. Based at the Grand Theatre they perform two shows a year on the main stage plus several smaller productions in its arts wing. The quality of these productions is remarkable given the age of the performers.

Full list of productions:

2002 – The Wizard Of Oz
2003 – Honk, 2003 – West Side Story
2004 – Sound Of Music, Little Shop Of Horrors
2005 – My Fair Lady, Singing In The Rain
2006 – Bugsy Malone, Fame, Jungle Book
2007 – The Wizard of Oz, We Will Rock You, Aladdin

2008 – Honk, Summer Holiday, The Aristocats
2009 – Into The Woods JR, Footloose
2010 – Billy Elliot

Penyrheol Light Operatic Society

Penyrheol Light Operatic Society was formed in 1988. Jac Jones was musical director, later president and David Thomas was director. The society was based in Penyrheol School and rehearsed and performed in its theatre. They performed operetta in their early days, with Merry Widow as the first performance. Pat Hart started directing in 1997 having been a member from 1988 to 1992. Roger Hart was appointed musical director in 1999 and this marked a move away from operetta to musicals. The society moved to the Taliesin Theatre in 2004.

Full list of productions:

1988 – The Merry Widow
1989 – Die Fledermaus
1990 – Orpheus In The Underworld
1991 – Gypsy Princess
1992 – Naughty Marietta
1993 – Gypsy Baron
1994 – The Desert Song
1995 – Goodnight Vienna
1996 – Carmen The Musical
1997 – Die Fledermaus
1998 – The Student Prince
1999 – Carousel
2000 – Fiddler On The Roof
2001 – South Pacific
2002 – The Music Man
2003 – The Pajama Game
2004 – A Funny Thing Happened On The Way To The Forum,
2005 – Calamity Jane
2006 – Sweet Charity
2007 – Seven Brides For Seven Brothers
2008 – Bugsy Malone
2009 – The Wizard Of Oz
2010 – South Pacific

Port Talbot and District Amateur Operatic Society

Port Talbot and District Amateur Operatic Society was started in 1947 by Mrs Aurelia Vowles John. In the intervening years the society has gone from strength to strength. Assisted by her deputy, Mr Norman John, who later became the society's musical director and then honorary patron, Mrs John took the society from its initial venue at the New Hall, Aberavon, via Margam College, to Sandfields comprehensive school hall. Each change of venue offered more modern facilities enabling the society to present shows, which would have previously been impossible to stage. In 1987, the society performed its first show at the Princess Royal Theatre. For the playing members, the stage was huge in comparison to what they had previously been used to, and for the first time the producer David Thomas, who served the society for 35 years in the role, did not have to worry about the lack of space available to him. The society's annual productions (and its Youth Theatre's annual productions) are still performed at the theatre and it is hard to imagine them staging their shows elsewhere. In addition to moving to different performance venues, the society's home has also changed many times along the way. For many years, in common with most musical societies at the time, they had nowhere to call home; rehearsals were held in various school halls, member's homes and even in the storeroom of a cycle shop! Then, in the early 1970s, courtesy of the former West Glamorgan County Council, the society was given the use of a building at the Eastern Schools complex, Taibach. It boasted large modern rooms and excellent facilities. However, a few short years later, much to the disappointment of members the building was declared unfit for the purpose, and the society was again without a place to call home. Following this the society set about finding an appropriate building to become their headquarters and eventually a run-down building behind Taibach Library was found. The Society first leased and improved it, then purchased it and turned it into a comfortable, up-to-date facility. The society is going from strength to strength. The senior society's annual production takes place in April each year, with the Youth Theatre's production in October.

Full list of productions:

1947 – Pirates Of Penzance
1948 – The Gondoliers
1949 – The Mikado
1950 – The Yeoman Of The Guard
1951 – Iolanthe
1952 – Patience
1953 – A Waltz Dream
1954 – Katinka
1955 – The Lilac Domino
1956 – The Gypsy Baron
1957 – The Quaker Girl
1958 – The Student Prince
1959 – The Desert Song
1960 – Goodnight Vienna
1961 – The Gondoliers
1962 – New Moon
1963 – The Merry Widow
1964 – The Arcadians
1965 – White Horse Inn
1966 – Naughty Marietta

1967 – Magyar Melody
1968 – Calamity Jane
1969 – Rose Marie
1970 – The Vagabond King
1971 – The Student Prince
1972 – Die Fledermaus
1973 – The Desert Song
1974 – Music For All (including Pirates Of Penzance)
1975 – Kings Rhapsody
1976 – Land Of Smiles
1977 – The Merry Widow
1978 – Carousel
1979 – A Waltz Dream
1980 – Fiddler On The Roof
1981 – Oklahoma
1982 – White Horse Inn
1983 – South Pacific
1984 – Brigadoon
1985 – My Fair Lady
1986 – The Great Waltz
1987 – The Music Man
1988 – Annie Get Your Gun
1989 – Half A Sixpence
1990 – Showboat
1991 – The Desert Song
1992 – Hello Dolly
1993 – Irene
1994 – Oklahoma
1995 – The Pajama Game
1996 – Charlie Girl
1997 – Carousel
1998 – Fiddler On The Roof
1999 – Oliver
2000 – Mame
2001 – Me And My Girl
2002 – Brigadoon
2003 – Anything Goes
2004 – South Pacific
2005 – Chess
2006 – Hello Dolly
2007 – Crazy For You
2008 – Calamity Jane
2009 – My Fair Lady
2010 – Oklahoma

Port Talbot Little Theatre

During the 1930's, Leo Lloyd gathered a group of people together in Port Talbot with an interest in theatre and drama. They became known as The Thespians and successfully entertained audiences in the town until they disbanded after the outbreak of the Second World War in 1939. Leo Lloyd, keen to keep drama alive, formed another group after the war and called it the Port Talbot Drama Club which evolved into Port Talbot Little Theatre in 1959 and has have been delighting audiences ever since. Originally the group performed in small halls, but now it uses the large stage of the modern Princess Royal Theatre.

1955 – Children To Bless You
1956 – Antigone
1957 – Night Must Fall, Torch Bearers, Touchwood
1958 – By A Hand Unknown, The Same Sky
1959 – Plaintiff In A Pretty Hat, Simon And Laura
1960 – All My Sons
1961 – The More The Merrier, Treble Chance, The Distant Drum, The Dark Lady Of The Sonnets, The Rehearsal
1962 – No details
1963 – A Man For All Seasons, Life With Father
1964 – Private Lives, Druid's Rest
1965 – The Glass Menagerie, Brush With a Body
1966 – A Letter From The General, The Bride And The Bachelor, The Flowering Cherry
1967 – Goodnight Mrs Puffin, The Reluctant Debutante, As Long As They're Happy
1968 – The Breadwinner, Tartuffe
1969 – Look Out For The Catch, Haul For The Shore
1970 – Boeing Boeing, Book Of The Month
1971 – Cat In The Bag, Under Milk Wood, Ride A Cock Horse
1972 – The Biggest Thief In Town, Toad In The Hole
1973 – The Man Most Likely To, Halfway Up A Tree
1974 – The Reluctant Peer
1975 – An Inspector Calls, Portrait Of Murder
1976 – Busybody
1977 – The Day After The Fair, Shadow In The Sun
1978 – The Enquiry, Lloyd George Knew My Father
1979 – No Time For Fig Leaves, Spring And Port Wine
1980 – And Suddenly It's Spring, When We Are Married
1981 – On Monday Next, I'll Get My Man
1982 – The Love Match, Blithe Spirit
1983 – Hobson's Choice, Ring Round The Moon
1984 – Caught On The Hop, Night Must Fall
1985 – Under Milk Wood, Separate Tables
1986 – Fish Out Of Water, Gaslight
1987 – Play On, Outside Edge
1988 – Post Horn Gallop, When We Are Married
1989 – Deathtrap, Beyond A Joke
1990 – Dangerous Corner, My Giddy Aunt
1991 – One O'clock From The House, See How They Run
1992 – How The Other Half Loves, The Late Edwina Black
1993 – Off The Hook, Night Watch
1994 – One For The Pot, Present Laughter
1995 – Family Planning, Move Over Mrs Markham
1996 – Run For Your Wife, Big Bad Mouse
1997 – Out Of Order
1998 – Trivial Pursuits, Murdered To Death
1999 – Funny Money, The Man Most Likely To
2000 – A Murder Is Announced, Rumours
2001 – When We Are Married, Two And Two Together

2002 – You're Only Young Twice, Stepping Out
2003 – A Sting In The Tale, One O'clock From The House
2004 – Cash On Delivery, 'Allo 'Allo
2005 – It Could Be Anyone Of Us, A Chorus Of Disapproval
2006 – I'll get My Man, Pullin' The Wool
2007 – Dad's Army, Beyond A Joke
2008 – Dinner Ladies, Tiptoe Through The Tombstones
2009 – The Titfield Thunderbolt, Love Begins At Fifty
2010 – The Vicar Of Dibley.

Taibach People's Theatre

Taibach People's Theatre was an offshoot of Port Talbot Little Theatre, initially called Taibach Young People's Theatre. Its guiding light was Leo Lloyd and its first production took place in 1959. Called Taibach People's Theatre after 1964 it produced dramas and comedies until the early 1990s.

1964 – Tons Of Money, Kith And Kin.
1965 – Blithe Spirit, The Diary Of Anne Frank
1966 – Lord Arthur Saville's Crime, Night Was Our Friend
1967 – Pickle In Paradise, No Escape, Wild Goose Chase
1968 – Meet Me By Moonlight, Lady precious Stream, And So To Bed
1969 – The Shifting Heart, Fools Paradise
1970 – A Stranger In The Tea, Big Bad Mouse,
1971 – Wanted: One Body, The Devils,
1972 – Every Other Evening, The Caucasian Chalk Circle
1973 – The Same Sky
1974 – How's The World Treating You, The Rape Of The Belt
1975 – Doctor In Love
1976 –
1977 –
1978 –
1979 –
1980 –
1981 –
1982 –
1983 – The Times Table
1984 – Pools Paradise
1985 –
1986 –
1987 –
1988 – Key for Two
1989 –
1990 – Tag Match
1991 – The Odd Couple

Taibach Young People's Theatre

1959 – Sailor Beware, Is Your Honeymoon Really Necessary?
1960 – Dry Rot, Hot Summer Night
1961 – Tilly Of Bloomsbury, The Ghost Train
1962 – Anna Christie, Watch It Sailor
1963 – When We Are Married, The Crucible

Briton Ferry Little Theatre

Formed in 1949, like many other groups Briton Ferry Little Theatre has had various homes over the years. First there was the Public Hall in Briton Ferry, then the former Palace Kinema in 1956. This was a strong and settled period in their history until, with the Kinema's demolition, they were forced to move to Cwrt Sart School in 1978. They produced two plays a year there until 1986 when they were forced to move again. There then followed an unsettled period with no home to call their own and they became strolling players. In 1993 they were afforded the opportunity to move into Briton Ferry Community Hall where they have been ever since. Notable names that have performed with the theatre are Robert Blythe and Bruce Miller. They also organised a festival of drama featuring James Bolam, Valentine Dyall, Ian Hendry, Annie Ross and Robert Lacey.

Full list of previous productions

1949 – No Medals
Thirteenth Chair
Quiet Weekend
Random Harvest
George And Margaret
The Heiress
The Importance of Being Ernest
September Tide
Family Portrait
Deep Blue Sea
Man In Grey
Beside The Seaside
On Monday Next
Maiden Ladies
Jinny Morgan
Wind Of Heaven
While The Sun Shines
Seagulls Of Sorrento
The Vigil
Job For The Boy
1960 –The Long And The Short And The Tall
All My Sons
Friends And Neighbours
Bride And Bachelor
Home And The Heart
Cradle Song
Sound Of Murder
Power Without Glory
Blithe Spirit
Hot Summer Night
Happiest Days Of Your Life
Love In A Mist
Duet For Two Hands
Intent To Murder
Diary Of Anne Frank

See How They Run
Billy Liar
1965 – Under Milk Wood
Roar Like A Dove
Woman In A Dressing Gown
The Long And The Short And The Tall
Fools Rush In
Dry Rot
Murder At The Vicarage
The Man
The Amorous Prawn
Johnny Belinda
Who Is Sylvia?
Tell Tale Murder
Goodbye Charlie
Night Must Fall (Youth Theatre)
1969 – Dead On Nine, , Sailor Beware!
1970 – Journey's End, Cat On The Fiddle
Let Sleeping Wives Lie
A Man For All Seasons (Youth Theatre)
All For Mary
Trap For A Lonely Man
Man Alive
Chase Me Comrade
Alfie
Not Now Darling
The Anniversary
Doctor In The House
Spring And Port Wine
I Am A Camera
Wanted – One Body
Uproar In The House
Shadow In The Sun
All Things Bright And Beautiful
One For The Pot
Suddenly At Home
Bang Bang Beirut
Friends And Neighbours
Barefoot In The Park
Lord Arthur Saville's Crime
The Odd Couple
Wishing Well
Uproar In The House
Come Blow Your Horn
Two and Two Make Sex
How The Other Half Loves
Round And Round The Garden
Trap For A Lonely Man
She's Done It Again
A Lady Mislaid
The Unvarnished Truth
Outside Edge
One For The Pot
Cabaret
They Don't Grow On Trees
Billy Liar
Intent To Murder
Taking Steps
Whose Life Is It Anyway?
Abigail's Party
Love In A Mist
Sweeny Todd
Toad Of Toad Hall
Treasure Island
Robin Hood
Dick Turpin
Wizard Wacky Meets King Arthur
Christopher Columbus
Gran's Will Be Done
My Three Angels
The Real Inspector Hound
1997 – Sweeny Todd, Post Horn Gallop, Pool's Paradise
1998 – Queen Of Hearts, The Unexpected Guest, My Friend Miss Flint
1999 – Red Riding Hood, In The Valley Of Past Shadows, The Chalk Garden
2000 – Sleeping Beauty, Caught On The Hop, After Eeyore
2001 – Dick Turpin, Family Planning, Barefoot in The Park
2002 – Wind In The Willows, They Don't Grow On Trees, Pack Of Lies
2003 – Wizard Wacky Meets King Arthur, Murder In Play, Holiday Snap
2004 – Dick Whittington, Last Tango In Little Grimley/ Last Panto In Little Grimley, An Inspector Calls
2005 – Christopher Columbus, Fat Lady Sings In Little Grimley, Nasty Things Murder, Curtain Up On Murder
2006 – Kidnapped At Christmas, Anagram Of Murder
2007 – The Tinderbox, London Suite, The Handyman
2008 – Robinson Crusoe, Make It Murder, The Guys
2009 – Jack And The Beanstalk, A Month Of Sundays, The Crucible
2010 – Sleeping Beauty.

Briton Ferry Musical Theatre Company

The company was established in 1948 as The Briton Ferry Amateur Operatic and Choral Society. It had been reformed from the old society, which had formed in the early 1920s and disbanded in 1938 prior to the outbreak of World War Two. Rehearsals and meetings were held at the Social Services hall, Cwm-y-Dwr, just off Neath Road and almost opposite where the company headquarters is today. The new company's first production, The Pirates Of Penzance was staged at the Public Hall in Briton Ferry in January 1949, with production costs about £700, which was a considerable amount of money at the time. It was a success and returned a healthy £450 profit, giving the society a fantastic start. In 1952 they were forced to seek alternative arrangements for rehearsal facilities as the Cwm-y-Dwr Hall became unavailable. It was decided that a permanent home was required and a plot of land was acquired at Villiers Gardens, together with the Whitford Hall, which stood on a site now occupied by Briton Ferry Roundabout. Throughout the summer of 1953 and under the supervision of contractors, members painstakingly dismantled the hall and re-erected it on the new site. At last the society had a home. Sadly in 1962 Balalaika was the last show staged at the Public Hall in Briton Ferry, as it was destined to be demolished. The following year saw them stage A Country Girl at The Gwyn Hall in Neath where they would stay until Oklahoma in 2006. The 1970s and 80s were a period of sustained growth and numbers. By 1994 it became obvious that the rehearsal hall was on its last legs, despite constant repairs. It was also proving to be too small for the needs of the flourishing society. A new larger home was sought to enable them to build their own sets and props, and make its own costumes as well, in the aim to achieve a more self-sufficient operating structure. The dream was realised in 1995 when together with a grant from the Foundation of Sport and the Arts, the society purchased the Flag Centre at Neath Road, Briton Ferry which was previously the Welfare Hall of the old steel works and even further back the original Wesleyan Church built in 1856. The next few years saw considerable work done to improve the interior and exterior of the new home with the help of grant assistance from the Arts Council Of Wales lottery fund and other smaller organisations. Above all that however was the hard work provided by the members of the Society. 2003 saw the need to change the public perception of the society's identity and they boldly changed its name to Briton Ferry Musical Theatre Company. In 2008 change came again as with the devastating loss of the Gwyn Hall, they now have a temporary new home at The Princess Royal Theatre in Port Talbot.

Full list of previous productions:

1949 – The Pirates Of Penzance
1950 – Merrie England
1951 – Tom Jones
1952 – Bless The Bride
1953 – The Vagabond King
1954 – Waltz Without End
1955 – Pink Champagne
1956 – Night In Venice
1957 – Land Of Smiles
1958 – Maritza
1958 – The Belle Of New York
1959 – Wedding In Paris
1960 – Naughty Marietta
1961 – Pajama Game
1962 – Balalaika
1963 – A Country Girl
1964 – New Moon
1965 – Rose Marie
1966 – Bless The Bride
1967 – Goodnight Vienna
1968 – White Horse Inn
1969 – Oklahoma
1970 – Sweethearts
1971 – Hello Dolly
1972 – Carousel
1973 – Viva Mexico
1974 – The Desert Song
1975 – The Maid Of The Mountains
1976 – Brigadoon
1977 – Calamity Jane
1978 – The Card
1979 – Lady Be Good
1980 – King's Rhapsody
1981 – The Music Man
1982 – Oklahoma
1983 – Charley Girl
1984 – Annie Get Your Gun
1985 – The Wizard Of Oz
1986 – The King And I
1987 – Hans Anderson
1988 – Gigi
1989 – Underneath The Arches
1990 – Oliver
1991 – The Sound Of Music
1992 – Anything Goes
1993 – Fiddler On The Roof
1994 – Guys And Dolls
1995 – Blitz
1996 – Hello Dolly
1997 – Half A Sixpence
1998 – The Pirates Of Penzance
1998 – The Boyfriend
1999 – Pickwick
2000 – Oliver
2001 – Carousel
2002 – My Fair Lady
2003 – Annie
2004 – The Music Man
2005 – Me And My Girl
2006 – Oklahoma
2007 – The Boyfriend
2008 – The King And I
2009 – Gigi
2010 – Summer Holiday

Neath Little Theatre

Neath Little Theatre began life as Neath Dramatic Society. It was founded by the town's Billings family in 1929. It became a formal society and changed its name in 1935. The theatre group was one of the few to continue performing plays throughout the Second World War. Its home is at its own purpose built theatre at Westernmoor Road, Neath. Internationally famous actor Michael Sheen appeared there in the early days of his career.

1936 – A Murder has been Arranged, The Devil's Disciple, A Bill of Divorcement
1937 – Lilies of the Field, Coronation production of five one-act plays: Military Medal; A Villa for Sale; The House with the Twisty Windows; Little Women; The Poacher, Bird in Hand
1938 – You Never Can Tell, Nine Till Six, Land of my Fathers
1939 – Mirror to Elizabeth, School for Husbands
1941 – Fresh Fields, Short Story
1942 – The Silver Chord
1943 – Ladies in Waiting, Ladies in Retirement
1944 – Tony Draws a Horse, Night Must Fall
1945 – Robert's Wife, The Light of Heart
1946 – They Came to a City
1947 – Inherit the Wind, The Shining Hour
1948 – Nine Till Six, The Unguarded Hour, A Man's House
1949 – The Distaff Side, Eden End, Love in a Mist
1950 – Duet for Two Hands, Rebecca, The Skin Game
1951 – Deep are the Roots, Mocking Bird
1952 – Captain Cavallo, The Late Edwina Black, The Righteous are Bold
1953 – The Strange Case of Blondie White, If This be Error, Coronation production: Frost on the Rose, Safe Harbour
1954 – Treasure Hunt, A Lady Mislaid, Madam Tic Tac
1955 – The Happy Marriage, Forced Landing, Berkeley Square
1956 – Ten Little Niggers, Dear Charles, Tartuffe
1957 – Toad of Toad Hall, Message for Margaret, Bonaventure
1958 – Intent to Murder, Book of the Month, Murder in the Cathedral, After my Fashion
1959 – The Living Room, My Three Angels, The River Line, Look Back in Anger
1960 – Sailor Beware, Summer of the Seventeenth Doll, Breath of Spring, And So to Bed, Affairs of State
1961 – Waiting for Gillian, Gigi, Not in the Book, Traveller Without Luggage
1962 – Farewell, Farewell Eugene, Separate Tables, Watch it Sailor!, A Taste of Honey, Love's a Luxury
1963 – Heartbreak House, The Aspern Papers, Offshore Island, Sound of Murder
1964 – The Keep, Brides of March, Double Yolk, His Excellency
1965 – Puss in Boots, The Shadow of Doubt, Goodnight Mrs Puffin, Shred of Evidence
1966 – Aladdin, Blithe Spirit, The Beaux-Stratagem, Winter Journey, House by the Lake
1967 – Sleeping Beauty, The Gazebo, Midsummer Mink, Silver Wedding, The Importance of Being Earnest
1968 – Cinderella, Semi Detached, The Rainmaker, The Anniversary, See How They Run
1969 – Jack and the Beanstalk, The Highest House on the Mountain, Shadow in the Sun, Boeing-Boeing, Touch of Fear
1970 – Queen of Hearts, The Burning Glass, School for Wives, Quiet Weekend, Romanoff and Juliet, When We Are Married
1971 – Babes in the Wood, Spring 1600, The Poker Session, Letter from the General, Person Unknown
1972 – Mother Goose, Home and the Heart, Birds on the Wing, The White Sheep of the Family, An Inspector Calls
1973 – Dick Whittington, The Killing of Sister George, Off the Hook, The House on the Cliff
1974 – Puss in Boots, The Queen and the Rebels, The Man Most Likely To, The Bride and the Bachelor
1975 – Aladdin, Who Killed Santa Clause?, Relatively Speaking, The Enquiry
1976 – Cinderella, Big Bad Mouse, The Day after the Fair, Move Over Mrs Markham
1977 – Robinson Crusoe, Gaslight, Lloyd George Knew my Father, The Children's Hour
1978 – The Teahouse of the August Moon, Portrait of Murder, The Corn is Green, Ladies in Retirement, Claudius the Bee
1979 – The Girl in the Freudian Slip, Roar Like a Dove, Barefoot in the Park
1980 – Dangerous Corner, The Rape of the Belt, The Winslow Boy, Bell, Book and Candle
1981 – Sweeny Todd, Don't Start Without Me, A bedfull of Foreigners, Miracle Worker, Table Manners
1982 – Pink String and Sealing Wax, Can you hear me at the Back?, All My Sons, Under Milk Wood
1983 – Time and Time Again, A Time to Kill, Come Blow Your Horn, Juno and the Paycock
1984 – A Murder is Announced, Beyond a Joke, Chase Me Comrade, House Guest
1985 – Key for Two, The Restless Evil, Lock Up Your Daughters
1986 – Plaza Suite, Death Trap, Hobson's Choice, Pardon Me Prime Minister
1987 – Fingers, Night Must Fall, The Shifting Heart, My Three Angels
1988 – Two and Two Make Sex, I Have Been Here Before, The Murder Game, On Golden Pond
1989 – The Odd Couple, The Happiest Days of Your Life, Educating Rita, One O'clock from the House
1990 – Philadelphia, Here I Come!, The Anniversary, Abigail's Party
1991 – 84 Charing Cross Road, Outside Edge, Last of the Red Hot Lovers, Billy Liar
1992 – The Late Christopher Bean, Veronica's Room, Touch and Go, Murder in Mind
1993 – Waltz of the Toreadors, Caught Napping, Absent Friends, September in the Rain
1994 – The Sunshine Boys, A Month of Sundays, Holiday Snap, Family Planning
1995 – Spring and Port Wine, Dead Ringer, Stags and Hens, Wait Until Dark
1996 – Arsenic and Old Lace, A Chorus of Disapproval, Go Bang Your Tambourine, A Night on the Tiles
1997 – The Prisoner of Second Avenue, A View from the Bridge, The Diary of Anne Frank, Trivial Pursuits
1998 – Bedroom Farce, Dial 'M' for Murder, Pack of Lies, Season's Greetings

The cast of Neath Opera Group's production of La Boheme at Craig-y-Nos in 1971. Bruce Dargavel is raising a glass and Anita Marvin is seated with white gloves. Anita is the mother of comedian Paul Whitehouse.

1999 – Up 'n' Under, The Business of Murder, Terra Nova, All in Good Time
2000 – Happy Jack, Dangerous Obsession, The Golden Pathway Annual
2001 – The Cemetery Club, The Wisdom of Eve, Butterflies are Free, All's Fair
2002 – The Lion in Winter, The Weekend, Breaking the String, The Prime of Miss Jean Brodie
2003 – Lucky Sods, Straight and Narrow, Silhouette, Entertaining Mr Sloane
2004 – Haywire, Forget-Me-Knot, Weekend Breaks, Thérèse Raquin
2005 – A Sting in the Tale, Sailor, Beware!, The Perfect Murder, Pastimes
2006 – Summer End, The Darling Buds of May, The Collector, Wishing Well
2007 – Quartet, Someone Else's Rainbow, The Glass Menagerie, Tonto Evans
2008 – The Unexpected Guest, Hay Fever, Pygmalion, Same Time, Next Year
2009 – The Turn of the Screw, Shut Your Eyes and Think of England, The Shape of Things, 'Allo 'Allo
2010 – The Beauty Queen of Leenane, Murder by Misadventure

Neath Amateur Operatic Society

Since its inception many people have contributed greatly to make Neath Amateur Operatic Society a success. It would be an almost impossible task to name everyone involved over the years but three men in particular have to be mentioned, namely Matthew Davies, Tom Dummer and Evan Lewis. In 1911 the three went to see a performance of Princess Ida by Swansea Amateur Operatic Society and as a result of this visit the seed was sown to start a society in Neath. Matthew Davies, a well known musician, discussed this new venture with members of his male voice choir and it was decided that a society should be formed. There was an enthusiastic response and subsequently a meeting was held at Gnoll Road Chapel schoolroom. Matthew Davies was appointed musical director and in 1912 the society staged The Mikado at Vint's Hippodrome. (later the site of the Windsor Cinema) In 1913 Neath Amateurs chose The Gondoliers as their show at the Gnoll Hall. Activities were suspended during the First World War, but 1919 saw a performance of The Yeomen of the Guard at the

Gwyn Hall. Shows continued to be staged at the Gwyn Hall until 1926 when the Gilbert and Sullivan opera Ruddigore was performed at the Gnoll Hall. In 1927 the Society entered the world of musical comedy with The Country Girl and shows such as Sibyl, Miss Hook of Holland, Princess Charming, Desert Song, A Waltz Dream, Nina Rosa and in 1938 The Maid of the Mountains. This was the last show before the outbreak of the Second World War in 1939. The society once again resumed activities in 1947 and rehearsals took place at a room above The Angel Hotel. Katinka was performed in November 1946 and hundreds of people failed to gain admission, with queues stretching from the Gwyn Hall to Bethania Baptist Chapel! In November 1949 Jerome Kern's Show Boat was staged at The Gnoll Hall. This proved to be a most ambitious project and was a great hit with the public. It was fitting that a Neath society should perform The Lisbon Story with music by Harry Parr Davies — Neath's own composer and in 1950 they held the Welsh Premiere with the composer himself making a visit. It was by now essential that the society should find its own headquarters and in 1954 the former Mechanics' Institute was purchased. Here there were better facilities for rehearsing and storage. The society's full list of productions:

1912 – The Mikado
1913 – The Gondoliers
1915 – The Pirates Of Penzance
1919 – The Yeoman Of The Guard
1920 – The Mikado
1921 – Iolanthe
1922 – Patience
1924 – Dorothy
1925 – Rose Of Persia
1926 – Ruddigore
1927 – A Country Girl
1927 – Katinka
1928 – Sybil
1929 – Miss Hook Of Holland
1930 – Princess Charming
1932 – The Desert Song
1933 – A Waltz Dream
1934 – The Yellow Mask
1936 – Nina Rosa
1938 – The Maid Of The Mountains
1946 – Katinka
1947 – Bitter Sweet
1948 – The Gypsy Princess
1949 – The Mikado
1949 – Showboat
1950 – The Lisbon Story
1951 – Magyar Melody
1952 – Chu Chin Chow
1954 – Wild Violets
1955 – Iolanthe
1955 – Kings Rhapsody
1956 – Annie Get Your Gun
1957 – The Maid Of The Mountains
1958 – Call Me Madam
1959 – The Merry Widow
1960 – The King And I
1961 – Kismet
1962 – The Vagabond King
1963 – Calamity Jane
1964 – Summer Song
1965 – La Belle Helene
1966 – Annie Get Your Gun
1967 – Orpheus In The Underworld
1968 – My Fair Lady
1969 – Song Of Norway
1970 – The Sound Of Music
1971 – The Grand Duchess Of Gerolstein
1972 – The King And I
1973 – Fiddler On The Roof
1974 – Oliver
1975 – Showboat
1976 – Mame
1977 – The Merry Widow
1978 – Die Fledermaus
1979 – Irene
1980 – Funny Girl
1981 – La Belle Helene
1982 – The Dancing Years
1983 – Hello Dolly
1984 – South Pacific
1985 – The Desert Song
1986 – Guys And Dolls
1987 – Call Me Madam
1988 – Pirates Of Penzance (Broadway version)
1989 – Mame
1990 – Robert And Elizabeth
1991 – Seven Brides For Seven Brothers
1992 – George M (Yankee Doodle Dandy)
1993 – Meet Me In St Louis
1994 – Chess
1995 – 42nd Street
1996 – Oklahoma
1997 – Gentlemen Prefer Blondes
1998 – Crazy For You
1999 – The Sound Of Music
2000 – Mack and Mabel
2001 – Scrooge The Musical
2002 – Copacabana
2003 – Hot Mikado
2003 – Jesus Christ Superstar
2004 – Aladdin
2004 – Titanic
2005 – Cinderella
2005 – Sweeney Todd
2006 – Jack And The Beanstalk
2006 – Tommy

2007 – Godspell
2008 – Scrooge The Musical
2009 – Honk (This show was cancelled just before opening night due to lack of ticket sales)
2010 – Jekyll

Swansea Youth Theatre

The Swansea Youth Theatre was founded in 1964 by a group of youngsters from Bishop Gore and Llwyn-y-Bryn Grammar schools. Originally known as the Tudor Players, the 25-strong teenage company was led by Gareth Armstrong, Eleanor Thomas and Gilly Adams. With a name change it became the very first independent youth theatre group in Wales. It thrived for 10 years and saw numerous productions, winning awards at regional drama festivals and playing two tours in Germany, based at Swansea's twin town of Mannheim. The group was the launching pad for a number of theatrical careers and a pioneer and model for the later county and regional based 'official' youth theatre companies which came to the fore in the last quarter of the 20th Century.

Welsh National Opera

The Welsh National Opera Company was the brainchild of the conductor Idloes Owen. It was originally funded by a Cardiff garage proprietor, Bill Smith, and administered by a volunteer secretary, Peggy Moreland. Its first performance was given in Cardiff on April 15, 1946 and was such a success that the company was swamped with amateurs seeking to join the chorus. All the chorus singers were amateur, as were many other members of what for years amounted to a part-time company. Drawing on the strong Welsh choral tradition, the WNO had two full choruses, one in Cardiff and the other in Swansea. Its initial Swansea seasons were at the Empire but moved to the Grand Theatre in 1957. In 1973 the chorus became professional and the WNO grew in stature until it earned itself an international reputation. It has regularly played at the Grand and its seasons continue to be one of the highlights of the Swansea theatre calendar. Its musical directors have included Warwick Braithwaite, James Lockhart, Richard Armstrong, Sir Charles Mackerras, Carlo Rizzi and Turgan Sokhiev. It is now recognised as one of Europe's great opera companies and some of its local leads include Dennis O'Neill and Rebecca Evans.

Neath Opera Group

Neath Opera Group was formed in 1960 by the late Dudley Hopkins while Vincent Thomas became its first secretary. From the beginning the artistic direction of the group was under the joint conductors Ivor John and his son Clive and the first few performances by the group took place at the Gwyn Hall from 1960 with assorted scenes from various operas, including Tosca and La Boheme. A venture of a more ambitious nature was then put forward by Dudley Hopkins. As a result, from 1963 the group transferred to Craig-y-Nos, using Madam Patti's theatre. So successful was the first Craig-y-Nos season, a tentative four-night stand, that the major work of Donizetti's Il Campanello Di Notta was later repeated in the theatre for BBC television. Over the years the seasons grew to a fortnight in length and would sell out weeks before the first night. The group was wholly self funded and relied heavily on the voluntary efforts of the members to put on these high quality performances. The principal roles were taken by professional artists from the likes of Covent Garden and Glyndebourne and cleverly were either big opera stars on the way down or fresh talent on the way up. Patrons would travel far and wide to experience the wonderful atmosphere of opera at this intimate 155-seat theatre and the Neath Opera Group provided the principality with an opportunity of experiencing the fruits of Italian opera. In 1975 they were joined by Roger Hart who along with Clive John continued with the group until its end in 1999. This came about when new owners took over Craig-y-Nos and decided they would no longer allow the theatre to be used for the annual opera fortnight and Neath Opera Group ceased with the last performance of The Merry Wives Of Windsor, although the group was unaware of that at the time and unfortunately did not have the chance to savour the last performance.

Full list of performances:

1963 – One Act – La Boheme, Il Maestro Di Capella and Il Campanello
1964 – The Tales Of Hoffman
1965 – Elisir D'Amore
1966 – La Traviata
1967 – The Count Ory
1968 –The Merry Wives Of Windsor
1969 – Faust
1970 – Martha
1971 – La Boheme
1972 – The Marriage Of Figaro
1973 – The Masked Ball
1974 – Pagliacci and The Tales Of Hoffman
1975 – Don Pasquale
1976 – The Magic Flute
1977 – The Bartered Bride
1978 – Rigoletto
1979 – The Pearl Fishers
1980 – Il Trovatore

Members of Neath Opera Group after a get-together at the Castle Hotel, Neath in the 1970s.

1981 – The Seraglio
1982 – Thomas and Sally and Dido and Aenas
1983 – Tosca
1984 – Die Fledermaus
1985 – La Boheme
1986 – No production except Gala Recital at the theatre with Dennis O'Neill accompanied by Ingrid Surgenor with chorus work by Neath Opera Group
1987 – No Production
1988 – No Production
1989 – Don Pasquale
1990 – Count Ory
1991 – Madam Butterfly
1992 – Norma
1993 – Gianni Schicchi and Il Campanello
1994 – The Bartered Bride
1995 – The Marriage Of Figaro
1996 – A Masked Ball
1997 – The Tales Of Hoffman
1998 – Tosca
1999 – The Merry Wives Of Windsor

Clydach (and Morriston) Amateur Operatic Society

Clydach and District Amateur Operatic Society was formed in 1917. Their earliest performances took place at Clydach Church Hall, later moving to the old Globe Theatre and Cinema in Clydach. In 1920 the society joined forces with the Operatic and Dramatic Society sponsored by the Mond Nickel Works Ltd., performing at the company hall for many years. In 1939 the society was suspended due to the outbreak of the Second World War. In 1982 it disbanded for four years then in 1986 reformed as Clydach and Morriston Amateur Operatic Society. The first show under the new title was Annie Get Your Gun in 1986, produced by Brian Sullivan. Brian produced every show thereafter until Godspell in 2005. The last presented by the society was Trivial Pursuits performed at Pontardawe Arts Centre in 2007.

Full list of productions:

1917 – Blodwen
1918 – Cavellera Rusticania and I Pagliacci
1919 – Faust
1920 – Blodwen
1946 – The Bohemian Girl
1948 – Maritana
1950 – Carmen
1951 – Faust
1952 – Nabucco (first performance of English translation in Britain March 20-22nd at Globe Theatre in Clydach)
1953 – Blodwen
1955 – Ernani
1957 – The Bohemian Girl
1958 – Pink Champagne
1959 – The Merry Widow
1960 – Naughty Marietta
1961 – The Gypsy Baron
1962 – Viktoria And Her Hussar
1964 – The Arcadians

1965 – The Student Prince
1966 – White Horse Inn
1968 – Ruddigore
1969 – Die Fledermaus
1970 – The Desert Song
1971 – Oliver
1973 – The Merry Widow
1974 – La Belle Helene
1975 – The Arcadians
1976 – Perchance To Dream
1977 – Fiddler On The Roof
1978 – Oklahoma
1979 – Finian's Rainbow
1980 – Carousel
1981 – Oliver
1982 – The Pajama Game
1986 – Annie Get Your Gun
1987 – The Sound Of Music
1988 – Some Enchanted Evening
1989 – The King And I
1990 – Oklahoma
1991 – Guys and Dolls
1992 – Oh! Susannah
1993 – Oliver
1994 – Fiddler On The Roof
1995 – Finian's Rainbow
1996 – Half A Sixpence
1997 – Anything Goes
1998 – Calamity Jane
1999 – A Funny Thing Happened On The Way To The Forum
2000 – Irene
2001 –The Wizard Of Oz
2002 – Oliver
2003 – South Pacific
2004 – The Boyfriend
2005 – Godspell
2006 – Return To The Forbidden Planet
2007 – Trivial Pursuits.

Melyncrythan Amateur Operatic Society

The Melyncrythan Amateur Operatic Society, Neath, was formed in 1923. They have performed annually except for the war years and a non-show year in 1980. Its formation, like many other cultural organisations, remains firmly rooted in Siloh Welsh Congregational Church Choir, Melyncrythan. The church choir was a frequent and successful competitor at Eisteddfodau. The conductress of the choir was Miss Ivy Davies, the daughter of John Davies, a successful local coal merchant and former Mayor of Neath.

Full list of productions:

1923 – Dogs Of Devon
1924 – Highwayman's Love
1925 – Rose Of Araby
1926 – La Cigale
1927 – Florodora
1928 – Our Miss Gibbs
1929 – The Arcadians
1930 – The Cingalee
1931 – The Geisha
1932 – High Jinks
1933 – Rose Marie
1934 – The Student Prince
1935 – Silver Wings
1936 – The Belle Of New York
1938 – Goodnight Vienna
1940 – The Belle Of New York
1948 – Goodnight Vienna
1949 – Sunny
1950 – Rose Marie
1951 – The New Moon
1952 – The Three Musketeers
1953 – The Desert Song
1954 – Nina Rosa
1955 – The Dubarry
1956 – Oklahoma
1957 – The Student Prince
1958 – The White Horse Inn
1959 – Rio Rita
1960 – Carousel
1961 – South Pacific
1962 – Guys And Dolls
1963 – Brigadoon
1964 – Showboat
1965 – The Music Man
1966 – The Desert Song
1967 – The Three Musketeers
1968 – Flower Drum Song
1969 – Count Of Luxembourg
1970 – Nina Rosa
1971 – Half A Sixpence
1972 – Camelot
1973 – Finian's Rainbow
1974 – Kiss Me Kate
1975 – Charley Girl
1976 – Call Me Madam
1977 – Guys And Dolls
1978 – Gigi
1979 – Half A Sixpence
1981 – Pickwick
1982 – Camelot
1983 – My Fair Lady
1984 – The Sound Of Music
1985 – Fiddler On The Roof
1986 – Carousel
1987 – Annie
1988 – Brigadoon
1989 – Irene
1990 – The New Mikado

1991 – My Fair Lady
1992 – Calamity Jane
1993 – Sweet Charity
1994 – The King And I
1995 – Billy
1996 – South Pacific
1997 – Singin' In The Rain
1998 – Me And My Girl
1999 – Annie Get Your Gun
2000 – Barnum
2001 – Pajama Game
2002 – Irene
2003 – Hello Dolly
2004 – Calamity Jane
2005 – Anything Goes
2006 – How To Succeed In Business Without Really Trying
2007 – By Jeeves
2008 – Thoroughly Modern Millie
2009 – A Slice Of Saturday Night
2010 – Annie

The Owen Money Theatre Company

The Owen Money Theatre Company was created in 2000 to produce high quality, dynamic productions of family orientated pantomimes during the winter between November and March, with a policy of promoting Welsh based and talented newcomers, supported by professional actors. Since then the company has established a proven background in successful pantomime playing at major venues in Wales: Theatre Brycheiniog, Brecon; The Coliseum Aberdare; Blackwood Miners Institute; The Lyric Carmarthen; Princess Royal Theatre, Port Talbot; Parc & Dare Theatre Treorchy; Congress Theatre, Cwmbran; the Muni Arts Centre, Pontypridd, the Grand Theatre, Swansea and the Pavilion, Porthcawl.

Full list of productions:

2000 – Aladdin
2001 – Cinderella
2002 – Jack And The Beanstalk
2003 – Dick Whittington
2004 – Aladdin
2005 – Robinson Crusoe
2006 – Peter Pan
2007 – Buttons Undone (adult panto), Jack And The Beanstalk, Cindrella
2008 – Buttons Undone (adult panto), Humpty Dumpty, Robinson Crusoe, Snow White and the Seven Dwarfs
2009 – Aladdin, Jack And The Beanstalk
2010 – Goldilocks and her Big Bear Behind, Robinson Crusoe, Dick Whittington

Cadoxton Opera Society

This society was formed by Alfie Jones and David John Lewis in 1907. They were both members of Cadoxton Church, which also supported the venture. The first production was Good Queen Bess and took place in the vicarage grounds. Subsequent performances were played at Vint's Palace in Windsor Road and then The Gwyn Hall, by which time Sir David Evans-Bevan had become the society's first president. Alfie Jones was for many years responsible for musical direction, choreography and production. The society performed grand operas only and all the demanding leading roles were sung by local people. There was so much local talent available that for decades they even had double casts. During the society's history there was never any amplification. The society became a casualty of the rising costs of putting on an annual show and in 2001 Die Fledermaus became its swansong. By this time professional artists were taking the leading roles and the large operatic orchestras fees no longer made the performances financially viable. Sadly this event, together with the demise of Neath Opera Group in 1999 – itself an off shoot of Cadoxton Opera Society – brought the performance of grand opera in Neath and District to an end.

Full list of performances:

1908 – Good Queen Bess
1910 – Martha
1911 – Maritana
1912 – Rose Of Castille
1921 – The Martyrs
1922 – Three Holy Children
1923 – Fridolin
1924 – Lurline
1926 – Carmen
1927 – The Martyrs
1928 – Fridolin
1929 – Lurline
1931 – Carmen
1932 – Il Trovatore
1933 – Ernani
1934 – Faust
1935 – Tannhauser
1936 – Carmen and La Traviata
1951 – La Traviata
1952 – Ernani
1953 – Martha
1954 – I Puritani
1955 – L'Elisir D'Amore
1956 – Aida
1957 – Mephistopheles
1958 – Carmen
1959 – I Pagliacci and Cavelleria Rusticana
1960 – Faust
1961 – The Bartered Bride

1962 – Martha
1963 – Il Trovatore
1964 – Force Of Destiny
1965 – Nabucco
1966 – The Pearl Fishers
1967 – La Favorita
1968 – Carmen
1969 – Norma
1970 – Cavelleria Rusticana and I Campanello
1971 – Samson And Delilah
1972 – L'Elisir D'Amore
1973 – Aida
1974 – La Traviata
1975 – Ernani
1976 – Faust
1977 – Lucia Di Lammermoor
1978 – Nabucco
1979 – Count Ory
1980 – Carmen
1981 – I Lombardi
1982 – L'Elisir D'Amore
1983 – Nabucco
1984 – I Pagliacci and Cavelleria Rusticana
1985 – Aida
1986 – Otello
1987 – The Pearl Fishers
1988 – Carmen
1989 – Die Freischutz
1990 – La Traviata
1991 – Faust
1992 – Martha
1993 – Nabucco
1994 – Il Trovatore
1996 – The Pearl Fishers
1997 – Ernani
1998 – La Traviata
1999 – Mephistopheles
2000 – Nabucco
2001 – Die Fledermaus.

West Glamorgan Youth Theatre

Established in 1975, under the leadership of founder director Godfrey Evans, the West Glamorgan Youth Theatre Company has built up an enviable reputation as one of the premier youth companies in Wales. The company has performed extensively within the West Glamorgan area and has undertaken national and international tours including two visits to Denmark.

Past members of the youth theatre have gone on to win Olivier and BAFTA awards, and many can be seen on television, in West End Musicals and with the larger national theatre companies. These include Joanna Page, Steffan Rhodri, Dave from Gavin and Stacey; Michael Sheen, Di Botcher, Steven Meo and Dr Who writer Russell T Davies. However, the youth theatre has never been seen merely as a training ground for the theatre, as many students have progressed to a wide range of different, equally successful careers. Whatever their profession, all former company members look back on their time with the theatre as being an exciting and vital part of their education. Following the retirement of Godfrey Evans in 1992, the youth theatre was directed for eight years by Derek Cobley and in September 2000, the development of the company was entrusted to an artistic directorate. The directorate comprised of ten youth theatre tutors with a wealth of experience within arts education, the theatre and in the direction of performance projects. Each is committed to maintaining the high standards which have characterised the work of the company. Such is the high regard in which the work of the youth theatre is held, that after local government reorganisation in 1996, the City and County of Swansea and Neath Port Talbot County Borough Council took the far sighted decision to continue facilitating the work of this nationally renowned company, thereby enabling young people of ability and enthusiasm in all aspects of theatre arts, to work together under the guidance of specialist tutors in a residential setting to create high quality projects. Over the last few years they have performed at various venues across Neath and Swansea

Resolven Operatic Society

The original idea to form the society came in 1925 with Captain D J Williams, a leading light in this. It launched in 1926 and the first show was The Pirates Of Penzance in 1927. The first musical director was Herbert Thomas who undertook the role until his death in 1950. During 1928 the planned performance of Iolanthe was abandoned due to the economic state of the country at the time and performances were suspended until they reformed as Resolven and District Amateur Operatic Society in 1938. Notable stalwarts of the society were Merfyn Jefferies, Clayton Thatcher, Idris Morgan and Mary Olwen Williams. Glyn Davies took over the role of musical director in 1950 and continued for the next 44 years. Viv Hill appeared every year from 1955 – 1994 in various leading roles and was later president, sadly the last few years saw a movement away from their operatic roots with more contemporary shows and the society's final show was The Wizard Of Oz in 1996.

Full list of performances:

1927 – The Pirates of Penzance
1927 – HMS Pinafore
1938 – The Mikado
1939 – The Gondoliers
1949 – The Pirates of Penzance

1950 – The Mikado
1951 – The Yeoman Of The Guard
1952 – Ruddigore
1953 – The Gondoliers
1955 – Merrie England
1956 – Trial By Jury and HMS Pinafore
1957 – The Rebel Maid
1958 – Dorothy
1959 – Mirette
1960 – Les Cloches De Cornville
1961 – The Yeoman Of The Guard
1962 – The Mikado
1965 – Ruddigore
1966 – The Gipsy Baron
1966 – The Pirates of Penzance
1967 – Passion Flower (Carmen)
1968 – A Night In Venice
1969 – The Gondoliers
1970 – Merrie England
1971 – Die Fledermaus
1972 – The Merry Widow
1973 – The Gipsy Baron
1974 – The Yeoman Of The Guard
1975 – Gipsy Love
1976 – The Mikado
1977 – The Count Of Luxembourg
1978 – The Grand Duchess
1979 – The Gondoliers
1980 – La Vie Parisienne
1981 – The Gipsy Princess
1982 – Naughty Marietta
1983 – Lilac Time
1984 – Die Fledermaus
1985 – Trial By Jury and HMS Pinafore
1986 – La Perichole
1987 – Valley Of Song
1988 – Gipsy Love
1989 – A Waltz Dream
1990 – The Merry Widow
1991 – Magyar Melody
1992 – Desert Song
1993 – Oliver
1994 – The King and I
1995 – The Sound Of Music
1996 – The Wizard Of Oz.

Port Talbot YMCA Players Dramatic Society

In 1921 Port Talbot YMCA set up a drama society known as the YMCA Players, and entertained the local people of Port Talbot and Aberavon until the 1960s. Between 1939 and 1946, it recorded that income from performances was in excess of £5,000 the equivalent today would be £40,000. The society welcomed a young actor with great ambitions to their ranks in 1955 and he made his stage debut with them that year in the play Emmanuel. His name was Anthony Hopkins who rose to become one of Great Britain's greatest actors. The society ceased productions in the 1960s. In 2009 the idea of a drama society within the YMCA surfaced again with Sir Anthony Hopkins lending his support as patron and Chris Needs MBE directing the first new production, Liberating Archie in October of the same year

1930 – The Liars
1932 – Othello
1933 – The Taming Of The Shrew
1934 – Granton Street
1935 – He Who Gets Slapped
1938 – White Collar
1940 – After October, Alibi
1941 – Aven't We All, Hay Fever
1942 – Family Affairs, I'll Leave It To You
1943 – Cedar So Strong
1945 – The Light Of Heart, Dear October Octopus
1947 – Elyah, Certain Nobleman
1951 – Come And Get It
1952 – Death Takes A Holiday
1953 – Village Wooing, Browning Version
1954 – The Greatest Show On Earth
1955 – Emmanuel
1956 – White Sheep of the Family
1957 – Dial M for Murder
1959 – While the Sun Shines, For Better For Worse
1961 – The Hollow, Present Laughter

Apart from the main auditorium, the Grand Theatre can offer the excellent modern facilities of the Arts Wing, pictured here, in its bid to draw fresh audiences. From exhibitions to youth theatre, it can cater for any number of artistic genre.

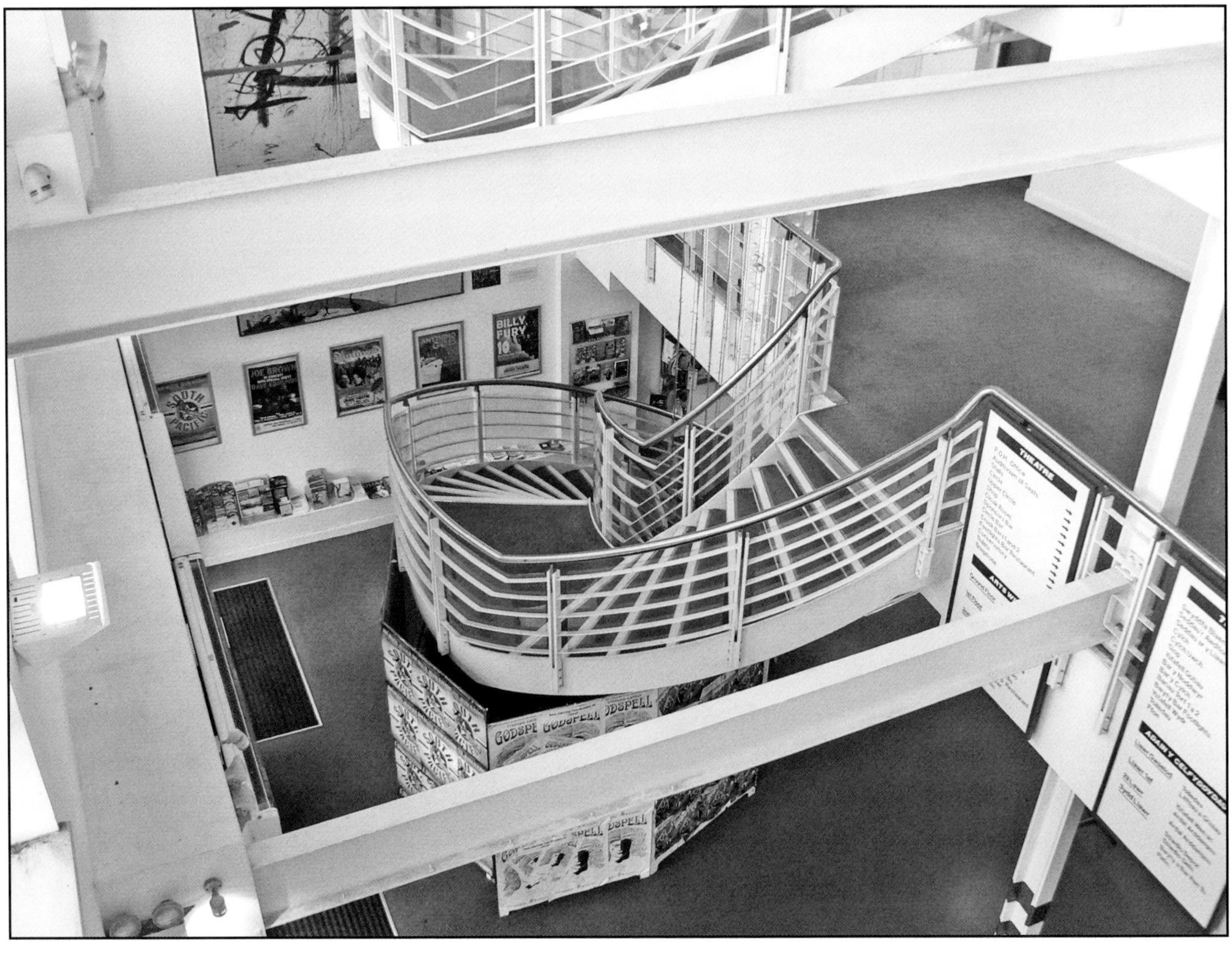

Act 17

A miscellany of top talent

The Swansea Bay area has always been a rich source of music and theatrical talent, something that is a tribute to the strength and passion for the performance arts that exists in the area. It has also proved a magnet for many of the world's top performers. Those who feature on the following pages are just some of the personalities linked in some way to the Grand Theatre. There have been many more.

Gilly Adams

Mumbles born, she began as an actress with Swansea Youth Theatre and made a few appearances at the Grand. She is especially remembered for her St. Joan in Anouilh's The Lark and as Laura in The Glass Menagerie. For more than a decade she was the artistic director of the Made in Wales stage company and long-term artistic associate of Welfare State International. She served as Welsh Arts Council drama director and as director of the BBC Wales Writers' Unit and drama producer for Radio Wales.

Jae Alexander

Born in Port Talbot, Jae began his musical career at 14 with Briton Ferry Musical Theatre Company. He has risen to become a musical director of critical acclaim,

with West End conducting credits including West Side Story, 1984, at Her Majesty's Theatre; The Mystery of Edwin Drood, 1987 at The Savoy, with Ernie Wise and Lulu; Follies, 1988 at the Shaftesbury, with Julia McKenzie and Eartha Kitt; Cats, 1989 at the New London; The Hunting of the Snark, 1991 at The Prince Edward, with Kenny Everett and David McCallum; Crazy For You, 1993 at The Prince Edward, starring Ruthie Henshall; Oliver, 1995 at The Palladium, with various Fagins including Jonathon Price, Jim Dale, Russ Abbot and Robert Lindsay and also Beauty and the Beast at The Dominion Theatre.

Sir Kingsley Amis

Amis was a novelist, poet, critic and teacher. London-born, he wrote more than 20 novels, three collections of poetry, short stories, radio and TV scripts, and books of social and literary criticism. Amis lectured in English at Swansea University from 1948 - 1961. During this time he wrote That Uncertain Feeling which was eventually made into the popular film Only Two Can Play starring Peter Sellers. It was filmed in and around Swansea and also re-made in the city for TV in 1984 reverting to its original title That Uncertain Feeling, which was again filmed in Swansea.

Leo Andrew

Neath born Leo Andrew's first foray into performing was with the Briton Ferry Musical Theatre Company in the late 1960s and early 1970s. He has carved out a long and successful career in theatre, concert, cabaret, radio and TV. His West End credits include playing leading and featured roles in eight West End musicals including Chess, Phantom of the Opera, Kiss of the Spiderwoman, On Your Toes, Poppy (RSC), Which Witch, Underneath the Arches and Joseph and the Amazing Technicolor Dreamcoat. He toured the UK in Jesus Christ Superstar as Jesus; Evita as Magaldi; and Joseph and the Amazing Technicolor Dreamcoat in which he was narrator. He also appeared in pantomime at the Grand Theatre in Robinson Crusoe with Kenny Smiles, Owen Money and Brian Conley in 1979/80.

Gareth Armstrong

This actor, broadcaster and writer, whose career has embraced the West End, Stratford upon Avon and worldwide tours for the British Council is another born in Swansea. His one man Shylock performance was a tour de force. He appeared in the 1971 repertory season at the Grand where his performances included a memorable Heathcliffe in Wuthering Heights. He was a founder member of Swansea Youth Theatre and can claim to have performed almost everywhere in Swansea where there is a platform! He worked extensively in Cardiff and became a well-known character in BBC Radio's The Archers.

Phillip Arran

Phillip's theatre work includes being a chorus member and understudy as Jacob in the West End production of Joseph and the Amazing Technicolor Dreamcoat. In pantomime, he has been lucky enough to work alongside some of the country's leading stars in principal roles at Dartford, Windsor, Isle of Man, Cardiff and back home at the Grand. During the winter of 1999 Phillip was part of the Stadium Theatre Company on the P&O cruise ship Oriana and circumnavigated the world. He is an established cabaret performer and has appeared in leading venues around the world. One of his favourites is the Hollywood Club in Kiev where his show was recorded and later televised throughout Europe. In 1996, he created his alter ego, CC Swan for Funny Girls in Blackpool.

Steve Balsamo

Actor, singer, songwriter Steve grew up in Swansea and began playing in bands in pubs and clubs. He appeared in amateur musicals and had walk-on TV roles in programmes such as the longest running BBC TV soap, the Welsh language Pobl y Cwm. At 21 he landed a role in the touring production of Les Miserables and then attended a singer-songwriter workshop for unemployed musicians run by the Princes Trust. He was noticed and was asked to open the Masters of Music Concert in Hyde Park in 1996 headlined by the Who, Alanis Morrisette, Eric Clapton and Bob Dylan. He then returned to the West End as the lead in Jesus Christ Superstar, winning acclaim and a recording contract. He became a leading rock musician, singer-composer with his band The Storeys, which toured with Elton John in 2008 culminating in a triumphant homecoming concert at The Liberty Stadium in Swansea.

Des Barrit

Born in Morriston, Desmond Barrit is one of the most versatile of British actors. He won an Olivier award for his Comedy of Errors and was acclaimed as the greatest Falstaff of his generation while working for the Royal Shakespeare Company. He was also praised for his work at the Royal National Theatre, in roles including that of Pseudolus in Sondheim's musical A Funny Thing Happened on the Way To The Forum. Desmond has starred in numerous films and TV shows and even played Colonel Pickering in My Fair Lady at The Hollywood Bowl. He is recognised as one of the best pantomime dames and producers, appearing at the Grand Theatre in Babes In The Wood in 1983/84 and Dick Whittington in 1981/82. Desmond also served in rep at the Grand Theatre.

Robert Blythe

Robert's first introduction to acting came when he joined Briton Ferry Little Theatre in the 1960s and became a great favourite among the local audiences. Eventually turning professional, his first TV role was in How Green Was My Valley in 1975. He followed this with a long list of roles on stage, television and in film. Port Talbot born Robert is best known in Wales for his comedy portrayal of Fagin in the cult series High Hopes that ran from 2002 – 2008 on

BBC Wales. He appeared at The Llewellyn Hall in Swansea in the Abbey Players production of Salad Days in 1970 and has appeared on television many times in Welsh and English language productions including Casualty, Eastenders, Midsomer Murders, Little Britain, The Bill and The Lifeboat.

Di Botcher

Specialising in comedy, Port Talbot born Di has appeared in roles in Little Britain, 'Orrible, Titty Titty Bang Bang, Belonging, in which she played Vanessa for six years, After You've Gone, Ideal, Bleak House, Pulling and High Hopes. Her first screen role was in the film Twin Town which was set in Swansea in 1997. In 2006 she appeared alongside Frank Vickery at the Grand Theatre in the play A Kiss On The Bottom and in 2008 appeared in a series of TV advertisements for the Post Office. She appeared again with Frank Vickery in Loose Ends at the Grand Theatre in May 2010.

Max Boyce MBE

Welsh comedian, folk singer and former miner, Max, born in Glynneath, specialises in rugby related humour and has an enormous following not just in Wales but across the rugby playing world. As well as a BBC TV series and a successful book of poems, songs and stories, he has enjoyed a varied career on stage and screen. Max's LP We All Had Doctors Papers, released in 1975, has the distinction of being the only comedy album to top the UK Album Charts! Max remembers the Grand, Swansea as a warm, intimate theatre and one of his favourite venues. In 1976 he performed his one-man show there for a week, selling out every night. Max is also supportive of new talent in Wales, giving Neath's Katherine Jenkins her first TV break.

Rob Brydon

Rob Brydon was born in Swansea, and attended Dumbarton House School along with Catherine Zeta Jones and Liz Fuller. He studied at the Royal Welsh College of Music and Drama, before joining BBC Wales as a radio and TV presenter. After moving to London he secured roles in a number of TV and film projects. He first caught the public eye with Marion and Jeff and Human Remains, winning comedy awards for both. He has also edited scripts for Little Britain. Rob became a national comedy favourite with The Keith Barret Show and in 2007 he was asked to play the character Bryn, in all three series of the popular Gavin and Stacey and developed the character into an integral part of the series. Rob has toured the UK in a sell out one-man tour, appearing at the Grand several times. He is also a successful voice over artist.

Richard Burman

A long career in musical theatre includes West End roles in Les Miserables, Phantom of the Opera and Beauty and the Beast. He performed all over Europe and enjoyed a number of successful cruise ship seasons before, in 2009 deciding to return home to Swansea, his birthplace. Richard was delighted to help out the city's Cockett Amateur Operatic Society in its award winning production of Beauty and the Beast. He took the part of the Beast, a role he had played in the West End. In 2010 he appeared in The Full Monty at the Dylan Thomas theatre and a triumphant one night version at the Grand.

Richard Burton CBE

He was born Richard Walter Jenkins in Pontrhydyfen near Port Talbot on November 10, 1925, the twelfth of 13 children. His mother died giving birth before he was two and he was brought up by his sister, Cecilia and her husband Elfed, while his father went to work as a coal miner. He took the surname Burton from the man who taught him acting. He rose to international stardom following his marriage to Elizabeth Taylor and became one of Hollywood's hottest properties. His stage work included Shakespeare at The Old Vic, Hamlet on Broadway and the musical Camelot. Burton only appeared at the Grand Theatre on one occasion, during its rep season on August 28, 1950, in The Seagull, where he starred as Constantine Treplef. In the same play were Kenneth Williams of the Carry On films and Wilfrid Brambell. He died of a cerebral haemorrhage in 1984, aged just 58.

David Callister

Swansea repertory favourite David Callister's links with the city and particularly the Grand Theatre stretch back to 1997 when he joined Ian Dickens Productions Ltd in their first season of repertory there. He has gone on to appear every year since and is one of a select band of actors whose mere entrance onto a stage is welcomed by applause. Norwich born, his most famous television role was as PC Kevin Anderson on ITV's The Bill, a role he played for eight months in the early 1990s. As a first class character actor he is particularly good at playing in farces and has seldom been short of roles to play. He has literally hundreds of theatre, film and TV credits to his name.

Wyn Calvin MBE

Wyn Calvin, the 'Welsh Prince of Laughter' has celebrated more than 60 years in show business. Born in 1928, at Narbeth in Pembrokeshire, he quickly rose to fame. Wyn related a story about the last pantomime at The Empire, Swansea – Jack And The Beanstalk – .where he played dame. A woman friend of his at the time suggested he should, at the curtain call, come down dressed in Welsh costume. He did, and it brought the house down. So on the last night Ossie Morris who was topping the bill, said to Wyn: "Let's come down together tonight." They did, but it didn't get the same reaction. Wyn played the Grand in pantomime on two occasions, in 1951/52 in Cinderella with Joan Laurie and Eddie Conor and again in 1960/61 in Jack And The Beanstalk with George Bolton. When, on February 6, 1952, King George VI died, he recalls arriving at the theatre and hearing people saying the King was dead. He remembers one bright spark chipping in with: "I hope he's got an understudy." Wyn also appeared at the Grand on April Fools day in 1968 with Diana Dors and Dennis Lotis, and in a Fabulous Fifties show during June 1987 with Clinton Ford, Ben Warriss, Cavan O'Connor and Llewellyn Williams. Wyn also did a week in April 1957 presenting 10 local acts in The Pick Of The Town featuring Swansea's Stars Of Tomorrow which proved very successful.

Cardini

Richard Valentine Pitchford, stage name Cardini, was born in Mumbles in 1895. He is credited by magicians all over the world with originating card magic as it is practiced today. He grew up in Swansea before he was called up for First World War duties, where he practiced magic in the trenches and after he was injured, continued perfecting his magic as he recovered in hospital. After the war he made his way to America, travelling around the world, through Australia, amazing other magicians with his dexterity and showmanship. What is even more amazing, is that Cardini did most of his magic routine while wearing gloves. Over time he developed a silent manipulation act with cards, billiard balls, and cigarettes unlike anything before it in the history of magic. His flawless technique, superb misdirection, and elegant style earned him enormous success and respect and a host of imitators. Cardini paved the way in Vaudeville for other magicians and during the 1930s and 1940s was considered by many to be the most imitated magician in the world. He played the White House eight times, gave a command performance before the King and Queen and was the second person to have his name up in lights at Radio City Music Hall. He also became president of The Society Of American Magicians in 1941. Cardini died in 1973.

Raie Copp

Raie Copp or Auntie Raie as she became known, was born Audrey Copp, started dancing at the age of 12 and made her professional stage debut just two years later. She was born into a London showbiz family. Her grandfather was a member of The Kentucky Minstrels and her mother was a comedienne. Changing her name to Raie certainly attracted attention and she worked continuously in theatres all over the UK. Her career saw her working with performers such as Norman Evans, Old Mother Riley and Kitty and Maurice Winnick's Band Show. While touring with the latter in 1945 Raie paid her first visit to the Swansea Empire. She appeared as a dancer on the famous 1940s BBC Radio show Happidrome with Harry Korris, Cecil Fredericks and Robbie Vincent and even appeared in the big screen version. In 1943 Raie also appeared in the film Somewhere On Leave with Frank Randle. She then joined the pantomime Jack and the Beanstalk with Alec Pleon, Ray Barry and Charles Harrison. They performed the same pantomime with the same cast for several years, finishing up at Swansea Empire in 1949/50. Raie met her future husband, Len in the cafe next to the stage door. At the end of the pantomime Raie was persuaded to open a dance school in Swansea by her friends. The Raie Copp School of Dance was an instant success and she never looked back.

Bruce Dargavel

Born in Briton Ferry, near Neath, Bruce became one of Wales' best known opera singers. In a long and distinguished career he appeared as principal for the Covent Garden Opera Trust, Sadlers Wells, Carl Rosa, Glynebourne and The Edinburgh Festival. One of his finest achievements was in the film The

Tales Of Hoffman when he was the singing voice of Robert Helpman. Beniamino Gigli once said of Dargavel: "He has a truly generous, magnificent voice of exceptional quality, a basso-cantata that is complete as regards quality, power and compass." In 1951 Bruce appeared in an amateur production of Faust with Clydach and District Amateur Operatic Society at the Globe Theatre, Clydach. Towards the end of his career he settled back in Neath and was persuaded to appear with Neath Opera Group at Adelina Patti's Craig-y-Nos theatre. He appeared in Martha in 1970, La Boheme in 1971 and The Marriage Of Figaro in 1972.

Allun Davies

Allun Davies fell in love with opera at a very early age. An influential moment occurred at the age of 11 when he was asked by his piano tutor, Unis Davies who was also a member of the Kenilworth Singers, if he would like to see the famous Australian opera diva Joan Hammond who was to appear as a guest artist at the Gwyn Hall in Neath. Allun who was born in the town was thrilled to be seated in the wings on a small chair. A seed was planted that night and Allun knew what he wanted from that moment on. At 14 he joined Cadoxton Opera Company and at 16 became the youngest member of the Welsh National Opera chorus – he performed with them at the Grand Theatre and in Cardiff. He was proud to meet up again with Joan Hammond when she appeared in Tosca for the Welsh National Opera. In 1965 Allun was a contestant on Hughie Green's Opportunity Knocks TV programme and became something of a sensation by winning the public vote for seven continuous weeks. The first song he sang on the show was the Richard Tauber classic Girls Were Made To Love And Kiss. Allun idolised Tauber and he was thrilled to receive a telegram and a white heather spray from Tauber's widow Diana Napier after that first show. Another highlight came in 1968 when Allun was chosen by the British viewing public to appear with Marty Wilde, Wayne Fontana and Brenda Marsh as the British contestants in the European Song Contest in Belgium. He continues to coach promising singers.

Harry Parr Davies

Born in Briton Ferry, near Neath, Harry was a musical prodigy; having composed whole operettas by the time he was in his teens. As a 17 year old shy youth he bought a day-return rail ticket from Neath to London. He arrived at The Winter Gardens clutching a song he had specially written for the star of the show, Gracie Fields, who was starring in the musical revue Walk This Way. It was a fortuitous meeting because inside her dressing room he discovered a piano being temporarily stored off stage. Gracie invited him to show off his talent. After that he became her full-time accompanist and travelling companion around the world. His best-known songs include Pedro the Fisherman, Wish Me Luck as You Wave Me Goodbye and Sing as We Go. For his song Smile When You Say Goodbye he received an advance royalty of £1,000, the highest sum paid at that time for a song. Among his stage shows were Black Velvet, The Lisbon Story, Her Excellency, and Dear Miss Phoebe. He composed music for the Gracie Fields film, This Week of Grace, and songs for other performers such as George Formby. He died at home in Knightsbridge, London, on October 14, 1955 and is buried at Oystermouth Cemetery, Mumbles.

Russell T Davies

Russell was born in Swansea and attended Olchfa School. He is a former member of West Glamorgan Youth Theatre. After taking a BBC directors' course in the 1980s his first foray into producing was in the successful BBC children's show Why Don't You? Russell is a prolific scriptwriter. His early successes included writing for children's television in the early 1990s including episodes of The Chuckle Brothers. In 1992 he moved to Granada Television, producing and writing for the successful children's TV drama Children's Ward. This was to change dramatically when he wrote Queer as Folk. Russell's list of TV writing credits after that include: The Grand, Mine All Mine which was filmed in Swansea, Coronation Street, Casanova, also starring David Tennant and The Second Coming, starring Christopher Eccleston. In 2005 he was chosen to resurrect the Doctor Who series, and as executive producer and writer he ignited the Doctor's appeal to a whole new generation. Spin-off series Torchwood, starring John Barrowman, and The Sarah Jane Adventures, have also proved highly successful. While truly at the top of his game he chose to stand down as executive producer of Dr Who in 2009.

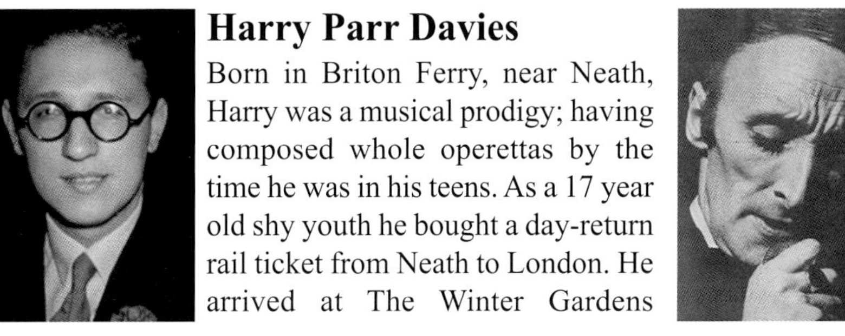

Ryan Davies

Glanamman born, Ryan Davies is a legend in Welsh entertainment history; probably the most talented all-round performer Wales has ever produced. Singer, actor, composer, songwriter, musician, comedian, conductor, radio presenter, television performer, sketch writer, he accomplished them all. He and comedy partner Ronnie Williams were the Welsh equivalent of Morecambe and Wise. Their television series Ryan and Ronnie was enormously popular, and their pantomimes at the Grand Theatre in the 1970s were some of the best ever produced there. Ryan's untimely death in 1977 sent shock waves throughout Wales. His signature tune which he sang at all his concerts was Myfanwy, thankfully caught on record when he performed it at The Top Rank Suite, Swansea, in 1975. In 2010 his manager Mike Evans organised a recreation of Ryan At The Rank, in the same venue, by then Oceana to relaunch all of Ryan's recorded works. His five pantomimes at the Grand Theatre are still recalled with great fondness by many of those who made up the sell-out audiences for them. He died while on holiday in the United States on April 22, 1977.

Mike Doyle

Mike Doyle appeared on the revived BBC talent show Bob Says Opportunity Knocks and won his heat. At the grand final he was runner up, however opportunity did knock, as this was the catalyst that he needed and his career went from strength to strength. He was presented with The Best Stage Newcomer Award at the British Comedy Awards in 1990 and was in good company as Jack Dee won the same award the following year. In 1991 he took part in the Royal Variety Performance in front of the Queen. Mike also had his own television series. He has a tremendous voice and has toured the UK in his own Mario Lanza tribute show. In the West End he appeared to great critical acclaim as The Big Bopper in Buddy. He has appeared many times at the Grand. This has included no fewer than five pantomimes which were: Aladdin in 2006/7, Jack and the Beanstalk in 2004/5, Cinderella in 2003/4, Peter Pan in 2001/2 and Snow White And The Seven Dwarfs in 2000/1. Carmarthen born, his one man shows at the Grand Theatre also proved very popular.

Cyril Dowler

In the 1930s he worked as a double act with Kay White, who later married the comedian Sandy Powell. After the Second World War he married Rhoda Rodgers and they presented another double act and produced their own touring revues and pantomimes. They presented four successive pantomimes at the Grand Theatre from 1953 onwards. He also appeared in a show at Swansea Empire in its final season.

Ceri Dupree

Born Ceri Jones in Swansea, his parents had met at a show in the Grand Theatre, and early happy memories for Ceri were of his visits there to see the annual pantomimes starring Ryan and Ronnie in the 1970s. During one of these, Ceri's father Malcolm who knew Ryan, went backstage and mentioned to Ryan that it was Ceri's birthday. During the show Ryan mentioned Ceri's name and that it was his birthday. Ceri says he lit up like a Christmas tree and it made his day. He particularly remembers the summer variety seasons at the Grand, put on by John Chilvers and he delighted in seeing the likes of Frankie Howerd, Larry Grayson, Ken Dodd and Bob Monkhouse. He is in no doubt that it was shows like these that nurtured his desire to perform. Ceri made his debut with the YMCA Players at The Llewellyn Hall, and also did a youth pantomime there. After some time spent studying performers like Stanley Baxter, Dick Emery and Danny La Rue he developed his own style of act and the glamorous Ceri Dupree was born. Ceri's first professional performance was at The Palace Theatre in High Street, Swansea, on September 9, 1983. He has also appeared in many West End nightclubs. His extensive wardrobe would not be out of place in any Hollywood Diva's home, with some of the outfits costing upwards of £6,000. He has often appeared at the Grand, once with his sister Ria, in the show Missleading Ladies.

Maudie Edwards

Elizabeth Maud Edwards was born in Florence Street, Neath on October 16, 1906; She first performed at the age of four in an act with her father and older sister, May. Maudie became one of Wales's best known and well loved entertainers. At one point she also ran her own theatre rep company. She could sing, dance, act and was a gifted comedienne. Throughout her career she performed with some of the world's greatest entertainers including Frank Sinatra. She regularly appeared on radio's Welsh Rarebit and provided the singing voices for a number of female stars. On December 9, 1960 she spoke the words: "Now the next thing you want to do is get a signwriter in. That thing above the door'll 'ave to be changed." They were the first words in the broadcast live opening episode of Britain's longest-running TV soap opera Coronation Street. In 1962 she appeared in the Swansea-set Only Two Can Play with Peter Sellers. She died in 1991.

Nigel Ellacott

Swansea-born actor, designer and pantomime specialist, Nigel is best known for his double act with Peter Robbins — the best ugly sisters in the business. He also runs an educational pantomime road show company which tours schools all over the UK. His inspiration was derived entirely from the John Chilvers pantomimes at the Grand Theatre. Nigel also runs the internet's largest pantomime website, its-behind-you.com. Sadly Peter Robbins died suddenly in April 2009, and after 30 years of being an ugly sister Nigel decided to carry on in pantomime, but in the pivotal role of dame. Nigel made his dame debut as Dolly Doughnut at The Kenneth More Theatre in Ilford, directed by his brother, that theatre's general manager Vivyan Ellacott.

Vivyan Ellacott

Vivyan was born in Gower, and is one of the few people to have performed at all three of Swansea's theatres – The Palace, The Empire and The Grand. He performed in five different rep seasons at Swansea Grand Theatre as an actor, directed several productions and was even musical director for three rep musicals. He was Assistant Manager and later Theatre Manager at The Grand from 1966 - 1973. Since then he has been manager and artistic director of the Kenneth More Theatre in Ilford. Vivyan commands the same respect as John Chilvers, and like John retains a boundless passion for the theatre.

Ivor Emmanuel

Ivor Emmanuel was born on November 7, 1927 in Taibach, Port Talbot. Shortly after, the family moved to Morgans Terrace in Pontrhydyfen. It was a tragic decision for the Emmanuel family. During the Second World War, in the early hours of March 17, 1942, the family were in bed. A few miles away the luftwaffe were unleashing their bombs over Swansea. A stray bomber flew overhead dropping his last two bombs. One landed on open ground near Pontrhydyfen, the other directly onto their home. A neighbour pulled Ivor and his brother out alive, but his mother, father, grandfather and sister were all killed. In 1947 Ivor had a memorable lead role in Port Talbot Amateur Operatic Society's production of the Pirates Of Penzance. In the same year he successfully auditioned for a role in Oklahoma at The Drury Lane Theatre, followed by a year long contract with the Doyly Carte Opera. Throughout the 1950s Ivor was in continual employment in West End musicals and in the 1960s he began to appear in cabaret and pantomime. He went to Broadway in 1966 to star in How Green Was My Valley. His TV career began with Dewch I Mewn and Gwlad Y Gan, but he shot to international fame in the film Zulu in 1964, leading the men in a stirring rendition of Men Of Harlech. Ivor loved to come home to Pontrhydyfen and found it a great wrench to leave again. In 1978/79 he appeared in the Pantomime Aladdin at the Grand Theatre. This was his last pantomime for not long after he turned his back on showbusiness and lived out the last years of his life in Benalmadena Pueblo in Spain. He died in 2007.

Bryan Evans

Bryan Evans was born in Swansea and while he was still a schoolboy became a champion swimmer, representing Swansea and West Wales in major competitions. He toured Germany as the lead singer/songwriter in a pop group called Rust, and then achieved great success as Claude in the UK National tour of the rock musical Hair. Bryan appeared in the pantomime Jack and The Beanstalk in 1975/76 at the Grand Theatre, alongside Ryan Davies. After a successful career in theatre Bryan became a successful businessman and settled in Swansea.

Rebecca Evans

Rebecca was born in Pontrhydyfen, near Neath in August 1963. She was training to be a nurse in a Swansea hospital, and singing as an amateur when she met internationally famous opera singing baritone Bryn Terfel at a concert that they were both performing in. Bryn convinced her to give up nursing and go to the Guildhall School Of Music and Drama. After leaving the school, this delightful soprano won The Welsh Singer Of The Year competition in 1989, and has since risen to become one of the UK's leading opera singers. Rebecca has performed all over the world and won a Grammy Award for Best Opera Recording in 2008. She has performed with the Welsh National Opera many times including visits to the Grand Theatre and also at the Royal Opera House, Covent Garden. On Friday May 1, 2009, Rebecca was awarded an honorary degree of Doctor of Music from the University of Wales. She has appeared at the BBC Proms and at the Edinburgh Festival.

Dai Francis

Dai Francis was born in Glynneath on February 23, 1928. He became a stalwart of BBC television's popular Black and White Minstrel Show in the 1960s and 1970s. His tribute to Al Jolson established him as Britain's foremost Jolson impressionist and he starred in summer season, pantomime and variety shows in most of the major theatres in the UK, including the Grand, in 1989. He also appeared in two Royal Variety shows. He died, aged 75, on November 27, 2003.

Alex Frith MBE

Alex was born in Barry and for many years lived in London. A major event in 1980 – the Iranian Embassy Siege – just a street away from her children's school, made Alex realise that London was not the place to bring up her children, Samantha and Alexandra. After a talk with her husband Dennis they decided to move to Wales. As they were already renting a property in Rotherslade, near Mumbles, they chose to move to Swansea permanently. Alex always had the creative ability to tell beautiful children's stories to her children which she could make up on the spot. She would tell tales of little characters from the beach at Mumbles which eventually turned into the Bumbles of Mumbles stories. Looking for something to do when she arrived in Swansea she turned up at The South Wales Evening Post building armed with a hand written story of The Bumbles Of Mumbles, which she gave to an editor at the paper. A short time later she was invited back to the newspaper and asked to write a page for children involving a new story every week. In 1986 she put forward an idea to the paper to turn her stories into a one-night show at The Grand Theatre. This first production was a great success and the manager of The Grand at the time, Paul Dayson, asked her to stage a couple more nights, which were again very fruitful. The show is now an annual event. In 1992 she decided to put on a show for the older children. This was to be a talent showcase that would celebrate the musical ability that abounded in the area. Billed as The Best Is Yet To Come, this show is now put on three times annually at the Grand Theatre. All of the proceeds go to charity. To date she has raised over £250,000. Alex was honoured with the MBE in 2008. In 1999 Alex hired Her Majesty's Theatre in London and staged The Best is Yet to Come there.

Liz Fuller

Liz Fuller was born in Killay, Swansea. She attended Dumbarton House school at nursery level and like everyone there at the time was pushed into the extra curricular activities of dance and drama, including the now very famous Catherine Zeta Jones. She went to Olchfa Secondary School and continued with her dance and drama lessons, excelling in all her exams, performing as a child in Joseph and the Amazing Technicolor Dreamcoat and A Night of a 100 stars at The Grand Theatre in 1988 along with numerous pantomimes down the years. She then moved over to The Grand Theatre School of Dance and continued taking part in stage productions including The Hobbit in May 1989. Liz fell into the world of modelling, almost by accident, however she was an instant success and continued to model across the UK, winning the Welsh competition for Miss Universe, allowing her to enter the final of Miss Great Britain. She has since turned to television presenting. Initially this was with a number of shopping channels. Later she became known nationally as a co-presenter on Channel Five's popular late night programme Quiz Call.

Helen Griffin

Swansea born, Helen Griffin is an actress, screenwriter and playwright. Brought up in Treboeth, she attended Bishop Vaughan School. She initially studied at nursing college alongside comedienne Jo Brand and was a psychiatric nurse until 1986, when her passion for acting took over. After many theatre performances and writing the play Killjoy, for Theatre West Glamorgan which later changed its name to Theatr Na Nog, she appeared in the Welsh cult classic Twin Town in 1997. Her first full length play was Flesh and Blood which she adapted into the screenplay for the film Little White Lies. This was filmed on location in Swansea and Cardiff. The film in which she also starred, won a Welsh BAFTA for her performance in 2006. Helen also appeared at The Edinburgh Fringe festival with Jo Brand in a collaborated play called Mental, based on their experiences as psychiatric nurses. On television she has appeared in Casualty, Gavin And Stacey, Dr Who, Satellite City, and has written for No Angels, Where The Heart Is and the short lived Night And Day. In 2003, Griffin performed a one-woman show, Caitlin, based on the life of Caitlin MacNamara, wife of Dylan Thomas

Hugh Griffith

After failing the English exam that would have led to university, Anglesey-born Hugh got a job in banking, and moved to London. He began to act with the St Pancras People's Theatre and finally gained a place at the Royal Academy of Dramatic Arts, coming top out of an intake of 300. Hugh had found his calling. He gained the Bancroft Gold Medal for the best Shakespearean actor of his year. His acting career was put on hold however as he served as a soldier in India and Burma during the Second World War. Hugh's first visit to Swansea was when he was sent as part of a bomb disposal and demolition squad to help clear up Swansea after the bombing of 1941. He drove a steamroller over the shattered streets. After the War, he returned to the stage as a member of the Royal Shakespeare Company going on to make the demanding role of King Lear his own. It was one he played at the Grand Theatre on October 31, 1949 and it was hailed as one of the best ever performances. Hugh then got married and went to live in Hollywood with his bride. He appeared in many films until his moment of crowning glory arrived in 1959 when he was cast in one of the most acclaimed films of the 20th century, Ben Hur. Hugh won an Oscar alongside Charlton Heston for his portrayal of the Sheikh. He was further nominated for his role in the 1963 film Tom Jones and took part in the 1968 version of Oliver. He also starred in The Last Days of Dolwyn, The Sleeping Tiger, Exodus, Cry of the Banshee, Wuthering Heights, Loving Cousins, The Titfield Thunderbolt and the Passover Plot. He was nominated for a Tony Award on Broadway in 1958 for Best Actor in Look Homeward, Angel. TV and rugby fans will remember him fondly for his role, alongside Windsor Davies and Sion Probert as Caradog Lloyd-Evans, the funeral director, in the 1978 comedy, Grand Slam. He died of a heart attack in 1980.

Claire Louise Hammacott

Born in Swansea, Claire graduated from the Welsh College of Music and Drama in 1992. Since then she has developed a career spanning all walks of musical life. Opera roles include Drusllia in L'Incoronazione di Poppea, Miss Wordsworth in Albert Herring, Susanna in The Marriage of Figaro and lastly, La Gioconda with Opera North. Claire's concert work has taken her around the UK, a series of concerts for the International Music Festival in Caracas, Venezuela and on two occasions she has sung for the Royal Family. She has appeared in the West End, Manchester and Edinburgh productions of Phantom of the Opera and the London production of Les Miserables. Her TV appearances include The Brian Conley Show, Mal Pope Meets, High Performance and A Day in the West End. Claire has also been a guest soloist on Radio 2's Friday Night is Music Night and has made a number of appearances at the Grand.

Griff Harries

In the late 1970s and early 1980s Neath born Griff Harries worked as a marketing officer at the Grand Theatre. During this time he became the saxophonist in its pantomime orchestra, subsequently becoming musical director and in 2009/10 he performed in his 26th consecutive panto there. Griff was a broadcaster for Swansea Sound and is founder and director/administrator of The Chamber Orchestra of Wales. He has played in the orchestra for a number of local amateur societies and provided an orchestra for many of the Neath groups which performed at the Gwyn Hall. For some, he has provided the musicians for more than 20 years.

Colin Hodges

Swansea born Colin is one of the few amateur performers whose mere entrance onto a stage warranted applause. Colin could easily have transformed into a professional career in entertainment had he chosen that path. His first performance was at the Swansea Empire when he was 10. One show involved a magician called the Great Lyle. Colin was mesmerised by this illusionist and when near the end of his act he asked for a volunteer from the audience, Colin, to his parents horror, jumped up onto the stage and assisted The Great Lyle. He first began to sing and act at Fabian's Bay Church, St Thomas. They would perform a very moving play based on the story of Mary Jones and Her Bible. It is reputed to be a true story of a young Welsh girl who saved for six years and then walked 25 miles to buy a bible in her own language. During 1955 Colin entered a talent show at the Swansea Empire hosted by Carrol Levis and won. Levis was very complimentary and told Colin he could join the tour around Britain's Empire theatres the next week. Colin turned him down as he wanted to finish his degree. His first role with Swansea Amateur Operatic Society was as Mr. Snow in Carousel at the Grand. His favourite role was that of Henry Higgins in My Fair Lady alongside Jean Thorley as Eliza in 1969 and Ria Jones in 1982. He appeared with Swansea Amateur Operatic Society for

30 years and also appeared in The King And I with a young Catherine Zeta Jones in 1981.

Mary Hopkin

Mary Hopkin was born in Pontardawe. As an 18 year old she appeared on Opportunity Knocks, where she came to the attention of Paul McCartney. She became one of the first artists to record on the Beatles' Apple record label, and her first single, Those Were The Days, became a No. 1 hit in the UK and reached number two in the American charts. Hits like Turn Turn Turn, Goodbye and 1970s Eurovision entry Knock Knock Who's There followed. She came second to Dana who sang All Kinds Of Everything in that contest. In 1971 Mary largely withdrew from the public eye to get married and have a family. She continued to record and occasionally performs as well. Mary now leads a very nomadic lifestyle, largely shunning the spotlight.

Sir Anthony Hopkins

One of Wales's most famous actors, acclaimed equally at the National Theatre and in Hollywood, Hopkins won an Oscar for his performance as Hannibal Lector in Silence Of The Lambs. The award in 1992 was for best actor in a leading role. His appearance in the film lasted only 11 minutes and is the shortest period for which an actor has won the award. He was born in Margam, Port Talbot and his first professional appearance came at The Palace Theatre, Swansea in the play A Lit Cigarette in 1961. He was knighted in 1993.

Glyn Houston

Although born in Tonypandy, on October 23, 1926, Glyn has a great many links with theatre in Swansea, appearing numerous times at the Grand Theatre, and as a guest star in a play at The Palace Theatre during the Maudie Edwards seasons. He also appeared in two pantomimes at the Grand. These were Babes In The Wood, in 1976 and Dick Whittington in 1987. He has appeared countless times in film and on TV since his debut in The Blue Lamp in 1950. He is also a very seasoned stage performer. Glyn is the brother of the late film actor Donald Houston. Perhaps Glyn Houston's most notable role was as Duncan Thomas, a hapless literary agent, in the 1980s British sitcom Keep it in the Family.

Gary Iles

Bridgend born, he entered the world of arts and entertainment in 1972 working in a variety of buildings in his home town including the Bridgend Recreation Centre and The Porthcawl Pavilion. Between 1979 and 1983 he was general manager at Southampton's Guildhall. This is a 1,500 seat multi-purpose venue presenting a mixed programme of variety, classical concerts and major dance events and competitions, many of them televised throughout Great Britain. From 1983 to 1986 he was building and activities manager at the National Concert Hall for Wales – St David's Hall in Cardiff. In June 1989 he was appointed general manager at the Grand Theatre, a post he still held in 2010.

Katherine Jenkins

Born in Neath and a former pupil of Alderman Davies' Church in Wales primary school, the Welsh mezzo soprano won a scholarship to study at the Royal Academy of Music in London, at the age of 17. At the age of just 23 Katherine signed the then largest record deal in United Kingdom classical recording history, reportedly worth £1 million. She has crossed over through the classical and pop charts, and has become the new forces sweetheart. She once shattered a chandelier while singing O Holy Night at Swansea's Brangwyn Hall. She performed at The Royal Variety Performance in 2005 in front of The Queen, and in 2008 signed the then largest classical record deal in history with Warner Music for a reported £5.8 million. She has toured globally and performed at some of the most prestigious venues including Sydney Opera House, The Millennium Stadium and Wembley Stadium. She has sold more than four million albums.

Clive John

Morriston born, Clive John was educated at Dynevor Grammar School and then later achieved a music degree at Cardiff University. He became a music teacher in Swansea and began a successful conducting career with various operatic societies in the area. He was twice awarded the conductor's prize at the Waterford Festival. He conducted Swansea Male Voice Choir for nine years and formed Neath Opera Group with the late Dudley Hopkins in 1961. Clive conducted, and then later produced as well, the fortnightly performances at Craig-y-Nos, which ended in 1999. His attention to detail and enthusiasm for music is astounding and in the early days of Neath Opera Group, when scores for various operas were only available in their native language, Clive would painstakingly translate them into English, then stick the English translation over the text on each score. Without his commitment some of the operas might have never been performed in English. Since 1985 Clive has also been conductor of Swansea Philharmonic Choir which regularly performs at The Brangwyn Hall.

Margaret John

Margaret John was born in Swansea and has been an actress for many years. She has appeared in countless television programmes, including Crossroads, Doctor Who with Patrick Troughton and David Tennant; Emmerdale Farm, Z Cars, Dixon Of Dock Green, The District Nurse, Blake's Seven, High Hopes, as Mrs Hepplewhite; Eyes Down with Paul O'Grady, Little Britain, the film Run Fatboy Run, and more recently as Doris in Gavin And Stacey. She now lives in Swansea after many years of living and working in London.

Kevin Johns, MBE

Swansea born, Kevin Johns is one of Wales' most popular entertainment personalities. A radio presenter with Swansea Sound where he has hosted his popular breakfast show for many years, he couples this with a successful career as an actor, comedian, compere, TV personality, Swansea City fan, committed Christian and pantomime dame. He has appeared in the Grand Theatre pantomime a record number of times, starting with the 1996/97 offering Robin Hood. He has also appeared at the theatre in the comic plays Toshack or Me and To Hull And Back as the character Vicar Joe, to critical acclaim.

Catherine Zeta Jones, CBE

Catherine Zeta Jones is the first actress from Swansea to win an Academy Award for her role as Velma Kelly in Chicago. She began her theatrical career in her hometown, first by winning various talent shows, then as a member of Gendros Catholic Amateur Operatic Society in its production of The Sound Of Music at the Grand in 1982, and again with the same company in Oliver in 1984. She had star quality even then, as she was mesmerising in whatever role she played, and owned the stage with her presence. She was fast tracked onto the West End stage and appeared in 42nd Street. Television followed by a major role in The Darling Buds Of May, then she progressed to feature films like Splitting Heirs, Entrapment, Traffic — starring her husband Michael Douglas; The Mask Of Zorro, Chicago and Ocean's 12. Catherine is an accomplished A-list celebrity and has a worldwide following which is testimony to her talent and determination.

Della Jones

Della Jones was born in Tonna, Neath. She studied at the Royal College of Music, where she won the Kathleen Ferrier Memorial Scholarship, and later in Geneva, where she made her professional debut in 1970, as Feodor and Olga. She joined the English National Opera in 1977, and the Royal Opera House in 1983, when she began appearing abroad notably in France, Italy, and the United States. She tackles a wide repertoire from baroque to contemporary works, with a speciality in the bel canto operas, notably of Rossini. In the mid 1970s she began a long association with Opera Rara, appearing in many long forgotten bel canto works, both on stage and on recording. She can be heard in the complete recordings of Donizetti and made a solo album titled Della Jones sings Donizetti, in all of which one can appreciate her impeccable coloratura technique and strong feeling for words and music. She also made albums such as Great Operatic Arias – Della Jones, for Chandos records.

Gary Jones

Gary Jones is a Swansea born actor best known for his recurring role as Sgt. Walter Harriman in Stargate SG-1 and Stargate Atlantis. He has also made guest appearances on such shows as Sliders, The Outer Limits, Andromeda and Dead Like Me. Gary was a member of the improvisation group Mission Improvable, which had a CBC comedy special prior to his role on Stargate SG-1. He joined Toronto's Second City Improv Company in the mid-1980s. Together with Second City he went to Vancouver in 1986 for the Expo. For six months, there were regular improvisation shows at the Expo Flying Club. After the Expo ended, Jones stayed in Vancouver and started his acting career with guest appearances in TV shows like Wiseguy, Airwolf and Danger Bay.

Ria Jones

Ria Jones is the sister of the flamboyant female impersonator Ceri Dupree. Her love of the theatre was developed through her parents who would take her and her brother to see the annual pantomimes at the Grand Theatre. Ria got her first opportunity to play the Grand as a 10-year-old when she was picked by John Chilvers to be one of the babes in Cinderella with Clive Dunn in 1977/78. Ria has many fond memories of John Chilvers who called her his 'Little Miss Dynamite.' She was sad, but proud to sing at his funeral in 2008. At the age of 19 she became the youngest actress ever to play the role of Eva Peron in the musical Evita. This was followed shortly after by her West End debut in the musical Chess, in which she played both Svetlana and Florence. She has had a long and sustained career in the West End and in national tours, including Cats, Les Miserables, Joseph and the Amazing Technicolor Dreamcoat and more recently as Mrs Overalls in Acorn Antiques and The Witches Of Eastwick. Ria has performed at the Grand many times.

Peter Karrie

Bridgend born, Peter Karrie started his career as a singer with the band Peter and The Wolves, which opened as a warm up band for, among others, The Rolling Stones and Tom Jones. After the band finished Peter fell on hard times and lived rough, busking on the streets of London, before getting his big break in the West End. Since then Peter Karrie's voice has been showcased in many of the greatest theatrical successes in contemporary musical theatre. The highlight of his career must rank as his highly acclaimed portrayal of The Phantom in Lord Andrew Lloyd Webber's record-breaking The Phantom Of The Opera. Peter first played the role at Her Majesty's Theatre, London and went on to play the role in Toronto, Singapore, Hong Kong and Vancouver. His performances have been described as 'definitive' and earned him the title of The World's Most Popular Phantom, pushing Michael Crawford into third place. Other high profile roles include Jean Valjean in Les Miserables and Che in Evita. Peter's links to Swansea are long standing. He has appeared in many Wales Theatre Company productions at the Grand, including Amazing Grace, The Contender and The Thorn Birds. This enormously popular singer-entertainer has also visited the Grand on a number of occasion with his successful one-man shows.

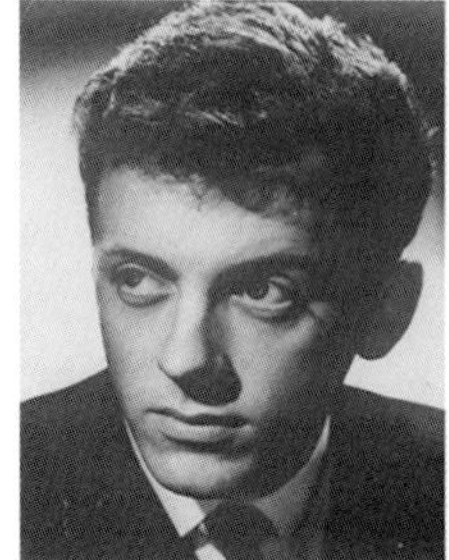

Freddie Lees

Freddie Lees, although Oldham born, became a great favourite with Swansea repertory audiences during the John Chilvers era, and was one of a select group who would receive an 'entrance round' or applause for just coming on stage in a play, when appearing in rep at the Grand. He always wanted to be involved in show business and after three years in the RAF, two of which were spent in the Suez Canal Zone, he joined a touring company for a year followed by a three-performance-a-day panto for five weeks in a different town every week. His third job took him to the Grand, Swansea, where he played a schoolboy in The Facts Of Life. He went on to appear in five pantomimes at the theatre. In the late 1950s he even did a season as stage manager. Freddie's last appearance in Swansea was in Educating Rita, directed by Menna Trussler. In the West End he was in Johnny the Priest, Norman is that You? and Billy, at Drury Lane. He then went on to Oliver and Chitty Chitty Bang Bang. In that production he played the toymaker, to rave reviews, during Michael Ball, Gary Wilmot, Jason Donovan and Brian Conley's consecutive stints as Caractacus Potts. He has appeared on TV many times, with two stints on Coronation Street in the 1970s playing two different parts. He also appeared in Little Britain, Old Gits and Hotel Babylon.

Anthony Lyn

Born in Swansea, his love for the theatre was nurtured by family visits to the Grand Theatre pantomimes in the 1970s. He joined the Gendros Amateur Catholic Operatic Society and appeared in some pantomimes staged at the Welfare Cinema in Ravenhill. Anthony has fond memories of Jackie Thomas who would write sketches for those distant pantomimes. Anthony's first performance at the Grand Theatre was with the Gendros Society in Kismet in 1980 followed by Charley Girl with the Abbey Players in the same year. Anthony appeared on stage with Catherine Zeta Jones at the Grand in 1982 in The Sound Of Music. He studied at the Welsh College of Music and Drama, in Cardiff. His stage career included West End and touring productions of Joseph and the Amazing Technicolor Dreamcoat, One Night with Rogers and Hammerstein, Oklahoma, Anything Goes and Les Miserables. Turning to directing Anthony was eventually offered a job working for Cameron Mackintosh. In 1999 he was offered the great opportunity to work with Disney on the Lion King at the Lyceum Theatre in London, as assistant to Julie Taymor.

Julie was the first woman to receive a Tony award for directing a musical – The Lion King – in 1997. It opened at the Lyceum in 1999 with Anthony as the resident director. In 2008 Anthony was an associate director of Mary Poppins on Broadway. He is an unsung Swansea theatrical success story who also appeared in the pantomime Dick Whittington at the Grand Theatre in 1987/88.

Lyn Mackay

Lyn is a classically trained pianist. At the age of 13, she wrote her first song and by the time she was 15, she played and sang at the Langrove Motel and Country Club three nights a week and later appeared on TV's Opportunity Knocks. Her stage name was Lyn Lawrence. During the 1970s and 1980s, she earned her living as a professional musician/ pianist/singer/ in the clubs of the South Wales Valleys along with the North-East and South West of England. She travelled extensively abroad, went to Oslo, Norway, for a month, was asked to go to Stockholm, fell in love with Sweden and as a result, spent almost five years there as the resident pianist/singer for the SAS Hotel chain in their prestigious piano bars. She was the resident pianist and singer at the Playboy Club, London where she went for a week and stayed six months and also did Sundays at Ronnie Scott's club. She did session work for EMI and then got the residency as pianist and singer at Kettners' in Soho. Lyn's first appearance at the Grand Theatre came in a touring revue called Spring Thaw in 1980. Around 27 years after her first appearance at the Grand she returned with her own creation Swansea Girls which was a great success.

Ruth Madoc

Ruth Madoc was brought up by her grandmother in Llansamlet, Swansea. Her parents were both involved in the medical profession. Ruth attended Bethel Infants School and then Peniel Green Junior School. She has wonderful memories of the Empire Theatre pantomimes, especially Puss In Boots in 1952/53 with Harry Secombe. Ruth went on to work with Sir Harry when they toured with Pickwick in the 1990s, visiting the Grand Theatre in 1995. Ruth left school at the age of 15 and started in repertory theatre almost straight away. Later she attended RADA, after which she spent three years with the Black and White Minstrels followed by a successful stage career where she has become a celebrated leading lady. Welsh television viewers will remember her appearances in Poems and Pints in the 1970s with Max Boyce and Ryan Davies. Nationally she is best remembered as Gladys Pugh in the huge BBC TV comedy success Hi-De-Hi. In 1976 Ruth paid her first visit as a performer to her 'home' theatre, the Grand. This was in the play Irma La Douce. She has been back many times since including making an appearance in the pantomime Robin Hood in 1996/97 with Little and Large. She was also cast by Russell T Davies to appear in the ITV Series Mine All Mine.

Sean Mathias

Sean Mathias is a British theatre director, film director, writer and actor who was born in Swansea. He directed the film Bent starring Clive Owen and Sir Ian Mckellen in 1997. He is a notable theatre director and has worked with the likes of Sian Phillips, Sir Ian McKellen, Alfred Molina, Richard E Grant, Ralph Fiennes, Kathleen Turner and Jude Law. He has directed on Broadway and the West End.

Steven Meo

Steven Meo was born at Morriston hospital in Swansea, brought up in the village of Ystradgynlais and studied at the Welsh College of Music and Drama in Cardiff. On completing his studies he was fortunate to secure a major role in the Welsh television hit Belonging, more television roles followed including Nice Girl, Holby City, High Hopes, Score, The Trouble with George, Spine Chillers and Grown Ups. Steven also appeared in an episode of Torchwood. In addition to his long list of television credits he has also worked extensively in theatre and on radio.

Ray Milland

He was born Alfred Reginald Jones at 5 Exchange Road, Neath in 1907. Before becoming an actor, he served in the Household Cavalry. An expert shot, he became a member of his company's rifle team, winning many prestigious competitions, including the Bisley Match in England. When his four-year duty service was completed, he tried his hand at acting and was discovered by a Hollywood talent scout while performing on the stage in London, went to America, and signed with Paramount Pictures. Although he never performed on stage in his home area, he was to become the first actor from Wales to win an Academy Award for Best Actor for his role in the movie Lost Weekend in

1945. Ray Milland who took his name from the Millands area near his home, has the distinction of giving the shortest acceptance speech at an Academy Award. He simply bowed and left the stage. He was a very busy performer and played nearly 200 screen roles in his long and distinguished career. Among these were the cult classic The Man With The X-Ray Eyes.

Owen Money MBE

Owen Money was born Lynn Mittell in Merthyr Tydfil. He started his career as a bass guitarist and lead singer with Merthyr band Crescendo. They merged with another local band The Rebels with Lynn, who was then known as Gerry Braden, on vocals. In the 1970s Lynn formed comedy show band Tomfoolery which quickly rose to become one of the UK's most successful comedy show bands, and often topped the bill at Blackpool's South Pier. In 1980 Lynn left to pursue a solo career as Owen Money. He soon went on to win the Clubland 'Comedian of the Year' award, performing alongside Shirley Bassey and Tom Jones. He has appeared in eight Grand Theatre pantomimes and made his debut on radio with the weekly Radio Wales programme Money For Nothing. The programme's popularity steadily increased and by 1997 he had won two prestigious Sony Gold Awards, one for Regional Broadcaster of the Year and the other for Best Music Sequence Programme of the Year. In 1979/80 Owen appeared in the pantomime Robinson Crusoe. In 2000, he set up his own Owen Money Theatre Company.

Gladys Morgan

Gladys was born in Swansea in 1898, and rose to become labelled the Welsh Queen of Comedy, although national recognition came late – it took over 40 years of touring in variety, concert parties and revues. She made an appearance on Mumbles Pier in 1923. Only 4ft 10in tall, she eventually found her place as a comedienne with her husband, Frank Laurie, as her comic feed. Gladys's big opportunity came when she was asked to audition in front of legendary producer Mair Jones for the popular radio show Welsh Rarebit. The show was a mixture of comedy, song and hilarious gurning, facial expressions. She was so successful that she earned a regular slot on the programme. She had an infectious laugh that really struck a chord with audiences and got them laughing too. With a vividly expressive face and toothless smile sometimes its effect on the audience lasted her whole performance! Throughout the 1960s the family, now joined by daughter Joan and son-in-law Bert Holman, were kept busy with pantomime and summer season including four sell-out tours of South Africa, where the family also had their own series on Springbok Radio called The Morgans. Gladys was approaching 70 at the time. She died in 1983.

Islwyn Morris

Islwyn Morris was a local actor who John Chilvers would call on from time to time to fill in during the repertory seasons. His first professional appearance was at The Palace Theatre, High Street, Swansea, during the Maudie Edward's season in the play No Orchids For Miss Blandish. He also ran a sweet shop in the nearby High Street Arcade as a sideline. This allowed him the opportunity to appear as a floating actor with John Chilvers at the Grand Theatre when needed. Islwyn is also Welsh speaking and has appeared in many Welsh television programmes including Pobl y Cwm and before that Fo a Fe with Ryan Davies. His most memorable role however was as Idris in the Welsh cult sit-com Satellite City for BBC Television.

Ossie Morris

Oswald John Morris was born at 173 Water Street in Port Talbot on July 18, 1906. In 1919 at the age of 13 he appeared in The Mikado with Afan and District Operatic Society. He had a love for bird whistling and mimicry, indeed his later catchphrase became 'Hush! I Must 'ave 'ush', After many local appearances with concert parties, Ossie's big break came at the age of 43 when he appeared on Hughie Green's Opportunity Knocks programme and his exposure to a wider audience attracted the attention of Bryan Michie who famously had given Morecambe and Wise their break at The Empire Theatre, Swansea in 1940. Brian invited Ossie to be a guest on his show at The New Theatre, Cardiff, where he was a success. The former £8 a week steelworker had arrived. After being appointed as resident comedian on Welsh Rarebit he began topping the bill on the variety circuit all over the country with Dorothy Squires and Wilson, Keppel and Betty. In 1950 he took part in the pantomime Red Riding Hood at the Grand Theatre. Following that he appeared in a further two pantomimes at the theatre and was also top of the bill at the final pantomime production at the Empire Theatre in 1957. Ossie died on April 7, 1968 aged 61.

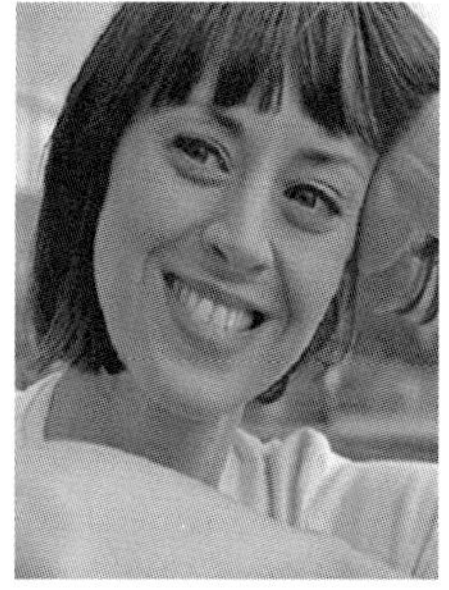

Siwan Morris

Siwan is another Glynneath success story, having grown up in the same town as Max Boyce. As a child she was inspired into becoming an actress by reading an article in the Neath Guardian newspaper highlighting Michael Sheen's rise to success. She graduated from Manchester Metropolitan University and built her career in London as part of the Royal Shakespeare Company. Having had great childhood memories of Mumbles and Swansea market, she was pleased that her big break came as Maria Vivaldi, one of the main characters in the TV series Mine All Mine, filmed in the city. It was written by Russell T Davies and starred Griff Rhys Jones. Siwan has appeared in Skins, Con Passionate, Caerdydd, A Mind To Kill, The Bill, Casualty, Belonging and Doctors and is an accomplished stage actress. Born in 1976, Siwan is fluent in English and Welsh. She has also performed as a singer with the Welsh electro-pop band Clinigol, appearing as a guest soloists on its debut album, Melys.

Con Murphy

Con was the Stage Manager at Swansea Grand Theatre from 1958 – 1983, and had worked occasionally backstage at Swansea Empire while a boy, as his grandfather (also called Con) used to work there. In the early years the job was part-time and casual, but a permanent post was created after 1969 when the theatre came under council control. He was excellent at his job, much admired, and respected as a genuine man of the theatre. At first he could seem a bit frightening, but underneath he was very kind hearted and great at encouraging beginners on the technical side of the business. He died a few years after retiring and in February 1988, Anthony Lyn staged a tribute show at the theatre in Con's memory. It was a mammoth event, starting at 7.30 and not finishing until 1.30am! The show was so long because everyone wanted to be in it. The finale had over 100 people on stage.

Richard Mylan

Richard Mylan was brought up in Swansea. At a very early age he took disco-dancing lessons with his sister, later taking up ballet lessons as well. His grandmother had a café five doors down from the Grand Theatre, called Connie's where Richard experienced many happy memories, as many famous people would pop in to eat there. In 1981 The Northern Ballet Company was appearing at the Grand when one of the cast had to pull out. Richard's grandmother suggested that the then eight-year-old Richard could play the part of the Egyptian Prince in A Midsummer Nights Dream at short notice. He took to the stage like a duck to water and was a great success. Richard also appeared in Oliver in 1984 with Gendros Catholic Amateur Operatic Society alongside Catherine Zeta Jones. The following year he appeared for the same company in Half A Sixpence. After that final show he was whisked off to London to study at the Urdang Academy of Ballet and Performing Arts. Straight after graduating he was cast in Starlight Express in the West End, where he stayed for four years. His television career has seen him appear in The Bill, Coupling, Belonging, Where The Heart Is, Border Café, Wild West and Grown Ups on BBC 3.

Eve Myles

Eve was born in Ystradgynlais, attending the same school as fellow actor Steven Meo. Theatrically trained at The Welsh College Of Music And Drama in Cardiff, Eve has since received great plaudits for her work with the Royal Shakespeare Company, and performed with Michael Gambon at the National Theatre. She played the part of Ceri in the long running BBC Wales TV series Belonging and after a small part in the Swansea filmed episode of Dr Who, The Unquiet Dead, Eve was cast by Russell T Davies to star in spin off series Torchwood. In 2008 she appeared in Merlin, and Little Dorrit both for the BBC.

Chris Needs MBE

Chris Needs was born in Cwmavon, near Port Talbot. He started out as a keyboard player, at one time accompanying Bonnie Tyler. After an appearance on Pobl Y Cwm, Chris turned to radio broadcasting and for six years was presenter for Touch AM. In 1996 he won the coveted Sony Silver Award for Best Regional Radio Presenter. It was the same year as he joined Radio Wales. After presenting a number of daytime shows for the station Chris turned to late night music and chat with The Friendly Garden Programme and has developed an on-air club of listeners. In 2005 he was awarded the MBE for services to broadcasting and charity in Wales. In 2007 Chris appeared in the Mal Pope musical Contender at the Grand Theatre adding yet another string to his bow.

Ivor Novello

Although born in Cardiff, Ivor Novello left a lasting impression on Swansea theatregoers with a breathtaking performance of The Rat at the Grand Theatre in 1924. He was also one of the very few Welsh artistes to universally be known by their first names – just say 'Dear Ivor' at the time, and immediately everyone knew you meant Ivor Novello. Another person who commanded the same kind of identity was the much-loved comedian Ryan Davies. Ivor was a composer, songwriter, actor, film star and producer. He was a legendary part of the first half of the 20th Century theatre. His song Keep The Home Fires Burning was one of the most successful of the First World War and his musicals Glamorous Night, The Dancing Years, Perchance To Dream and Kings Rhapsody filled West End theatres in the 1930s and 40s.

Dennis O'Neill CBE

Pontarddulais born, Dennis O'Neill has carved out a glittering career as an operatic tenor of the very highest order and is world renowned as a fantastic leading man. He has performed worldwide in places such as the Royal Opera House in London, the Metropolitan Opera in New York and is a regular guest star with the Welsh National Opera. He has also made frequent guest appearances with the Bavarian State Opera and appeared with the Vienna State Opera. Dennis has delighted audiences at the Grand Theatre on many occasions including its 100th Anniversary show in 1997. Dennis is deeply involved in the development of future opera singers and is director of the International Academy of Voice at Cardiff University. He gives masterclasses worldwide and adjudicated in prestigious international competitions.

Joanna Page

Joanna Page was born in Mumbles, Swansea. As she grew up her acting aspirations were realised when she joined the West Glamorgan Youth Theatre. She also appeared at the Grand Theatre in a Bumbles Of Mumbles show with Alex Frith. After a few minor appearances on television, she landed her first film role in the Brit flick Love Actually in 2003. More television and theatre followed including a role as Candy, the daughter of Griff Rhys Jones, in the Russell T Davies-penned series Mine All Mine, which was filmed in Swansea in 2004. Joanna was a hard working jobbing actress until in 2007 she was well and truly launched into the public eye as Stacey in the runaway comedy success Gavin and Stacey. Since then many more offers flooded in for this extremely talented and likeable actress. She also had a leading role in the 2001 BBC Production of The Cazalets, about a disparate well to do English family during the Second World War.

Gail Pearson

Born in Neath she studied at University College, Cardiff and the Royal Northern College of Music in Manchester. Her professional début was as Gilda in Rigoletto with the Welsh National Opera. She has since performed many times with the Welsh National Opera, English National Opera, Scottish National Opera, Opera North and in numerous concerts worldwide. In 2002 she created the role of Mary Wollstonecraft Godwin in the world premiere of Sally Beamish's new opera Monster with Scottish Opera. In April of 2009 Gail returned to Neath to perform with Neath Amateur Operatic Society at St David's Church in The Merry Widow. Her father, Mel Pearson was musical director with Briton Ferry Musical Theatre Company for many years.

Julie Paton

Born and brought up in Swansea, Julie joined The Raie Copp School of Dance and went on to appear with numerous amateur companies at The Grand Theatre including Gendros Catholic Amateur Operatic Society and The Abbey Players. In 1986/87 she appeared alongside Christopher Biggins and Les Dennis in Mother Goose at the Grand. Leading roles followed in both the West End and touring productions of Joseph and the Amazing Technicolor Dreamcoat, Oliver, Kiss of the Spiderwoman and Godspell which came to Swansea on a tour in May 1988. The star of the show on that occasion was her future husband, Rock 'n' Roll star Alvin Stardust. Julie has since appeared around the world with him. The couple have a daughter, Millie.

Howard Phillips

Howard was born in Llansamlet, Swansea, and attended the same primary school as Ruth Madoc. His career in amateur theatre started in 1961 with an appearance in The Abbey Players first production The Boyfriend. He studied under singing tutor and famous opera singer John Myrddin and later Cassie Simon. Howard's first principal role was as Nicely Nicely Johnson in Swansea Amateur Operatic Society's production of Guys And Dolls at Swansea Grand Theatre in 1967 and his rendition of Sit Down You're Rocking The Boat is still fondly remembered. He has appeared for many societies including Uplands Arts, Neath Amateur Operatic and Penyrheol Light Operatic. In 1974 without his knowledge Cassie entered Howard into the National Eisteddfod at Carmarthen. He was selected as one of the finalists, and was the eventual runner up. It was a feat he was later to repeat twice at the Eisteddfod. In 1990 Howard studied for a degree in history at Swansea University and also joined an agency that brought him some professional work on film and TV. Including roles in Pobl y Cwm, Cowbois ac Injuns and A Mind To Kill. In 2005 Howard was asked by the Welsh FA to sing the country's National Anthem before the World Cup qualifier against Azerbaijan at The Millenium Stadium. He has also done the same at The Liberty Stadium and Parc y Scarlets.

Sian Phillips CBE

Sian Phillips was born in Betws near Ammanford, and attended Pontardawe Grammar School. She was inspired to take to the stage by her annual visits to see the pantomimes in Swansea. At an early age she performed on radio and television for the BBC. Sian has had a long and illustrious career on film, television, theatre and radio and is cherished as one of Wales' greatest living actresses. One of her most acclaimed performances was as Marlene Dietrich in the West End and on Broadway. She was married to Peter O'Toole for many years and they have two children.

Mal Pope

Mal Pope was born in Brynhyfryd, Swansea and was discovered by Radio 1 DJ John Peel as a fresh faced teenage musical genius. He was quickly signed up by Elton John's newly formed record company Rocket Records. After many years living, performing and recording in London he decided to move back home to Wales, first becoming a researcher for BBC Radio Wales, and later a producer. Television followed, with him having his own show for HTV, The Mal Pope Show. In 1995 he produced his first musical Copper Kingdom which was staged at the Grand Theatre in June of that year. Mal wrote the music to author Iris Gower's words. He followed it up with the successful Amazing Grace in 2005 and again a year later. In 2007 he wrote a new musical on the life of the boxer Tommy Farr called Contender. It starred Mike Doyle in the title role and was praised by the critics. Mal's career has included tours with Art Garfunkel, Belinda Carlisle and Merrill Osmond and he has an impressive back catalogue of his own albums. In 2009 his musical Cappuccino Girls was staged at Swansea Grand Theatre, with a new version of the title track recorded by Swansea singing sensation Bonnie Tyler.

Sion Probert

An actor since the age of 11, Sion has appeared in leading roles with The Royal Shakespeare Company, The English Shakespeare Company and various theatres in the West End and worldwide. Sion went to Clwyd Primary School in Swansea with Philip Sayer and they remained life long friends – Philip was also best man at Sion's wedding. He has featured in hundreds of plays, documentaries, short stories, serialisations and poetry programmes for BBC radio. His varied television and film appearances span many years, and include roles in Welsh, French, Spanish and Italian. Sion has received awards for his contributions as a writer, performer and director in all aspects of the media. He is best remembered for his iconic performance as Maldwyn Novello Pugh in the BBC film Grand Slam in 1978. He has performed at the Grand Theatre on a number of occasions.

Radcliffe and Ray

Dick and Ray Radcliffe were Swansea born brothers. They worked a popular vocal and piano act in the style of Layton and Johnstone. Their regular radio broadcasts and successful gramophone record sales made them a very successful act on the extensive Empire and variety circuits in their day. The pair were regularly employed alongside Norman Evans in his well known road show and even conquered the United States.

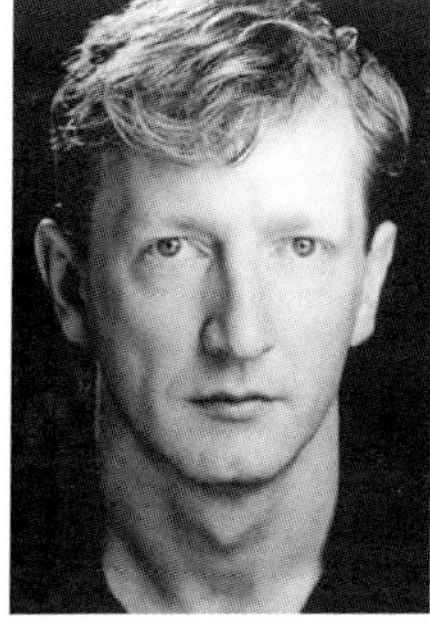

Steffan Rhodri

Steffan Rhodri was born in Morriston, Swansea. He attended Exeter University studying drama and English. He was a company member at Theatr Powys for four years where he learned his craft. Steffan appeared in the film Twin Town, filmed in Swansea. Since then he has become a familiar face on Welsh television with roles in Pobl y Cwm, Con Passionate and Belonging among many others. On stage he has appeared all over the country and at the Grand Theatre on a number of occasions including Rape of The Fair Country in 1997 and Communicating Doors in the same year. His most recognisable role on television was as Dave Coaches on Gavin and Stacey and he played Reg Cattermole in Harry Potter and the Deathly Hallows.

Kathryn Rice

Kathryn is a freelance director working in the fields of both drama and musical theatre. She initially trained alongside her father, the well-known director David Thomas MBE and then undertook training at Warwick and Loughborough universities, continuing to develop her skills working alongside various professional directors. Kathryn directs the Sir Harry Secombe Youth Musical Theatre Trust which is based at the Grand Theatre. Its productions have included Fame, The Wizard of Oz, We Will Rock You and Summer Holiday. Other directing credits with Cockett Operatic Society include Me and My Girl, Hot Mikado and Jekyll and Hyde. Kathryn, her mum and sister formed a company, Master Act in memory of her father. The company's inaugural production of The Boyfriend was a sell-out and the company intend to continue to bring small, quality musicals to theatres in Wales. Kathryn has also directed the Grand Theatre production of Swansea Girls, a musical by Lyn Mackay based on the lives of four women living in Swansea. In addition she directed a touring production of The Wales Spectacular Variety Show and Bound for Broadway at the Grand Theatre for Silver Stage and Screen Productions.

Rachel Roberts

Rachel Roberts was born in Llanelli. Her father was Rev Richard Rhys Roberts. She trained at the Royal Academy of Dramatic Art where she was awarded the Athene Seyler Award for Comedy. She first appeared in repertory at The Grand in 1950, taking part in plays like Family Portrait, Bonaventure and Crime Passionel. She married the stage actor Alan Dobie in 1955, which lasted until 1961. Her screen debut came in the 1953 film Valley of Song. Rachel appeared in the film Saturday Night and Sunday Morning in 1960 to critical acclaim and won the first of her two BAFTA's for Best British Actress. She met and married Rex Harrison in 1962 and was nominated for an Oscar as Best Actress in This Sporting Life. Rex was also nominated for Best Actor in a leading role for Cleopatra at the same award ceremony in 1964. Unfortunately neither won. After many screen appearances she returned to the Grand Theatre stage on September 29, 1969 in Who's Afraid Of Virginia Woolf, which ironically starred her former husband Alan Dobie along with Joanna Van Gyseghem. Rex reportedly came to the theatre and watched Rachel through every performance. Rachel's mother lived in Townhill then, and she arranged for the Grand's management to provide seats for her mother to come to see her. After her divorce from Rex Harrison in 1971 she continued in supporting roles in films including Doctor's Wives, Murder on the Orient Express, Picnic at Hanging Rock, Foul Play, When a Stranger Calls together with Charlie Chan and the Curse of the Dragon Queen. She also appeared in Yanks with Richard Gere in 1979. Sadly she suffered in her private life and in 1980, aged 53, she committed suicide.

Philip Sayer

Philip Sayer was born in Swansea on October 24, 1946. His early schooling was at Clwyd Primary in Penlan. His potential talent as an actor was recognised by Kenneth Pearce, one of his teachers there. After a few shows with Swansea Little Theatre, Philip became assistant stage manager at the Grand during the repertory season of 1963, under the guidance of John Chilvers. After studying at the London Academy of Music and Dramatic Art, he appeared in the West End as Frank-N-Furter in the Rocky Horror Show, until the strain of working in high heels every night brought on a serious back injury, which forced him to withdraw from the show. On TV he appeared on many programmes in the 1970s like Van Der Valk, Crown Court and Rock Follies. On the big screen he appeared in The Hunger and Shanghai Surprise. He was also acclaimed as a Shakespearian actor, and after he died in 1989, his friend Sir Ian Mckellen hosted a tribute show at the Aldwych Theatre in Philip's honour.

Sir Harry Secombe

Harry Donald Secombe was born at 7 St Leger Crescent in the St Thomas area of Swansea on September 8, 1921. Harry was one of four children, although his sister Joan died when she was just four years old. He had an older brother, Fred and a younger sister Carol. Harry's father was a good artist, who did drawings for the South Wales Evening Post, and his mother was the manageress of Peacock's

Bazaar in Swansea Market for a while. He had a very happy childhood. During the Second World War he met Spike Milligan and the seeds of the future Goon Show were sown. Along with Harry the show catapulted Peter Sellers and Michael Bentine to stardom. Harry's career took him through comedy, television, musical theatre, chart success and film, most famously as Mr Bumble in Oliver in 1968. Later in life he appealed to a new audience as host of TV's Sunday evening Highway programme. He appeared at Swansea Empire in the pantomime Puss In Boots in 1952/53, and at the Grand Theatre in Pickwick in 1995 with Ruth Madoc and Glyn Houston. Harry, who was knighted in 1981 suffered a stroke in 1997 from which he did not really recover. He died in 2001. His legacy to Swansea is The Sir Harry Secombe Trust set up in his name for up and coming performers to experience appearing on the big stage of the city's Grand Theatre.

Michael Sheen OBE

Michael Sheen was brought up in Port Talbot, and has followed in the tradition of the town for producing world class acting talent. Sheen has specialised in playing iconic British characters on the big screen. These have included Kenneth Williams in Fantabulosa, Tony Blair in The Deal and The Queen, David Frost in Frost/Nixon and in 2009 as Brian Clough in The Damned United. He was awarded an OBE in the Queen's Honours list in 2009. His father is Jack Nicholson lookalike Meyrick Sheen. Michael's early career saw him perform at Neath Little Theatre, Swansea's Taliesin Theatre, and The Princess Royal Theatre, Port Talbot in amateur productions. He has a child with his former partner, actress Kate Beckinsale who was the daughter of Porridge star Richard Beckinsale.

Kenny Smiles

Kenny was born and raised in Swansea. Early in the 1980s, after three successive pantomimes at the Grand, and having established himself as a great favourite with the city's audiences, he decided to follow in the footsteps of the legendary Tom Jones and see what life was like for a Welsh entertainer in the USA, and especially Las Vegas. Kenny's luck was in and he established a completely new career as a cabaret artist. In the years that followed he became one of the most sought-after entertainers for the luxury cruise ship market. After many years of living in America he returned to Wales to live in Newport. He still entertains on luxury cruise ships. His act developed into a purely off the cuff routine and he only rehearses his songs. Kenny lists his proudest achievement as topping the bill in the pantomime Puss in Boots at the Grand in 1981/82.

Ray Smith

Ray Smith was born in Trealaw in the Rhondda in 1936 and had a busy and successful career on stage and television. His first regular TV role was in 1959 as PC Smith in the series Nick Of The River. He did two rep seasons at the Grand Theatre under the direction of John Chilvers. He appeared in the 1960 series How Green Was My Valley and also in the 1975 remake, this time in the memorable role of Dai Bando. His most recognised role nationally was as Detective Superintendant Gordon Spikings in the hit television series Dempsey and Makepeace. Ray also appeared in many, diverse and challenging roles and it was a great loss to the acting profession when he died of a heart attack in 1991 aged just 55.

John Sparkes

John Sparkes was born in Swansea and started out on his journey in the world of entertainment as a stand-up comedian, being nominated for the Perrier Award in 1987 for his first solo Edinburgh show. He has risen to become a well established face on television famously for the characters of Siadwell in the Naked Video Show and Barry Welsh in Barry Welsh is coming. John has also made a number of one man show appearances at Swansea Grand Theatre. Many will recall him as the voice of Fireman Sam in the children's cartoon series. He returned to the Grand in 2006 with his television show Ghost Story, where he investigated the ghostly goings on at the theatre. He spent the night alone there with a camcorder.

William Squire

William Squire was born at 13 Florence Street, Neath in 1917, just three doors down from where Maudie Edwards was born. He was for many years an important figure in Britain's major theatre companies, though rarely a leading man. He was among the leading supporting Shakespearian actors of his time. In 1956 he played Captain Cat in the first stage adaptation of Under Milk Wood at the Edinburgh Festival, and toured the UK, stopping off at Swansea

Empire Theatre in September, it also starred Donald Houston. In 1961 he took over the role of Arthur – vacated by Richard Burton – on Broadway in the musical Camelot starring alongside Julie Andrews. On film William appeared in The Battle Of The River Plate and Where Eagles Dare. His most recognisable role however was in the television series Callan as the boss of Edward Woodward.

Dorothy Squires

Born in Pontyberem, Llanelli, she became a band singer for Charlie Kunz and then for Billy Reid. Hugely popular, she sold thousands of records and topped the bill around the country. She also performed in front of a young Elvis Presley who insisted that she perform This Is My Mother's Day. In 1953 she married the actor Roger Moore, who was 12 years younger than her. Many people felt she neglected her own career to promote his. If that was the case she succeeded and he became a film star. They parted in 1961 but she refused to give him a divorce until 1968. In an effort to restart her own career she hired the London Palladium for her one-woman show and packed the place. She even got a recording, My Way, in the Top Twenty. However, she became unreliable, prone to sue everyone at the slightest provocation, and eventually became ill with cancer. She spent her last years living off the charity of one of her loyal fans. She is nowadays regarded as Wales' version of Judy Garland. She regularly appeared at Swansea Empire Theatre, though Dorothy Squires' only appearance at the Grand came on March 27, 1967. She died, aged 83, on April 14, 1998.

Stan Stennett MBE

Stan Stennett was born on July 30, 1925 in Cardiff. He was brought up in Gorseinon, Swansea, by an aunt after his mother died in childbirth. Stan has fond memories of his time in the city. He sold sweets at the local cinema and in return would get free entry to the matinees. This was to fuel his dream to be an entertainer, hoping to emulate stars such as Gene Autrey. While in Swansea he saved up to buy a guitar and taught himself to play. Then came service in the Second World War. After his demob in 1947 he entered a talent contest at The Royal Gwent Talent Show in Newport, which he won. One of the judges on that day was Mair Jones who was one of the producers of radio's Welsh Rarebit programme who offered him a spot as resident comedian on the show. Stan appeared in variety all over the country with acts like Johnny Ray, Benny Hill, Charlie Chester and Tommy Cooper. He returned to Swansea in the pantomime Red Riding Hood in 1950/51 at the Grand. He appeared with Morecambe and Wise in Babes In The Wood in 1955/56, this time at the Empire Theatre. On television he appeared in The Black and White Minstrel Show, Coronation Street, and Crossroads. Two more pantomimes followed at the Grand Theatre; Mother Goose in 1959/60 and Robinson Crusoe in 1969/70. He returned to the Grand in 2009 in his Bless 'em All variety show nearly 60 years after his first appearance there.

Mike Sterling

Mike Sterling was born in Glanamman, but moved to Swansea as a child. His love for singing was developed at the age of seven when he used to entertain the guests at his parents hotel. His first professional engagement took place at the Cwmfelin Social Club, Swansea at just 14. He was launched to stardom when he won New Faces in 1987 and since then has been an artiste in theatre, television, concert and recording, most notably known for his interpretation of The Phantom in Lord Lloyd Webber's The Phantom Of The Opera, with over 1,000 performances in the role at Her Majesty's Theatre and on tour. Mike has performed alongside stars like Dame Shirley Bassey, Michael Ball, Barry Manilow, Eric Clapton and Michael Flatley. He produced a fabulous homecoming concert at the Grand Theatre in 1996. He has fond memories of the theatre as a youngster from watching Ryan Davies in pantomime there. A highlight of this homecoming concert was Mike performing a duet of Unchained Melody with his long term singing coach, Welsh operatic tenor and former Opportunity Knocks winner, Allun Davies from Neath. In 2008 Mike appeared in Beijing as Fagin in Oliver.

Brian Sullivan

Swansea born, Brian Sullivan was educated at Gowerton Boys Grammar School and made his acting debut aged just 15. Brian trained for the stage at the Leatherhead Repertory Theatre with well known drama coach Marion Naylor. His radio and television work includes The Life and Times Of Lloyd George, Three Up, Two Down and Return To Treasure Island. He has worked with Dirk Bogarde, Lee Remick, Dyan Cannon, Elke Sommer, Richard Todd and Robert Hardy among many others. He was once Swansea City Council's entertainments

entertainments officer and produced and directed three pantomimes at the Grand Theatre in the 1980s. As entertainments officer he brought to the area shows by Tom Jones, Shirley Bassey, The Everly Brothers and Don Williams. Brian also produced numerous shows with the Clydach and District Amateur Operatic Society.

Dave Swan

Dave Swan was brought up in Swansea. At school he was the class clown and loved the fact that he could make people laugh. To appease his father he started an apprenticeship as a painter and decorator, and would call bingo at night, cultivating his act. He was a comedian who developed his act through the tough valley clubs in the 1960s. He rose to become a successful club comedian and was asked by John Chilvers to appear in the pantomime Puss In Boots at the Grand in 1970. He went to Las Vegas on a trip in 1978 and liked it so much he moved there with his wife Jan and worked continuously until his death from cancer in 2008. He often worked with performers like Frank Sinatra, Sammy Davis Junior, Tony Bennett, Roy Orbison and Billy Eckstine and opened shows for many Vegas legends.

Myfanwy Talog

Myfanwy Talog was one of Wales' best loved actresses, appearing in both Welsh and English language productions. She was especially known as the wayward daughter, Phyllis Doris, in the Ryan and Ronnie TV series and from the Welsh soap opera Dinas as well as being the narrator of the Welsh cartoon series Will Cwac Cwac. She appeared in two repertory seasons at the Grand Theatre, under the directorship of John Chilvers, and was a great favourite with Swansea audiences. She was the long-term partner of actor Sir David Jason and died of breast cancer at the early age of just 51 on March 11, 1995.

David Thomas MBE

David Thomas was born in Brixton, London, on December 10, 1931. His mother was a dresser to a firm of theatrical costumiers, delivering and collecting costumes from theatres. As a young boy David was fortunate to come into contact with the legendary actress Sybil Thorndike and her husband Lewis Casson. The family moved to Swansea in 1937 and settled in Brynmill. In 1943 during the Second World War he joined Brynmill and Uplands Youth Club when it staged its first Gilbert and Sullivan production The Gondoliers. In 1949 the club changed its name to the Uplands Arts Club. He progressed to play virtually every lead role in the Gilbert and Sullivan repertoire, later becoming producer, director, chairman and president over the 60 years that followed. In 1961 David and a few friends formed the Abbey Players. He also produced shows for Port Talbot Amateur Operatic Society from 1965 - 2000. Other companies he directed for included Carmarthen Amateur Operatic Society, Clydach Amateur Operatic Society, Penyrheol Light Opera, Neath Master Players, Neath Opera Group and Cadoxton Opera Society. In June 1995 he was awarded an MBE for services to amateur theatre in Wales.

Dylan Thomas

Dylan Thomas was born in Swansea and became Wales' best known writer. In 1932 he joined Swansea Little Theatre based in Southend, Mumbles and acted in a number of plays including Noel Coward's Hay Fever. After a very short career as a journalist with The South Wales Evening Post he left in late 1932 to write poetry full time. His first poem, published in England was And Death Shall Have No Dominion in 1933. His lasting legacy is his play for voices Under Milk Wood which was first produced for the stage at the Edinburgh Festival in 1956. It came to the Swansea Empire Theatre the same year, before transferring to the West End. It has been performed at all the Swansea theatres many times since and in 1972 transformed into a film starring Richard Burton and Elizabeth Taylor. Dylan has long qualified for the title of Swansea's most famous son.

Eleanor Thomas

Swansea born actress and teacher, Eleanor began her performing as an amateur performer and made a great impact as Shakespeare's Juliet in a production for Swansea Youth Theatre and Swansea University and was then invited to join the rep company at Swansea Grand Theatre. She appeared in six different seasons there under the direction of John Chilvers, being especially remembered for her performance as Heloise in the epic production Abelard and Heloise. Her career included seasons in the West End and also with various UK productions, along with several pantomimes as principal girl until she took on the demanding everyday roles of mother and teacher.

Rachel Thomas OBE

Rachel Thomas was born at Alltwen, Pontardawe, in 1905. She first rose to prominence in 1933 when the BBC invited her to read the lesson in a service from Minny Street Chapel in Cardiff. Listeners demanded to know more about the owner of this wonderful voice. She made her film debut in the 1940 film Proud Valley, which starred the American singer Paul Robeson. (Robeson incidentally made a personal appearance at The Plaza Cinema in the Kingsway, Swansea in 1939). Her other films included The Halfway House, Blue Scar, Tiger Bay, and the film version of Under Milk Wood with Richard Burton and Elizabeth Taylor in 1972. In 1960 she was central to the success of BBC TV's How Green Was My Valley and was awarded the OBE in 1968. Rachel appeared in rep at the Grand on several occasions, finally at the age of 82 with Harriet Lewis in Arsenic And Old Lace. For many years she was a stalwart of the Welsh TV soap Pobl y Cwm. She died on her 90th birthday after a long illness following a fall. Her motto was 'Not good when you can do better.

Jean Thorley

Jean Thorley was born and brought up in the Sandfields area of Swansea. Her love of music took her to the Welsh College of Music. Her first foray onto the stage was as part of the chorus in the Swansea Amateur production The Maid of The Mountains at Swansea Empire Theatre in 1955. At the age of 16 Jean won a Lili Marlene competition at The Carlton Cinema on the back of which she was offered a contract to go to London. Her father felt that she was too young to go and London's loss was Swansea's gain. Jean became a regular principal player with Swansea Amateur Operatic Society alongside Colin Hodges, seeing the society through a purple patch in its history with a long run of sellouts. Jean represented Swansea in the television series Top Town in 1959. In 1965 she was visited at home by John Chilvers and offered a principal role in the Grand pantomime Puss in Boots alongside Jess Conrad, a role she was to turn down as she was bringing up her two children, Mark and Julie. In 1971 she appeared on Opportunity Knocks in the same show as Les Dennis and on the back of it was offered an entertainment spot on a three week Mediterranean cruise. Throughout the 1970s she appeared in cabaret alongside Dick Emery, Mike and Bernie Winters, Bob Monkhouse and Norman Vaughan in a series of midnight matinees across Swansea in venues including The Albert Hall and the Brangwyn Hall. Her last role with Swansea Amateurs was in Camelot in 1974. She later became a singing coach at the Grand Theatre.

Menna Trussler

Menna Trussler was born in Swansea and eventually joined Fforestfach Amateur Drama Club which staged plays at the Welfare Cinema. After many years Menna joined Swansea Amateur Operatic Society and was given a role in Fiddler On The Roof at the Grand Theatre in 1973. Four years later on April 22, 1977 Menna got a call from John Chilvers offering her a position as assistant stage manager at the Grand, the date is significant, as later in the day the news came through that Ryan Davies had died in America. She has since gone on to a successful career on film, stage and television, including Pobl y Cwm, Doctors, Casualty and Torchwood. Menna made three pantomime appearances at her beloved Grand Theatre, with Puss In Boots in 1981/2, Dick Whittington, 1982/3, and she was also the Fairy Godmother in Cinderella in 1984/5. Menna was in all three series of the award winning comedy series Little Britain. She also appeared in both Jennifer Saunders's series Jam and Jerusalem. Big screen appearances include Human Traffic, and August with Sir Anthony Hopkins.

Bonnie Tyler

Bonnie Tyler was born in Skewen, near Neath as Gaynor Hopkins on June 8, 1951. Her father was a miner and her mother harboured a love of opera which she shared with Bonnie her two sisters and two brothers. In 1976, Tyler was spotted in The Townsman Club in Swansea by the songwriting and producing team of Ronnie Scott and Steve Wolfe. She has had a hugely successful career as a singer, since her first hit Lost In France in 1976. She is instantly recognisable on record due to her raspy vocal style. It's a Heartache in 1977 made her an international star, reaching number three in the US singles chart. In 1983 she recorded the album Faster Than the Speed of Night which entered the UK album chart at No.1 making her a Guinness Record holder as the first ever British female solo artist to have an album enter the UK chart at No. 1. From that album her biggest hit Total Eclipse Of The Heart reached No. 1 in the UK, USA, France and Australia. Bonnie appeared on the Grand stage in November 2009 in Mal Pope's musical Cappucino Girls. A multi-award winner, Bonnie tours all over the world, but still loves to return home to Swansea.

Melanie Walters

Melanie was born and brought up in Swansea. After studying drama at Aberystwyth University she got the first acting job she auditioned for and her career began. She lived in London for many years, working extensively in theatre, radio and on television where her many roles included appearances on The Bill, Coronation Street, Casualty, Belonging, Dangerfield and Jack Of Hearts. She decided to move back home to Swansea to bring up her son. Melanie now juggles her acting career with her role as director of a company which runs pilates classes. Her most high profile acting role is as Stacey's mother Gwen in the runaway sitcom success Gavin and Stacey for BBC TV. One of her favourite stage roles was at the Grand Theatre, playing the part of Rita alongside Freddie Lees in Educating Rita in 1992. Melanie who also has a regular role as one of the mothers in popular TV soap Hollyoaks landed the starring role in the Grand's 2010/11 pantomime, Snow White and the Seven Dwarfs.

Ronnie Williams

Ronald Clive Williams was born in Cefneithin, Llanelli, on March 29 1939. After trying various jobs including one as a junior reporter on his local newspaper and as a conductor with the James bus company in Ammanford, at the age of 19 Ronnie went to Cardiff College of Music And Drama. After that he freelanced as a continuity announcer with the BBC. He then got together with Ryan Davies in the mid-1960s and they became the nation's favourite double act. Known simply as Ryan and Ronnie they dominated Welsh TV and the cabaret scene for many years. Their place in Swansea theatre folklore was cemented when they tackled the pantomimes at the Grand Theatre – Cinderella in 1972/73 and Dick Whittington in 1973/74. They were the longest running pantomimes in the country at the time. Ryan and Ronnie parted company in 1974 due to Ronnie's ill health. He did sporadic work over the next few years, appearing at the Grand in 1988 in a show in memory of Con Murphy. His partner that day was Ryan's son Arwyn in a recreation of their act. His last appearance was a poignant one. The final scenes of the movie Twin Town took place on Mumbles Pier with him conducting a choir singing Myfanwy (ironically Ryan's signature tune) in 1997. Ronnie was suffering from severe depression and tragically took his own life on December 28, of that year.

Rex Willis

William Rex Willis was born on October 29, 1924 in Ystrad in the Rhondda Valley. His father Captain Billy Willis owned a number of cinemas in the Welsh valleys, and also the Grand. Rex was a great sportsman and went on to achieve 21 Welsh international caps, some as Captain. His father passed control of his entertainment business interests to Rex in the 1960s. Rex was fortunate that The Grand was run so brilliantly by John Chilvers, that he had little to do in regards to the day-to-day operation of the Theatre, He was, however a hard-nosed businessman, and negotiated fiercely with Swansea City Council when they eventually bought the theatre in 1978 for just under £100,000.

Cherry Willoughby

Cherry Willoughby began her career as a dancing double-act with her sister, Hazel. She turned to choreography during the Second World War and worked extensively for ENSA, the organisation set up to entertain servicemen and women. She then staged dances in the West End for Stanley Baxter and Jewel and Warriss, and appeared on stage opposite George Formby in Zip Goes A Million at the Palace Theatre, London. In 1964 she choreographed her first Grand Theatre pantomime Aladdin and worked alongside John Chilvers for the following 18 successive pantomimes. The Cherry Willoughby Dancers were an almost permanent fixture of the 'JC Years' at the Grand. Cherry continued working as a choreographer until she was well into her seventies, and died in 2003 aged 95. She also directed and choreographed several productions for Melincrythan Amateur Operatic Society and Clydach and District Amateur Operatic Society including the Melyn society's memorable Charlie Girl at The Gwyn Hall, Neath in 1975. She is fondly remembered by all involved with her productions.

The Grand auditorium packed with patrons – a scene to delight every single one of the managers who has ever held the reins at the theatre.

Looking from the back of the auditorium towards the curtained stage at the Grand Theatre.

Act 18

Full list of Grand productions

From its very first production right up to its latest show, the Grand Theatre, Swansea, has always been a place where people from the city and surrounding satellite towns have been drawn in their quest for entertainment. Its offerings down more than 11 decades have been many and varied; countless world famous stars have appeared on its stage and delighted audiences. Here for the first time is a complete list of every production at the theatre except pantomimes which are listed elsewhere.

1897: Opening Ceremony, The Geisha, The Land Of Nod, The Strange Adventures Of Miss Brown, Between The Light, The Span Of Life, The Shop Girl, My Friend The Prince, The Sign Of The Cross, A Trip To Chinatown, The King Of Crime, My Girl, Jim The Penman, The Mikado, The Ballet Girl, Monte Carlo, Two Little, Vagabonds, Tom, Dick and Harry, La Poupee, A Gaiety Girl, Shaft No.2 Company, The Shamrock and The Rose.

1898: True Blue, Boys Together, Saints And Sinners, The Prince and The Pauper, The Prisoner Of Zenda, The Gay Parisienne, When London Sleeps, Maritana, I Pagliacci, Cavalleria Rusticana, Faust, Tannhauser, Bohemian Girl, Il Trovatore, My Jack, Mary, Queen Of Scots, Hamlet, Lear The Forsaker, East Lynne, School For Scandal, The Destroying Angel, A Marriage Of Convenience, Madam Sans-Genes, The Iron Maiden, The French Maid, The Lady Slavey, Camille, Charlotte Lorday, The Lady Of Lyons, Greed Of Gold, The Mikado, The Sorcerer, Yeoman Of The Guard, The Private Secretary, Tommy Dodd, Garden scene from Faust, Prison scene from Maritana, Balcony scene from Romeo and Juliet, Othello, Merchant of Venice, The Hunchback, Macbeth, Hamlet, Merchant Of Venice, As You Like It, Richelieu, Macbeth, As You Like It, Richelieu, School For Scandal, La Poupee, A Little Ray Of Sunshine, Red Spider, The Transit Of Venus, How London Lives, Boys Together, Proof, The Golden Ladder, Two Little Vagabonds, Under The Red Robe, Little Minister, Under The Czar, The Geisha, The Tree Of Knowledge, The New Mephisto, The Circus Girl, Fedora, The Lady Of Lyons, The Silver King, The Sign Of The Cross, Between The Lights, The Coastguard, The Magistrate, The Guv'nor, Ours.

1899: A Woman Of No Importance, My Friend the Prince, The Swiss Express, The Belle Of New York, A Woman's Error, Lord and Lady Algy, Faust and Margaret, Sporting Life, Soldiers Of The Queen, Or Briton And Boer, Morocco Bound, What Happened To Jones, Tommy Atkins, The Idler, Liberty Hall, The Ambassador, The JP (Charley's Uncle), The Highwayman, Faithful James, The Liars, The Girl Of My Heart, Circus Girl, Dangers Of London, Slave Girl, The Three Musketeers, Christian's Cross, The Case Of Rebellious Susan, Scales Of Justice, The Only Way, The Little Minister, Pygmalion and Galatea, The Runaway Girl, Our Boys, Little Miss Nobody, The Gay Grisette, A Royal Divorce, The Cuckoo, Charley's Aunt, Falka, The Geisha, The Greek Slave, The Gay Lord Quez, Why Smith Left Home, The Broken Melody, The Shaughraun, Rogue Riley, The Colleen Bawn, The Boys From Wexford, Saints and Sinners, The Belle Of New York.

1900: Belle Of New York, The Great World Of London, Carmen, Stanella, Faust, Maritana, Lohengrin, Bohemian Girl, What Happened To Jones, The Favourite, Honour Thy Father, The American Heiress, The Christian, A Royal Divorce, La Poupee, David Garrick, The Bungalow, The Iron Founder, Still Waters Run Deep, Lady Of Lyons, Lord And Lady Algy, East Lynne, The Degenerates, At The Foot Of The Altar, Danny Fifth, The Private Secretary, Sweet Lavender, Lady Of Ostend, My Friend The Prince, Shadows Of A Great City, Curse Of Drink, Wages Of Sin, The

World Against Her, The Poor Streets Of London, The Octoroon, The Ticket Of Leave Man, The Little Minister, In Old Kentucky, Defender Of The Faith, A Pair Of Spectacles, A Woman Of No Importance, Three Little Britons, Bootle's Baby, Magda, The Second Mrs Tanqueray, Brother Officers, The Power And The Glory, Wheels Within Wheels, Two Little Vagabonds, A Runaway Girl, One Of The Best, Miss Hobbs & Madam Butterfly, The Belle Of New York, The Rose Of Persia, The J.P., On Her Majesty's Service, Greed Of Gold, Quo Vadis.

1901: Quo Vadis, The Worst Woman In London, A Trip To Chicago, The Sign Of The Cross, Davy Garrick, The Rivals, She Stoops To Conquer, School For Scandal, An Emperors Romance, La Poupee (the Doll), The Elder Miss Blossom, The Likeness Of The Night, Ben-my-chree, The World Of London, Tannhauser, Carmen, Lohengrin, Cricket On The Earth, Faust, Cinq Mars Or The Conspiracy, Facing The Music, Mrs Dane's Defence, Proof Or A Celebrated Case, The Red Coat, The Private Secretary, Sacrament Of Judas, Hamlet, Our Boys, Lord Edward, True Son Of Erin, Rory O'More, The Shaughraun, The Colleen Bawn, Green Bushes, Under False Colours, My Friend The Prince, The Silver King, Somebody's Sweetheart, London After Dark, The Unknown, East Lynne, Day To Day, The Orphans Of Paris, Called Back, Rob Roy, Iolanthe, Delivery From Evil, The Guilty Man, A Man's Shadow, The Silver King, In The Soup, Honour Thy Father, The Second Mrs Tanqueray, Magda, Brother Officers, San Toy Or The Emperors Own, A Message From Mars, A Night Out, Florodora, Lady Huntworth's Experiment, The Circus Girl, A Runaway Girl, Shop Girl, A Woman Adrift, The Second In Command, The Emerald Isle, The Night Of The Party, The Wilderness, Uncle Tom's Cabin.

1902: A Pair Of Spectacles, When London Sleeps, The Sign Of The Cross, The Greed Of Gold, The Merchant Of Venice, Twelfth Night, Romeo And Juliet, Much Ado About Nothing, The Toreador, Kitty Grey, Sherlock Holmes, An Eye For An Eye, San Toy, The Dandy Fifth, In A Woman's Grip, Are You A Mason, The Cape Mail, Patience, The Messenger Boy, Davy Garrick, The Rivals, The School For Scandal, Edmund Kean Tragedian, A Reformed Rake, Fair Play, The Geisha, A Royal Divorce, The Red Lamp, A London Actress, Master Of The Chain, The Shop girl, The circus Girl, A Runaway Girl, A Modern Magdalen, The Stolen Birthright, Why Woman Sins, A Little Outcast, The Little Minister, The Worst Woman In London, The Grip Of Iron, Livermore Brothers, Two Little vagabonds, The belle Of New York, Hamlet, Paulo and Francesca, The Merchant Of Venice, The Merry Wives Of Windsor, Richard The Third, Twelfth Night, The Lady Of Ostend, A Message From Mars, San Toy, Florodora, The Gas Grisette, Mice And Men, That Wretch Of A Woman, Charley's Aunt, The Blind Witness, Ben-My-Chree, A Woman Of No Importance, Sweet Nell Of Old Drury.

1903: The Three Musketeers, Called Back, HMS Irresponsible, The Sign Of The Cross, Tannhauser, Cinq Mars, Carmen, Cavalleria Rusticana & I Pagliacci, The Marriage Of Figaro, Lohengrin, Faust, In A Woman's Grip, Waterloo, The Bells, Louis XI, The Merchant Of Venice, Still Waters Run Deep, The Elder Miss Blossom, Mrs Hamilton's Silence, A Woman Adrift, Under The Red Robe, A Trip To Chinatown, The Fatal Wedding, Under Two Flags, Mons Beaucaire, David Garrick, In The Shadows Of Night, The Marauders, My Friend The Prince, The Sorrows Of Satan, The New Clown, The Eternal City, Our Flat, The Marauders, Sowing The Wind, The Light That Failed, Too Many Cooks, Held Up, The Silver King, Her Second Time On Earth, Two Little Vagabonds, Quality Street, A Chinese Honeymoon, Just Like Callaghan, The Lights Of London, The Marriage Of Kitty, Three Little Maids, The Christian, San Toy, The Admiral Crichton, My Lady Mollie, Sherlock Holmes, La Poupee, A Life's Revenge, When We Were 21, A Message From Mars.

1904: The Taming Of The Shrew, Julius Caesar, The Merry Wives Of Windsor, Macbeth, Hamlet, Julius Caesar, The Toreador, Zaza, The Ring That Binds, Tannhauser, Cavalleria Rusticana & I Pagliacci, Maritana, Don Giovanni, Lohengrin, Faust, Carmen, Dick Hope, The Elder Mrs Blossom, A Scrap Of Paper, Lady Of Lyons, Home Sweet Home, A Girl's Cross Roads, Between Two Women, Uncle Tom's Cabin, The Eternal City, Resurrections, Private Secretary, The Mikado, Monsieur Beaucaire, Mice And Men, Caste, Ours, School, The Gondoliers, Iolanthe, Yeoman Of The Guard, Princess Ida, Patience, The Mikado, Zaza, A Royal Divorce, The Master Criminal, Trooper Hunt's Widow, Saved From The Sea, Liberty Hall, The Sin Of Her Children, In The Ranks
, Sunday, The Fatal Wedding, Seal Of Silence, A Sailor's Sweetheart, His Excellency The Governor, The Darling Of The Gods, The Lady Of Ostend & The Cruise Of Saucy Sally, The Merchant Of Venice, Becket, The Lyons Mail, Waterloo, A Country Girl, Much Ado About Nothing, The Good Hope, The merchant Of Venice, Two little Vagabonds, Sapho, A Chinese Honeymoon, The Belle Of New York, Under The Red Robe, David Garrick, Nell Gwyn, A Path Of Thorns, East Lynne, No Mans Land, Maritana.

1905: Carmen, Lohengrin, The Daughter Of The Regiment, Faust, La Traviata, Il Trovatore, Bohemian Girl, Cavalleria Rusticana & Pagliacci, La Traviata, Mignon, Maritana, Lohengrin, Carmen, Girl From Kay's, Dahomey, The Housekeeper, Still Waters Run Deep, Les Cloches De Cornville, If I Were King, Three Little Maids, Sapho, The Sign Of The Cross, Sergeant Brue, The Christian, Duke Of Killicrankie, Facing The Music, A Hot Night, Merely Mary Ann, The Merchant Of Venice, As You Like It, Romeo And Juliet, The Merry Wives Of Windsor, The School For Scandal, Little Mary, Beauty And The Barge, The Girl From Chicago, The Garden Of Lies, Under The Czar, Jane Shore, The Shaughraun, Nell Gwyn, The Colleen Bawn, The Silver King, Lucky Durham, The Idle, A Pair Of, An Actor's Pardon, When London Sleeps, Are You A Mason, A Wrecker Of Men, Beside The Bonnie Briar Bush, Mice And Men, A Silent Accuser, A Country Girl, Cousin Kate, A Royal Revenge, The Adventures Of Lady Ursula, David Garrick, As You Like It, Nell Gwyn, The Mikado, The Gondoliers, Patience, Iolanthe, The Yeoman Of The Guard, The Freedom Of Suzanne, The Great Awakening, East Lynne, The Throne Of Terror, The Days Of Cromwell, Madam Bernice De Pasquali, The Duchess Of Dantzic.

1906: The Cingalee, The Lady Of Ostend, The Cruise Of Saucy Sally, The Orchid, Sunday, The Yeoman Of The Guard, Dick Hope, The Housekeeper, The Ironmaster, My Cousin Marco, The Breed Of The Tresham, Oliver Twist, The Earl And The Girl, The Wearin' O' The Green, The Walls Of Jericho, The Youngest Of Three, Daredevil Dorothy, Mr Hopkinson, The Little Bread Winner, The Price Of Her Soul, Leah Kleshna, Our Boys, Caste, The Biggest Scamp On Earth, Peggy Machree, The Manxman, The Plucky Nipper, Lost In London, The New Clown, Maritana, The Lilly Of Killarney, The Bohemian Girl, Carmen, La Fille De Madame Angot, The Daughter Of The Regiment, Faust, Camille, The Old Curiosity Shop, Sowing The Wind, In The Soup, A Queen's Vengeance, Boxing Film Oscar Nelson V Jimmy Britt, Two Little Vagabonds, The Sin Of Her Childhood, Hamlet, David Garrick, Othello, The Merchant Of Venice, Twelfth Night, The Merchant Of Venice, Hamlet, Mollentrave On Women, The Coal king, The Swiss

Express, His House In Order, The Bauble Shop, Lucky Durham, The Night Of The Party, When Knights Were Bold, San Toy, The White Chrysanthemum, Sunday, Uncle Tom's Cabin, Public Opinion, All Of A Sudden Peggy, The Streets Of London, Monte Cristo, His Majesty's Guest, The Little Michus.

1907: The Walls Of Jericho, The Lion And The Mouse, The Gondoliers and Trial By Jury, Brigadier Gerrard, The Trumpet Call, The Private Secretary, The Sign Of The Cross, The New Barmaid, The Master Builder, Somebody's Sweetheart, Boxing Film Oscar Nelson V Joe Gans, The Officer's Mess, Beside The Bonnie Brier Bush, Mdlle Lumiere, Claudian, The Youngest Of Three, Sir George Of Almacks, The Lady Of Ostend, A Marriage Of Convenience, Still Waters Run Deep, A Bunch Of Violets, The Second Mrs Tanquery, The Tyranny Of Tears, Captain Swift, The Glass Of Fashion, A Fools Paradise, The Profligate, Benefit concert for John Roberts, The Importance of Being Earnest, Driven From Home, Lady Windermere's Fan, The Love That women Desire, Are You A Mason, The New Housemaid, The Marriage Of Kitty, The Belle Of New York, The Prince Of Pilson, Leah Kleshna, Catch Of The Season, John Glaydes Honour, Broken Melody, See See, Hamlet, Taming Of The Shrew, David Garrick, The Merchant Of Venice, Othello, Twelfth Night, David Garrick, His House In Order, The Duchess Of Dantzic, Lucky Durham, The Walls Of Jericho, Lights Out, The Night Of The Party, The Lion And The Mouse, Mr Popple(Of Ippleton).

1908: The Christian, The Silver King, A Grand Sacred Concert, The Girl From Kays, Harbour Lights, Grand Sacred Concert, The Little Muchus, Sherlock Holmes, The Hypocrites, Monsieur Beaucaire, The Prisoner Of Zenda, The Lady Of Lyons, The School For Scandal, David Garrick, The Gay Gordons, A Royal Divorce, Grand Benefit Concert, Faust, Maritana, Beside The Bonnie Brier Bush, The Pirates Of Penzance, The Dandy Fifth, Mrs Ponderbury's Past, The Gayer Of The Gay, Her Son, The Mystery Of Edwin Drood, East Lynne, This Never Never Lasts, The Village Priest, Trilby, The Midnight Wedding, Man And Wife, In The Soup, Diana Of Dobson's, Florodora, Leah Kleshna, The Dairy Maid's, Charley's Aunt, You Never Can Tell, Miss Hook of Holland, The Bondman, With Edged Tools, The Merry Widow, Irene Wycherley, Merchant Of Venice, Hamlet, Romeo And Juliet, As You Like It, Othello, The Thieves, Lady Frederick, Mrs Dot, The Gay Lord Quez, Caste, A Pair Of Spectacles, Henry Of Lancashire, The Sorrow Of Sabia, Nana, A Dolls House, Hedda Gabler, The Master Builder, Peter's Mother.

1909: The New Housemaid, The Fatal Wedding, The Prodigal Son, Samson, The Cingalee, The Hypocrites, Raffles, The Sins Of Society, Sweet Lavender, Liberty hall, The Magistrate, Brewster's Millions, Butterflies, The Christian, Convict 99, Beside The Bonnie Brier Bush, Merchant Of Venice, David Garrick, Julius Caesar, Dorothy, Message From Mars, My Wife, The Breed Of The Thresham's, The Only Way, The Flag Lieutenant, The Chatelaine, Benefit Concert, Her Majesty's Guest, Sexton Blake, The Stepmother, His Excellency The Governor, Admiral Guinea, Fanny And The Servant Problem, The Explorer, Our Miss Gibbs, Candida, Cupid And The Styx, Havana, A Country Mouse, The Builder Of Bridge, With Edged Tools, Carmen, Lohengrin, Faust, The Masked Ball, Tannhauser, Maritana, An Englishman's Home, Man To Man, Somebody's Sweetheart, Under The Red Robe, Diana Of Dobson's, Brewster's Millions, John Glayde's Honour, An Anniversary Concert, Her Love Against The World.

1910: Political Meeting, A Royal Divorce, The Merry Widow, When Knight's Were Bold, The Dairymaids, The Woman In The Case, You Never Can Tell, The Sign Of The Cross, Thro' The Divorce Court, The Dollar Princess, The Little Damozel, Driving A Girl To Distraction, The Luck Of Roaring Camp, The Midnight Wedding, The Mikado, The Little Duke, The Private Secretary, Tom Jones, Those Terrible Twins, The Cruise Of The Constance, Drink, Ben-My-Chree, A Sacred Pictorial Service, On His Majesty's Service, Hush Money, Niobe (all smiles), The Silver King, The Speckled Bird, A Sherlock Holmes story, A White Man, The Greater Love, Our Miss Gibbs, Leah Kleschna, Miss Hook of Holland, Mr Preedy And The Countess, She Stoops To Conquer, The Road To Ruin, School For Scandal, A Reformed Rake, Davy Garrick, Sherlock Holmes, King Of Cadonia, The Fires Of Fate, The House Of Temperley, Old Heidelberg, The Geisha, A Greek Slave, Lord And Lady Algy, The marriage Of Kitty, The Prince And The Beggar man.

1911: Grand Opera in English, The Girl in The Train, Tantalizing Tommy, Priscilla Runs Away, The Merry Widow, Arsene Lupin, The Captain Of The School, The Chocolate Soldier, Darcy Of The Guards, Smith, The Ruin Of Her Life, The Arcadians, Charley's Aunt, The Boy King, Iolanthe, Just To Get Married, The Sins Of London, A Woman's Way, The Speckled band, The Man From Mexico, Her Love Against The World, The Sailor's Wedding, The Convict's Daughter, The Little Mother, Through Death Valley, The Gambler Of The Golden West, A Homespun Heart, The Little Prospector, Her Fatal Marriage, A Message From Mars, What The Butler Saw, East Lynne, Beau Brocade, A Royal Divorce, The Beggar Girls Wedding, Florodora, Peggy, The Witness For The Defence, The Unwritten Law, The Lily, Our Miss Gibbs, Brewster's Millions, The Chocolate Soldier, Inconstant George, The Dollar Princess, Passers By, A Butterfly On A Wheel, The Bishop's Move, Iolanthe, The Mikado, The Yeoman Of The Guard, The Mikado.

1912: The Last Of Luxembourg, Mrs Wiggs Of The Cabbage Patch, The Quaker's Girl, The Sign Of The Cross, King Of The Wild West, The Perplexed Husband, The Whip, The Balkan Princess, Merrie England, Baby Mine, The Passing Of The Third Floor back, The Lifeguardsman, Tantalizing Tommy, The Arcadians, The Girl In The Train, Il Trovatore, Maritana, Faust, I Pagliacci and Cavalleria Rusticana, The Barber Of Seville, Faust, Carmen, The Mousme, The Easiest Way, The Glad Eye, Under Two Flags, Brought To Book, For Wife And Kingdom, Home Sweet Home, A Soldier Of France, The Guiding Star, A London Actress, Rogues and Vagabonds, Siberia, The Ticket Of Leave Man, King Of The Gypsies, The Silver King, East Lynne, Bunty Pulls The Strings, Find The Woman, The Prince and The Beggar Maid, The Bear Leaders, A White Man, The Hope, The Sunshine Girl, When Knights Were Bold, A Butterfly On A Wheel, The Chocolate Soldier, Milestone, A Country Girl, A Waltz Dream, The Unwritten Law, The Barber Of Seville, The Lily Of Hamlet, Bella Donna, Amateur Dramatic and Drama Week, With Edged Tools, Kismet.

1913: The Count Of Luxemburg, The Gay Gordon's, Little Miss Llewellyn, The Quaker Girl, The Dollar Princess, The Merry Widow, Ready Money, The Whip, Les Cloches De Cornville, The Barrier, Every Woman, The Midnight Wedding, Miss Hook of Holland, Faust, Carmen, Elijah, Bohemian Girl, Tannhauser, Il Trovatore, Maritana, The Glad Eye, The Pink Lady, A Royal Divorce, The Easiest Way, The Miracle, Raffles, Sexton Blake, Candida, Cupid And The Styx, Hindle Wakes, Nature's Zoo, The Master Of The Mill, After Midnight, Convict 99, Hush Money, Tracked By Wireless, Allah's Orchard, The Flag Lieutenant, Oh! Oh! Delphine, East Lynne, Bunty Pulls The Strings, Find The Woman, The Duke, A Scrape O' The Pen, Oh I Say, Eliza Comes To

Stay, A Waltz Dream, Open Windows, The Sunshine Girl, The Typhoon, Man And Superman, A Butterfly On A Wheel, Bought And Paid For, The Girl In The Taxi, The Chocolate Soldier, His Indian Wife, The Quaker Girl.

1914: Gypsy Love, Peter Pan, Bella Donna, Officer 666, Maritana, Carmen, Romeo And Juliet, The Puritan's Daughter, The Dance Of Death, Elijah, The Bohemian Girl, The Sign Of The Cross, The Pearl Girl, The Girl From Utah, The Glad Eye, Mr Wu, The Dancing Minstrels, George Dance's Company, The Girl On The Film, The Soldier Princess, The Whip, Within The Law, The Easiest Way, Inconstant George, Milestones, The Gondeliers, The Scarlet Pimpernel, Bunty Pulls The Strings, A Place In The Sun, The Turning Point, The Master Of Iron, Change, Sorrows of Satan, East Lynne, The Maid Of The Mill, The Speckled Band, The Beggar Girl's Wedding, The Three Musketeers, Monte Cristo, Oh Oh Delphine, Mr Wu, Oh I Say, The Arcadians, Captain Scott In The Antarctic, The Girl In The Taxi, A Pair Of Silk Stockings, Raffles, The Ever Open Door, Brewster's Millions , The Land Of Promise, The Dollar Princess, The Coastguards Daughter, Mary Goes Forth, The Dust Of Egypt, The Blindness Of Virtue, Four nights of War footage, The Story Of The Rosary.

1915: Pygmalion, The Marriage Market, Mr Wu, Gypsy Love, Three Little Britons, The Pearl Girl, The Girl From Utah, Sherlock Holmes, Alias Jimmy Valentine, Charley's Aunt, Grumpy, The Count Of Luxembourg, The Second Mrs Tanqueray, Eliza Comes To Stay, Carmen, The Daughter Of The Regiment, Faust, Lily Of Kilarney, The Puritan's Daughter, The Bohemian Girl, Maritana, Diplomacy, Potash and Pearlmutter, The Merchant Of Venice, Hamlet, Henry The Fifth, Richard The Third, Henry The Fifth, The Gay Parisian, Lucky Durham, Leah Kleshna, The Barrier,Little Miss Ragtime, Searchlights, The Younger Generation, Cherry Kearton, A Royal Divorce, The White Girl Slave, What Every Woman Wants, Broadway Jones, Passers By, Three Spoonfuls Three, Florodora, It's a Long Way To Tipperary, The Land Of Promise, Oh I Say, Bella Donna, A Pair Of Silk Stockings, Gamblers All, Quinney's, The Spanish Main, A Country Girl, Tonight 's The Night, A Little Bit Of Fluff, Outcast, The Cinema Star, Hindle Wakes, The Man Who Stayed At Home, A Butterfly On The Wheel, Gypsy Love, The Merry Widow, The Great Adventurer, Elijah, The Second In Command, Lucky Durham, The Lion And The Mouse, Sealed Orders.

1916: Betty, Peg O' My Heart, Brewster's Millions, The Arcadians, Potash and Pearlmutter, Pygmalion, Diplomacy, More, Stop Thief, The Taming Of The Shrew, Grumpy, The Scarlet Pimpernel, HMS Pinafore, Britain Prepared, The Story Of The Rosary, The Belle Of New York, The Marriage Market, The Rosary, The Love Thief, Uncle Tom's Cabin, The Chaperon, Are You A Mason?, My Artful Valet, Somewhere A Voice Is Calling, East Lynne, A Mill Girls Wedding, The Land Of Promise, Sunday, A Father Of 90, The Girl On The Film, Romance, Peg O' My Heart, Nobody's Daughter, The Silver King, Betty, A Little Bit Of Fluff, My Lady Frayne, Maskelynes Mysteries, The Rotters, Caroline, Once A Thief or Kick In, The Case Of Lady Camber, The Spring Song, The Birth Of A Nation, The Basker, The Confessions Of A Wife, The Dumb Girl Of Portici, When The Heart Is Young, Romance.

1917: Potash And Pearlmutter, The Happy Day, Potash And Pearlmutter in Society, Mrs Pomeroy's Reputation, It Is For England, Woman Power, A Sense Of Humour, The Rotters, A Message From Mars, The Old Country, Her Husband's Wife, The Black Sheep Of The Family, The Ware Case, Sacred Concert in Aid Of Daily Post War Prisoners Fund, Peg O' My Heart, Hobson's Choice, David Garrick, Rigoletto, La Boheme, Il Trovatore, Martha, Two Little Wooden Shoes, Madam Butterfly, Cavalleria Rusticana, Bohemian Girl, All Of A Sudden Peggy, Ye Gods, General Post, Tiger's Cub, Jerry, Quinney's, Damaged Goods, Alias Jimmy Valentine, Her Only Son, For Love Of Peg, Under Two Flags, The Crackswoman, Mr Barnes Of New York, The Birth Of A Nation, The Pearl Girl, The Cinema Star, Intolerance, Caste, The Barton Mystery, Inside The Lines, The Misleading Lady, His Mother's Rosary, Peg O' My Heart, San Toy , A Greek Slave, Tina, Ghosts, Sherlock Holmes, Bluff, Young England, For Sweethearts and Wives, Baby Mine, Ann or Thro' The Window, Beauchamp and Beecham, Three Weeks, Cavalleria Rusticana & I Pagliacci, Tannhauser, The Bohemian Girl, Tosca, Rigoletto, Lady Of Killarney, Moonshine, Seven Days Leave.

1918: The Maid Of The Mountains, London Pride, Tonight's The Night, The Girl From Ciros, Eliza Comes To Stay, My Lady Frayle, The Arcadians, Broadway Jones, Charley's Aunt, Wild Heather, Bubbly, Five Nights, General Post, Betty, Cook, Damaged Goods, Monty's Flapper, Romance, The Little Brother, Remnant, Oh I Say, A Royal Divorce, Florodora, The Silver King, Nothing But The Truth, The Yellow Ticket, Carminetta, Inside The Lines, My Old Dutch, The Maid Of The Mountains, The Story Of The Rosary, The Boy, The Thirteenth Chair, Betty At Bay, High Jinks, Tales Of Hoffman, Madam Butterfly, Faust, Carmen, Mignon, Tales Of Hoffman, Il Trovatore, By Pigeon Post, Seven Days Leave, The Man From Toronto, A Cigarette Makes Romance, The Burgomaster Of Stilmonde, The Rapperee Troopers, The Professors Live Story, The Lilac Domino, Hearts Of The World, The Bing Boys Are Here.

1919: Hindle Wakes, Peter Pan, Fair And Warmer, Yes Uncle, C.O.D. Cash On Delivery, The Fatal Wedding, Going Up, A Southern Maid, Billeted, The Luck Of The Navy, Telling The Tale, Toto, Eliza Comes To Stay, Dear Brutus, Daddy Long Legs, A Country Girl, His Last Leave, Henry Of Navarre, The Christian, Tales Of Hoffman, Cavalleria Rusticana & I Pagliacci, Il Trovatore, Mignon, Carmen, Tales Of Hoffman, Maritana, Soldier Boy, Sailor Lad, Les Rouge Et Noirs, In The Night Watch, My Old Dutch, The Girl From Ciro's, All Aboard, By Pigeon Post, The School For Scandal, As You Like It, She Stoops To Conquer, The Merchant Of Venice, The Rivals, The School For Scandal, The Law Divine, A Chinese Honeymoon, Roxanna, A Temporary Gentleman, Les Rouges Et Noir, Arlette, The Maid Of The Mountains, Peg O' My Heart, Scandal, The Plaything Of An Hour, The Yellow Ticket, Tales Of Hoffman, Faust, Maritana, The Three Monks, The Marriage Of Figaro, The Daughter Of The Regiment, Il Trovatore, The Merry Widow, Gypsy Love, Shanghai, The Luck Of The Navy, Daddalums, The Purple Mask, The Freedom Of The Seas, The Female Hun, The Yeoman Of The Guard, Oh Joy.

1920: Seven Days Leave, The Arcadians, Daddies, The Lilac Domino, His Little Widows, Tails Up, A Southern Maid, Uncle Sam, High Jinks, La Tosca, Blodwen, Yes Uncle, La Poupee, Little Women, The Man From Toronto, The Gondoliers, Iolanthe, The Mikado, The Gondoliers, Iolanthe, The Mikado, The Naughty Wife, Tannhauser, Rigoletto, Cavalleria Rusticana & I Pagliacci, Romeo And Juliet, The Tales Of Hoffman, Faust, Bohemian Girl, Martyr's, Nurse Benson, The Merchant Of Venice, Hamlet, Twelfth Night, The Taming OF The Shrew, The Tempest, Julius Caesar, Hamlet, A Sinner In Paradise, The Divorce Question, A Fools Paradise, The Girl For The Boy, The Natural Law, Never Say Die, Il Trovatore, Maritana, The Rose Of Castille, Lohengrin, Samson and Delilah, La Traviata, Lilly Of Killarney, Toto, Paddy The Next Best Thing,

The Bird Of Paradise, Abraham Lincoln, The Jest, Scandal, Mr Pim Passes By, Tilly Of Bloomsbury, A Southern Maid, Rose Of Araby, Lord Richard In The Pantry, The Cinderella Man, Kissing Time, The Taming Of The Shrew, Macbeth, The Merchant Of Venice, Hamlet, As You Like It, The Tempest, Macbeth, The Boy, The Merry Widow, Gypsy Love, The Private Secretary, Carnival, La Tosca, Mignon, Suzanne's Secret & I Pagliacci, The Tales Of Hoffman, La Boheme, Madam Butterfly, Carmen, Princess Ida, Dorothy, Les Cloches De Corneville, Tom Jones, Merrie England, The Young Person In Pink, Chu Chin Chow.

1921: Our Peg, A Pair Of Sixes, Catch Of The Season, Tilly Of Bloomsbury, The Passing Of The Third Floor Back, Afgar, Romance, Tatters, Blodwen, Elijah, Irene, Warriors Day, Daddy Long Legs, The Yeoman Of The Guard, The Mikado, The Gondoliers, Iolanthe, The Mikado, The Yeoman Of The Guard, The Gondoliers, Hullo America, The Right To Strike, Peg O' My Heart, Macbeth, As You Like It, King Henry V, The Tempest, Hamlet, King Henry V, The Merchant Of Venice, Julius Caesar, Charley's Aunt, Scandal, Morocco Bound, Oh Julie, A Mother Should Tell, Tarzan Of The Apes, At The Hour Of Midnight, An Unmarried Mother, The Plaything Of An Hour, Pygmalion, Fanny's First Play, Toto, Don Q, French Leave, At The Villa Rose, Rose Of Araby, The Garden Of Allah, The Knave Of Diamonds, The White Headed Boy, Kissing Time, The Blue Lagoon, Mary Rose, Sybil, Carmen, Cavalleria Rusticana and I Pagliacci, Tannhauser, Rigoletto, Il Trovatore, Tales Of Hoffman, The Daughter Of The Regiment, Lord Richard In The Pantry, The Man Who Came Back, Paddy The next Best Thing, A Night Out, A Bill Of Divorcement, The Ninth Earl, Haddon Hall, The Sign Of The Cross, Seven Nights In London, The Savage And The Woman.

1922: A Safety Match, The Edge Of Beyond, The Very Idea, Bulldog Drummond, The Wrong Number, The Romantic, Young Lady, Getting Married, The Romantic Young Lady, Getting Married, The Importance Of Being Ernest, The Romantic Young Lady, Peddlers Pie, Woman-To-Woman, My Nieces, The Medium, What Did Her Husband Say, The Vigil, Private Room Number 6, E and O.E, The Sign On The Door, Uncle Ned, The Naughty Wife, The Belle Of New York, A Little Bit Of Fluff, The Scarlet Pimpernel, The Passing Of The Third Floor Back, Of Mice And Men, David Garrick, The Call Of The Room, The Merchant Of Venice, As You Like It, A Midsummer Nights Dream, Hamlet, Julius Caesar, A Midsummer Nights Dream, King Henry V, Hamlet, Seven Days Leave, Up In Mabel's Room, Nightie Night, Polly With A Past, Lily Of Killarney, Carmen, Lohengrin, Il Trovatore, Martha, Samson And Delilah, Faust, The Skin Game, A Mother Should Tell, At The Villa Rose, The Mormon And His Wive's, Three Wise Fools, Mrs Winterbottom's Woes, The Private Secretary, Sally, Brown Sugar, If Winter Comes, The Garden Of Allah, The Merry Widow, Gypsy love, The Faithful Heart, David Copperfield, The Bat, The Mikado, The Gondoliers, The Yeoman Of The Guard, The Gondoliers, Trial By Jury And Pirates Of Penzance, The Mikado, The Yeoman Of The Guard, The Lady Of The Rose, Samson And Delilah, Cavalleria Rusticana & I Pagliacci, Lohengrin, Tannhauser, Tales Of Hoffman, Mignon, Maritana, Paddy The Next Best Thing, Mary, Scandal, Butterfly On A Wheel, Peg O' My Heart, Ambrose Applejohn's Adventure, Tons Of Money, Martha, Made In England, Pedlars Pie.

1923: French Leave, Bulldog Drummond, Loyalties, The Mikado, Patience, The Sign On The Door, The Beggar's Opera, Charley's Aunt, The Edge Of Beyond, The Dover Road, The Way Of An Eagle, Old Bill M.P., The Co-Optimists, Through Romantic India, The Wandering Jew, The Call Of The Road, Of Mice And Men, Rosemary, The Passing Of The Third Floor Back, David Garrick, The Love Habit, Mignon, Rigoletto, Carmen, Lily Of Killarney, Madam Butterfly, Il Trovatore, Bohemian Girl, Macbeth, King Henry V, Macbeth, Othello, A Midsummer Nights Dream, Othello, Julius Caesar, The Merchant Of Venice, The Swansea Welsh Drama Society, Lass O' Laughter, Quality Street, If Winter Comes, Eliza Comes To Stay, Are You A Mason?, School For Scandal, She Stoops To Conquer, The Rivals, School For Scandal, Caste, The Sheik, Raffles, Monsieur Beaucaire, Magda, The Second Mrs Tanqueray, Uplifted, Gabrielle, La Poupee, Secrets, The Cat And The Canary, The Happy Ending, Tons Of Money, The Bad Man, The Marriage Of Kitty, The Cabaret Girl, The Lady Of The Rose, The Dancers, The Bat, The Maid Of The Mountains, Polly, The Laughing Lady, Bluebeards 8th Wife, The First Kiss, Tom Jones, Her Temporary Husband, The Sign Of The Cross, Battling Butler.

1924: Omar Khayyam, Paddy The Next Best Thing, The Story Of The Rosary, Good Luck, Grand Orchestral Concert, The Rat, The Lie, The Magician, Catherine, Romance, Friend Of The People, A Cousin From Nowhere, Our Betters, The Honourable Mrs Tawnish, Outward Bound, Welsh Drama Week, The Scarlet Pimpernel, Sweet Lavender, The Passing Of The Floor Back, The Yellow Poppy, The Yellow Ticket, What A chance, A Royal Divorce, Brown Sugar, The Prince And The Beggar Maid, Seven Days Leave, Boy O' My Heart, Why Men Love Women, The Walls Of Jericho, Her Love Against The World, The Life guardsman, Confusion, The Witness For The Defence, The Walls Of Jericho, The Hawk Of The Desert, Leah Kleshna, The Hawk Of The Desert, Under Two Flags, The Hawk Of The Desert, The Return, Her Temporary Husband, Betty, White Cargo, The Green Goddess, Il Trovatore, Tales Of Hoffman, Faust, Maritana, Madam Butterfly, The Bohemian Girl, Tales Of Hoffman, Bella Donna, The Mikado, The Yeoman Of The Guard, Cox and Box, HMS Pinafore, The Mikado, Ruddigore, Toni, Katinka, Bluebeard's 8th Wife, Who's My Father, The Fake, The Lillies Of The Field, Mrs Done's Defence, The Blue Butterfly, The Last Waltz, Irene, The Rebel Maid, The Sport Of Kings.

1925: Peter Pan, Madam Pompadour, Tons Of Money, The Sea Urchin, Sally, Stop Flirting, The Merry Widow, The Rising Generation, The Private Secretary, The Creaking Chair, The Farmers Wife, The Maid Of The Mountains, It Pays To Advertise, Welsh Drama Week, The Outsider, Nothing But The Truth, Witness For The Defence, Nothing But The Truth, Witness For The Defence, Twelfth Night, Julius Caesar, Merchant Of Venice, As You Like It, Macbeth, A Midsummer Nights Dream, Merry Wives Of Windsor, The Thirteenth Chair, The Adventurous Are, The Second Mrs Tanqueray, Gypsy Princess, Plus Fours, So This Is London, Three Weeks, A Butterfly On A Wheel, The Land Of Promise, The Woman In The Case, In The Night, The Man From Toronto, Bought And Paid For, Patricia, White Cargo, The Right Age To Marry, Possessions, Cavalleria Rusticana & I Pagliacci, Madam Butterfly, Il Trovatore, Faust, Carmen, Maritana, Samson and Delilah, Educating A Husband, The River, Lilac Time, No 17, The Street Singer, The Folly Of You, Monsieur Beaucaire, Alf's Button, Just Married , Primrose, Little Nelly Kelly, Sweet Nell Of Old Drury, The Bride, His Highness Below Stairs, No No Nanette, The Margate Peddlers, Iolanthe, Stop Flirting.

1926: Doctor Syn, The Thief, The Laughing Lady, Katinka, Mixed Doubles, The Gorilla, The Blue Bird, Dracula, Lavender Ladies, Katja The Dancer, No No Nanette, The Cardinal, The Ghost Train, Cock O' The Roost, The Pelican, Madam Pompadour, It Pays To Advertise, Charley's Aunt, In The Next Room, Saint Joan, Scotch

Mist, Raffles, Mrs Dane's Defence, The Walls Of Jericho, Once A Thief, The Barrier, Mrs Gorringes Necklace, The Case Of Lady Camber, East Lynne, Welsh Drama Week, The Farmers Wife, Honour, Betty In Mayfair, The Widow's Cruise, Rose Marie, Sun Up, The Gondolier, Patience, Ruddigore, Cox And Box, Pirates Of Penzance, Patience, The Gondolier, Ask Beccles, Alf's Button, Lilac Time, The Last Of Mrs Cheyney, Mercenary Mary, White Cargo, The Street Singer, The Naughty Wife, A Cuckoo In The Nest, Just Married, Cabaret Up To Date, The Rising Generation, The Ware Case, Variety Boy Scout Show.

1927: Katja, The Lash, Is Zat So, Wild Flower, Loose Ends, The Ghost Train, The Belle Of New York, A Greek Slave, The Last Waltz, The Ringer, Mr What's His Name, The Wooing Of Catherine Parr, Doctor Syn, Welsh Drama Week, Lido Lady, Aloma, No No Nanette, Easy Virtue, The Whole Town's Talking, It Pays To Advertise, The Black Spider, The Silver King, The Second Mrs Tanqueray, An Ideal Husband, The Thief, The Yellow Ticket, John Claydes Honour, The Fake, The Outsider, The Student Prince, Dawn, Yvonne, Yellow Sands, The Joker, Escape, Sunny, The Constant Nymph, Mercenary Mary, Gala Nights, The Best People, Just A Kiss, Tannhauser, The Barber Of Seville, Cavalleria Rusticana and I Pagliacci, Carmen, The Valkyrie, The Barber Of Seville, Faust, The Blue Train, The Last Of Mrs Cheyney, And So To Bed, The Terror, Rookery Nook, Royal Italian Circus, Meet The Wife, Scout Week.

1928: The Girlfriend, Lido Lady, Potiphar's Wife, Interference, The Blue Mazurka, Broadway, The Farmer's Wife, Young England, Lady Luck, The Scarlet Pimpernel, Welsh Drama Week, Prince Charming, White Cargo, The Silent House, A Tale Of Alsatia, The Man Who Took A Chance, The Ringer, Aloma, The Ghost Train, The Sign Of The Cross, Macbeth, Julius Caesar, Compromising Daphne, The Monster, The Garden Of Eden, Carnival, Pygmalion, Man And Superman, Mrs Warren's Profession, Pygmalion, You Never Can Tell, Mrs Warren's Profession, Thark, When Blue Hills Laughed, Carmen, Faust, Madam Butterfly, La Boheme, Samson And Delilah, Rigoletto, Il Trovatore, Dracula, The Big Drum, None But The Brave, Two White Arms, Alibi, You Never Can Tell, Candida, Pygmalion, Arms and The Man, Mrs Warren's Profession, Widower's Houses, Man And Superman, Lady Be Good, Marigold, The House Of The Arrow, My Son John, The Wrecker, Tip Toes, Yellow Sands, Lady Mary, Lord Babs, The Crooked Billet, Rose Marie, Good Morning Bill, Charley's Aunt, The Terror, Sunny, Sleeping Partners, Other Men's Wives, Swansea Scout Show, Welsh Drama Presentation.

1929: Swansea Hospital Concert, The Squeaker, So This Is Love, The Man Who Changed His Name, To What Red Hell, Oh Kay, Interference, Baby Cyclone, Princess Ida, Thark, 77 Park Lane, Lumber Love, The Real McCoy, Plunder, The Silent House, Welsh Drama Week, The Desert Song, The Burglar, The Letter, The Fourth Wall, Compromising Daphne, The Flying Squad, Knight Errant, Bird In Hand, The Twister, A Welsh Singer, When Knights Were Bold, The 100th Chance, Blackmail, Rookery Nook, He Walked In Her Sleep, Juno And The Paycock, Journey's End, The Farmers Wife, The Trial Of Mary Dugan, Hit The Deck, Lucky Girl, The Chinese Bungalow, Rope, Marigold, Young Woodley, A Damsel In Distress, Keepers Of Youth, The Sacred Flame, The Vagabond King, The Last Hour, This Thing Called Love, The Patsy, The High Road, Passing Brompton Road, Within The Law, The Man At Six.

1930: Peter Pan, A Cup Of Kindness, The Flag Lieutenant, Persons Unknown, Pygmalion, Man And Superman, Mrs Warren's Profession, You Never Can Tell, Mrs Warren's Profession, Pygmalion, Man And Superman, The Calender, The Duchess Of Dantzic, The Private Secretary, Sorry You've Been Troubled, The First Mrs Fraser, Tarnish, Welsh Drama Week, Plunder, Sweet Nell Of Old Drury, The Woman In Room 13, Treasure Island, The Squeaker, Symphony In Two Flats, French Leave, Journey's End, Baa Baa Black Sheep, My Wife's Family, The Green Lamp, The Stranger Within, When Blue Hills Laughed, Paddy The Next Best Thing, The Burglar, Sarah Ann Holds Fast, Tell Me The Truth, Eliza Comes To Stay, On The Spot, Her First Affair, Third Time Lucky, Suspense, The Man In Possession, A Warm Corner, Cape Forlorn, Twelfth Night, The Merchant Of Venice, The Tempest, Twelfth Night, The Merchant Of Venice, The Tempest, She Stoops To Conquer, Silver Wings, The Limping Man, Murder On The 2nd Floor, Two Deep, Mr Cinders, The Middle Watch, The Girl Friend, The Patsy, Sarah Ann Holds Fast, Honours Easy, Alibi, The Purple Mask, A Midsummer Nights Dream, Simba.

1931: The Silent Witness, Almost A Honeymoon, The Arcadians, Man And Superman, Misalliance, Pygmalion, The Doctor's Dilemma, Getting Married, The Doctor's Dilemma, Man And Superman, Odd Numbers, Nine Till Six, None So blind, Abie's Irish Rose, Darling I Love You, Welsh Drama Week, Traffic, Lilac Time, Seven Days Leave, Daddy Long Legs, Proof, The Black Moth, Lord Richard In The Pantry, Lady Windermere's Fan, The Rosary, A Sinner In Paradise, If Four Walls Told, Her Past, The Lie, A Woman Of No Importance, Bulldog Drummond, The Naughty Wife, Moths, Spring Cleaning, Gentleman Jim, The Hypocrites, Carnival, The Story Of The Rosary, His House In Order, A Bunch Of Violets, Loose Ends, Smouldering Fires, The Man From Toronto, Polly With A Past, The Barrett's Of Wimpole Street, The Underdog, The Faker, The Christian, Paddy The Next Best Thing, The Walls Of Jericho, The Manxman, The Cat And The Canary, The Maid Of Cefn Ydfa, Maria Marten, The Life Guardsman.

1932: Tilly Of Bloomsbury, A Butterfly On A Wheel, The Yellow Ticket, Tom, Dick and Harry, The Silent House, Baby Mine, The Last Of Mrs Cheyney, The Silver King, Interference, The Squall, Nobody's Daughter, The Passing Of The Third, The Light Of The World, The speckled Band, Welsh Drama Week, Under Two Flags, Concert In Aid Of The Denville Homes for, Aged Actors, Easy Virtue, The Man Who Stayed At Home, The Bird Of Paradise, The Face At The Window, Peg O' My Heart, The Blindness Of Virtue, The Crooked Billet, Rain, Outcast, A Butterfly On A Wheel, Il Trovatore, Faust, Maritana, Il Trovatore, Faust, Maritana, Rigoletto, Carmen, The Bohemian Girl, Rigoletto, Carmen, The Bohemian Girl, Madam Butterfly, La Traviata, Lily Of Killárney, Madam Butterfly, La Traviata, Lily Of Killarney, Tales Of Hoffman, The Barber Of Seville, Daughter Of The Regiment, Tales Of Hoffman, The Barber Of Seville, Il Trovatore, Faust, Carmen, Rigoletto, Tannhauser, Maritana, Tales Of Hoffman, Il Trovatore, The Barber Of Seville, Lily Of Killarney, Tales Of Hoffman, Carmen, Rigoletto, Bohemian Girl, Maritana, Eliza Comes To Stay, John Glayde's Honour, The Barrier, Brown Sugar, The Trial Of Mary Dugan, Diplomacy, Grumpy, The Sign On The Door, Three Wise Fools, The Silent Witness, The Rookery Nook, My Old Dutch, A Royal Divorce, The Eleventh Commandment, Facing The Music, The Improper Duchess, The Barrett's Of Wimpole Street, While Parents Sleep, Dangerous Corner, Autumn Crocus.

1933: Lilac Time, Michael And Mary, Blackmail, Welsh drama Week, Her First Affair, The Ghost Train, The Last warning, A Bill Of Divorcement, Bought And Paid For, Important People.

1934: Choral and orchestral concert, Welsh Drama Week.

1935: Welsh Drama Week.

1936: Welsh Drama Week.

1937: Welsh Drama Week.

1938: Welsh Drama Week.

1939: Welsh Drama Week.

1940: Welsh Drama Week.

1941: No theatre performances exclusively a cinema.

1942: No theatre performances exclusively a cinema.

1943: No theatre performances exclusively a cinema.

1944: No theatre performances exclusively a cinema.

1945: No theatre performances exclusively a cinema.

1946: No theatre performances exclusively a cinema.

1947: No theatre performances exclusively a cinema.

1948: Frieda, My Wife's Family, See How They Run, The Shop At Sly Corner, Smilin' Through, Jane Steps Out, Pygmalion, They Walk Alone, Arsenic And Old Lace, The Guinea Pig, Pink String And Sealing Wax, While The Sun Shines, This Happy Breed, The Night Must Fall, Grand National Night, A Hasty Heart, The Man From The Ministry, Claudia, Rope, Anna Christie, Blithe Spirit, Rebecca, Ten Little Niggers, The Corn Is Green, Thunder Rock, When We Are Married, The Shining Hour, French Without Tears, The Crime Of Margaret Foley, Love In Idle, An Inspector Calls, The Sacred Flame, The Light Of Heart, The First Mrs Fraser, Ladies In Retirement, Pride And Prejudice, Fools rush in, Present laughter, The Little Foxes, You Can't Take It With You, All Through The Night.

1949: Arms and the Man, Murder Without Crime, Continental Ballet Company, George and Margaret, Wishing Well, The Last Of Mrs Cheyney, The Years Between, On The Spot, The Linden Tree, The Winslow Boy, Miranda, The Shop At Sly Corner, Rain on the Just, The Eagle Has Two Heads, Storm in a Teacup, Jane Eyre, Bird in Hand, Juno And The Paycock, The Amazing Doctor Clitterhouse, Dark Summer, Doctor Angelus, Saloon Bar, Fumed Oak, The Browning Version, Gaslight, The Scarlet Pimpernel, Winterset, Fresh Fields, Desire Under The Elms, Quiet Weekend, Goodbye Mr Chips, Black Limelight, Clutterbuck, The Paragon, Guilty, By Candlelight, Duet For Two Hands, King Lear, The Chiltern Hundreds, The Importance of Being Earnest, Ghosts, The Arabian Night, The Druid's Rest, The Man Who Came To Dinner.

1950: The Rose Without A Thorn, Candida, Doctor's Joy, The Old Ladies, Born Yesterday, The Second Mrs Tanqueray, The Whirligig of Time, The Circle, The Enemy of the people, Daughters of the parsonage, On Approval, Oliver Twist, Welsh Drama Festival, The Happiest days of Your life, Lovers leap, Mary Rose, They fly by Twilight, The Respectable Prostitute, See how they run, Murder at the vicarage, The Continental Ballet Company, It's you I want, Adventures of Tommy Trouble, Pygmalion, The Sacred Flame, Reluctant Heroes, Worm's eye view, Family Portrait, Little Lambs Eat Ivy, The Seagull, Blithe Spirit, St Joan, Hello Out There & Harlequinade (double bill), Bonaventure, Crime Passionnel, Castle In The Air, Twelfth Night.

1951: The Rambert Ballet, The Student Prince, Queen Elizabeth Slept Here, Party Manners, Here We Came Gathering, Home At Seven, The Devil's Bride, Shw' Mae Heno, No, No, Nanette, Mrs Warren's Profession, I Must Have Hush, A Guardsman's Cup Of Tea, Bed, Board and Romance, Welsh Drama Week, King Of The Castle, Don't Listen Ladies, Fair And Warmer, Black Chiffon, While Parents Sleep, The Dominant Sex, This Was A Woman, Count Your Blessings, The Family Upstairs, Suspect, High Temperature, Dangerous Corner, The Perfect Woman, Private Lives, Double Door, London Wall, George and Margaret, The Heiress, Eliza Comes To Stay, Mother Of Men, The Tolerant Husband, The Shining Hour, Love Let Loose, A Murder Has Been Arranged, The Holly And The Ivy, Tons Of Money, The Late Christopher Bean.

1952: Full House, Without A Prince, Love From A Stranger, It's a Boy, Granite, Love In A Mist, Wandering Jew, Laburnum Grove, Two-Dozen Red Roses, The Silver Chord, The Girl Who Couldn't Quite, Payment Deferred, What Anne Brought Home, Larger Than Life, Coals Of Fire, In Death They Were Not Divided, Titus Andronicus, The Magic Cupboard, The Gathering Storm, The Cat And The Canary, School For Husbands, Rookery Nook, The Two Mrs Carrolls, Isle Of Umbrellas, Fifty Mark, Doctor Brent's Household, Up The Garden Path, The Enchanted Cottage, The Good Young Man, To Kill A Cat, The Dover Road, Lady Audrey's Secret, Gooseberry Fool, Night Was Our Friend, Crystal Clear, A lady Mislaid, The Chinese Bungalow, For The Love Of Mike, Peg O' My Heart, French For Love, Spring At Marino, Murder Out Of Time, Don't Call Me Madam, Johnny Belinda, Welsh Drama Week, The Hasty Heart.

1953: Charley's Aunt, To Dorothy a Son, The Winter Journey, The River Line, The Bat, The Male Animal, Maria Marten, The Vigil, When Knights Were Bold, Random Harvest, The Seventh Veil, White Sheep Of The Family, Interference, The Outsider, Smilin' Through, Will Any Gentleman, Queen Elizabeth, A Woman Or Two, The Young Madame Conti, The Patsy, White Cargo, The Green Pack, The Fan Dancer, The Day Is Gone, Husbands Don't Count, A Little Bit Of Fluff, The Hollow, Rain, Maiden Ladies, To What Red Hell, The Gift, Murder Mistaken, Written For A lady, Sleeping Partnership, The Letter, The Barretts Of Wimpole Street, Too Young To Marry, Mantrap, The Case Of The Frightened Lady, Her Past, Reefer Girl, Golden Rain, Ghost Train, Jane, Death Takes A Holiday.

1954: Ambrose Applejohn's Adventure, Meet Mr Callaghan, The Man In Grey, Paddy The Next Best Thing, The Maniac, The Painted Veil, The Fanatics, The Happy Marriage, The Vigil, Separate Rooms, Safe Harbour, Tell Tale Murder, The Seven-Year Itch, Four Winds, Down Came A Blackbird, Madame Tic-Tac, The Wild Oat, No Other Verdict, The Happy Prisoner, Deadlock, Dial 'M' For Murder, The Dashing White Sergeant, Someone Waiting, For Better Or Worse, Honeymoon Beds, East Of Suez, Spring Model, Give Me Yesterday, Deliver My Darling, Where There's A Will, Her Shop, A Man With Red Hair, Beside The Seaside, Rebecca, Jane Steps Out, Voices On The Wind, The Burning Glass, The Running Tramp, Pygmalion, All Done With Mirrors, Murder Story, As Long As They're Happy, The Wind And The Rain, The Soul Of Nicholas Snyder's.

1955: Pin-ups From Paris, Late Love, The Prisoner, Yes And No, Maid Of Cefn Ydfa, Its Never Too Late, Outward Bound, High

Temperature, Come Back Little Sheba, Whispering Gallery, Jinny Morgan, Tilly Of Bloomsbury, Human Passion, Vice In The Street, The Party Spirit, The Secret Tent, Relations Are Best Apart, Someone At The Door, Dangerous Corner, Swansea Theatre Scandal, Yours Faithfully, The Dark Horse, Serious Charge, A Bed For Two, Bed, Board And Romance, Granite, Manor Of Northstead, Witness For The Prosecution, Third Party Risk, Intimate Relations, Alibi, Lord Arthur Saville's crimes, I Am A Camera, The Rotters, The Fall Of The Sparrow, The Ticking Clock, Jane Eyre, The Squall, Peril At End House, Poor Dad, I've Been Here Before, On Approval, The Four Poster.

1956: It's a Small World, Life Begins At fifty, The Golden Earring, Smith, Love On The Never-Never, Children Of Wrath, Widows Mite, Mad About Men, Sabrina Fair, Lady Look Behind You, Friendly Relations, Desire In The Night, Blackmail, I Hold You Prisoner, Jackie, Wuthering Heights, Autumn Crocus, Holiday For Simon, Ten Green Bottles, The Age Of Indiscretion, The Shining Hour, Draw The Blinds Slowly, Daughter Of My House, September Tide, Black Chiffon, Reluctant heroes, The Shadow Of Doubt, The Tender Trap, Dead On Nine, All For Mary, Mrs Moonlight, Doctor Morelle, The Love Match, Doctor Angelus, Spider's Web, My Three Angels, The Whole Truth, Death Of A Rat, Love In A Mist, Indoor Sort, Nobody's Fool, Nightmare, The Moon Is Blue.

1957: We Proudly Present, Ten Little Niggers, Trespass, No Escape, The Facts Of Life, No Trees In The Street, Hip Hip Hooray Circus, Belle Of New York, Disc Doubles, Welsh Drama Festival, Pick Of The Town, Four Jones Boys, Girls In Cellophane, The Bed, Legs That Thrill, Ballet Rambert, Murder On The Nile, Master Of Arts, South Sea Bubble, Ring For Catty, Reluctant Debutante, Strange Request, Waters Of The Moon, Book Of The Month, A Man About The House, Waiting For Gillian, Tabitha, The Man, Mr Kettle And Mrs Moon, Black Coffee, Dance Of Death, Touch Of Fear, Plaintiff In A Pretty Hat, Doctor In The house, Double Image, Breakfast In Bed, Wind Of Heaven, A likely Tale, Murder When Necessary, Welsh National Opera, Look Back In Anger, The Opium Eaters, Our Dear Delinquents, A Picture Of Autumn, Bell, Book And Candle.

1958: The House By The Lake, Cosh Boy, Oklahoma, The Diary Of Anne Frank, The Rainmaker, This Happy Home, Summer Of The Seventeenth Doll, Silver Wedding, Subway In The Sky, Separate Tables, Wanted; One Body, For Pete's Sake, Towards Zero, Johnny Belinda, Night Of The Fourth, Nude With Violin, The Shadow Between, Picnic, Paddle Your Own Canoe, The Food Of Love, A Hatful Of Rain, Hippo Dancing, Dry Rot, The Chalk Garden, Sailor Beware, Beth, Something To Hide, The Little Foxes, Mrs Gibbon's Boys, Murder At The Vicarage, The Bride And The Batchelor, Variations On A Theme, The Lovebirds, Time Murderer Please, Welsh Drama Week, Dear Delinquent, Family On Trial, Three Way Switch, The Bad Seed, A Touch Of The Sun, Mist Over The Mistletoe.

1959: Dancing Years, Die Fledermaus, Rigoletto, I Lombardi, Cavalleria Rusticana & I Pagliacci, Nabucco, The Tunnel Of Love, Speaking Of Murder, George Dillon, Verdict, Ride A Cock Horse, Flowering Cherry, Gigi, By A Hand Unknown, A View From A Bridge, The Hollow, The Gentle Savage, You, Too Can Have, A Body, Tea And, Sympathy, Breakout, Bus Stop, Breath Of Spring, Murder On Arrival, The Open Cage, Friends And Neighbours, How Say you?, The Telescope, Caught Napping, The Light Of Heart, Not In The Book, The Love Match, The Ten Commandments, Welsh Drama Festival.

1960: Hit The Deck, The Unexpected Guest, Guilt And Gingerbread, The French Mistress, The Sound Of Murder, Power Without Glory, The Grass Is Greener, Loves A Luxury, Five Finger Exercise, The Pleasure Of His Company, Murder At Midnight, Basinful Of The Briny, Roar Like A Dove, Spider's Web, The Corn Is Green, High Temperature, And Suddenly It's Spring, The Chinese Bungalow, This Thing Called Love, A Shred Of Evidence, Rookery Nook, The Circle, The Complaisant Lover, Key Of The Door, See How They Run, Love From A Stranger, A Taste Of Honey, Murder At Quay Cottage, Charley's Aunt.

1961: The Battle, La Boheme, Nabucco, Madame Butterfly, Il Trovatore, Carousel, The Geese Are Getting Fat, Jane Eyre, Brides Of March, Roots, Murder Delayed, The More The Merrier, Peg O' My Heart, This Year Next Year, Cat And The Canary, Pools Paradise, A Clean Kill, The Shining Hour, Peril At End House, Rebecca, Crystal Clear, Piccadilly Alibi, Small Hotel, Wuthering Heights, Off With The Motley, Night Must Fall, Bed Board And Romance, Witness For The Prosecution, Saturday Night At The Crown, The Seventh Veil, Happy The Bride, The Bargain, The Aspern Papers, Watch It Sailor, Time To Kill, The Hostage, Pygmalion, The Bride Comes Back, Alibi, Welsh National Drama Week, French For love, Celebration, Settled Out Of Court, The Perfect Woman, Little Women.

1962: William Tell, Nabucco, The Marriage Of Figaro, Giselle, Light Fantastic, Swan Lake (Act II), Night And Silence, Rentcontre, Shindig, Les Sylphides, Eaters Of Darkness, Peepshow, The Fair Maid, White Horse Inn, Doctor In The House, Someone Waiting, The Miracle Worker, Simple Spyman, Two Faces Of Murder, The Irregular Verb To Love, Those Damn Joneses, The Gazebo, Don't Tell Father, Murder By Accident, Billy Liar, The Extraordinary Seaman, Hocus Pocus, Ghost Squad, A Guardsman's Cup Of Tea, The Big Killing, School For Spinsters, Murder At The Vicarage, Pillar To Post, The Amorous Prawn, Doctor At Sea, Towards Zero, The Man In Grey, The Deep Blue Sea, The Keep, A Murder Has Been Arranged, A Jolt For The Joneses, The Glass Menagerie, Becket or The Honour Of God, Guilty Party, Write Me A Murder, The Keep (revival), The Doctor And The Devils, Life With Father, The Rough And The Ready, The Miser.

1963: Lohengrin, Escape From The Harem, La Traviata, William Tell, Giselle and The Nutcracker Suite, The Merry Widow, The Cadets Show, Outward Bound, Rock A Bye Sailor, Cry For Love, Photo Finish, Turn Left For Piccadilly, Trilby, Two Stars For Comfort, The House On The Cliff, All Things Bright And Beautiful, Dr Joey, She Stoops To Conquer, The Seashell, Breaking Point, The Tulip Tree, Miss Pell Is Missing, Semi-detached, Ring Out An Alibi, Love Locked Out, Murder On The Nile, Goodnight Mrs Puffin, Signpost To Murder, The Barretts Of Wimpole Street, Brush With A Body, Come Blow Your Horn, Policy For Murder, Period Of Adjustment, The Private Ear And The Public Eye, The Lark, Jupiter Laughs, How Are You, Johnnie?, The Marriage Go Round, Trap For A Lonely Man, Maiden Ladies, The Hot Tiara, David Copperfield, A Party For Christmas.

1964: Barber Of Seville, Il Trovatore, Marriage Of Figaro, La Boheme, Macbeth, La Traviata, Il Seraglio, Marriage Of Figaro, Annie Get Your Gun, All In Good Time, Go Back For Murder, Home And The Heart, Where Angels fear To Tread, The Shot In Question, Bachelors Gay, Key Witness, Flat Spin, Woman In A Dressing Gown, The Proof Of The Poison, The Rivals, Waiting For Yesterday, No Time For Love, And Sat Down Beside Her, Druid's Rest, Licence To Murder, The Trouble With Dad, The Maid Of Cefn

Ydfa, The Dream House, Rule Of Three, The Patient, The Rats, Afternoon At The Seaside, Welcome Little Stranger, Rattle Of A Simple Man, The Sleeping Prince, Bachelor Flat, Amber For Anna, Mary Mary, By Whose Hand?, The Heiress, The Queen And The Welshman, The Wishing Well, Portrait Of Murder, Man Alive, Suspect, Never Too Late, One For The Pot, The Kingdom Of God.

1965: Fidelio, Madame Butterfly, Tosca, Macbeth, Rose Marie, Western Theatre Ballet, Olde Time Music Hall, The Reluctant Peer, Merry Murder Go Round, The Sacred Flame, Ten Little Niggers, I love You Mrs Patterson, The Wind Of Heaven, Busman's Honeymoon, The Diplomatic Baggage, East Lynne, Murder Murder Quite Contrary, Return Ticket, Past Imperfect, Make Me A Widow, The Night Of The Iguana, Plunder, The Unexpected Guest, Hot And Cold In All Rooms, Busybody, According To The Doctor, High Temperature, A Shot In The Dark, Public Mischief, Dangerous Corner, Stranger In My Bed, The Girl Who Couldn't Quite, Wings Of The Dove, Poor Bitos, The Late Christopher Bean, Travelling Light, Person Unknown, Doctor At Sea, Spider's Web, Second Honeymoon, The Bronte's.

1966: La Traviata, The Bartered Bride, Die Fledermaus, Moses, Fidelio, The Student Prince, Olde Time Music Hall, Come On Jeeves, The Hollow, When We Were Married, Maigret And The Lady, The Family Upstairs, The Touch Of Fear, By candle Light, The Good Old Summertime, The Right Honourable Gentleman, The Full Treatment, The Creeper, Fools Rush In, Accolade, As Black As She's Painted, Breakfast In Bed, Hostile Witness, The Cat And The Canary, Verdict, Wolf's Clothing, The Whole Truth, Morgan And Moses, The Letter, Pajama Tops, The Lodger, Traveller's Joy, Dead On Nine, The Rehearsal, Barefoot In The Park, A Friend Indeed, One For The Pot, A Severed Head, Murder Mistaken, Cat On The Fiddle, Treasure Hunt.

1967: Don Giovanni, La Boheme, Don Pasquale, Moses, Olde Time Music Hall, Dorothy Squires Show, Guys And Dolls, Snow White and the Seven Dwarfs, And suddenly it's Sandy Powell, The Chris Shaw Show, Harlequin Ballet, Scene '67, Arms And The Man, Towards Zero, Boeing Boeing, Home At Seven, Dial M For Murder, The Killing Of Sister George, The Ghost Train, The Winslow Boy, Say Who You Are, Give Me Yesterday, The Importance Of Being Earnest, Blithe Spirit, The Adventures Of Tom Jones, Doctor In love, Goodbye Mr Chips, Chase Me, Comrade, Murder For The Asking, The Anniversary, Arsenic And Old Lace, Sleeping Partnership, The Poker Session, Let's Get A Divorce, The Homecoming, I Am A Camera, Laura, Northanger Abbey, A Lily In Little India, On Monday Next.

1968: Romeo And Juliet, Rigoletto, Nabucco, Carmen, Oklahoma!, The Diana Dors Show, Old Time Music Hall, Wait Until Dark, My Three Angels, An Inspector Calls, The Odd Couple, She Stoops To Conquer, The Promise, Murder On The Nile, I'll Get My Man, Gaslight, Relatively Speaking, Jane Eyre, In At The Death, A Day In The Death Of Joe Egg, Let's All Go Down The Strand, Pink String And Sealing Wax, Hay Fever, Keeping Up With Father, The Amorous Prawn, Jane Steps Out, The Unexpected Guest, All For Mary, Someone Waiting, The Bride And The Batchelor, Sabrina Fair, Subway In The Sky, Rebecca, The School For Scandal, Relative Values, Dracula, The White Liars, Toys In The Attic, Pride And Prejudice, Candida.

1969: Old Time Music Hall, This Story Is Yours, Dawn Dweud – Gift Of The Gabb, My Fair Lady, Spider's Web, Who's Afraid Of Virginia Woolf?, The Au-Pair Man, Lord Arthur Saville's Crimes, Black Chiffon, The Sport Of My Mad Mother, The Man, The Queen And The Welshman, Shadow In The Sun, Enemy, Welsh Drama Festival, The Constant Lover, A Phoenix Too Frequent, Return Journey, Mistress Of The Inn, Circus Extravaganza, A Christmas Carol, Marriage of Figaro, La Traviata, Macbeth, Hamlet Prince Of Denmark.

1970: How He Lied To Her Husband, Don Juan In Hell, Happy Days, Purgatory, The Maids, Daniel Owen (in Welsh), The Barber Of Seville, Nabucco, Carmen, Breakaway, The Lesson, La Ventana, Beauty And The Beast, Ten Little Niggers, Summer Song, Chapman's Old Tyme Music Hall Revue, Plaza Suite, All In Good Time, The Dragon Who loved Music, Meet The Scribble Kids, Peter And The Wolf, Pilgrim's Progress, The Bride Makes Three, Midnight Variety Show, Doctor In The House, A Boston Story, Spring And Port Wine, The Flip Side, Cat On A Hot Tin Roof, Out Of The Question, Dead Silence, Duet For Two Hands, Blue Denim, The Wrong Side Of The Park, Alfie, Murder Without Crime, Let Sleeping Wives Lie, The Prime Of Miss Jean Brodie, Forty Years On, Bless This House, Ghost's, What The Butler Saw, Private lives, The Boys In The Band, The Beggar's Opera, Somebody Waiting, The Importance Of Being Earnest, Arms And The Man, Juno And The Paycock, Welsh Drama Festival 1970, La Boheme, Die Fledermaus, The Recruiting Officer, Chips With Everything, Under Milk Wood (SLT), The Merchant Of Venice (SLT), Billy Liar, Madness Of May, As Black As She's Painted, The Wooden Dish, Treasure Island, Roar Like A Dove.

1971: The Constant Wife, The Rose And The Ring, Y Claf Di-Glefid Imaginary Invalid performed in Welsh, The Good Young Man, Carousel, Olde Tyme Music Hall Revue, Meet The Gang, Witness For The Prosecution, The Innocents, Beauty And The Beast, Giselle, Boris Gudunov, The Magic Flute, Simon Boccanegra, Aida, Make No Mistake, Conduct Unbecoming, The Man Most Likely To, The Lion In Winter, Wuthering Heights, Hadrian The Seventh, The Glass Menagerie, A Bequest To The Nation, Not Now Darling, The Dolls Of Swansea, Mother Courage, Oh What A Lovely War, Romeo And Juliet, Partners, The Pajama Game, Welsh Drama Festival 1971, Journey's End, The Empty Suit, Dark Elegies, Embrace Tiger And Return To Mountain, Dance and Dancers, 'Tis Goodly Sport, Four According, Pierre Lunaire, Bertram Batell's Sideshow, A Pig In A Poke, Under Milk Wood, Unexpectedly Vacant, Village Wooing.

1972: Sunday Evening Concert, Ballet For All With Dancers, New Moon, Uncle Vanya, Meet The Gang, Forget Me Not Lane, Home On The Pig's Back, Who Killed Santa Claus, Dial M For Murder, Salad Days, End Of Conflict, Turandot, Rigoletto, Aida, Who Killed Santa Clause?, The Investiture, Butterflies Are Free, Vanity Fair, A Streetcar Named Desire, 75th Anniversary Celebration 1897-1972, The Entertainer, She's Done It Again, Abelard And Heloise, The Relapse Or Virtue In Danger, Charley's Aunt, Adventures In The Skin Trade, Twelfth Night, Back To Square One, Misanthrope, There's A Girl In My Soup, Grand Variety Show, Cheshire Foundation Homes, Death On Demand, Cock A Doodle Doo, Go Bang Your Tambourine, Live Like pigs, One Of The Family, Carry Me Back To Canning Town.

1973: Don't Just Lie There Say Something, Fiddler On The Roof, The Starving Rich, Butley, Murder Sails At Midnight, Meet The Gang 1973, Nutcracker Act III, Ways Of Saying Bye Bye, Le Carnival, Background To A Ballet, Giselle, Glasstown, Lilac Time, Rigoletto, Madam Butterfly, Don Carlos, The Secretary Bird, Ring Round The Moon, Great Expectations, Getting On, Hobson's

Choice, Uproar In The House, Murder On The Agenda, Present Laughter, A Voyage Round My Father, A Man For All Seasons, The Pearl Fishers, Idomeneo, Die Fledermaus, Don Carlos, The Mating Game, Gwl Ddrama Gymraeg, As You Like It, Ballet For All, Panache, Tribute To Saunders Lewis, Subway In The Sky, Pygmalion, Wanted, One Body, Loves A Luxury, Flowing Cherry, The Ghost Train, Loot, One Night Show.

1974: London Cotemporary Dance Theatre, Camelot, Gaslight, The Tilted Scales, Meet The Gang 1974, Night Fall, The Lads From Fenn Street, La Boheme, L'Elisir D'Amore, The Pearl Fishers, The Beach Of Falesa, L'Elisir D'Amore, La Boheme, An Inspector Calls, Midsummer Night's Dream, The Sacking Of Norman Banks, Suddenly At Home, Night Must fall, How The Other Half Lives, Lloyd George Knew My Father, Say Goodnight To Grandma, Hay Fever, The Dickie Henderson Show, The Golden Years of Music Hall, That's Life The Al Read Show, Hylda Baker Show(Russ Conway stepped in at last minute), Time And Time Again, The Day After The Fair, My Fat Friend, The Flying Dutchman, The Elixir of Love, La Boheme, Simon Boccanegra, The Flying Dutchman, I'll Sleep In The Spare Room, Welsh Drama Week, The Scribble Kids Story Book, Melodies Of The Minstrels, Snow White and The Seven Dwarfs, Hamlet, Rosencrantz And Guildenstern are Dead, The School For Scandal, Hair.

1975: Humphrey Lyttleton, Calamity Jane, Murder At The Vicarage, Meet The Gang 1975, Macbeth, Godspell, The New Minstrel Show, The Good Old Days, Two And Two Make Sex, London Contemporary Dance Week, Charles Dickens, The Grand Duchess Of Gerolstein, Cosi Fan Tutte, Manon Lescaut, The Flying Dutchman, French Without Tears, London Assurance, Habeas Corpus, Move Over Mrs Markham, Halfway Up The Tree, Freddie Davies, The Dora Bryan Show, Television Startime, Ryan, Crown Matrimonial, A Swansea Family, The Importance Of Being Earnest, Swingle II, Manon Lescaut, Othello, Jenufa, The Grand Duchess Of Gerolstein, Romeo And Juliet, The Rainmaker, Pride And Prejudice, David Nixon Show, The World Of Gilbert And Sullivan, Aneurin Bevan Struggles Against The Iron Heel.

1976: The Tempest, Hello Dolly, I Am A Camera, A Taste Of Honey, The Long And The Short And The Tall, Sleeping Beauty, Soft Blue Shadows, Othello, Meet The Gang 1976, Albert Herring, The Seraglio, Jenufa, Il Trovatore, Othello, Anna Christie, Absurd Person Singular, Don't Start Without Me, Private Lives, The Late Edwina Black, The Glass Menagerie, Next Time I'll Sing To You, Who Saw Him Die?, Five Finger Exercise, Entertaining Mr Sloane, Wait Until Dark, The Mating Game, Sleuth, Summer Variety, The New Vaudeville Band, Freddie and The Dreamers, Irma La Deuce, Godspell, Darling Mr London, Spiders Web, Il Trovatore, Orpheus In The Underworld, The Seraglio, La Boheme, The Wild Duck, Northern Dance Theatre, Welsh Drama Week, Bats In The Belfry, The Phantom Tollbooth, Max Boyce, The Murder Game, The Breakers, Love's Labour's Lost, My Cousin Rachel.

1977: Song Of Norway, King Lear, Dial M For Murder, Meet The Gang 1977, Double Edge, The Chiltern Hundred, Absent Friends, The Barber Of Seville, Orpheus In The Underworld, Albert Herring, I Masnedieri, Joseph And The Amazing Technicolor Dreamcoat, Boeing Boeing, Porter Must Go, Table Manners, Living Together, Round And Round The Garden, There Goes The Bride, Children's Puppet Theatre, Charlie Drake, The Thoughts Of Chairman Alf, Cilla Black, Harry Worth, The New Seekers, The Late Christopher Bean, Shades Of Laughter, Blithe Spirit, The Pearl Fisher, Rigoletto, The Barber Of Seville, Northern Ballet Company, Gwyl Ddrama Gymraeg 1977, Sleeping Partner, The Snow Queen, Caricature Puppet Theatre, Vince Hill, Jimmy Tarbuck, Time To Kill, Flarepath, In Praise Of Love.

1978: Doctor In The House, Meet The Gang 1978, Showboat, Donkey's Years, Under Milk wood, The Unexpected Guest, A Midsummer Night's Dream, La Boheme, The Marriage Of Figaro, Hair, The Adventures Of A Bear Called Paddington, Otherwise Engaged, Just Between Ourselves, The Bed Before Yesterday, The Frankie Vaughan Show, The Peters and Lee Show, Frankie Howerd Laughter Show, A Touch Of Spring, Funny Peculiar, Equus, Il Trovatore, La Boheme, The Barber Of Seville, Tchaikofski and His Ballet's, Ashton: The Dream Era, Gwyl Ddrama Gymraeg 1978, Pygmalion, Pippi Longstocking, Windsor Davies And Don Estelle(Windsor Davies had to pull out and was replaced by Norman Vaughan), Sextet, A Murder Is Announced, How To Succeed In Business Without Really Trying, The Man Most Likely To.

1979: Richard III, Witness For The Prosecution, South Pacific, The Magic Flute, Turandot, The Turn Of The Screw, Mzumba, Max Boyce, Your Place Or Mine?, The Mikado, HMS Pinafore, Jumpers, Who Killed Agatha Christie?, Blithe Spirit, The Desert Song, Rebecca, Busybody, Breezeblock Park, Bedroom Farce, Leslie Crowther Featuring Arthur Askey, Roger De Courcey And Nookie Bear, Lennie Bennet, Faith Brown Show, Joseph And The Amazing Technicolor Dreamcoat, The Gingerbread Lady, Side By Side By Sondheim, The Pearl Fishers, The Makropoulos Case, La Traviata, Coppelia, Giselle, Festival Of Welsh Drama, Godspell, Anthony and Cleopatra and Caesar and Cleopatra, Ten Times Table, Jet Set, The Pajama Game, Fings Ain't Wot They Used To Be.

1980: Monkey Walk, Dylan And Liz, Brigadoon, Rookery Nook, Big Bad Mouse, Hinge And Bracket, The Krankies, Ernani, Eugene Onegin, The Coronation Of Poppea, Jasper Carrot, Night And Day, Spring Thaw, Kismet, A Bed Full Of Foreigners, Whose Life Is It Anyway?, Black Coffee, Joking Apart, Privates On Parade, Eisteddfod Genedlaethol Dyffryn Lliw, Patti Boulaye Show, Brotherhood Of Man, Summer Spectacular, Joseph And The Amazing Technicolor Dreamcoat, You're A Good Man Charlie Brown, Tosca, Rigoletto, The Servant (world premiere), Alexandra Roy, Culhwch And Olwen, Mary O'Hara, Welsh Drama Festival 1980, Dirty Linen and New Found Land, The Happy Apple, Gwyl 80, Charley Girl, Further Adventures Of A Window Cleaner.

1981: Close Of Play, Romeo And Juliet, The King And I, Murder Mistaken, The Marquis, The Caine Mutiny Court Martial, Ipi Tombi, Leo Sayer, Hot Gossip, Danny Grossman Dance Company, Tommy Steele, Kiss Me Kate, Beyond A Joke, La Traviata, The Barber Of Seville, Loot, The Dresser, Once A Catholic, Peril At End House, Iris Williams With The Dallas Boys, Bob Monkhouse, Pam Ayres, The Boyfriend, Outside Edge, The Rocky Horror Show, Fidelio, Madame Butterfly, Midsummer Night's Dream, Dracula Or a Pain The Neck, Welsh Drama Festival 1981, Playing The Game, Hansel And Gretal, Fur Coat And No Knickers, Little Me, The Hitch Hikers Guide To The Galaxy.

1982: A Tribute To John Chilvers, Deathtrap, The Crucible, My Fair Lady, Hinge And Bracket, Caught In The Act, Stage Struck, Grease, Twelfth Night, The Hollow, Anyone For Dennis?, Casanova's Last Stand, The Sound Of Music, Duet For One, The Gentle Hook, The Elephant Man, Middle Age Spread, Welsh National Eisteddfod, Larry Grayson And Friends, Des O'Connor, Cilla Black, Godspell, The Last Of The Red Hot Lovers, She Stoops To Conquer, The Nutcracker,

Welsh Drama Festival 1982, The Night They Raided Minsky's, Sweeny Todd, Sleuth, The Wizard Of Oz, Cards On The Table.

1983: During the major renovations at the theatre a small season of Grand Repertory was transferred to the Dylan Thomas Theatre: Educating Rita, Tomfoolery, California Suite, Abigail's party, Can You Here Me At The Back, 84 Charing Cross Road, Same Time, Next Year.

1984: Steaming, Rattle Of A Simple Man, Guys And Dolls, Verdict, The Selfish Shellfish, Dear Ivor, Another Country, Forget Me Not Lane, The Sleeping Beauty, Oliver, La Boheme, La Traviata, Jenufa, Jesus Christ Superstar, Midsummer Night Dream, Black Comedy & Harlequinade, Wait Until Dark, Run For Your Wife, Lulu, Frankie Vaughan, Ken Dodd, Cabaret, Cider With Rosie, London Contemporary Dance, The Merry Widow, Ernani, La Boheme, The Greek Passion, Masterclass, Paul Daniels Magic Show, Children Of A Lesser God, Policy For Murder, No No Nanette, The Magic Of Doyly Carte, Oklahoma, Max Boyce, The Paper town Paper chasers.

1985: Cabinet Mole, Carousel, Babes In Arms, Vince Hill and His Solid Gold Music Show, Love At A Pinch, Joseph And The Amazing Technicolor Dreamcoat, Why Not Stay For Breakfast, Having A Ball, London Contemporary Dance Theatre, Mr Cinders, Half A Sixpence, Rigoletto, Norma, Tosca, Annie, Hinge and Bracket, Habeas Corpus, The Anniversary, Olde Tyme Music Hall, Titter Time with Frankie Howerd, The Basil Brush Show, Compo Plays Stupid, The Railway Children, Gypsy, Jasper Carrot, Ballet Rambert, An Evening With Queen Victoria, The Lion The Witch And The Wardrobe, Macbeth, Swan Lake, Coppelia, Val Doonican, Jane Eyre, Jimmy Cricket, Romantic Comedy, Stardust Road, The Gingerbread Men, Pamela Stephenson, Doctor In The House, Sweet Charity, Cosi Fan Tutte, Rigoletto, Madam Butterfly

1986: The Nutcracker, Othello, Cosi Fan Tutte, I Puritani, The Greatest Nite Of The Year,(The Grand then offered its patrons a studio season while the last part of the renovations were being completed, where the audience were seated on the stage area, 300 only, and the plays would take place in the middle)One Flew Over The Cuckoo's Nest, Boys In The Band, Trafford Tanzi, Stags and Hens, The Fantasticks, The Happiest Days Of Your Life, Canterbury Tales - The Grand Re-opened fully complete, after its £5 million pound facelift with the Pantomime "Mother Goose" starring Les Dennis and Christopher Biggins on December 17 1986.

1987: Swan Lake, Kings Rhapsody, Noises Off, The Basil Brush Show, Supergran, A Murder Is Allowed, Seven Brides For Seven Brothers, A Gala Evening For Dr Barnado's, Bobby Davro, London Contemporary Dance Theatre, Daisy Pulls It Off, Beauty Is The Business, The Golden Fortune, The Rocky Horror Show, Fiddler On The Roof, The Fabulous Fifties, Carmen, Le Nozze Di Figaro, La Boheme, Deadly Nightcap, Arsenic And Old Lace, The Man, Boeing Boeing, The Tart And The Vicars Wife, Roy Castle, Keith Harris and Orville, Free Lunchtime Concert, Dennis O'Neil Charity Show, Die Fledermaus, Copy Cats, An Evening With Adelina Patti, Die Fledermaus, Fidelio, A Taste Of Wales, Fidelio, The Cunning Little Vixens, The Three Degrees, The Cunning Little Vixens, The Marriage Of Figaro, Die Fledermaus, An Affront To Culture, Sunrise And Shipwreck, The Grand Style Of Jazz, Cantabile, Shanghai Kunju Theatre, Danny La Rue, See How They Run, Friends To The End, The Rambert Dance Company, The See Saw Tree, Grand Xmas Fashion Show, Victoria Wood, The Haunting Of Hill House, Twelfth Night, She Stoops To Conquer, South Pacific, Joseph and the Amazing Technicolor Dreamcoat, Max Bygraves and Friends, Bad Day At Black Frog Creek, Bumbles Of Mumbles.

1988: Night Of 100 Stars, Funny Peculiar, St David's Day Concert, Entertaining Mr Sloane, Hello Dolly, Tosca, Salome, The Supremes, Eugene Onegin, Hale And Pace, Sounds Like Strauss, Salome, Frankie Vaughan, Tosca, Don Giovanni, Blood Brothers, Bobby Davro, Godspell, Charlie and The Chocolate Factory, London Contemporary Dance Theatre, Camelot, West Side Story, Duncan Norvelle, Holmes And The Ripper, Fur Coat And No Knickers, Deathtrap, Breezeblock Park, Gigi, Danny La Rue, Billy Liar, n One Bed And Out the Other, The Rocky Horror Show, Winnie The Pooh, The Secret Diary Of Adrian Mole Aged 13 ¾, Wife Begins At Forty, Witness For The Prosecution, A Man For All Seasons, Page 3 Murder, Ain't Misbehaving, Joan Collins Fan Club Julian Clary, Welsh National Opera Week, John Dowie, Evening Post Fashion Show, HTV Best Of The Fringe Awards, HTV Presents The Art Of Excellence, The World Of The Actor, And The Opera Singer, The World Of The Comedian And The Theatre Of Musicals and Reviews, The World Of The Actor And The Television Director, Die Puppenfee (The Fairy Doll), The Selfish Shellfish, Dinosaurs And All That Rubbish, BBC Radio Wales 10th Anniversary, Having A Ball, Rosser And Davies, Little Shop Of Horrors, Mame, Mr Fothergills Murder, The Bumble Of Mumble '88.

1989: Postman Pat Live, Chunks And Chips, St David's Day Concert, One O'clock From The House, The Glass Menagerie, Annie Get Your Gun, Stiff Option, The War Of The Roses, An Ideal Husband, Of Mice And Men, To Kill A Mocking Bird, Blithe Spirit, Hobson's Choice, Guy Mitchell, Chas And Dave, Freddie Starr, The Business Of Murder, The Hobbit, Hale And Pace, Dangerous Obsession, Showboat, Whitbread Senior Citizen's Talent, Ivor The Engine Show, The Minstrel Stars, No Sex Please We're British, One O'clock From The House, Breaking The String, Up In The Gallery, La Boheme, Adriane Auf Naxos, La Sonnambula, Seraglio, Cowardy Custard, Dracula, Frankenstein, Robin Hood And His Mucky Men, The Adventures Of Pinocchio, Joseph And The Amazing Technicolor Dreamcoat, Suspects, One For The Road, Up And Under, A Taste Of Honey, HTV recording of a festival of Jazz, Evening Post Clothes Show, Free Grand Theatre Open Day, John Sparkes, Russ Abbot, Lucia Di Lammermoor, The Bartered Bride, Der Freischutz, A Simple Man, Legends Of Motown, The Ideal Gnome Expedition, Lend Me A Tenor, Annie, Phil Cool, Craft Fair, Bumbles Of Mumbles III, Joan Collins Fan Club Julian Clary, Frankie Vaughan.

1990: Fireman Sam To The Rescue, An Evening With Barry McGuigan, St David's Day Gala, The Drifters, Spring Craft Fair, Daniel O'Donnell, Family Planning, Kiss Me Kate, Humphrey Lyttleton, Who Killed Agatha Christie?, Anthony Newley in Concert, Born In The Gardens, Ladies Night, Peter Pan The Musical, Spiders Web, Keith Harris And Orville, Der Freischutz, The Barber Of Seville, Cosi Fan Tutte, Prisoner Cell Block "H", George Hamilton IV, The Entertainer, David Jacobs, Bobby Davro, Chas 'n' Dave, Julian Clary, Hale and Pace, Hence Forward, Superted, Lenny Henry, The Merry Widow, Watching, The Pirates Of Penzance, The Mikado, HMS Pinafore, Trial By Jury, On The Piste, Northern Ballet Company, Shirley Valentine, S4C Yn Cyflwyno O'r Grand, Barbara Dickson, Tribute to the Music Of Bert Kaempfert, Matt Monro Junior, Run For Your Wife, Trev and Simon's Stupid Party, The Care Bears, Grease, O'r Grand, Yogi Bear, Coriolanus, The Winters Tale, Russ Abbot's Madhouse, HTV recording "2nd To None" 3 nights of Music(Owain Arwel-Hughes, Osian Ellis and Julian Lloyd Webber), Easy Terms, From The

House Of The Dark, Carmen, The Marriage Of Figaro, Cinderella, Prince Igor, Swansea Fringe Comedy, Postman Pat, Evita, Guys And Dolls, Gerry's Christmas Cracker, Brendan Shine, Bumbles of Mumbles.

1991: Hazel O'Connor, All's Fair, The Lion The Witch And The Wardrobe, The Horse And His Boy, In The Mood, Dracula Spectacular, The Three Degrees, Blitz, Godspell, Gala Concert for St David's Day, Gene Pitney, An Evening With Vic Damone, Madam Butterfly, Compagnia D'Opera Italiano Di Milano, Wonderful West End, The Rod, Jane And Freddy Show, Spring Craft Fair, A Slice Of Saturday Night, The Drifters, White Horse Inn, The Great Gatsby, Grease, Cannon And Ball, Roy Chubby Brown, Rainbow, Rita McNiel, Ria Jones, Gilbert O'Sullivan, Driving Miss Daisy, Daniel O'Donnell, La Fanciulla Del West, La Traviata, Count Ory, Carmen, Frankie Howerd, The Woman In Black, Jim Davidson, Portrait Of Anna Pavlova, The Dubliners, Hale And Pace, The Gondoliers, Iolanthe, Sir Harry Secombe OBE, Joseph And The Amazing Technicolor Dreamcoat, Chas And Dave, The Cherry Orchard, Ruby Wax, The Pirates Of Penzance, Live Theatre Youth Day, The Little Shop Of Horrors, The Magic Of The Musicals, Sleuth, The Solid Silver 60s Show, Richard Digance, Summer Craft Fayre, Risky Business, Home and Away The Musical, Under Milk Wood, Cider With Rosie, Ladies Night, Fun In The Foyer, Wedding Fair, Pinocchio, Bouncers, Chicago, Jaws and Claws, Owen Money, Privates On Parade, Romeo And Juliet, The Archers, The Gingerbread Man, Jack Jones, Phantom Of The Opera, Max Boyce Rugby World Cup Tour, NSPCC (Swansea) Fashion Show, Power Proms, Film and TV Greats, John Sparkes, Dr Hook with Ray Sawyer, Idomeneo, Rigoletto, Die Fledermaus, Writers Workshop, Jazz, A Kiss On the Bottom, Jimmy Jones, Revue Night, Ceri Dupree Spectacular, Kikunokai, New Orleans Mardi Gras, Elkie Brooks, Glenn Miller Orchestra, NSPCC Variety Show, David Essex, Twelfth Night, The Wizard Of Oz, Joe Longthorne, The Bumbles Of Mumbles, Rod, Jane And Freddy, Wonderful West End 2, Tammy Wynette.

1992: Fireman Sam, After I'm Gone, After Eight, A Night Out, Stepping Out, The Best Little Whorehouse In Texas, Ken Dodd, Sooty And Friends, Jimmy Jones, Trev and Simon, The Mary Whitehouse Experience, Hollywood And Broadway, Jethro and The Wurzels, Keith Harris and Orville, Dame Hilda Bracket, Huckleberry Hound and The Magic Wood, The Butterfly Children, Mike Doyle and Friends, The Fancy Man, The Rocky Horror Show, Murder By Misadventure, BFG, Rose Marie, Rik Mayal, O'r Grand, BBC Concert Orchestra, Ra Ra Zoo Gravity Swing, The Little Mermaid, David Alexander, 3rd Live Youth Theatre Day, Grand Circle Bar Cabaret Revue, Rab C. Nesbitt, Ernani, Iphigénie en Tauride, Madame Butterfly, Simon Drakes Secret Cabaret, Hot Stuff, My Mother Knew I Never Should, Nunsense, Steel Magnolias, Sleeping With Mickey Mouse, Postman Pat, Educating Rita, Thunderbirds Fab, Educating Rita, Timmy Mallet Show, Cosi Fan Tutte, Carmen, Cabaret, Comedy Store Players, Macbeth, The Tempest, Jack Dee, Toy Train and Craft Fair (10-4), The Syd Lawrence Orchestra, Jacques Loussier and The Swingle Singers, Gene Pitney, An Evening With Gary Lineker, Tutti Frutti, The Laughter Show, The Magic Of The Musicals, Foster and Allen, Humph and Helen, Les Patineurs, Donizetti, Variations and the Witchboy, Swan Lake, Welsh National Opera Week, Bootleg Beatles, I Can Give You A Good Time, Macbeth, Sean Hughes, A Funny Thing Happened On the Way to the Forum, The Ladies Of Legend Ceri Dupree, David Alexander, Alfie, Incantation, Bumbles Of Mumbles, Grand Christmas Fayre (am), Craft Fayre.

1993: Eddie Izzard, Billie Jo Spears, Jethro, Bugsy Malone, The Nutcracker, A Night On The Tile, Cantabile, Peter Pan, Gala Celebration For St David's Day, Elkie Brooks, In The Mood, Diversions Dance Company, The Drifters, Brigadoon, Sinderella, Death Of A Salesman, David Essex, La Boheme, Un Ballo In Maschera, La Favorita, Erik The Viking, Roy Chubby Brown, As You Like It, Romeo And Juliet, Solid Silver 60s Show, Glenn Miller Orchestra In Concert, The Hollies, Phantom Of The Opera & Papageno, Rod, Jane And Freddy, The Sleeping Beauty, A Tribute To The Blues Brothers, A Tribute To The Carpenters, Julian Clary, Allsorts, Abertawe'n Fflam, Elvis The Musical, The Pirates Of Penzance, Orpheus In The Underworld, The Chippendales, Aspects Of Love , Lipstick Dreams, Family Planning, Quest For The Dragon 2, Mr Men, Ken Dodd, Rumpelstiltskin and Puppet Cabaret, The Magic Roundabout, Inside Job, The Complete Works Of William Shakespeare, Gala Evening Of Ballet, Julius Caesar, Romeo and Juliet, My Glittering Passage, Buddy – The Buddy Holly Story, Falstaff, Onegin, Lucia Di Lammermoor, Paul Merton, Coppelia, Ben Elton, Trivial Pursuits, Toy And Train Fair, Not In Front Of The Children, Tutti Frutti, Lindisfarne And The Strawbs, Half a Sixpence, Paying The Rent Lily Savage, Eddie Izzard, Charity Show In Aid Of The Christian Lewis Trust, Bumbles Of Mumbles, The Chippendales, A Star Is Torn Ceri Dupree.

1994: A Tribute To Hylda Baker, From The Commentary Box, The Wonderful West End, Midge Ure, Solid Silver 70s Show, Weavers, Valentines Day Writing Workshops, Beauty And The Beast, Only The Lonely, The Hollies, Beauty And The Beast, Sleeping Beauty And Swan Lake, In The Mood, Olde Tyme Music Hall with Danny La Rue, Sean Hughes, The Magic Flute, The Barber Of Seville, That'll Be The Day, 'Allo 'Allo, Return To The Forbidden Planet, Jeff Hooper, The Sound Of Music, Solid Silver 60s Show, Postman Pat, Hinge And Bracket, Hollywood & Broadway 2, Stars Of The Bolshoi Opera, Joe Longthorne, A Tribute To Patsy Cline, A Tribute To The Blues Brothers, Noddy, Elkie Brooks, Little Shop Of Horrors, Manifesto, The Glenn Miller Orchestra, Loose Ends, Jack Dee, Mal Pope and the Jacks in concert, The Legends Of Rock, Fascinating Aida, Great Balls Of Fire, Der Rosenkavalier, Tosca, La Finta Giardiniera, Bouncers, Misery, Animal Farm, Godspell, Shirley Valentine, Four For the Road, Ken Dodd, Mr Men In Toyland, Hot Stuff Ceri Dupree, Present Laughter, Breaking The String, Run For Your Wife, Jo Brand, The Concert They Never Gave, The Rocky Horror Show, Russian Army Cavalcade, Rambert Dance Company, Russ Abbott, South Pacific, The Beat Goes On 94', Hank Marvin, Solid Gold Rock 'N' Roll, That'll Be The Day, Stars From The Commitments, Steeleye Span.

1995: Dazzle, The Family Way, Don Giovanni, A Tribute To Hylda Baker, A Glamorous Night, The Syd Lawrence Orchestra, The Hollies In Concert, Ty Olwen Appeal Concert, Beef And Lamb In A Stew, Playdays, The Good Old Days, St David's Day Gala, Joe Pasquale, Eddie Izzard, Raymond Froggett, Romeo And Juliet, Pickwick, Solid Silver 60s show, Fireman Sam, The Comedy Store Players, 42nd Street, A Tribute to Freddie Mercury And Queen, Le Nozze Di Figario, The Yeoman of the Guard, The Billy Pearce Laughter Show, Cinderella On Ice, The Magical World Of Musicals, The Canterbury Tales, Lily Savage, Roy Chubby Brown, The Chuckle Brothers, Jukebox Giants, The Magic Of The Musicals, Evita, Romeo and Juliet, Gene Pitney in Concert, Lily Savage, Joe Pasquale, Vanessa Mae, Joe Longthorne, Passion Killers, Jimmy Tarbuck And Gerry And The Pacemakers, Copper Kingdom, The Ultimate Tribute Show, Images Of Dance, Roots and Wings, Youth Drama Project, West End Showstoppers, Brideshead Revisited, That'll Be The Day, Ken Dodd, Family Planning, Mr Men And

Little Miss's, Tommy Steele, Voulez Vous, Cleo Laine and Johnny Dankworth, Out Of The Soul and The Spinning Head, Two Of A Kind, Summer 60s Storybook Schwitzer, Rita, Sue and Bob Too, Ben E. King and Dakota Staton, The Magic Of The Musicals, Celtic Crossroads Concert, Bob Downe, The Glenn Miller Orchestra, How To Live, Opera De La Luna, Rod, Jane and Freddy, Sean Hughes, Love Forty, Jethro, Cinderella And Gala Programme, Return To The Forbidden Planet, HTV presents Swansea Festival, HTV presents Words From Swansea, Nabucco, Madam Butterfly, West Glamorgan Community Dance, Hot Shoe Shuffle, Two Old Farts In The Night, The Beverley Sisters, A Night At The Music Hall, Diversions Dance Company, The Chippendales, The Magicians, Nephew, The Lion The Witch And The Wardrobe, Harry Hill, The Real Thing, Carousel, Foster and Allen, Hank Marvin, The Bumbles Of Mumbles, Stars from The Commitments, Elkie Brooks, The Complete Works Of Shakespeare (Abridged), The Bootleg Beatles.

1996: Peter Karrie, The Blues Brothers, Australian Pink Floyd Tribute, Bobby Davro, Sean Hughes, Arabian Nights, Rose Marie, Solid Gold Rock And Roll Show, Playdays, Godspell, Swansea Grand Youth Theatre, BBC Radio Two Presents BBC Big Band, Gaga, Joe Pasquale, Fat Barry's Soul Band, Hinge and Bracket, Barnum, David Essex in Concert, Rambert Dance Company, Oliver, My Cousin Rachel, The Counterfeit Stones, The Stars Of The Future, A Night At The Music Hall, Five Guys Named Moe, Julian Clary, The Rocky Horror Show, The UK Chinese Acrobatic Company, Joe Pasquale Cavalleria Rusticana & I Pagliacci, Faust, The Rake's Progress, The Drifters 1996 Tour, The Ultimate 60s Concert, The Chuckle Brothers, What A Feeling, The Seventies Spectacular, Country Music, Dracula, In The Mood, Plan 9 From Outer Space, Margarita Pracatan, Joe Pasquale, Carmen, Budgie The Little Helicopter, The Essential 60's Concert, There's A Girl In My Soup, Roy Chubby Brown, Magic – Queen Tribute, Lee Evans, Prisoner Cell Block H The Musical, Absent Friends, Iris Williams, Ferry Cross The Mersey The Musical, 7th Annual Youth Drama, Jess Conrad & His Band, Liberty Mountain, Stars Of The Russian Opera, Syd Lawrence Orchestra, The 30th Anniversary World Cup Winners Tour (An Evening With Peter Bonetti, Geoff Hurst & Martin Peters), Kovari, Mike Sterling In Concert, Men On Film, Wind In The Willows, Rock Showcase, 11th Annual Summer School Grand Theatre Dance, Murder At The Theatre, Owen Money & His Band, Firebird And Puppet Cabaret, Glad All Over, A Sensational Evening In The Company Of The Barron Knights & The Searchers, I Have Been Here Before, Easy Terms, Ladies Night, Savoy Opera Favourites, Essential 60s Concert, Ken Dodd, Fat Barry's Soul Band, Jenny Éclair, Lee Hurst, Dracula or How's Your Blood Count, Georgia State Dance Company, Gary Wilmot Showstoppers, An Evening With Henry Cooper, Red Riding Hood, The Hollies, Mr Men Music Land, Mad Monty's Morning Children's Show, Acker Bilk's Jazz Jamboree, Reduced Shakespeare Company, La Boheme, Die Fledermaus, Magical World Of The Care Bears, Joe Longthorne, Phantom Of The Opera On Ice, Paul Daniels and Debbie Magee, Bob Downe, Diversion Dance Company, Voulez Vous, Bryn Yemm, My Fair Lady, Old Time Music Hall, Freddie Starr Live And Devilish, Nursery School Concert, Harry Hill, Bumbles Of Mumbles, Beatles Anthology, Lee And Herring Live, Mad Monty's Xmas Party, Merry Xmas Everybody, Fire Brigade Road show, John Sparkes, The Chippendales.

1997: Stars From The Commitments, Trainspotting, Fairport Convention, Madama Butterfly, The Moldovian, Judie Tzuke, (Swansea's Best Mal Pope & The Jacks, Ceri Dupree & Bob Webb), Fleetwood Bac, Meat Loaf Tribute, La Classique, Albina Dmitrieva, Victor Filimonov,, Yelena Kaminskikh, The Australian Pink Floyd Show, The Best Is Yet To Come, Murder At The Theatre, Alice In Wonderland, Rape Of The Fair Country, A Midsummer Nights Dream, Beowulf, Elkie Brooks, A Midsummer Nights Dream, Beowulf, Me And My Girl, Showaddywaddy, Across The River, (The Barron Knights, Ricky Valence, Bert Weedon & Susan, Maughan), Think No Evil Of Us, Ga Ga, Pinocchio, Ben Elton, Hollywood & Broadway Wayne Sleep & Lorna Luft, Coppelia, Toy Soldiers & Dreaming, Hank Marvin, Jazz, Solid Silver 60s, Roy 'Chubby' Brown, Botham & Lamb, Max Boyce, Carmen, Rigoletto, Iphigenie En Tauride, Joseph & The Amazing Technicolor Dreamcoat, Old Time Music Hall, Joe Pasquale, Ultimate 60's, The Chuckle Brothers, Rambling On Tour, Fat Barry's Soul Band, Bible The Complete Works Of God, The Rabbit And Pork Tour Chas and Dave, What A Feeling!, Romeo And Juliet, Anthony and Cleopatra, The Drifters, Three Steps To Heaven, Playdays, Ruthie Henshall, Spirit Of The Dance, Three British Tenors, Sinatra, The Best Is Yet To Come, Jo Brand, Les Ballet Africa's, David Essex, Summer Musical Magic, Jimmy Jermaine, Magic, Blood Brothers, Budgie The Helicopter, Youth Drama Project 1997, Sgt Pepper's Lonely Hearts Club Band, Grand Summer Garden Party, The Boyfriend, (Grand Centenary Concert A Gala concert celebrating the 100-year centenary of the Theatre. It starred Ria Jones, Mike Sterling, Lee Honey-Jones, Glyn Houston, Menna Trussler, Ruth Madoc, Jason Howard, Dame Gwyneth Jones and Dennis O'Neill), Educating Rita, Communicating Doors, The Spider's Web, Mr Men and The Magic Toyshop, The Dresser, Tap Dogs, Silhouette, Tina Turner Tribute, Wuthering Heights, A Little Night Music, The Blues Brothers Final Tour, Margarita Pracatan, Charity Fashion Show, Expressions Dance Company, An Adult Evening With Billy Pearce, Voulez Vous, Jim Davidson, 42nd Street, Rumplestiltskin & Puppet Cabaret, Matters Matrimonial, Fascinating Aida, Randwyck, Solid Gold Rock 'N' Roll, Lucky Sods, Rose Royce Shalamar & The Real Thing, The Owl And The Pussycat, Legends The Tribute, Lee Hurst, Rambert Dance Company, Magic Of The Ballet, One O'Clock From The House, La Traviata, Jethro, Under Milk Wood, Camelot, Festival Of Dance All Winners Gala, Just The Three Of Us, Greg Proops, Bumbles Of Mumbles, Julian Clary, Fat Barry's Soul Band, Roy Wood.

1998: A Child's Christmas In Wales, Let The Force Be With You, An Evening With Dickie Bird, Diversions, The Best Is Yet To Come, It Started With A Kiss, Carmen, Beauty And The Beast, (Solid Silver 60's Show Helen Shapiro, The Searchers & The Swinging Blue Jeans), Jeff Hooper Big band show, Pastimes, Grand Variety Concert, Shopping and F***ing, That'll Be The Day, Family Planning, Fame, Boogie Nights, Crazy For You, The Care Bears, Tosca, Billy Budd, The Coronation Of Poppea, Ken Dodd, Tommy Steele, Elkie Brooks, Charity Fashion Show, The Hollies, The Classic Soul Show, After The Orgy, The Herbal Bed, Jason Hughes, Gayle Tuesday, David Strassman, Roy Chubby Brown, Dancing In The Streets, The Rocky Horror Show, The Chuckle Brothers, Richard Digance, Whitbread Senior Talent Show, Glam-A-Mania, Cinderella Ballet, Magic, The Best Is Yet To Come, Mike Doyle Tribute to Mario Lanza, Babe The Sheep Pig, Owen Money In Concert, Cider With Rosie, Funny Money, Michael Barrymore, Under African Skies, Give My Regards To Jolson, Wizadora, Iris Williams And The Black Mountain Male Chorus, Gas Station Angel, Studio Images of Dance, Joseph And The Amazing Technicolor Dreamcoat, Testosterone, Ladies Night, Youth Drama Project, Don't Dress For Dinner, Humpty Dumpty Nursery Rhyme Show, How The Other Half Loves, Dial M For Murder, What The Butler Saw, And Then There Were None, Nursery Rhyme Land,

Tales From The Jungle Book, Jasper Carrot, The Spice Of Music Hall With Stan Stennett and Johnny Dallas, D.V.L.A Number Plate Auction, Time Of My Life, Pullin' The Wool, Paul Merton, The Pirates Of Penzance, Rock And Roll West End, Madam Butterfly, Jenufa, Un Ballo In Maschera, Max Boyce, Evening Post Catwalk, Jethro, Magic Of Sinatra, Ardal O'hanlon, Playdays, Rob Newman, Gaga, Bjorn Again, The Great Kovari, Liberty Mountain as Elvis, The Lord Mayor Gala Concert, The Woman In Black, Hello Dolly, The Best Is Yet To Come, Loose Ends, Shake, Rattle and Roll, Bumbles Of Mumbles, The Drifters, Simply The Best, Fat Barry's Soul Band.

1999: Weavers, Aida, Weavers, Think Floyd, The Little Mermaid, (Glitz Blitz & 70's Hitz Suzi Quatro, Alvin Stardust & The Rubettes), BBC Big Band, Let The Force Be With You, Best Of Welsh, The Best Is Yet To Come, Anthology Of The Beatles, Barnum, A Kiss On The Bottom, Terry Pratchett's Guards!, Swansea Festival Of Dance, The Musicals, Illegal Eagles, (The Solid Silver 60's Peter Noone, Freddie & The Dreamers, Billy J Kramer & The Dakotas & Brian Poole with Electrix), Lumen And Nowhere But Here, Woolpackers, Joe Pasquale Is The Nerd, The Merry Widow, Norman Collier, Bob Downe, Ladies & Giblets, Postman Pat, Back Out Of Hell, (Sixties Gold The Fortunes, Gerry & The Pacemakers, The Merseybeats & Mike Pender's Searchers), Magic, The Ugly Duckling, The Memphis Belle Swing Orchestra, Peter Grimes, La Boheme, Hansel & Gretel, 4 Steps To Heaven, (A Night At The Music Hall Cannon & Ball, The Roly Polys & The Batchelors), George Meets Humph, Giselle, Viennese Strauss Gala, Sleuth, Loot, Pam Ayres, Danny La Rue, Comedy Club, Rocking On Heaven's Door, The Chuckle Brothers The Trouble At Sea Tour, For Don A Celebration, The Dubliners, Three Men In A Boat, Tales Of Hoffman, The Chippendales, Magic Of The Musicals, Wizadora, The Best Is Yet To Come, Happy Days, Joseph And The Amazing Technicolor Dreamcoat, Peter karrie Unmasked, Bill Wyman And The Rhythm Kings, Hinge And Bracket 25th Anniversary Concert, Senior Citizens Talent Show, Playdays, Phil Cool, Images Of Dance, The Reduced Shakespeare Co., The Mikado, Give My Regards To Jolson, Voulez Vous, Joe Brown and The Bruvvers, Youth Drama Project, Into Space, The Ultimate Hen Party, Tan Dance, Dangerous Obsession, The Three Little Pigs, Round And Round The Garden, Charley's Aunt, The Unexpected Guest, No Sex Please We're British!, Billy Pearce, Twelfth Night, Beyond The Barricades, Grease, Max Boyce, Ceri Dupree Totally Frocked Up, Roy Chubby Brown, Billy Fury Experience, Gene Pitney, The Bootleg Beatles, Nabucco, A Year To Remember, A Night On The Tiles, An Inspector Calls, Fat Barry's Soul Band, Dr Hook with Ray Sawyer, Tower, Step By Step and Boyz Only, The Barron Knights, The Best Is Yet To Come, Pavlov Ballet Swansea, Abigail's Party, (Solid Gold Rock and Roll Marty Wilde, Joe Brown, John Leyton, Eden Kane and Vernon Girls), Macbeth, Sankofa, The Hollies, Gaga, Stars Of The Commitments, Oklahoma, Craig Charles, A Childs Christmas In Wales, Phil Jupitus, Dominic Kirwan, La Traviata, Millennium The Musical, John Coshlan's Quo, Sleeping Beauty, Roy Wood Spectacular, Bumbles Of Mumbles.

2000: Mark Lamarr, Diversions Dance Company, Anthology Of The Beatles, The Swansea Show, Bad Finger, Elkie Brooks, The Illegal Eagles, Three Of The Best Three one-act plays starring Frank Vickery, Beastly Behaviour, Dishonourable Ladies, Flesh And Blood, The New Rocky Horror Show, Madama Butterfly, The Pulse, Jethro's Bull'cks to Europe Tour, (Solid Silver 60's Show Gerry And The Pacemakers, Peter Sarstedt, The Searchers & The Swinging Blue Jeans), (When Irish Eyes Are Smiling The Batchelors, The Nolans and Jimmy Cricket), The Royal Family, Reach Out, Freddie Starr, Bananas In Pajamas, The Blues Brothers Musical, Swansea's Pavlov Ballet Company, Calamity Jane, Romeo and Juliet, The Best Is Yet To Come, Everything Must Go, Abbasolutely, Cosi Fan Tutte, Turandot, The Barber Of Seville, Jim Davidson, De*witched and Millennium, The Musicals II, The Adventures Of Noddy, Blood Brothers Starring Linda Nolan, In Sunshine And In Shadow, Pinocchio, Shakin Stevens, Naked Flame, Jazz At The Grand, Welsh Rugby Past Present and Future Featuring Graham Henry, Spirit Of The Dance, Howard Marks, The Nualas, Dance Competition, The Chuckle Brothers, The Rat Pack Tribute, A Night At The Music Hall, Joe Pasquale, The Oyster Catchers, Beyond The Barricade, Magic Queen Tribute, Swansea Russian Ballet Company, The Rat Pack, Sian Phillips, Electric Lipstick, Van Morrison, Stand By Me , The Phoenix and The Carpet, Shakespeare Review, Senior Citizens Talent Contest, Think Floyd, Voulez Vouz, (A Gala Concert Max Boyce, Dennis O'Neill, Victor Spinetti and Mike Doyle), Annual Youth Drama Project, Gorseinon College Of Performing Arts, Tribute To The Carpenters, Patrick Moore The Great Universe, Ultimate 60's Show, Playdays, Spring and Port Wine, Deathtrap, Stagestruck, Wife Begins At Forty, Murder At The Vicarage, Rosie And Jim's Music Party, Brilliant Creatures, Sing-A-Long-A Sound Of Music, Ken Dodd, Shane Richie, An Intimate Evening with Mark Rattray, Rockin' On Heaven's Door, The Marriage Of Figaro, Cirque Eloize Exentricus, As You Like It, Supergirly, All's Fair, West Side Story, The Tale Of Little Red Riding Hood, The Best Is Yet To Come, Lee Hurst Tour 2000, Ga Ga, Charity Fashion Show, The Counterfeit Stones, Dominic Kirwan, Aida, Regards To Jolson, The 39 Steps, Together 2000, Wayne Dobson, Roots And Wings, Dangerous Journey, Elkie Brooks, Ed Byrne, Abbasalute, Defending The Caveman Mark Little, Joe Longthorne, Gypsy, Gilbert & Sullivan Evening, Ceri Dupree The Full Diamante, David Essex, The Naughty Rhythms Tour, The Other Beatles, Owen Money & Friends, Harry Hill in Bird Strike, Bill Bailey The Bewilderness Tour, The Pulse, The Nutcracker Swansea's Ballet Russe, A Child's Christmas In Wales, Dream Xmas, Tales Of Maths & Legends, Bumbles Of Mumbles.

2001: Joseph And The Amazing Technicolor Dreamcoat, Rumours Of Fleetwood Mac, Saturday Night At The Movies, Fat Barry's Soul Band, Comedy Charity Concert, VIP's Of Jazz, Swansea Ballet Russe, Saints And Sinners, (Iesu Grist Siwpyrstar Jesus Christ Superstar in Welsh), Roy Chubby Brown, Diversion Dance Company, Madam Butterfly, Illegal Eagles, Great Balls Of Fire Tribute, Abba Mania, Polka Dot Shorts, The Best Is Yet To Come, S Club Party and Billie Tribute, Tommy Tiernan, The Real Monty Comes Again, Musical Biography of Roy Orbison, The Billy Fury Story, Boogie Night Fever, The Hollies, Sing-Along-A Sound Of Music, Salute To Sinatra, Bananas in Pajamas, La Traviata, Beatrice And Benedict, The Marriage Of Figaro, The Lady Vanishes, Mothers and Daughters, My Fair Lady and Iolanthe, Supergirly, Solid Silver 60's Show, Missleading Ladies Ceri Dupree and Ria Jones, La Boheme, Joe Pasquale, Jethro, Fever The Making Of Peggy Lee, Postman Pat, Spirit Of The Dance, The Chuckle Brothers, West End Encore, Shania Twain Tribute, An Audience With Julian Cope, Twm, Little Red Riding Hood, What A Feeling!, Family Planning, Look Who's Coming To Dinner, Jazz Legends In Concert, Looney Tunes Children's show, Bjorn Again, Pure Puccini Opera Classics, Swan Lake, Maria Ewing, Mortimer's Miscellany, Blues Brothers – Sweet Home Chicago, Peter Karrie, Nobody's Perfect, Puppetry Of The Penis, Vivaldi By Candlelight, Beyond The Barricade, Wheels On The Bus, Paul Daniels, Lenny Henry, The Squadronaires, Images Of Dance, The Borrowers, Swansea's Ballet Russe, Young Person's Tribute to Sir Harry Secombe,

Rebecca, Table Manners, Night Must Fall, A Murder Is Announced, Run For Your Wife, Murder By Misadventure, Elkie Brooks, A Night At The Musicals, The Dream Concert, (All Star Variety Show Vince Hill, Dianne Lee & Rick Price, Ken Goodwin, Wayne Dobson & Jack Seaton), Promo Donnas, Patsy Cline Music And Memories, Love Me Tender, Gaga, Van Morrison, High Society, Erogenous Zones, The Glenn Miller Tribute Orchestra, Romeo And Juliet, (Solid Gold Rock'n'Roll Show Marty Wilde, Joe Brown, John Leyton, Eden Kane And The Vernon Girls), Blackmore's Night, Chiquitita, An Evening With Jack Dee, Seven Brides For Seven Brothers, Fist Of The Dragon, A Portrait Of Ivor Novello, The Carpenters Tribute, David Essex The Wonderful Tour, The Sooty Show, Lord Of The Flies, Debbie McGee's Ballet Imaginaire, Beyond Broadway, Sing-a-long-a Sound Of Music, Dusty The Concert, The Best Is Yet To Come, Silly Circus, Cooking With Elvis, (Bonnie Tyler Although this appeared in a flyer Bonnie the show was cancelled), Magic A Kind Of Queen, The Ceri Dupree Show, Coppelia Swansea's Ballet Russe, Simply The Best, Think Floyd, Turandot, Carmen, Grease, Fiddler On The Roof, Mike Doyle And Friends, Ready Steady Dance, Wayne Sleep and Melanie Stace, Death Of A Salesman, Dream Xmas, Voulez Vouz, Bumbles Of Mumbles Show, Welsh National Opera Chorus.

2002: The Enormous Crocodile, Talent' Wales Final, Rumours Of Fleetwood Mac, The Real Abba Gold, Joseph And The Amazing Technicolor Dreamcoat, Charity Gala Concert, The Drifters, Roy Chubby Brown, Pure Puccini, Salute To Sinatra, Pop Starz, The Return Of Return To The Forbidden Planet, At The Hop, An Evening With Gordon Giltrap, Superstars, Westenders, The Best Is Yet To Come, Polkadot shorts, Lindisfarne, Tales Of Blooming Science, Fat Barry's Soul Band, Illegal Eagles, Diversions, Louise, The Lavender Hill Mob, (ReelinandaRockin Gerry Marsden, Mike D'Abo, Mike Pender, Brian Poole, Dave Berry & The Nolans), Mack & Mabel, Giselle, Trivial Pursuits, Jim Davidson, An Audience With Danny La Rue, Westside, Noddy & The Treasure Chest, Ken Dodd Happiness Show, Jethro's Beyond The Edge Tour, Africa Africa, Sing A Long A Abba,The Magic Of The Musicals, (Call Up The Groups The Barron Knights, The Tremeloes, The Fortunes & Marmalade), Nabucco, Tosca, Five Blue Haired Ladies Sitting On A Green Park Bench, Blood Brothers, My Beautiful Laundrette, Rope, The Manfreds, Freddie Starr Unwrapped, Barbara Dickson, The Bible, Hank Marvin, Pop Starz, The Sleeping Beauty, Kak Raider '02 Joe Pasquale, VIP's of Jazz, (Hey Rock'n'Roll Showaddywaddy, The Deevettes, Jason Steele & Lisa Radclyffe), Raiders Of The Lost Bark, Reservoir Dogs, The Ghosts Of Ruddigore, The Dreamboys, Bjorn Again, Noel James & Company, Big Band Crazy, Grand Theatre Dance School, A Tribute To Richard Rogers, (The Solid Gold Comedy Show Jimmy Cricket, Duncan Norvelle, Frank Carson, Paul Adams & Norman, Collier), Sweet Caroline, Des O'Connor, Side-By-Side, An Audience With Tony Benn, Pam Ayres, Yours Silver Stars Talent Contest, That'll Be The Day, The Second Young Entertainers Tribute To Sir Harry Secombe, La Traviata, Barber Of Seville, One Night Only, Spirit Of The Dance, The Squadronaires, Playdays, Beyond The Barricade, Rockin' On Heaven's Door, Swansea's Ballet Russe, Toreadors, T-Birds & Tyranny, Concert With The Orchestra Of Welsh National Opera, Rigoletto, Gangstars, When We Are Married, Living Together, The Ghost Train, One For The Road, Double Double, Postman Pat in Where's Jess?, The Dream Concert, The Wizard Of Oz, A Night To Remember, Owen Money, La Fille Mal Gardee Swansea Ballet Russe, Elvis, Beyond Broadway, Dance Passion, Lee Evans The Wired And Wonderful Tour, Lets Go Round Again, Norma, Cleo Laine and Johnnie Dankworth, Aida, Brief Encounter, Ga Ga, Sweet Home Chicago, Jeremy Hardy, What Mother Never Told You, David Essex, The Sooty Show, (Solid Gold Rock'n'Roll Bobby Vee, Chris Montez, Bryan Hyland, Johnny Preston, The Chiffons and the Vees), Annie, National Youth Ballet, Think Floyd, The Best Is Yet To Come, Pub Landlord Al Murray, Level 42, James and The Giant Peach, Permanent Revolution V2R, Vienna Boys Choir, Chwarae Chwaer, The Red Army, Die Fledermaus, Tosca, Madam Butterfly, Scrooge The Musical, Mike Doyle And Friends, Billy Bragg And The Blokes, Single Spies, The Nutcracker Swansea's Ballet Russe, Bumbles Of Mumbles, Westenders at Christmas

2003: Talent Wales The Final, Chorus Concert Welsh National Opera, Fame The Musical, Carmen, Roy Chubby Brown, The Glenn Miller Tribute Orchestra, Mamma Mia The Concert, Festival Of Dance, An Evening With Hannah Gordon & Peter Barkworth, Hold Tight It's 60s Night, A Night Of Angels, Ed Byrne, Circus Hilarious, Turn On The Taps, One Night Of Queen, Peter Green Splinter Group, Phantom And The Opera, Welsh Musical Theatre Young Singer Of The Year, The Best Is Yet To Come, The Buddy Holly Story, Jethro, Swan Lake Swansea's Ballet Russe, A Midsummer Nights Dream, Wild Horses Spring Tour eve, A Clockwork orange, Uri Geller, The Illegal Eagles, Paddington Bear, (ReelinandaRockin Gerry Marsden, Dave Berry, Mike D'Abo, Brian Poole, Mike Pender & The Nolans), Carousel, Derren Brown, The Winters Tale, Carmen, The Elixir Of Love, Cavalleria Rusticana And I Pagliacci, Jenufa, Moscow Ballet La Classique, George's Marvellous Medicine, An Evening With Christine Hamilton, (Mersey Beat The Swinging Blue Jeans, The Merseybeats, The Fourmost's & The Pete Best Band), The Rocky Horror Picture Show Timewarp. 30th Anniversary, Mal Pope & The Jacks, Marion And Geoff Tour, The Blues Brothers Show, (Solid Silver 60'sThe Searchers, Dave Dee, Dozy, Beaky, Mick & Tich, Wayne Fontana & Barry Ryan), Julian Clary, Spirit Of The Dance, Star Doors The Chuckle Brothers, Summer Holiday, Spanish Lies, Clive James & Pete Atkin, Counterfeit Stones, (Glitz Blitz & 70's Hits The Sweet, The Rubettes, Showaddywaddy), The Musical Manhattan, Magic – A Kind Of Queen, The Royal Ballet School, Rick Wakeman, The Nutcracker, Stones In His Pockets, Bobby Davro, The Cavern Beatles, Kevin Bloody Wilson, Voulez Vous, The Big Chris Barber Band, The Golden Years Of Variety, Heaven Can Wait, Judith Durham, Silver Stars Talent Contest, The Musicals, La Boheme, The Best Is Yet To Come, An Audience With Ann Widdecombe MP, Men In Coats, La Fille Mal Gardee Swansea's Ballet Russe, Fat Barry's Soul Band, Noddy & The Magical Day, The Funny Guys, Children Of Eden, Mars: The Next Frontier, The Drifters 50th Anniversary, 89 Minutes To Save The NHS, Mercury, Livin La Vida Loca, (Stage Stars Julie Paton, David Massey, Joanna Lee & Jay Marcus), Sailor Beware, My Cousin Rachel, It Runs In The Family, Tickledom, Trap For A Lonely Man, The Decorator, West Side Story Harry Secombe Youth, Rigoletto, Peter Karrie & Friends, At The Hop, Mugenkyo Taiko Drummers, Max Boyce Celebrates 30 Years In Show Business, Madama Butterfly, Manami Hama, Elvis Tribute, Owen Money & The Soul Sharks, An Evening With Bob Geldof, Meat Loaf Tribute, Bollywood Nights, Wizard Of Oz Sing-A-Long, Playing Burton, The Best Is Yet To Come, Under Milk Wood, The Amazing Chinese Acrobats, Ga Ga tribute to Queen, Jim Davidson, David Essex, The Squadronaires, (Call Up The Groups Tremeloes, Barron Knights, Marmalade & Fortune), Dream Out Loud, Tonto Evans, A Night Of Angels, The Manfreds, Abba Tribute, The Full Diamante Ceri Dupree, The Marriage of Figaro, Il Trovatore, Parsifal, Annie Get Your Gun, Saturday Night Fever, Grand Charity Concert, Joe

Longthorne, Rockin' On Heaven's Door, The Bumbles of Mumbles, The Nutcracker Ballet Russe, Beyond Broadway.

2004: Joseph And The Amazing Technicolor Dreamcoat, Australian Pink Floyd Show, Kings Of Swing, Cinderella Goes Pop, Barbara Dickson, The Circus Of Horrors, Dennis Locorriere The Voice Of Dr Hook, Circus Hilarious, A Viennese Strauss Gala, All The Great Books - The Reduced Shakespeare Company, Ysgol Y Strade, Roy Chubby Brown, Turandot, Gala Performance Swansea's Ballet Russe, Welsh Musical Theatre, Bananas In Pajamas, Malachi, The Woman In Black, St David's Day Concert, Zipp 100 Musicals, All That Jazz, The Hollies, Mal Pope With Steve Balsamo, The Best Is Yet To Come, Jongleurs On The Road, Shakespeare 4 Kidz Macbeth, Shakespeare 4 Kidz Midsummer Nights Dream, Jethro Off The Wall Tour, An Evening With Mike Sterling, Spirit Of The Dance, The Vagina Monologues, Swing Mania, Derek Acorah, Swan Lake, Jesus Christ Superstar, Tony Hadley and Peter Cox, The Civic Celebration, Shakespeare's R & J, Eugene Onegin, Hansel And Gretel, Madam Butterfly, Dave Willetts, Side-By-Side, Super Troupers, Bill & Ben & Andy Pandy, Oh What A Night With Kid Creole, Van Morrison, Derren Brown Live, Dynion Euroman, Ultimate Energy, Magic A Kind Of ELO, Grand Charity Celebration, Belinda Carlisle, That's Life, Think Floyd, The Cavern Beatles 2004, Beyond The Barricade, Tribute To Riverdance, One Night Of Queen, Freddie Starr, Jongleurs On The Road, Marty And Joe Are Back, Cosi Fan Tutte Swansea City Opera, The Sleeping Beauty On Ice, Tell Me On A Sunday, My Fat Friend, Illegal Eagles, The Animals 40th Anniversary Tour, Coppella Swansea Ballet Russe, Glenn Miller Tribute, The Chamber Of Horrors-The Chuckle Brothers, Pullin' The Wool, Stones In His Pockets, From Basin Street In Broadway, Tosca, The Best Is Yet To Come, The Spencer Davis Group and The Yardbirds, The Best Musicals Ever- The Westenders, Silver Years Talent Contest, Fine Young Cannibals, Abba The Story, Dream Street, Bill Bailey Part Troll, Diane Lazarus, Pinocchio, Heartbeat, Elkie Brooks, The Little Shop Of Horrors-The Harry Secombe Youth Musical Theatre Company, Images Of Dance, Night At The Philharmonic, Blithe Spirit, Killing Time, Don Quixote Swansea Ballet Russe, Out Of Order, The Turn Of The Screw, Outside Edge, The Gentle Hook, Googlewhack Adventure Dave Gorman, The Wheels On The Bus, Singalong In Sing Song City Divas, The Morriston Big Band with Owen Money, The Sound Of Music-Sir Harry Secombe Youth Musical Theatre Company, Giselle Swansea Ballet Russe, Gervase Phinn, Puppetry Of The Penis, High Spirits, Moscow By Night, Mamma Mia, Twelfth Night, Cymbeline, The Merchant Of Venice, Keith Barret show Live, Turandot, Iphegenie En Tauride, Ariadne Auf Naxos, The Drifters, Swing Like Crazy, VIP's Of Jazz, Cinderella Ballet, The Sleeping Beauty Ballet, Mum's The Word, Sixties Gold P.J.Proby, The Troggs, Herman's Hermits & The Ivy League, A Night At The Musicals, The Best Is Yet To Come, (Best Of The 80's Tour Toyah, Nick Heyward, Curiosity Killed The Cat & Altered Images), A Night At The Opera, Givin' It Tour, Love Forty, Mark Thomas, The Bootleg Beatles, Russian Cossack State Dance Company, Dial M For Murder, Swansea Sound 30 Years On The Radio with Kevin Johns, Aida Opera, Cavalleria Rusticana & I Pagliacci, (Solid Gold Rock'n'Roll Show Showaddywaddy, Eden Kane, John Leyton & Freddy Cannon), BBC Big Band, The Blues Brothers, The Elvis Collection, The Scarlet Pimpernel, Rumours Of Fleetwood Mac, Abba, The Bumbles Of Mumbles, Christmas Concert, The Nutcracker Swansea Ballet Russe, The Chippendales.

2005: Night Of Angels, La Fille Mal Gardee Swansea's Ballet Russe, The Circus Of Horrors, Something's Afoot, The Calculating Mr One, Tony Hadley V Martin Fry & ABC, Sing-a-long-a Sound Of Music, The Best Is Yet To Come, An Evening With Mo Mowlam, Sharon Neil, GaGa, Madama Butterfly, Jongleurs Comedy On The Road, (Roy Chubby Brown cancelled due to illness), Sleeping Beauty, Welsh Musical Theatre Young Singer Of The Year, Laughing All Over The World, A Viennese Strauss Gala, St David's Day Concert, Mike Doyle In Concert, (Glitz, Blitz and 70's Hits The Sweet, Rubettes and Sailor), Kings Of Swing, Derek Acorah, Paul Childs and Friends, Dave Spikey, (Solid Silver 60's Show Gerry and The Pacemakers, The Searchers, The Merseybeats and The Swinging Blue Jeans), An Evening With Jane McDonald, The Slipper And The Rose, Amazing Grace, An Inspector Calls, Three Other Tenors, From Welsh National Opera, Tony Christie, Van Morrison, Manhattan Nights, Supertroupers, (Call Up The Groups Barron Knights, The Fortunes, The Tremeloes and Marmalade), Elvis The Vegas Years, Grand Charity Show, Stones In His Pockets, Broadway, Jekyll And Hyde, The Manfreds, Phoenix Dance Theatre, Jack Dee Live, The Barber Of Seville Swansea City Opera, One O'clock From The House, Freddie Starr, A Midsummer Night's Dream, Jongleurs Comedy On The Road, The Complete Works Of William Shakespeare (abridged), The Kings Of Swing, Pirates Of The River Rother-The Chuckle Brothers, The Improvisers, The Magic Flute, Iolanta, Rigoletto, At The Hop, Diane Lazarus, The Best Is Yet To Come, A Grand Concert, Mad About The Musicals, U2 Two, Spirit Of The Dance, Magic, Glenn Miller Tribute Orchestra, Dr Bunhead's Recipe For Disaster, Roy Chubby Brown rescheduled performance, Jethro, Silver Stars Talent Contest, Thank you For The Music, The Little Humpbacked Horse, Grand Theatre School Of Dance, Art, Singing In The Rain-The Harry Secombe Youth Theatre Company, Mugenkyo Taiko Drummers, Movie Magic, Tan Dance Taking part, Images Of Dance , Beauty And The Beast, Present Laughter, Jane Eyre, Jim Davidson, Just Desserts, I'll Be Back Before Midnight, Caught On The Net, My Fair Lady-The Harry Secombe Youth Theatre Company, Porgy And Bess, Tony Stockwell, The Drifters, Night At The Musicals, Max Boyce, Carmen, The Elvis Collection, The Rat Pack Party, Postman Pat, Ken Dodd, Gaslight, Joe Pasquale, Ardal O'Hanlon, Voulez Vous, The Red Army, The Best Is Yet To Come, A Diaghilev Gala Swansea Ballet Russe, Annie, A Bilingual Hamlet, Greg Lake, Killer Queen, All Through The Night, The Pearl Fishers Swansea City Opera, The Illegal Eagles, Thatha, Guys And Dolls, Mal Pope, Jimmy Carr, The Merry Widow, The Barber Of Seville, Romeo And Juliet, Ben Elton, Bumbles Of Mumbles, Merry Xmas Everybody-Slade, Mud and T-Rextacy, Christmas Gala with Swansea ballet Russe, Life Of Ryan And Ronnie, Al Murray The Pub Landlord.

2006: The Holly And The Ivy, The Story's, The Sir Harry Secombe Musical Youth Theatre Company, An' That's Jazz, Omid Djalili, Chris Needs & Friends, Colin Fry, Alexander O'Neal, Swan Lake, The Nutcracker, The Bert Kaempfert Orchestra, Rumours Of Fleetwood Mac, Ga Ga, The Magic Of The Musicals, Rent A Ghost, The Gruffalo, The Best Is Yet To Come, Jethro, Owen Money & The Soul Sharks, Paul Childs, (The Solid Silver 60's Show Gerry & The Pacemakers, Dave Dee, Dozy, Beaky, Mick & Titch, Wayne Fontana & PJ Proby), Mrs Jessop & The Maths Lesson of Doom, Night Of Angels, Young Singer Of The Year Final winner Connie Fisher, La Boheme, Think Floyd, The Jive Aces, The Hollies, Mike Doyle, The Bootleg Beatles, Titanic The Musical, The Mighty Boosh, Broadway, Natya Kala, The Best Blues Brothers Show In The World….Ever, A Grand Concert, Fireman Sam To The Rescue, Tunes Of Glory, Seven Brides For Seven Brothers, The Marriage Of Figaro, Jephtha, The Flying Dutchman, Stuart Little, Beyond Reasonable Doubt, An Evening With Joan Collins, The Magical

Dance Of Ireland, Completely Hollywood Reduced Shakespeare Company, Moscow By Night, A 40th Anniversary Musical Evening Mal Pope & Steve Balsamo, Young Talent Show, The Jungle Book, Rigoletto, A Kiss On The Bottom, A Grand Wedding Fayre, Lady Chatterley's Lover, Derren Brown, Derek Acorah, Dara O'Briain, Elvis In Concert Show, Soweto Gospel Choir, Love Of A Nightingale, Roy Chubby Brown, The Chuckle Brothers, Abba Mania, The Kings Of Swing, Jongleurs Comedy On The Road, This Is My Song A Tribute to Sir Harry Secombe, The Best Is Yet To Come, Cinderella Swansea Ballet Russe, Bugsy Malone-Sir Harry Secombe Musical Youth Theatre Company, Tony Stockwell, Joe Longthorne, Images Of Dance, The Rhythm Of Life The Grand Theatre School Of Dance, Saturday Night Fever, Oliver, Richard Digance, Giselle Swansea Ballet Russe, One Night Of Queen, The Rock n Roll Years, The Glenn Miller Tribute Orchestra, Magic Of The Dance, Bedroom Farce, Wuthering Heights, Funny Money, A Party To Murder, Star Quality, Paddy McGuinness, One Man Star Wars Trilogy, Hot Chocolate, The Canterbury Tales, Dora's Pirate Adventure, Fame The Musical The Harry Secombe Youth Theatre Company, RNIB Charity Concert With Sion Probert, Die Fledermaus, Illegal Eagles, Magic A Kind Of Queen, Thank You For The Music, Luv Esther, Blood Brothers with Linda Nolan, Puppetry Of The Penis, Gina Yashere – I Don't Think So, Jimmy Carr Gag Reflex, The Spencer Davis Group, La boheme, Chorus, La boheme, Jim Davidson, A Child's Christmas In Wales, Amazing Grace, A Christmas Carol, Spirit Of The Dance, Family Planning, The King And I, Mark Thomas, Joe Brown, The Daughter Of The Regiment, Swansea City Opera, The Bumbles Of Mumbles, (Merry Xmas Everybody Mud, T-Rextasy & Slade), Lenny Henry.

2007: Lenny Henry, Toshack Or Me, A Night To Remember –a tribute to murdered Swansea teenager Ben Bellamy, September Tide, Jimmy Carr, Showbiz-The Harry Secombe Youth Theatre Company, Romeo And Juliet, Swan Lake, Onke Ose, Voulez Vous, The Mark Jermin Stage School Awards, Joseph And The Amazing Technicolor Dreamcoat, A Viennese Straus Gala, The Tempest, Magical Midsummer Mayhem In The Woods, Jethro, Killer Queen, Steven Seagal(Hollywood tough guy) And his band Thunderbox, The Bootleg Beatles, Sing-a-long-a Sound Of Music, Aida, The Drifters, Off The Wall, Welsh Musical Theatre Singer Of The Year, Stephen Howe, The Last Pirate, The Storys, Sarah Kendall, Peter Grant, Rambert Dance Company, The Big Drip, Peter Pan On Ice, Thoroughly Modern Millie, The Big Ballet, Honor Blackman story, (Solid Silver 60's Show with The Searchers, Wayne Fontana, Merseybeats, John Walker Of The Walker Brothers and The Dakotas), The Image Of Cliff Richard And The Shadows, Max Boyce, Madam Butterfly, Carmen, Khovanshchina, Tracey Beaker Gets Real, Contender-Mike Doyle and Peter Karrie, Could It Be Magic, Stardust, London Community Gospel Choir, Friday Night Is Music Night, Joe Longthorne, The Kings Of Swing, Mugenkyo Taiko Drummers, An Enchanting Evening Of Tchaikovsky at The Ballet with Swansea Ballet Russe, Granny Annie, Marty Wilde & The Wildcats, Phoenix Dance Theatre, Masters Of The Musical, Freddie Starr, Spooky Goings On 2, The Wizard Of Oz-The Sir Harry Secombe Musical Youth Theatre Trust, Swansea Institute Of Performing, Tosca, Magic A kind Of Queen, The Best Is Yet To Come, Make Way For Noddy And Friends, Colin Fry, An Evening With Gervase Phinn, The Great Gilbert And Sullivan Show, Abba Mania, Images Of Dance, Buddy, The Billie Holiday Story with Rain Prior (the daughter of legendary American comedian Richard Pryor), Beyond The Barricade, Elkie Brooks, Real Diamond, Talon The Best Of The Eagles, Glenn Miller Tribute Orchestra, Humph 'N' Acker, Bound For Broadway, Ken Dodd's Happiness Show, The Railway Children, High School Musical, Cash On Delivery, Coppelia with Swansea Ballet Russe, The Lady Boys Of Bangkok, The Decorator, The Secretary Bird, Dangerous Corner, Dead Guilty, The Elvis Collection, Tweenies Live, Annie, An Audience Wuth Sian Phillips, Ross Noble, Spirit Of The Dance, Rumours Of Fleetwood Mac, Mad About The Musicals, Gaga, Jake And Elwood's Best Blues Brothers In The World Ever, Carmen, A Night On The Tiles, Abba Forever, Mal Pope, The Servant Of Two Masters, Essence Of Ireland, The Best Is Yet To Come, Circus Hilarious, Ceri Dupree, A Chance To Dance, South Pacific, Jenny Éclair, Dynion, Godspell with Stephen Gately, Jimmy Carr, Swansea Girls, Anything Goes, Bumbles Of Mumbles.

2008: The Masters of the House, The Sir Harry Secombe Trust perform songs from hit musicals, The Magic Flute Swansea City Opera Company, Jimmy Carr, (Call up the Groups-Barron Knights, Fortunes, Marmalade & Tremeloes), Toshack or Me!, To Hull and Back, Jethro, Scrap Arts Music, Sharon Neill, On the Stage and Off, Oh What a Night!, Romeo and Juliet, The Sleeping Beauty, Cerys Matthews, Best is Yet to Come, Bill Wyman's Rhythm Kings, Dad's Army, On the Trail of the Countback Kid, Madama Butterfly, La Traviata, Mike Doyle In Concert, The Circus of Horrors, Welsh Musical Theatre Young Singer Of The Year Competition - The Final, The Bootleg Beatles, Rambert Dance Company, Gordon Hendricks. Elvis Tribute, Hello Dolly, Over the Rainbow The Life Story of Eva Cassidy, Buddy Holly and the Cricketers, Basil Brush, Angelina Ballerina's Star Performance, Voulez Vous, Roofless, Roy Chubby Brown, The Californians, John Culshaw Comedy Impressionist, Derek Acorah, Hamlet Shakespear4kids, Under Milk Wood, (Solid Silver 60's Show Gerry and The Pacemakers. The Swinging Blue Jeans, Dave Berry and Dave, Dee, Dozy, Beaky, Mick and Tich), Derren Brown Mind Reader Tour, Buttons Undone, The Magic Flute, Eugene Onegin, Falstaff, Danny The Champion Of The World, Paul Merton Impro Chums, Dave Spikey, Think Floyd, Viva Las Vegas Live, The Chuckle Brothers Indiana Chuckles and The Kingdom Of The Mythical Sulk, Aspects Of Love, Fireworks At The Ballet Swansea Ballet Russe, Ricky Tomlinson's Laughter Show, Roots and Wings, Thomas The Tank and Friends, The Afternoon Show With Chris Needs, Peter Karrie, (Sensational 60's Show The Tremeloes, The Merseybeats and The Dreamers), Those Musical Gals, Richard Digance, Oklahoma, The Rat Pack, Images Of Dance, Rupert Bear Follow The Magic, Simply Ballroom, Onke Ose, One Night Of Queen, Westenders, The Beat Is Yet To Come, Thank You For The Music, The Spirit Of Pavarotti, Little Howard and the Magic Pencil of Life and Death, Swansea Girls, Honk Sir Harry Secombe Trust, The UK Beach Boys, Lazytown Live, Rockin' on Heaven's Door, Morriston Phoenix Choir, We're All In This Together, One-Man Star Wars™ Trilogy, See How they Run, The Business of Murder, Daisy Pulls it Off, Don't Look Now (cancelled), Diane Lazarus, Run for Your Wife, Chas and Dave in Concert, Bless 'em All With Stan Stennett, Jive Talkin', Tim Vine – Punslinger, Beyond The Barricade, Tony Stockwell, Gala Variety Performance, Summer Holiday The Sir Harry Secombe Trust, Romeo and Juliet, La Boheme, Killer Queen, Erogenous Zones, Jim Davidson, Puppetry Of The Penis, Under Milk Wood Dance, Russell Howard, CBeebies at the Theatre, Joe Pasquale Back On The Road, The Big Ballet, Barber Of Seville, Otello, The Best Is Yet To Come, The Jungle Book, Simon Yates Beyond The Void, My Brilliant Divorce, The Motown Show How Sweet It Is, The Reduced Shakespeare Company present The Bible The Complete Word of God' (abridged), Jimmy Carr, Joe Brown, Beauty And The Beast, Dara O' Briain, Oliver, Rob Brydon, L'elisir d'amore (Elixir of Love) Swansea City Opera, Lee Memphis King,

The stars from The Commitments, Talon: The Best of the Eagles, Ladyboys of Bangkok, Hayley Westenra, Colin Fry, Bumbles Of Mumbles, Andy Abraham, Merry Xmas Everybody Mud2 T-Rextasy and Slade.

2009: Paul Carrack, The Nutcracker Swansea Ballet Russe, Sing a Long a Sound Of Music, Sounds Of The Glenn Miller Era, Coppelia, Swan Lake, Murder With Love, Stephen K Amos, An Evening With Tony Benn, Four Poofs and a Piano, A Gala Night at the Musicals Sir Harry Secombe Trust, Jethro, Peter Grant, Stones In His Pockets, The Nelson Riddle Orchestra, Masters Of The House, The Best Is Yet To Come, Bjorn Again, Vienna Strauss Gala, Magic A Kind Of Queen, The Drifters In Concert, Teenage Love Affair Dani Dee School Of Dance, Welsh Musical Theatre Young Singer Of The Year, Aida, Carmen, Sally Morgan, Rhod Gilbert and the Award Winning Mince Pie, Jake and Elwood The Best Blues Brothers Show in the World Ever, Max Boyce, Circus Of Horrors, (Solid Silver 60's Show The Searchers, Wayne Fontana, The Merseybeats and John Walker), The Jimi Hendrix Experience, The Californians, A Vision Of Elvis, Chris Needs and Friends, Golden Days Of Music Hall with Stan Stennett and Johnny Tudor, Cirque De Glace, Noises Off, HMS Pinafore, The Thorn Birds, The Elixir Of Love, Salome, The Marriage Of Figaro, Chuckle Brothers chuckle Trek, Only Men Aloud, All The Fun Of The Fair with David Essex, Trivial Pursuits, The Naked Truth with Lisa Riley, Gaga, The Worlds Greatest Elvis Gordon Hendrix, Blood Brothers with Maureen Nolan, Turandot, Ross Noble, Ceri Dupree, Shaken Not Stirred, Joe Longthorne, Milkshake Live, Shaolin Warriors, The Songs Of Sister Act, Tony Stockwell, Masters Of The Musical, Alice's Adventures in Clubland, Side-By-Side, Roy Chubby Brown, The Best Is Yet To Come, String Of Pearls, Broadway Lights and Hollywood Nights, Scales and Scandal, Abba Mania, Seven Brides For Seven Brothers, Images Of Dance, 5x60 Dance Evolution, Off The Wall-Spirit Of Pink Floyd, An Evening With Pam Ayres, Noise Ensemble – The Percussion Spectacular, The Cavern Beatles, Le Grand Cirque, Magic of the Dance, The Life and Music Of Ivor Novello, The Vagina Monologues, Here Come The Boys, The Great Pretender, Strictly Murder, Hayley Westenra, You Don't Bring Me Flowers, Rattle Of A Simple Man, Oyster Bay, The Tart And The Vicar's Wife, Write Me A Murder, Forces Sweethearts, Pools Paradise, Derek Acorah, Mad About The Musicals, Tweenies Live, The Doctor and the Devils, Tim Minchin, Footloose The Sir Harry Secombe Trust, Jane Macdonald, Babe The Sheep Pig, The Ukulele Orchestra of Great Britain, Afternoon Delights with Kevin Johns, Mike Doyle, Variety Magic Jimmy Cricket, Don Maclean and Dana, Fashion Spectacular, Shirley Bassey Tribute, Think Floyd, Ken Dodd, Over The Rainbow - The Life Story of Eva Cassidy, Diane Lazarus, Abba Forever, The Elvis Years, The Best is Yet to Come, Musicals in Motion, La Traviata, Madam Butterfly, Soweto Gospel Choir, Sing-A-Long-A Rocky Horror Picture Show, Fascinating Aida, Chas and Dave, Boogie Pete Live, Stewart Lee, Rhod Gilbert The Cat That Looked Like Nicholas Lyndhurst, David Essex, Bob The Builder Live, Company, How Green Is My Valley? Independent Ballet Wales, Rat Pack Vegas Spectacular, India Dance Wales: Life, Andy Parsons, Hooray For Hollywood, Tonto EvanS, Vagina Monologues, Kevin Bloody Wilson, One Night Of Queen, Alistair McGowan, The Stylistics, Bill Wyman's Rhythm Kings, Pam Ann, LazyTown Live! - The Pirate Adventure, Kismet, Cappuccino girls, The Nutcracker Swansea Ballet Russe, Colin Fry & TJ Higgs, A Family Christmas Concert with Steve Dewitt, Bumbles Of Mumbles, Beyond The Barricade, Steeleye Span.

2010: Elkie Brooks, The Winner Takes It All, Paul Carrack, Buddy Holly and the Cricketers, West End to Broadway The Sir Harry Secombe Trust, Mark Jermin stage school awards, Side By Side, Joe Brown In Concert, That'll Be The Day, Jimmy Carr, Tim Vine, Derren Brown Enigma, Circus Hilarious, The Pearl Fishers Swansea City Opera, Stephen K Amos, Chinese New Year Concert, The, Best Is Yet To Come, Welsh Musical Theatre Young Singer Of The Year, Living TV's Most Haunted (cancelled), The Circus Of Horrors, The Stones Tribute Band, Jethro, How Sweet It Is, Sgt Pepper's Lonely Hearts Club Show, A Slice Of Welsh Rarebit, The Searchers, Snow White On Ice, To Kill A Mocking Bird, Porridge with Shaun Williamson, Kenny Ball, Chris Barber & Acker Bilk(postponed), An Audience with Sally Morgan, Solid Gold Country Legends, (Solid Silver 60's Show Dave Berry, Mike Pender, Brian Poole, Peter Sarstedt backed by Vanity Fare with The Swinging Blue Jeans and The Troggs), Des O'Connor, The Woman In Black, Talon The Best Of The Eagles, Noddy In Toyland, Abba Mania, Back For Good, Frankie Boyle, A Night out with Tommy Cooper Jus' Like That!, Tosca, Carmen, Pirates Of Penzance, Boy George, Paul Merton's Impro' Chums, Katy Brand, What Black Women Want, Real Diamond-John Hylton, An Audience With The Chuckle Brothers, Loose Ends, The Hairy Bikers Big Night Out, Die Roten Punkte, Pop Star!(cancelled), Billy Elliot The Sir Harry Secombe Trust, Jim Davidson, One Night In Vegas, Brendan Cole Live and Unjudged, Piaf, Hi-De-Hi(cancelled), Roy Chubby Brown, We'll Meet Again, The Full Monty, Dancing Queen, The Storys Final Show, A Night At The Opera, Lee Memphis King (cancelled), The Dream Boys, The Best Is Yet To Come, Billy Elliot The Sir Harry Secombe Trust, The Ladyboys Of Bangkok, 5x60 Dance Evolution 3, Oh Lord What A Knight, Curtain Up, Peppa Pig, Godspell, Sounds Of The Glenn Miller Ere, ELO Tribute, Bon Jovi Experience, Dance Energy Production, The Late Edwina Black, Dolly! The Show, The Trouble With Old Lovers, Inside Job, Love's A Luxury, Murdered to Death.

Act 19

Index

T

U

V

W

X

Y

Z

For more information on the Grand Theatre and all things theatrical, both professional and amateur in the Swansea Bay area, visit

www.swanseasgrand.co.uk